Dockyard

Dog

Lyle Garford

Published by:
Lyle Garford
Vancouver, Canada
Contact: lyle@lylegarford.com

ISBN 978-0-9936173-8-6

Cover by designspectacle.ca

Book Design by Lyle Garford
www.lylegarford.com

First Edition 2016
Printed by Createspace, an Amazon.com Company.
Available on Kindle and other devices.

Dedication

This is for my wife Kathy.

Chapter One
June 1784
Aboard HMS Wind Off The Coast Of Antigua

The sway of the mast got worse the higher he went. Much worse.

"Bastard," he swore under his breath, although it mattered little as no one could hear him and the insistent strength of the wind carried his voice away anyway. Cursing his Captain yet again the young officer risked a glance upwards, hoping the remaining distance would seem less daunting the closer he got to the maintop and the tiny perch already occupied by a lookout.

Mistake. The masthead, still over ten feet away, swayed in a steady arc back and forth against the high, thin cloud in the sky. Had the ship been at a standstill the mast would still have swayed in the wind; with the ship under way at almost nine knots the mast was a living thing. This time the officer cursed himself, as he knew better. Pausing to settle the churning in his stomach, he clutched the rope ladder hard.

"Get on with it, you idiot," he muttered.

Climbing well over a hundred feet to the top of the mainmast of a warship at sea was a terrifying experience and he knew it mattered not how many times you had done it before. Most sailors found it frightening, but he knew a few fools made light of it and usually ended up being dead fools. Anyone serving on a British Royal Navy warship with any sense soon learned one simple lesson. All tasks required absolute caution and respect, and paying attention to small details was essential. The officer shook his head; a warship held far too many ways for the unwary to get killed.

With effort he took several deep breaths and focused on the thick mast in front of him. The churning finally subsided and he resumed his climb, thankful yet again at learning to master the nausea touching at times even the most experienced sailors. The officer smiled as he resumed his climb, knowing he could still do it. The alternative was vomiting from his current perch, which would guarantee a wide splatter on the deck and people below. The wrath of his furious Captain wouldn't bear even thinking about.

Twenty-two year old Lieutenant Evan Ross already knew his wrath well, having borne the brunt of it on many occasions. A rebellious spark deep inside kept the thought alive, though. Doing something to precipitate a way out of his current harsh situation was tempting. Evan had been ecstatic when word came he would replace the former third Lieutenant of HMS Wind three months ago after the man succumbed to fever, but the euphoria didn't last. Being assigned to a frigate, the swift hunters of the Royal Navy, should have been a dream posting. In reality they were the worst three months of his young life.

Right from the start the Captain seemed bent on venting his anger over anything going wrong with his ship on the new Lieutenant, and nothing Evan did worked to change his mind. The Captain's puzzling, irrational behaviour toward him was a frustrating mystery until the Second Lieutenant George Paxton took pity and pulled him aside for a quick moment after one manifestly unfair episode where Evan took the worst of the blame.

5

"You know, Mr. Ross, it may seem like it, but Captains don't always get their way."

Wary and alert, Evan risked a swift look around to ensure they were unheard before turning back to the Second Lieutenant.

"I take it that means the Captain was thwarted in some way recently, sir?"

Paxton took his own quick look about before replying. "Hmm, you wouldn't know this, but our senior mid Walsh is the son of our Captain's sister. The Flag didn't approve the Captain's request. Seems the Flag already had lots of unemployed Lieutenants around."

A brief, weary smile creased his face. "Thought you might want to know that." With a quick nod and one last look around he walked off to busy himself elsewhere before anyone noticed the two in deep conversation.

With the truth behind his situation much, much clearer Evan sighed as he considered the implications, knowing patronage was a huge part of advancement in the Navy. Midshipman Walsh was excellent at his duties and ready for greater challenges such as an acting Lieutenancy. Evan could see his Captain in a much different light as a result, because in putting Walsh forward for promotion the Captain was only doing what was expected of him, to find and promote talented people. No one would question the propriety of a family relationship being involved; Captain Woods was not the first and wouldn't be the last officer to push forward a relative for promotion. Making his new Lieutenant's life hell wasn't expected of him, but doing so was a backdoor way to get what he wanted. The Captain in reality wanted some excuse to clap him in chains or beach him and promote his favourite. The Captain owed Evan nothing.

And Evan could do nothing about it, knowing The Articles of War governing the lives and behaviour of people on board a Royal Navy warship gave the Captain enormous power over the ship and its people. His word was law.

Reaching the maintop with relief, Lieutenant Ross shoved aside his frustration. Eight years in the Royal Navy, serving since he was thirteen years old, had taught him patience was key to dealing with a demanding Captain. Bland responses and painstaking attention to duty was the only way to combat the abuse. This, and a firm resolve he wasn't going to be beaten.

Climbing onto the platform he squeezed his body in beside the seaman already sitting on the perch. The sailor gave him a quizzical look for a long moment, before a look of panic appeared on seeing the stony look he got in return.

"Sir," said the sailor, offering a hasty salute.

"Report, Smith," said Evan. "What have we got here?"

Another brief flicker of confusion crossed the sailor's face, but this time he responded quickly. "She's a Yankee, sir, like I called when I spotted her. You can see that from the trim of the ship. Sails, too. No one else has them cut like that. Pardon for asking, but is that what you came up to find out, sir?"

"Smith, you know bloody well why the Captain sent me up here is none of your concern," snarled Evan, although he quickly relented and told himself it wasn't fair to take his frustration out on the sailor.

"I presume he wants to know as much as possible about the situation well in advance of getting there," said Evan as he pulled out his telescope.

But even as he turned attention to his task Evan knew the sailor was probably still curious and raising a skeptical eyebrow behind his back. The man was right, too; sending a ship's officer to the top of the mainmast to scout something was most often a waste of time, as an officer would be unlikely to see more than an experienced lookout. Evan knew too the man was smart enough to realize this was also the likely source of the Evan's gruff responses. But as a professional seaman Smith would never openly criticize an officer, let alone the Captain. Doing so would bring a swift and brutally harsh response.

Evan studied the situation as he trained his telescope on the ship they were fast bearing down on. The Captain had shifted course as soon as the hail from the lookout came, but gave no indication of what he was concerned about. The French and the Americans were still active all over the Caribbean, so breaking the ship's homeward voyage to check out what this strange sail was up to wasn't anything anyone on the ship would deem odd. The Treaty of Paris signed in September 1783 formally ended hostilities between the combatants involved in the American Revolutionary War, but this certainly didn't mean the hard feelings and suspicion were gone.

The ship being in this place was indeed odd, though. The lookout did well to spot the strange ship, anchored in one of the many small bays dotting the coastline of the Caribbean island of Antigua. From a distance it would be challenging to see a ship against the background of palm trees and dense undergrowth.

"Pardon me for asking again, sir," said Smith. "What do you think she's up to? Maybe they're smuggling something, sir?"

Evan grunted in response, still peering hard through his telescope. "I'd say you're right, Smith. Looks to me like they've been offloading cargo on the beach. Yes, there's a big pile of stuff and a bunch of people around it. Looks like a sloop and they're Yankees all right. That's their flag. Hello, they've finally woke up and spotted us," he added with amusement. "There's a jolly boat pushing off from the beach like they've got the hounds of hell after them."

"Maybe the Captain will teach them to pay attention, sir," said Smith.

Evan took one final, close look at the American ship before glancing over to see a wolfish grin on the sailor's face.

"Could be," said Evan with a smile, allowing a hungry look to grow on his own face. "One last bit of action before we go home would be good."

Heeding the lesson the Americans were learning Evan gave the horizon a scan in all directions to make sure he wasn't missing anything, but the ocean was otherwise empty. He couldn't resist pausing for a few brief moments to drink in the view. Climbing to the masthead was unquestionably terrifying, but the reward was always an incredible view and a sense of exhilaration. Evan felt the same way every time; every cell in his body was keenly alive.

"Right. Carry on, Smith," said Evan, pocketing his telescope and swinging himself off the platform to begin the long descent back to the deck. A rush of top men climbing the mast to attend to the sails slowed his passage down.

Finally reaching the deck he straightened his uniform on his way to the quarterdeck where a knot of officers were clustered, all staring intently at the ship they had found. Captain Woods, as was his right, was standing by himself on the windward side, equally focused on the scene before him.

"Report," grunted John Harder, the ship's First Officer, not even bothering to glance in Evan's direction.

"Sir," he replied, saluting as he came to a stop. "Strange sail is definitely a Yankee. Appears to be a trading sloop. I think they may be smuggling—"

"You think, Mr. Ross?" said the Captain, his voice oozing sarcasm, as he came over to join the little group. "I had no idea you could. Of course, I didn't ask you to think, I asked you to check the situation and report back in a timely manner. You've dawdled so long about it what they're doing is already plain for everyone to see. It's obviously a trading sloop and they're obviously smugglers! Unless you actually have something else to report?"

"Sir, very little else, sir. There's a large pile of crates and goods stacked up on the beach. There are no other sail about, sir," replied Evan, maintaining a consciously bland look on his face.

"Sir, very little else, sir," mimicked the Captain, shaking his head. "Bloody useless."

"Captain," interrupted the First Officer, still training his telescope on their target. "From all the bustle on yonder sloop I'd say they are clearly thinking about getting underway."

Evan was grateful for the interruption as Captain Woods strode back to the windward side of the quarterdeck and turned his attention to the American ship.

"Mr. Harder," said the Captain with a grim snort of amusement moments later. "Explain to them they aren't going anywhere."

"Sir," replied the First Officer, turning to the waiting group of officers. "Mr. Ross, pass the word for the gunner to put a shot across his bow."

Evan found the gunner already working to obey the command. The ship's gunner Johnson, a warrant officer with over twenty years experience, had anticipated the order and wasn't about to be caught unprepared. He and the ship's bosun had already brought together a gun crew ready to leap into action when the order was given. A well-trained gun crew could load and fire a gun in less than three minutes, and it wasn't long before one of the forward six-pound chase cannons roared out. The round dropped into the bay and raised a geyser of spray less than a hundred feet in front of the American's bow, right off his starboard side.

"Well shot, Mr. Johnson!" called the First Officer. He studied the ship before him for a few moments before snapping his telescope closed. "They appear to be standing down, Captain. Orders, sir?"

The Captain paused a moment in thought before turning to offer another grim smile to his First Officer. "Well, we need to see what these buggers are up to, don't we? Take a boarding party and check them out, Mr. Harder. I think they're trying to get around that Navigation Order in Council I mentioned when we spoke a while back."

"Bloody cheek smuggling in broad daylight, if that's what they're doing, sir."

"Greedy, grasping, arrogant shits. No respect for tradition. We gave them everything and they— Gah! Don't get me started. Right, any nonsense from them and you smile and tell them the July 2, 1783 Order in Council concerning Navigation says they're in trouble. They'll pretend to know nothing and want to keep their contraband, but that's not going to happen. While you're dealing with them I'll have Mr. Paxton here take a party to the beach to pick up everything they've offloaded. If we let it sit there too long I'm sure it'll all sprout legs and disappear."

"Uh, so I fully understand in case they argue some point I know nothing about could I get a little more background on this Order in Council, sir?" said the First Lieutenant.

"Hmm, yes, you should have a little background. Before the war the Yankees were thick as the goddamn mosquitos in these islands trading their goods. The greedy damn plantation owners on most of the islands out here are always in need of proper timber and food they can't get here, and especially things like salt fish, which they feed to their slaves."

The Captain paused to give a disapproving grunt and shake his head. "Slavery, I ask you. Anyway, the Yankees get goods like rum, sugar, coffee, spices, and coconuts in return. Well, you get the picture."

The Captain paused once more to let a savage smile crease his face while nodding his head in the direction of the ship awaiting them. "What these Yankee rebels are about to learn is they can't have it both ways, right? They can't expect we're going to let them continue trading to their hearts content because we had to kiss and make up. The Order in Council specifies all trade with the Americans to and from our islands must be on British registered ships with British crews. Of course, that also means our good

King is able to collect the appropriate customs duties."

Instant understanding appeared on the faces of everyone listening. The duties were notoriously heavy and universally disliked by everyone involved in trade.

"I know what you're thinking, gentlemen, but make no mistake here. This may seem a bit beneath the regular duties of a King's ship, but that couldn't be further from the truth. I think the treasury, which pays the bills for all of us to be here and do our jobs, is seriously depleted. Enough, I'm sure you understand now so let's be about it, shall we?"

"Thank you, Captain. I think we all understand much better now. I may take who I want with me, sir?"

The Captain waved an indifferent hand. "As you see fit. And make sure you check everyone's papers on that ship. I won't be surprised if half of that damn crew is Royal Navy deserters. You know what to do. I'll be in my cabin."

He gazed about with disinterest. "It's too bloody hot out here today. Let's get this sorted and be on our way. Three years out here is long enough. I'd like to be home in Kent before the end of July."

"Amen to that, sir," nodded his First Officer in reply, before issuing a flurry of orders.

As the ship came to anchor Evan was commanded to join the party as backup for Harder. Squeezing into the cutter already lowered into the water was a party of eight Royal Marines and their commanding officer, Lieutenant Fulham. Another half dozen sailors rounded out the group. As soon as everyone was aboard they began rowing smartly toward the American ship.

Several angry looking faces lined the rails of the sloop. A few were more inscrutable, but they all shared one common feature. No one looked happy.

"Right," said Lieutenant Harder. "Everyone armed? Weapons loaded everyone? I don't think this lot is going to give us trouble, but we'd better be ready for it."

The cutter hooked on to the sloop at the boarding ladder and he looked at the waiting, tense faces around him one last time.

"Marines, follow me smartly."

By the time Evan reached the deck the First Officer was already in heated conversation with a grizzled, scruffy looking older man who was presumably the Captain. Evan took a quick look at his surroundings to assess the situation. The crew was mostly clustered behind the older man and looked as scruffy as their leader. Their ship, however, was decidedly not scruffy. A little touch up paint wouldn't hurt, but any ship in steady service always needed some touch up. Everything about it spoke of professional care and attention, certainly as good as any Royal Navy ship afloat.

"This is an outrage, I tell you!" shouted the old man. "You have no right to impede our passage, let alone board anybody you feel like. We're honest traders doing our job! Haven't you got some privateers you can go chase?"

"Oh, please," groaned the First Officer. "Sir, you are in British waters and are therefore subject to our laws. You are clearly flying an American flag and you are obviously smuggling goods to unknown parties resident on Antigua. You are in clear violation of the Order in Council concerning Navigation."

"But I've never heard of this damned Order of yours!"

"Not my problem," barked Lieutenant Harder, his patience gone. "Your cargo is forfeit. Right, I want to see your ship's papers and I want them now, sir."

The Captain of the sloop visibly deflated, knowing the pointlessness of continuing. "Damn you. Our families will go hungry because of you. Your consul in Boston shall be hearing about this outrage. This isn't over, because we'll sue if we have to. Come on, then, they're in my cabin."

Harder turned to Ross and the Marine officer Fulham. "Mr. Ross, take a party to search the ship thoroughly." He gestured with a flick of his hand towards the cluster of still visibly angry American sailors. "Mr. Fulham, have your men guard this lot and keep them from interfering. Check their papers while I deal with the Captain."

Evan turned and gestured to a tall and lanky, light brown skinned sailor standing nearby, one of the master's mates on the Wind. To find a black sailor on a Royal Navy warship was not unusual. The Navy was always in need of men due to attrition from death, desertion, or illness and as long as a man did his job, no one cared what he looked like.

"Mr. Wilton, you're with me. We'll search forward."

Turning, he looked at the bosun standing nearby. "Jackson, take Payne and search aft. Report back to Lieutenant Harder. Anything suspicious you call for help."

Ten minutes later Evan and the sailor Wilton compared notes on what they'd found once they worked their way back to the deck. The hold was mostly empty except for the usual stores a ship would have in place for a long voyage. The sailor's berths also held only the small personal effects one would expect. Unless something was found aft, Evan surmised they had caught the smuggler having already unloaded their cargo, but still in the process of loading for the return trip home.

Coming on deck they found the First Lieutenant deep in discussion with the Marine officer Fulham. The two sailors Evan had detailed to search aft were already back, standing a respectful distance away from the First Officer's side.

"Ah, Mr. Ross, here you are. Report, please."

It took only moments for Evan, with Wilton at his side, to detail the little they had found.

"Hmm, well, the two that searched aft found much the same, except this lot did in fact start loading goods for the homeward trip. A few casks of rum and some molasses were already stored away aft. Papers confirm they are who they say they are, traders out of Boston, so we've got them red handed. Lieutenant Fulham has checked the paperwork on the crowd we found on deck and they all seem to be in order. If they're forgeries they are quite good ones. It seems they really are American born. On the other hand, Jackson and Payne didn't find only cargo aft. They found two more hands doing their best to stay out of sight."

Harder paused to grunt with annoyance at some papers he held up for Evan to see. "They claim to be innocent and swear they weren't trying to hide from us. Their papers don't look legitimate to me, but I can't put my finger on why."

"Could I take a look, sir?" said Evan. "I had to look over a lot of Yankee paperwork in my last ship."

Wordlessly the First Officer handed Evan the paperwork. After a few moments scrutinizing them, Evan looked up at Harder.

"Sir, it's the stamps of the town seals on their birth certificates, I think. Forgers won't have access to the real stamp, of course, so they have to try to either hand draw it or make their own forged stamps. The paper itself looks rather cheap, too. Some forgeries are better than others. Where are these two men? I'd like to question them."

"Over there, behind Jackson and Payne. Go ahead."

Turning, Evan walked toward the two sailors as they stood aside and pointed at the two men they had found. As they came into view Evan's jaw dropped open. The two men reacted with equal surprise and shock on their faces.

"Cromwell? Anderson? You bloody— Sir, these men are deserters from my last ship!" shouted Evan.

The two men overcame their shock fast. Both punched the men guarding them and wrestled their weapons from their grasp.

"Back off, the lot of you! You bastards aren't taking us back!" shouted the one called Cromwell as he waved a sea pistol about.

Recovering from his shock Evan stepped forward, pulling out his own gun in turn. "Give it up you fools, there's nothing for it—"

The sharp report of Cromwell's gun galvanized the rest of the men on deck into action, paralyzed momentarily by how fast the situation had changed. Evan gasped in sudden pain and surprise, clutching his left arm. Blood was fast staining his uniform above his left elbow where the shot had struck.

The rest of the British crew was already rushing forward. A Marine wielding his musket like a bat hammered the sailor Cromwell hard on the head and he dropped to the deck bleeding from the force of the blow. The second deserter, Anderson, was aiming directly at Evan when the black sailor Wilton brushed past trying to enter the fray with his cutlass. Anderson's gun barked just as another Marine jostled his arm and deflected his aim.

Anderson's shot found a target in all the confusion. Wilton gasped in pain and fell clutching his right thigh as the blood began seeping through his fingers. A millisecond later Lieutenant Fulham shot Anderson point blank in the chest. A flash of surprise crossed his face as a dark red stain blossomed on his shirt and he crashed to the deck. The shock of being shot finally overcame Evan and he fell to one knee beside Wilton.

A few of the remaining American sailors were already involved in support of their mates, scuffling with several of the Marines. The fully galvanized Marines soon took command of the situation, using their muskets as clubs. Knowing they would lose the American Captain shouted for attention, loudly ordering his men to stand down. By the time they finally complied three of their number were crumpled on the deck, holding bruised and bleeding heads, while the remainder were clustered together. All of them were scowling in mute anger.

"Idiots," growled Harder as he shook his head, glaring at the two deserters on the deck.

"You call them idiots, you murdering shits?" shouted one of the American sailors, holding his side in obvious pain where a musket butt had been hammered into his ribs. "Maybe if you didn't flog people for bloody nothing they wouldn't desert!"

"We beat you buggers before and we could do it again," growled another American sailor.

"Shut your goddamn mouths, all of you, or they'll be shut for you!" growled Harder in obvious frustration. With a sigh, the First Officer frowned as he assessed what needed to be done.

Evan groaned in pain and shock as he and the sailor Wilton were tended to by one of the older and more experienced sailors. The man finished tying off tourniquets on both and looked up as the First Officer stalked over.

"Permission to get these two over to the ship for the surgeon right away, sir? They've already lost a fair bit of blood and need attention soon, sir."

Lieutenant Harder grunted agreement and signaled to a group of the remaining British sailors. "Get them to the ship and then get back here right away. Tell the Captain what happened and that I'll return on board shortly with a full report. Mr. Ross, Mr. Wilton, we'll get you some attention right away."

Evan grimaced, clutching his arm, and mumbled his thanks to Harder.

"What about the deserters, sir? Should we take them with us?" asked another of the sailors.

Harder turned and walked over to the two men still lying on the deck.

"No," he said, surveying the scene before him with a grim smile. "Mr. Fulham has ended any need for urgency over the one he shot. This other fool is still out cold. Better for him if he doesn't wake up. The Captain will probably have him dancing with a rope around his worthless neck real soon anyway. No, we'll bring him over with us once you return."

Harder surveyed the scene one last time and offered another bleak smile to the waiting men. "If I can find some chains I'll load him down with them while we're waiting. Now be off with you."

Evan and Wilton were already lapsing in and out of consciousness from shock and blood loss as they were manhandled into the boat and rowed quickly across to the Wind. Captain Woods waited, drawn on deck from the sound of the gunshots. He wore an inscrutable look on his face as Evan was helped past on his way to the surgeon.

"Sir," gasped Evan, unable to salute as he was still holding his shattered and bleeding arm. The Captain's expression didn't change as he watched the two men disappear below, listening to the report of what happened on the American ship.

By the time they were dropped onto the surgeon's tables in his space on the orlop deck the two men were groggy, but still conscious from the painful jostling endured in getting there. The surgeon, a grizzled older man, looked them over with a professional eye. Evan was conscious enough to realize where he was and what was about to happen.

"Mr. Manley," said Evan, in what was a bare whisper with his strength fast disappearing. "I beg of you, sir. Please don't take it off."

The surgeon paused a few moments more before responding with a sigh. "I wish I could agree to that, Mr. Ross. I think the ball may have shattered the bone of your arm beyond hope and if I don't deal with this I fear you will lose more than your arm. I will assess you carefully, but I will also do what is necessary, sir. Be happy I am as skilled a surgeon as I am and that there are few in the Royal Navy better than I. Now drink this rum my surgeon's mate has for you and I will be back to you shortly."

As the surgeon moved to look over his other patient his assistant stepped forward without asking and insistently made Evan drink a large dose of rum. Rough and heady, the standard issue Navy rum on Royal Navy warships packed a heavy punch. As shock and the strong rum overcame him Evan still retained enough focus to realize the surgeon was talking about the unconscious, injured black sailor lying on the other table beside Evan in the surgery.

"Hmm, well, this one is lucky. The shot went right though his thigh and how that missed a major artery I'll never understand. Looks like a clean wound, too. He doesn't seem to have anything inside his wound to fester. Right, he won't be much of a problem. We'll come back to him in a bit. Blackwell, help Mr. Wilton enjoy another nice big tot of rum. That should make him oblivious while I deal with Mr. Ross."

As the rum continued to carry him into his own oblivion Evan retained enough awareness to realize the surgeon was back at his table and probing the wound, enough to give him twinges of pain even through his drunken stupor.

"Sorry lad, I had to do that to be sure. Don't want to do this, but there is no choice. Blackwell, give him a little dose of that laudanum I've been hoarding. He's going to need it."

***

Manley busied himself organizing his tools, waiting several minutes to ensure the drug was taking effect. He knew Evan was doubly fortunate to have both a surgeon good at his job and to have one with some of the most precious, effective pain killing medicine available anywhere on hand. As Manley waited he let his thoughts drift and he shook his head, marveling for the thousandth time at his personal downfall. But he knew if it had not happened he never would have joined the Navy and come to appreciate life at sea.

A successful practice serving London's high society had once been his reality. Manley knew his undoing had been naively thinking people would understand his desire to help the poor on the side through political advocacy and action. A newsman with unsympathetic political leanings noticed his work helping prostitutes unable to afford skilled services when their precautions didn't work. Soon, clever stories implying his relationship with the underworld of London involved far more nefarious activity began appearing. The ensuing scandal and attention was crushing.

Manley shrugged it off, knowing he was far too late to be complaining about fleeing to service in the Navy in order to save himself. Turning his attention back to his patient, a quick check showed Lieutenant Ross had slipped into complete unconsciousness. With a sigh he shook his head and turned to his assistant.

"Blackwell, bring my saw over here, please. I'm afraid it's time to put it to use again."

Chapter Two
July 1784
Aboard HMS Boreas off the coast of St Kitts

The young Captain scowled and clenched his fists in impotent rage as the forward chase guns roared yet again, adding to the acrid smell of spent gunpowder drifting back to the quarterdeck. Like the others, the shots fell far too short.

"We need better armament, damn it," he muttered to himself.

But this was a thought for another day, as a hard decision was at hand. Darkness was falling fast enough to save the mystery ship they were chasing. All his prey had to do was not light his night lanterns, wait till full darkness, and change course. By dawn they would be far away and their hunter would find only empty seas in all directions.

With a sigh the Captain turned, stalked over to a waiting knot of officers and addressed his Third Lieutenant. "Order the gunner to stand down, Mr. Fleming."

"Sir," the officer replied, saluting as he left to pass the order on.

"This is downright annoying, isn't it, sir?" said his First Officer.

"Indeed, sir," grumbled the Captain. "He was lucky we came across him so late in the day. Even an hour or so earlier and we'd have had that bugger, whoever he was."

The Captain lapsed back into silence, thinking back on the last few months. Both he and crew of HMS Boreas, a swift frigate bearing twenty-eight guns, were anxious to prove their mettle. Commissioned March 18, 1784 with a young Captain only twenty-five years old and new to the ship, they had sailed from England to Barbados in the Caribbean to report for duty as part of the Leeward Islands Station.

On reaching Barbados their orders were to sail when ready for the island of Antigua and to base themselves henceforth in the British naval base and Dockyard at English Harbour, south east of the capital St. John's. As Post Captain of the largest warship based in Antigua it meant the young Captain would be in overall command of the Northern Division of the Leeward Island Station, answerable only to his Admiral in Barbados.

He knew his tasks would be many and varied once in place. London wanted intelligence reports on the activities of French warships in the area. Diplomats on the various islands in his domain needed the flag and, most importantly, British sea power to be on regular display. British merchant shipping needed assurance they would have protection from privateers and occasional piracy still plaguing the area when opportunity arose. Most such activity had long since been stamped out, but predators were always on the lookout for the unwary. The Navy also desperately wanted the naval Dockyard at English Harbour expanded and strengthened faster than the current pace of work.

But his biggest and most difficult task was to enforce the Navigation Order in Council and eliminate smuggling from the area. His orders from the Admiralty in London were emphatic he was to do everything in his power to achieve this.

The First Lord of the Admiralty, Richard Howe, was a patron of the young Captain. Thinking back to the meeting sitting with the First Lord, his orders in hand, the Captain knew his patron was making extra effort to ensure he understood exactly what he was to accomplish.

"Your orders don't say this, but you need to understand how vital your mission is to the nation."

The young Captain remembered letting his eyes widen as he watched the First Lord give him a smile without warmth.

"What I'm about to tell you is for your ears only. The sugar islands account for a quarter of the entire trade of our country. We need the wealth they generate to help replenish our coffers, sir. The country is almost bankrupt. Yes, it is that bad and we are that desperate. And we need to deal with this soon. Mark my words, sir. We are not done with the bloody French yet. Not even close. Yes, Admiral Rodney thrashed them at the Isles de Saintes and that gave us much to bargain with at the end of the war, thank heaven, but the frogs are only rebuilding. They have their own problems to deal with so it won't be soon, maybe even a few years, but they will be back to plague us. So you understand, sir? You have many tasks, a Captain always does, but crushing these smugglers is the priority."

As the First Lord paused for a moment the young Captain realized he was being scrutinized, but he was used to it and knew what kind of picture he presented. Slim and relatively short, the young Captain was not an imposing physical figure. But everyone noticed on first meeting him the aura of strength and energy he consciously radiated, along with an air of command only true leaders carried. When walking into a room he made deliberate effort to project the strength of his presence, enough to instantly demand everyone's attention.

"Yes, we have need of someone with energy and drive to take charge in Antigua, Captain. Are you that man?"

The Captain smiled. "You know I am, sir."

Shaking his head to bring himself back to the present, the Captain turned to his First Officer once again. "Enough. Let's get back on course to Antigua."

After issuing orders to this effect the First Officer turned back to his Captain. "Sir? What do you think that was all about? Why did he run when we challenged him, if you don't mind my asking, sir?"

"Hmm. I can't be sure, Mr. Wilkins, but one of our tasks out here is to put a stop to smuggling in the area. He wasn't flying a flag, but if that wasn't a Yankee trader then I'm no sailor. He's probably learned we're serious about dealing with this and knew well he had to run."

"Isn't he pushing it, sir? There's still some time, I suppose, but we're at the beginning of hurricane season now and it's not safe out here."

"You're absolutely right, Mr. Wilkins. But being a trader is all about making money. He's probably trying to make one last fat profit off people wanting to stock up on his goods so they don't run out. He takes a risk and they pay a premium, right?"

"I see, sir."

"Speaking of risk, we too are taking one being out here this late. So it's off to the safety of English Harbour until the hurricane season is over for us." Pausing for a moment, the Captain frowned into the dim distance where his prey had all but disappeared.

"As for him, he'll be back and so will we. The deck is yours, sir. I'll be in my cabin."

***

Minutes later the Third Officer returned to the quarterdeck, and seeing the Captain was gone, he approached the First Officer.

"Lieutenant Wilkins? So what did the Captain think that was all about?"

The First Officer smiled and explained. In their short time serving with this relentless, aggressive new Captain both men had learned much about him. They had no doubt he would find whoever had escaped them today and deal with them.

"Not to worry, Mr. Fleming," said Lieutenant Wilkins with a predatory grin. "I think we both know this Captain will be absolutely unyielding in pursuit of prey. Let's hope we have plenty!"

And most of all, both men knew with utter certainty Captain Horatio Nelson hated losing.

***

They approached the island with a greater press of sail than Nelson liked, but the winds were light. Both he and his sailing master had been to English Harbour before and neither was looking forward to it. Nelson knew he had to approach with caution and be absolutely certain to stay in the deepest part of the channel as they sailed past Fort Berkeley on the point into Freeman's Bay. Even with the presence of the local pilot taken on board before they began their approach this was still a daunting task, even for skilled sailors. Charlotte Point and the Pillars of Hercules rock formations on the other side of the entrance loomed less than a thousand feet away. Once past the point an immediate course change of almost 180 degrees was required to get into the safety of the anchorage, but the maneuver was notoriously difficult. Nelson was well aware the wind almost always disappeared when entering the bay, right as the ship was struggling to either tack or wear onto a new course.

Either way, without fail attempting the entrance was a dangerous nuisance sure to make the day far less pleasant. Nelson knew even the best sailors were sometimes reduced to sweating with fear and helpless cursing as they struggled to safety.

But Nelson also understood the struggle was worth it. English Harbour became a desirable location when the Navy discovered what a truly safe haven it could be from the dread power of the devastating hurricanes plaguing the Caribbean every year. September was the worst month, but they were known to occur as early as July and even as late as November some years. Several years prior a particularly brutal storm saw every ship anchored in ports around Antigua drag their anchors and suffer major damage while those in English Harbour suffered little if any. Seeing the clear benefit, the Navy began clamoring for its further development as an anchorage.

With the winds light Nelson feared they would have to be warped into harbour, but this time they managed to avoid it. With everyone entirely focused on getting the ship anchored they paid little attention to the details of their surroundings. Finally freed from the demands of sailing the ship, the relieved officers began looking about.

Within moments of being anchored a swarm of rowboats with black men at the oars surrounded the ship. Sugar, molasses, coconuts, all manner of local fruit, and fresh fish were all on sale. Varying sizes of jugs and hollowed out coconuts filled with rum were featured prominently. Several of the boats also held black women who made it clear they were for sale too. A number of the crew were already hanging over the side of the ship and beginning the bartering process.

The midshipmen were all clustered at the railings too, salivating at the prospect of trading some well-fed ship rats they had captured for fresh victuals. Catching rats to supplement their diet was a long-standing tradition for midshipmen throughout the fleet. The technique was remarkably simple; a baited hook lowered on a line into the hold soon got results.

"Mr. Fleming," said Nelson, looking them over with a wary eye. "Keep that lot at bay until we get ourselves sorted out here. We're going to be here a while and I will be able to offer shore leave, but I need some time to make arrangements for that."

A number of ships of varying sizes and shapes dotted the harbour. A schooner was careened over on the far side of Freeman's Bay on Galleon Beach with a few workers busy cleaning its exposed bottom. Not far from their anchorage the largest of the ships in the harbour, a brig, was moored directly to the wharf in front of the main Dockyard buildings. Past the Dockyard was the inner harbour where yet more small ships were moored.

Nelson was still looking about for what had changed since his last visit to this station when his First Officer interrupted, his voice conveying an odd mix of puzzlement and concern.

"Captain? Correct me if I'm wrong, but I understood you to be the new senior officer on station here, sir?"

Nelson gave him a quizzical look. "Yes, of course. That is my understanding. Why?"

"Hmm, well, there's not much wind today so I could be wrong, but unless I am very mistaken that brig moored at the wharf has a commodore's pennant flying at the masthead."

Nelson whipped about to stare hard at the ship. As he did a stronger puff of wind fluttered the flag, leaving no doubt about it being a commodore's pennant. Anyone with this rank would automatically be Nelson's superior officer on the station. Nelson's eyes bulged in stunned surprise for a brief moment before he exploded in anger.

"What the bloody— Mr. Wilkins, what's the name of that ship?"

"Uh, looks like it's the HMS Latona, sir. That would be Captain Sands, I think. But he's junior to you, isn't he, sir?"

"He certainly bloody well is," growled Nelson as he recovered his composure. "And he is certainly not a commodore. I don't know what he thinks he's doing, but he'd better have a good explanation for it. Mr. Wilkins, have my coxswain ready my gig. We'll sort this out right now."

With his First Officer appearing very glad someone else would be on the receiving end of the dressing down sure to follow Nelson stalked to the side of his ship, climbing into his gig with icy determination.

The Captain's impatience was obvious and the boat crew pulled hard to get Nelson the short distance to the shore. Within minutes he was standing on the deck of the brig. The surprised ship's crew did their flustered best to accord him proper honours as required for a senior officer, but Nelson could see they were caught off guard. The ship was clearly out of discipline as no one was wearing anything remotely resembling a dress uniform.

The anxious First Officer stepped forward to greet their visitor and introduce himself. If he hadn't done so Nelson would never have picked him out as an officer. The man was wearing a baggy old pair of trousers and a loose white shirt with stains too numerous to count.

Seeing Nelson's frigid stare at his clothes, the young Lieutenant tried a sheepish smile. "Sorry for our attire, sir. I am Lieutenant Hill. The ship is out of discipline and we weren't expecting you. Our dress wear is on shore being laundered."

Nelson continued to glower at him and the smile melted away. "Captain Sands has been made aware you have come on board and should be here—"

"I am here now sir," interrupted a young officer still pulling on his uniform coat as he strode up while his First Officer breathed an audible sigh of relief to no longer be on the spot. "Captain Nelson, sir, it has been far too long. Welcome to Antigua."

"We'll get to that," said Nelson, a warning tone in his voice putting everyone on edge. "I am here for an explanation, sir. Why is that flying at your masthead?" Turning to the side he pointed at the pennant fluttering limply in the light breeze.

Captain Sands was puzzled as he looked where Nelson was pointing and, still appearing confused, he finally looked back at Nelson. "I'm sorry, sir, I don't— Oh! You mean the commodore's pennant, sir?"

Seeing the acknowledgement in Nelson's eyes, he gathered his thoughts for a moment before continuing. "Is this a concern, sir?"

"Of course it's a bloody concern, sir!" barked Nelson. "I don't know what you think you're doing flying that but you'd better have a good explanation.

31

Captains, even senior Captains on station, do not have the right to pretend they have a higher rank than they do."

The worried look on Captain Sands face cleared a little. "Of course, sir. The pennant is not my doing, sir. I was ordered to fly it by Captain Moutray, the Commissioner and senior officer in charge of the Dockyard, sir. It is he that is performing the role."

Nelson sucked in his breath and his eyes widened to the point the men on deck all braced for the explosion of anger sure to follow, but Nelson quickly mastered himself and shook his head.

"What bloody nonsense. That flag must come down, sir."

Captain Sands gave him an anxious look in return. "Sir, Captain Moutray is our senior by over twenty years as a Captain. I—"

"I don't care if he's been a Captain for a hundred years!" he said with heat, before pausing to calm down again.

"Sir, do you not understand? You and I are active service, commissioned sea officers. Captain Moutray is a civilian, in charge of an administrative, support arm of the Navy. You and I do not under any circumstances take orders from civilians. It is the other way around. And in fact, as of right now, there is only one person in overall command here and that would be me. So, Captain Sands, since I am not a commodore, that flag comes down, now, sir."

"I understand, sir," replied Captain Sands, turning to nod at his First Officer. Within moments the flag was down and being stored away as Sands turned back to Nelson.

"Um, I assume you will be briefing Captain Moutray? Would you like me to attend with you, sir?"

Nelson offered him a grim smile. "Not necessary, sir. I will ensure the good Captain understands where things stand."

Nelson turned to leave, but paused as he glanced at the scruffy attire of the officers around him. "I'm sorry to have had to disturb you and your men on what I'm sure is a well deserved day off. We must dine together soon, though. Good day, sir."

Back on shore Nelson paused and straightened his uniform. During his short time on shore the wind had dropped even more and the sticky heat was stifling. A trickle of sweat was already running down his back and the shirt under his uniform felt like it had melted to his skin. As he began walking toward the main Dockyard buildings he paused with a hand to his head. Detouring quickly back to his gig and the waiting crew he could see them fanning themselves in the sweltering heat.

"Anderson," he said, addressing his coxswain. "I am remiss. My haste to find out what in blazes was happening has left you and the men forgotten and sweating here in this vile heat. My God, it's only just past noon and the heat will get worse, too. You have my permission to take them to the shade of those palm trees over there and to roust up some water for them. I don't think I will be away long here, but I can't be sure."

Nelson turned to leave, but stopped himself once again. "And Mr. Anderson? Let's make sure it really is only water, shall we? I don't want to be smelling rum on anyone's breath on the way back to the ship."

The grateful men quickly began climbing onto shore as several called out thanks to the Captain, but he was already on his way to the Dockyard.

***

The men were soon settled in the shade, greedily slurping water from a small tub offered to them by workers in the Dockyard. The coxswain smiled as he looked at the building Nelson disappeared into on the other side of the Dockyard. Anderson had served in the Navy almost twenty years on several different ships, with many different officers. Royal Navy Captains were a diverse group and no two were alike. Each had their unique characteristics and ways they approached their role.

Anderson knew this Captain was different in some most interesting ways. He was both firm and fair right from the start, and he had stayed this way, always a good sign. Some Captains were notoriously inconsistent in how they did things. Captain Nelson also knew what he was doing. The coxswain was aware the Captain had gone to sea when he was thirteen years old and had the crew's respect as a sailor, a real 'tarpaulin man', as experienced professionals were called. More than a few Captains were promoted for reasons of patronage long before they were ready for such a role.

The crew also noticed the energy and strength of purpose the Captain radiated. Even the ship's sailing master, a grizzled professional with twenty-five years experience to his credit, had learned to pay close attention when the Captain made a suggestion.

What had everyone's attention, though, was the way he led the men under his command. The crew soon realized this Captain actually respected even the lowliest common seamen and the work they did. He also cared about the welfare of the men. The simple act of stopping to care for the boat crew when much weightier matters were on his mind spoke volumes to the men. Numerous examples of this kind of care had convinced even this hardened crew of the Captain's sincerity and his respect for them. This was what made this particular Captain a rare creature indeed.

"Here, mate," said one of the sailors lounging in the shade, interrupting Anderson's thoughts. "What say we go together on one of those coconuts filled with rum? The Captain will never notice."

Anderson laughed and merely shook his head. Sailors would do anything for a drink.

***

Reaching the entrance to the main Dockyard building Nelson made his way to where he knew the main offices were located. The Dockyard commissioner's clerk saw him coming and glanced up from where he sat at his desk, a puzzled look on his face. Nelson paused a moment in front of him.

"Is Captain Moutray in?"

The clerk looked Nelson up and down a moment before replying. "Well, yes, but he's busy. The rest of his day is already occupied. I'm afraid you'll have to make an appointment for another day."

Nelson's eyes widened for a moment before he leaned closer to the clerk.

"Say 'sir' when you talk to me."

The clerk leaned back in his chair, flustered. "Sir, I'm sorry. It's just I wasn't expecting anyone else, sir."

Nelson grunted and walked around the desk toward the door to Captain Moutray's office. The appalled clerk leapt from his chair and stepped in front of the door to block his way.

"Sir! Please! Captain Moutray gave strict instructions he wasn't to be interrupted!"

Nelson scowled at the clerk. "Tell me, fool, have you ever felt the touch of the lash?"

The clerk's face fell in fear as a bead of sweat appeared on his forehead. "Sir, no sir."

"Well, what you need to know is with my arrival I am the senior in command here and if you don't get out of my way immediately, you will learn what it's like soon enough."

Nelson entered the office as the clerk stepped aside in haste. Inside two men were seated on either side of the desk commanding the room. Both wore loose fitting shirts open at the neck and they appeared relaxed in conversation. A partly filled decanter was on the desk between them and the rich scent of amber rum permeated the room. Both men held full glasses in their hands. The men looked up, appearing surprised at the interruption as Nelson walked up to the desk.

"Gentlemen."

The younger of the two men was the first to react, getting to his feet. "Who— what do you think you're doing barging in here?"

The much older officer seated behind the desk also stood, but he offered his hand in greeting. "Stand down, Mr. Burns. Captain Nelson, it has been far too long. This is my First Officer here in the Dockyard, Mr. Gerald Burns. What brings you to Antigua, sir?"

Nelson smiled as he shook hands with both men. "Orders, of course. This is my new command, sir."

"Command? You mean station under my command, do you not? I am after all your senior."

Nelson's smile hardened. "Captain, you know how this works. You are a civilian appointment in this role, and active commission sea officers do not take orders from civilians. Tell me, did you actually have direct orders to fly the commodore's pennant?"

Captain Moutray seemed momentarily confused and paused to think a moment before responding. "Well, no, if you must know. I am senior on station, though, and there are several vessels stationed here. It's only right I signify presence of an overall command officer. Admiral Hughes is aware, of course. He had no problem with it."

Nelson gave a tiny snort of amusement. "Captain, we know each other too well for this. Since I am now senior in command of this station and I am not a commodore, Captain Sands has been informed and the pennant has been hauled down. I will inform the Admiral of my decision."

"Well, I disagree, Captain Nelson, but as you say, we know each other too well. Far be it for me to interfere with the doings of active sea officers. But enough of this trivial nonsense, you simply must dine with us. My good wife Mary will be so surprised and happy to see you again. Perhaps I could invite the Governour and a few locals? Mr. Burns, you and Mr. Long must join us. Mr. Long is my other Lieutenant, Captain Nelson. He is out and about on the business of the Dockyard right now. We are a busy place."

Nelson glanced down at the decanter of rum and their glasses. "Yes, I see that."

"Would you care for a drop, sir?"

"Hmm, a bit early for me, sirs. And yes, I'm sure the Dockyard is a busy place, but its going to get busier, sir. Among other things my orders direct me to expand the facilities here at a rather faster pace than we've had up to now."

Captain Moutray wore an inscrutable look on his face as he responded. "Fascinating. I think many people will be interested to hear more about your orders. How about three nights from tonight? That will give us time to get word out and prepare. Can I send my servant around to pick you up for dinner, sir?"

"Yes, I would welcome that. We must ensure we all have the same understanding. And yes, I would very much welcome seeing your good lady once again. Until then, gentlemen."

***

Lieutenant Burns turned to his commanding officer as the door closed behind Nelson and the two men sat down once again.

"Sir, forgive me, but I confess I am shocked. Perhaps I am missing something, but it seems to me that man's arrogance knows no bounds. He has no respect for you or our work."

Captain Moutray laughed. "Gerald, you really must learn to deal with things as they come. Of course he's arrogant. There's no lack of that in the Navy. And, trust me, this man is not stupid."

The Captain paused a moment in thought before looking intensely at his officer. He knew the shortcomings of his First Officer well and smiled at the thought of what was to come. "Yes indeed, I know one thing for certain, Mr. Burns. I think things are going to get most interesting around here."

***

The evening was warm, almost to the point of being stifling. Fortunately, Captain Moutray's home was on the side of a hill near the capital St. John's, affording at least some breeze to give relief.

The number of people at dinner grew to over twenty seated at the long table. The island's Governour, Thomas Shirley, was present along with four local plantation owners, a senior officer from the local military garrison, a senior customs official, and all of their wives and escorts. The group filled the room to capacity. Captain Sands from the Latona had also been invited to attend and was joined by John Collins, Captain of the smaller HMS Rattler, returned from a patrol with barely sufficient time to change into his dress uniform.

Conversation was light as they mingled before dinner and then later around the table as they were all starved for the latest news from home. Nelson knew he would be pumped for information and won gratitude for having thought to bring several extra newspapers from home for the locals to devour.

The Commissioner's wife, Mary Moutray, was the sun around which the younger men in the room revolved. Over twenty years junior to her middle aged husband she shared the vibrancy of youth with the young Navy officers. She was also strikingly good looking and seemed to have a genuine affection for the young naval officers, who were all intent on finding ways to make her smile. Nelson's two younger Captains, Sands and Collins, enjoyed their alcohol and the more they drank the more gregarious they became. A stiff competition for her attention quickly developed.

The real business of the dinner came afterwards, as the men retired with their drinks to the main sitting area of the house, leaving the women to their own devices. Captain Moutray looked around the room as everyone settled in.

"Well, gentlemen, are we all comfortable? Drinks refilled? Excellent." Turning to Nelson, he offered a brief smile. "Captain, you have our undivided attention. We'd all like to hear about your orders and your plans to achieve them."

Nelson smiled in return as he looked at the watching faces. Most gave no indication of their thoughts, but they all had one thing in common. None of them were smiling.

"Gentlemen, I look forward to working with all of you. My orders are straightforward. As I mentioned to Captain Moutray the other day the Admiralty desires the Dockyard facilities expanded and they want it done soon. Antigua and English Harbour are strategically well placed in this part of the Caribbean to meet the needs of the Navy now and in future. It is in everyone's best interests that this need be met, of course."

Two of the plantation owners reacted with grunts of disbelief while a few others in the room groaned openly, allowing grimaces to flash across their faces before they all mastered themselves.

"I will of course be doing my utmost to protect shipping and trade in the Northern Leeward Islands. I intend to make our presence felt on and around all of the islands. The number of privateers and pirates operating in the area has dropped considerably from what I understand, but we must be vigilant. We need to show the flag to keep our diplomats happy. The Admiralty also wants the usual regular reports on, hmm— naval matters in the area. I have some surveying duties to perform, too."

Keeping a deliberately bland look on his face, Nelson paused and looked around the room.

"And, I have been tasked with enforcing the Order in Council regarding Navigation which I'm sure you're all aware of."

"And we've never seen such a pile of rot, sir," said John Roberts, one of the plantation owners, in a burst of anger. "These fools in London are going to ruin us, sir. Ruin, I tell you! They'll kill our businesses with this nonsense and then where will they be?"

"I can't believe the Navy has the bloody gall to intervene in what is a purely commercial matter, sir," said another of the owners, his irritation clear in his voice. "The Customs tariffs and their collection is not your affair."

"Captain Nelson," said Governour Shirley, interrupting before Nelson could respond. "As you can see, there are strong feelings on the islands around here about this, so let me help you understand. The islands do not produce everything needed to run the plantations, so the owners have no choice but to trade with the Americans. These gentlemen need the free ability to trade without onerous duties burdening them in order to get back on their feet. Damage from hurricanes the last few years has been widespread and crops have suffered significantly in the area. They are only now getting back to where they were even five years ago and they need our support, sir."

"Governour Shirley, have you not made representations to London about this?" asked Nelson.

"Of course, sir, of course. I have not met with much success yet, it is true, but I continue to make efforts to help them understand. I am hopeful they will come around. Making the owners use only British crews and ships angers the Americans. They know we need them and have already threatened to add their own ridiculous duties in retaliation. And making the owners here pay even higher duties will bankrupt them all. Do you see, sir? I ask you, what is your intent? In light of this, I hope you will be circumspect about your orders? All we ask is take your time about following them while we sort this out."

Nelson sighed and took a sip of his drink. "Gentlemen, I understand your issues and I have some sympathy. We all have our jobs to do, don't we? But I simply cannot agree to what you ask. My orders are clear and the understanding I was given is they come from the highest levels of government. I can only assume your representations have been heard and dismissed, sir."

Several men in the room groaned and a number tried to speak. The Customs man, George Lawson, managed to shout them down and turned to Nelson.

"Sir, as His Majesty's senior Customs Officer here I confess I am shocked the Navy is involving itself in an area that is so clearly the domain of Customs. It has always been our role to enforce collection of duties and to ensure attempts to circumvent the rules are kept in check. I really don't understand why your involvement is necessary."

Nelson regarded the Customs official with barely disguised contempt. "Well, perhaps, sir, the government thinks you need some help."

The Customs man's eyes widened, but he pressed on, unwilling to concede. "Captain Nelson. Surely you see this is really in the domain of the Customs Office. If you must do this you should at the least be operating with the authority of a deputation from Customs. I recommend you request such from London before you take action. I'd be happy to assist with preparing it if need be."

Nelson could no longer contain himself, offering a laugh as he shook his head in wonder. "Sir, the only 'deputation' I require is what my orders say. And they are very, very clear."

Several of the men in the room groaned once again and, as one, the four plantation owners looked at each other and got up to leave.

"I've never heard such nonsense," said one, pulling on his coat, his face flushed with anger.

"Bloody Navy. Same as ever," growled another.

"Well, sir, you've made yourself understood," said the owner named Roberts. "So let us be understood. Good luck getting everything you need done in the Dockyard without our help. Good luck getting anything done with anything. You'll not have our support. Captain Moutray, our thanks to you and your good wife for a fine dinner."

Several of the others began leaving as well and the next few minutes were occupied with farewells as they climbed into their coaches for the journey home. Captain Moutray pulled Nelson to the side and begged him to stay a few moments, so Nelson agreed.

"Sir, a word of advice if I may," said Moutray as they stood on the porch watching the last of the guests leave. Nelson nodded in reply.

"We know each other well, don't we? We've had our disagreements in past and still do, but we have always been friends, have we not? So I offer this with that in mind. The plantation owners take this issue quite seriously and their needs are real. They, and their supporters you saw tonight, will actively throw roadblocks in your way. These men have resources you cannot hope to match."

Nelson smiled and shook his host's hand in departure. "Well, we'll see about that."

Chapter Three
August/September 1784
Antigua

Dreams. He was shifting and swirling from one impossible situation to another. A vague sense of danger and threats surrounding him on all sides gave the feeling of being cornered. But most of all, an overwhelming, constant anger filled him. The problem was a sense of building pressure and of a tiny light touching his consciousness. Some outside influence was trying to force him to do something. The temptation to resist and remain in his unconscious stupor was strong, but whatever the unknown force was simply wouldn't let him. He felt his head lifted, cradled in someone's hand, and as he opened his eyes a stream of water began flowing down his throat.

"Gakkk—" he croaked as the shock of returning to consciousness made him choke on the unexpected water.

The old black woman pouring the water stopped as she saw his eyes focus on her, still holding his head up to drink. "Well, well, look who's awake. I think you're going to make it after all. Would you like some more water?"

Still reeling and disoriented from the shock of waking, Evan took a moment to digest what she had said and realized his mouth was completely parched of moisture. He managed another croak and the briefest of nods in response.

The woman smiled and replied with the rich accent of people born in the islands. "I thought so. Drink up, son, it'll do you good."

Several large sips later he finally let his head slip back to the pillow. The mere act of drinking had exhausted him. Seeing he was done she rearranged the mosquito netting around him back into place.

"Excellent. Now, back to sleep for you. I think tomorrow morning will be soon enough to check on you again."

As she spoke Evan realized the only light was coming from a candle the old woman picked up and carried out with her as she left the room. As total darkness fell Evan slipped back into unconsciousness, still wondering what had happened.

The next morning he opened his eyes and focused on the ceiling above him, trying to understand why it looked wrong. With sudden insight he understood; what he saw was not the familiar ship's deck ceiling he expected. Looking around he realized the room was suffused with full daylight and a gentle breeze was blowing throughout from the open window. Still groggy and befuddled, Evan struggled to move, but found little strength to do so.

Becoming frustrated, he opened his mouth to call for help, but once again all he could get out was a croak. Moving what little saliva was in his mouth around, he made a supreme effort to speak.

"Hel—hello?" was still all he could manage, lifting his head a few inches off the pillow before collapsing back once again.

The door opened and the same old black woman from the night before peered in. Seeing him awake she offered him a broad smile. "I was right! You are awake. I'll be right back."

Moments later she bustled in with a jug of water and eyed him carefully. "Well, I think you

46

really are going to stay alive after all. Right, lets get you fixed up here."

She was soon pouring more water down his throat and gauging his reaction. Seeing he remained conscious she wet a cloth and wiped his face with it, which made him realize he had a rough, uneven growth of beard. The sensation was wonderfully refreshing, though, and Evan found the strength to turn and look at the old woman.

"Who—who are you? Where am I?" he managed to rasp out.

The old woman laughed. "Full of questions, aren't you? My name is Betty and I'm your nurse, of course. Here, if you're going to keep talking we may as well sit you up a little." Walking over to a cabinet in one corner of the room she pulled out some pillows and set about propping him up in the bed.

Evan was still trying to process the thought he needed a nurse as she was hauling him upright, when the memory of the fight came crashing back. Looking down as she lifted him up he saw only a heavily bandaged, small stump where his left arm had once been.

"Oh God!" he groaned, as the full realization of what had happened struck.

"Yes, Mr. Ross, you've had a tough time," said the old woman as she finished propping him up with enough support to ensure he was stable.

"Good Christ, I asked him not to take it off," said Evan as a wave of black despair at the ramifications of having lost his arm sunk in. "God, I've lost everything."

"Everything?" said Betty, a look of compassion in her eyes if not in her voice. "That's a bit of an exaggeration, don't you think?"

"You don't understand," replied Evan with a tone of angry dejection in his voice. "I'm an officer. Officers need two arms, not one. This is the excuse my Captain was looking for. He'll get rid of me for certain now."

As he said it a sudden look of horror crossed his face and he stared fiercely at the old woman. "Wait, where am I and where is my ship?"

"Mr. Ross, this is Antigua and you are in the hospital at Shirley Heights, near the Dockyard. This is the new hospital that they are just finishing building. The old hospital right outside the Dockyard was pretty full so they sent you here, since it was close enough to being done to serve your needs. As for your ship, it's long gone. I expect they are back in England by now."

Evan groaned and closed his eyes. "Oh, God."

"Your ship stopped here long enough to offload you and the contraband they captured. I'm told the ship's surgeon didn't think you would survive the journey home and he felt you'd have a better chance here with us. He feared you would suffer from infection and he was right. You've been very, very sick Mr. Ross."

Evan sighed in disbelief. "It wasn't the surgeon, it was my Captain. He told the surgeon to make up some excuse to leave me behind."

"Well, however it happened, you're here now. Oh, I forgot to mention you're not alone. Your sailor Mr. Wilton is here too."

"Wilton? What— oh, he was shot too! What did they leave him behind for?"

The old woman shrugged. "They told me it was the same reason for both of you. Are you hungry? Feel like you could eat something?"

Even as she spoke Evan realized he was ravenous and he nodded. The old woman smiled to see his sudden hunger and stood up.

"I'll go see what we can find to feed you. I've been spooning broth into you for a few weeks now, so I think it's time you had something more substantial."

"Weeks? Good God, how long have I been unconscious?"

"Today is August the first, Mr. Ross. You're young and strong and that helped you through this. But like I said, you were very sick. After we get some real food in you we'll have a look at that dressing on your wound."

A few minutes after she left the door to the room opened once again, but this time the black sailor Wilton peered in and entered when he saw Evan awake. He did so cautiously as his right arm was fully occupied managing the crutch he was using. He was able to plant his right foot on the floor, but put only minimal weight on it.

"Lieutenant Ross! I'm glad to see you've pulled through, sir," he said, gingerly dropping into the chair beside the bed and saluting.

"Mr. Wilton," said Evan. He studied the man before him for a few long moments before looking pointedly at Wilton's leg. "That ball was meant for me, wasn't it? You saved me."

Wilton shrugged and made to brush it off, but Evan continued. "Don't play it down. It's come back to me. That bastard's gun was aimed at my heart."

"Sir, I thought I could stop him. I reacted, same as anyone else would. I hadn't seen where he was aiming until I got past you. Lucky for me that Marine jostled his arm or I wouldn't be sitting here right now. Just doing my job, sir."

"Well," said Evan. "I am in your debt, Mr. Wilton. I wouldn't be lying here if you hadn't. I don't know how to repay you. Mind you, I don't have a future anymore. Perhaps it would have been better to take a shot to the heart."

Wilton stared at Evan for a moment before responding. "Forgive me for saying this, sir, but that's nonsense. We'll get ourselves out of here and back to a ship once we're better."

Evan shrugged in response. "Maybe you, perhaps, but me? No one is going to want a one armed officer, Mr. Wilton."

"Maybe no one will want a lame master's mate, sir. But I won't know unless I try, right?"

Evan closed his eyes and sighed. From somewhere deep inside a little voice responded to the sense of loss and the temptation to simply give in flooding through him. The voice pushed back the fear.

With a deep breath, Evan opened his eyes and looked over at the sailor waiting patiently for him to respond. "You are right, of course. Can't give up. Allow me my moment of weakness, Mr. Wilton. Well, it would seem the two of us are in this together. Nothing for it, we'll have to get better and find our way out of this mess."

"Deal?" said Evan as he stuck out his hand.

Wilton hesitated a moment, smiled, and grasped his officer's hand hard. "It's a deal, sir."

Evan looked down at Wilton's leg, a puzzled look on his face. "So what is the prognosis for your leg? The ball obviously didn't hit a major artery or the bone. You wouldn't have that leg still if it had. But you're still hobbling around on a crutch?"

"Yes, sir. You are correct I was fortunate the shot went straight through without hitting bone. It got infected like your wound, though I don't think mine was as bad."

A worried look stole over his face for a moment as he paused to gingerly rub the thick bandage wrapped around his thigh. "The doctor seems to think I may have some bad damage on the inside, though. I may be walking with a limp for the rest of my life."

The door opened as Betty brought in a steaming tray filled with food. A heaping plate of fresh fruit accompanied two large bowls filled with an aromatic fish soup with bread and butter on the side. Both men looked at it like starving wolves and she laughed, giving the black sailor a big smile. "Yes, Mr. Wilton, I knew you'd be hungry so I brought enough for the two of you!"

Despite the deep depression Evan was struggling with he couldn't stop a tiny smile from surfacing on seeing how Wilton had obviously wriggled his way into her heart.

After their meal Betty removed his old bandage. The small stump of his arm was still an angry reddish colour, but Betty assured him this was much improved from when he first arrived in the hospital. The wound was still painful enough her ministrations aggravated it. Seeing him wince, she stopped to give him a spoonful of laudanum to ease the pain. As she finished applying a fresh bandage to his wound he quizzed her further.

"Betty? Has anyone from the Dockyard come by or asked about me or Mr. Wilton?"

"Sorry, no," she replied, stepping back to examine her handiwork.

51

"Did anyone say anything about who I'm to report to when they brought us?"

Betty could only shrug. "I think you're going to have to show up and ask them."

"Right, well, maybe in a day or two I'll check with them."

Betty laughed and shook her head.

"What?" he said, looking annoyed.

"Mr. Ross, you barely had the energy to eat and get out of bed long enough to use the chamber pot today! I don't know if you noticed it, but you're a lot thinner now than when you came in here, despite my good care. It's going to take you a long time to get back to where you were. If those people in the Dockyard are so busy they can't ride up here to check on you that's their problem, don't you think? You don't want to try doing too much until you're ready for it and I don't know what point there would be showing up and asking for something to do when you aren't up to it."

Evan hung his head a moment before replying. "You're right. I guess I'm not thinking clearly yet."

"I know I'm right, I'm the nurse around here, remember? Maybe tomorrow, note I said maybe, we'll see if we can get you up on your feet and moving around. Your sailor Mr. Wilton has found himself a nice shady bench to sit on outside and I'm sure he'd enjoy some company."

Giving him a broad smile, she left the room once again.

***

The passing days became passing weeks. Evan and the sailor Wilton spent several days sitting on the bench outside the front entrance of the hospital watching the construction activity still going on around the hospital and on Shirley Heights. No one came to ask or enquire after either of them, and their concern grew with each passing day. Slowly, ever so slowly, the two men grew closer in a friendship between officer and seaman, which in normal circumstances would have been unthinkable.

Evan was also slowly growing accustomed to not having his left arm. He was fortunate to be right handed so he didn't have to learn how to make do with a weaker hand. Being without two hands made a huge difference in so many tasks, though. The simple act of carrying something while trying to open a door or even climbing in and out of bed all took longer to do. Evan found himself thinking about how to do even the smallest of tasks, many of which previously wouldn't even have required conscious effort.

Although Betty insisted his arm was healing well he continued experiencing pain for which he took a dose of laudanum every night to help him sleep. With sleep came nightmares, impossible situations filled with vaguely menacing forms. He woke many nights drenched in sweat. He soon discovered Mr. Wilton was experiencing similar nightmares and difficulty with sleeping. On several occasions both men found themselves feeling angry and on edge for no apparent reason.

As the two men grew increasingly restless a doctor finally stopped by on his rounds to check on the two men in the first week of September. Pronouncing himself satisfied with progress the man made to get up and leave.

"Doctor?" said Evan, stopping him before he could walk out the door. "Are we fit for duty? Are you reporting on this to the Navy?"

"Eh? Heavens, no, I'm not a Navy doctor nor am I reporting to anyone. It's part of my practice to help care for patients here. I knew you two were the only ones here at the moment and that you were going to be here for a while. Betty would have contacted me if there were any problems, which is why I haven't been by for a while. Anyway, no, I will not be doing a report unless someone wants to pay me to do that. As to 'fit for duty' I— hmm, let me think."

The doctor paused a few moments to study the two men. "The earliest either of you should consider presenting yourself for duty is the end of September. Between now and then both of you should continue to eat well. Make sure you rest. I'm going to tell Betty to slowly wean both of you off the laudanum so you'll sleep better. It really is imperative you get your rest. You can begin periodic exercise to build your muscles again. I'd say both of you probably lost almost twenty pounds and it's going to take a while to get that back."

The two men looked at each other and realized the truth; the clothes they both wore hung loose about their frames. As the doctor left Evan turned and looked at Wilton.

"Right. I don't know about you but I've had enough of sitting around not knowing our fate. I don't care what anybody says, I'm going to the Dockyard offices tomorrow and tell them we'll be available end of the month. If they won't come to us we will have to go to them."

Mr. Wilton smiled. "Thank God, sir. I don't think either of us are the kind of people to sit around doing nothing. Do you want me to come with you, sir?"

"No. Don't worry, I'll bring you into the conversation and find out for both of us."

***

Early the next day Evan removed his dress uniform from his sea chest and with Mr. Wilton's help pulled it on. The empty sleeve dangling loose didn't seem right so Mr. Wilton used a pin to fold it up and make it more presentable. Brushing himself off, Evan was about to leave when Betty walked in and frowned at him.

"And where do you think you are going?"

"Only to the Dockyard office, Betty. We can't take this waiting anymore. We need to let them know we're here and will be available soon."

Betty continued frowning at him for a few moments, but slowly her face softened. "Well, you are getting better and I guess I'd be talking to the wall anyway. You're going to go do this regardless of anything I say."

She paused a moment and folded her arms, looking stern once again. "It's a fair ride to the Dockyard office and it's hot out there. Are you taking some water and Mr. Wilton with you? Mr. Ross, I insist. You two both think you're stronger than you really are."

"Nonsense, Betty, I can manage on my own."

This time she put her hands on her hips, unwilling to give in. "Who's the nurse here, you or me? Besides, Mr. Wilton could use a change of scenery like you."

With a sigh Evan agreed. "I bow to your wishes. Have you something we can take some water in?"

Ten minutes later they had horses borrowed from the engineers working on the Heights

55

fortifications and were riding down the hill to the Dockyard offices in the distance. The early morning sun wasn't too intense, so the ride was pleasant enough with little sips of water periodically to sustain them. Finding a way to mount his horse with only one arm proved a frustrating experience, but Evan finally managed it after a few tries without help.

"Sir?" said Mr. Wilton. "What are we going to do if they have nothing for us?"

"God, I don't want to think about it. I don't know. Return to England, I guess. There's nothing there for me, though. What about you?"

As he said it, he turned and looked at him as if for the first time. "Here we've spent all this time together and I don't know much about you. In fact, I don't even know your first name."

"James, sir. James Wilton."

"James Wilton. That's a good name. What's your story, James? You're black, but you don't have the accent of the islands. And you've obviously been in the Navy long enough you know your way around. It takes time and skill to become a master's mate. Are you an escaped slave? Don't worry, the secret will be safe with me."

"No, sir," said Wilton, a touch of pride in his voice. "I'm as British as you, sir. My Dad was a Navy officer, a Lieutenant like you. His name was Richard. He'd been stationed out here and when he returned he brought my Mom back to England with him. She was already pregnant with me. She actually was a slave, but he bought and freed her before I was born."

Evan wore a surprised look and raised an eyebrow in response. "And how did that go over with his family?"

"Better than you might expect. A few of them wanted absolutely nothing to do with coloured people in the family, but most of them had no problem and welcomed us with open arms. Anyway, my father died when I was only ten years old. He was off on a long mission to the East Indies. He got the fever in Bombay and never recovered. Mom got pneumonia and died one winter a few years later so I'm on my own now. The family did all right by me, though. They made sure I went to school, so I can read and write as good as anyone."

Evan looked at him with renewed interest. "How did you end up in the Navy as a sailor? If you were the son of an officer you could have followed in his footsteps."

Wilton gave Evan a quick, wry smile. "Well, because it could happen doesn't mean it will, sir. It's true, the family tried for me, but they didn't have much influence with anyone. The family did all right with money, but none of them were rich enough to have the pull to get attention for me. So none of the captains were willing to take me on as a midshipman. I could have gone for a merchant ship, but I figured with a war on the horizon the Navy was for me. Volunteered when I turned fourteen. I guess I wanted to follow in Dad's footsteps. With both of them gone there was really nothing to keep me in England so here I am."

"Forgive me for asking here, but can you prove all of this?"

Wilton looked hard at Evan before responding. "Yes, sir. I have all the paperwork. I've got my birth certificate, which lists both of my parents. I have my parent's birth certificates and I even have my Dad's commission papers. Do you mind if I ask you why, sir?"

"Well, this is a lesson learned, Mr. Wilton. I made assumptions about you. I thought you were just a simple sailor, but I see I was wrong. And the reason I'm asking is so I can file this away for the future. I told you I owed you, Mr. Wilton. I don't know if or how this information could ever be useful, but it may be some day."

As they reached the entrance to the Dockyard, dismounted, and tied up their mounts, a scruffy dog moved out of the shade and came to greet them. As he neared the men they realized the dog was obviously a mongrel. He had several scars crisscrossing his body, one of which revealed where it had somehow lost one of its hind legs. Despite missing a limb the dog had adapted and was able to move about with a hopping gait at a remarkable speed. Evan absentmindedly scratched behind the dog's ear before both men walked off. Asking for directions to the Dockyard Commissioners office they made their way to the entrance. Inside, the same imperious clerk who had stopped Nelson awaited them. A disdainful glance and raised eyebrow was all they got, as he made it evident they were to state their business.

After introducing them both Evan explained their desire to see the Commissioner. The clerk's expression changed little in response, but he did flip through a ledger book beside him. With a sniff he closed the book and looked at Evan.

"The Commissioner is busy. There's simply no room in his schedule for at least a week. I'm afraid you'll have to make an appointment and come back later. Frankly, I'm not even sure he'll want to see you. You aren't part of his staff."

"Well, that's exactly it, you see. We aren't sure whom we should report to, but we'd like to do our duty. Isn't there someone else we could see?"

As Evan spoke the door opened and one of the Dockyard shipwrights left the office. "All right, look here," said the clerk with a resigned sigh. "The Commissioner has a brief break right now so let me go in and explain your request. I'll see what he says. Please take a seat."

"That's kind of you," said Evan as the clerk walked into the Commissioner's office.

A few minutes later he returned, closing the door behind him and looking at the two men. "Well, I was right. He's far too busy to see you. He suggests you talk to one of his senior officers. His name is Lieutenant Gerald Burns. You are to explain your situation to him and seek his guidance. I'm afraid that's the best we can do."

"Thank you, we appreciate your help. And where can we find Lieutenant Burns?"

"The office across the hall and two doors down. But I don't think he's there right now. I believe he's due back in a half hour if you'd care to wait in his office."

"We shall. Thank you again."

Making their way to the Lieutenant's office, which was open, they made themselves comfortable as best they could in the two hard backed chairs in front of the officer's desk.

James eventually broke the companionable silence. "Sir? We talked about me, but now you have me curious in return. You seemed quite concerned your career in the Navy may be over. I think you said you have nothing to go back to, if you don't mind me asking that is?"

Evan sighed, shifting in his chair to get more comfortable. "The Navy is all I have, Mr. Wilton. There's not much to tell, really. I'm the third son in our family and you undoubtedly know what that means. And yes, my parents are gone too. That bad chest fever and cough that came through a few years ago took them both. So my oldest brother John inherited the bulk of the estate and the title."

Evan paused and shook his head. "He's an arsehole. I don't even like talking about him. If he'd had his way the rest of us in the family would've been left out in the cold. Fortunately, my Dad had the will so well prepared he couldn't find a way to break it, at least not without costing him far too much money. So the rest of us have our annual allowance from the estate as long as we live and John has decided to give up on trying to rob us of it. It's not a large allowance, but with that and my Navy pay I get by comfortably. My brother Francis is in the Horse Guards posted God knows where now. My sister Fran married an officer in the 1st Foot and is with him at Gibraltar, or at least that's where they were last I heard."

Pausing for a moment he gave James a tiny smile. "So it was the Navy for me. I wanted to do something. See the world. So yes, I've been in the Navy since I was thirteen and you can see why I'm concerned. All that I am today is really due to the Navy and my own hard work. If this was to end there won't be anyone to turn to. Like you, I guess."

As James nodded in reply Lieutenant Burns walked in through the open door. The two men stood and saluted the surprised officer. Looking annoyed at the intrusion he brusquely demanded an explanation for their presence as he waved them back to their seats. As Evan explained the situation a look of boredom grew on his face and he rudely stared out the window.

Burns gave a condescending grunt and returned his gaze as Evan finished. "Well, sir, I'm not surprised Captain Moutray had no idea what to do with you since I don't either. Neither of you have any expertise that could be of use around here. We are a highly specialized operation here, sir."

"I understand, sir. We were both thinking more along the lines of active service on a ship."

"Well, you'd have to talk to Captain Nelson about that, I should think. He's the new senior officer for the active service around here."

The look on Lieutenant Burn's face was unmistakably a sneer, but before Evan could question him further the Dockyard officer continued.

"In case you're wondering he's not here right now. He's a madman, if you ask me. He dashed off to St Kitts yesterday, God knows why. It's still hurricane season out here, you know. Anyway, I'm afraid you're out of luck there."

"Ah, would that be Captain Horatio Nelson, sir?" Seeing the Dockyard officer nod he continued. "Well, that's interesting. Do you know when he'll be back, sir?"

"No idea," said Burn's with a dismissive wave of his hand. Sitting back in his chair he eyed both of them with a contemplative look. "See here, I'm a little puzzled. You have both been badly injured. Do you seriously think you'll be able to resume your careers?"

The two men looked at each other before Evan looked back at Burns. "Yes, sir, we do."

"Huh. Well, I must be honest with you both. I think that doubtful. You maybe don't want to hear that, I know. I really think you should be realistic about this, however. We are at peace, gentlemen. I'm given to understand there's no shortage of fully able-bodied officers seeking employment these days. And lame sailors, even master's mates, well. I think the preference is the same as it would be for officers."

"Sir, I appreciate your frankness, but we'd still like to talk to Captain Nelson. Would you be so good as to let him know of our presence and that we expect to be ready for duty, whatever it may be, by the end of September?"

"Of course, Lieutenant, of course. Now, if that's all I have a frightfully busy day ahead of me."

The two dispirited men arose and gave him thanks once again as they departed.

James looked at Evan as they returned to their mounts. "Do you know this Captain Nelson, sir?"

"No, not personally, but his reputation seems to be growing around the fleet. The word is he's a fighting Captain. If you're on his ship you'll find yourself in action likely sooner rather than later. Well, we're going to have to prove ourselves to him, aren't we?"

The ride back to the hospital seemed twice as long as both men were lost in glum thoughts and worries for the future. Neither man could say anything to stop the deep, black depression winding its tentacles around every thought, dragging their spirits into what felt like the depths of the sea.

Chapter Four
September/October 1784
Antigua

The days blurred together. Betty was insistent they exercise themselves as much as possible and ever so slowly they began to bring tone back to their muscles. The weight slowly returned too, courtesy of Betty's plentiful cooking. Although she was a rather uninspired cook she always ensured they had plenty to eat. But the lack of purpose to their days and worry for the future began to weigh on both men.

The nightmares and the anger had waned, but not disappeared as she weaned them both off the laudanum. Betty rushed into Evan's room one night, drawn by the sound of a loud crash. She found him sitting at his desk, blankly staring at the wall with his hand on his head in despair. The noise drawing her in was the result of Evan sweeping everything off the desk to smash to the floor.

"Mr. Ross? Mr. Ross!"

"Ah— what?" said Evan. The surprise was clear on his face, as if he was surfacing from a deep sleep. He stared at his hand before looking at the mess on the floor, vacantly trying to understand what had happened. Betty could only give him a long hug and put him to bed, after administering another small dose of the laudanum to give him ease.

No one from the Dockyard or any of the ships at anchor contacted them and the resulting frustration from the sense they were forgotten was the worst. Some days they walked down the hill to the nearest beach where they swam and sunned themselves. Other days the two men grew into the habit of walking every evening to the top of the Heights, where the lookout was slowly being built, to watch the sun go down and stare longingly at the ships in the harbour.

What came out of their time together was their friendship. The shared bonds of injury and the worry of being cast aside as useless drew them together. The closeness of the two men was apparent to the engineers and workers doing construction on the Heights, raising a few eyebrows. Officers and the men they led were not supposed to be friends.

The commanding officer of the engineers, an amiable, older man with a thick Scottish accent, approached them when they first began poking around the fortifications. Learning their situation, he raised his eyebrows and smiled.

"Sure, lads, feel free to poke about. If you feel like helping you're welcome to pitch in! Haul a few rocks for us."

Neither man cared about the puzzlement their relationship generated around them. James had shown his birth certificate and other documents to Evan after their first trip to the Dockyard and Evan filed the information away in his mind for the future. The fact James's father had been an officer changed the dynamic of the relationship and made friendship much easier to explain if asked.

But no one did. The construction work commissioned for the fortifications at the Heights and the nearby Block House was extensive and commanded the full attention of the military engineers. Their focus at the moment was on building the military barracks to accommodate the full garrison when the time came. Some of the major fortifications were already done, such as the Block House, situated on a slightly lower hill near the

Heights and intended as a signal station and defence for the approaches to English Harbour from the north and east. The Heights themselves, however, were most impressive. The hill towered a full thousand feet above the sea and commanded an amazing view of the Dockyard and the Harbour. Falmouth Bay glittered in the far distance past the Harbour.

The injured men saw the cannon the engineers would eventually have in place when the work was done would dominate the Harbour entrance without difficulty. An attacker of the facilities could also face a chain stretched almost a thousand feet across the entrance, from Fort Berkeley on one point to the other side of Freemans Bay and the Pillars of Hercules. The chain was an excellent defence against nighttime cutting out raids and during the day it would slow an attacking force significantly. The attackers would have to be determined indeed to force their entrance.

But the work was proceeding slowly and some days not at all. Curious, Evan approached the senior engineer one day for an explanation. He grimaced and spat in disgust.

"I was only half joking that day we first met when I suggested you haul some rocks for us. What few men we have to do the job simply aren't enough. The slaves the plantation owners lend us do the real work. The problem is they don't really want to lend them to us. It's only because Governour Shirley makes the owners support us that this is happening. These shipping rules that the government wants enforced aren't helping matters, either. The plantation owners are getting extremely good at inventing reasons why they can't free their slaves for our use. But we do what we can."

As he finished speaking a small party of slaves went past them pushing a heavy barrow full of limestone, used for fill between the stones of the growing fortifications, up the slope of the hill. A white man, not in uniform, came behind. Whenever he thought one of the slaves was shirking he struck the man with a cane hard across the back. When one of the slaves slipped on the gravel slope, falling hard on his face, the overseer began beating the stricken man and shouting at him to get up and back to work.

"Easy there, man," said the Scottish engineer. "Give the lad a chance to get up."

The overseer looked over to where the three men were standing and grunted in disgust. "If you want this place built you'll shut your face and let me get on with it. Start showing these animals leniency and there'll be trouble." Turning back he scowled and resumed beating the slave as the man struggled to his feet.

The barrow began moving once again and the man paused, turning his scowl to the watching men. "Besides, they are the property of my master and as one of his overseers, I can do whatever I want with his property. So mind your own business."

Turning away without waiting for a response the man strode after the still struggling slaves.

"Pleasant fellow, what?" said the engineer.

The two sailors were shocked. "Good Lord, are these plantation overseers all like that?" asked Evan.

"Hmm," replied the engineer. "I couldn't say 'all', but from what I've seen on the projects I've worked on out here the last few years I'd say there's a fair number. I don't like it, but this is the way it seems to work out here. The slaves are the ones that get the jobs done. I don't know why they need to be treated so badly, though. Mind you, sailors get beatings too for shirking, do they not?"

"Well, yes, the bosun and his mates keep the crew in line, for certain," replied Evan. "But that's different. There are rules, sir. And British sailors are not property, either. It looked to me like the only rules those slaves have to live by are whatever suits that man at any given time."

By the last week of September both men could take it no longer. Both felt stronger and while neither truly felt as they did before they were injured, they did feel strong enough to stand before a senior officer and report for duty. Borrowing horses once again, they made the journey back to the Dockyard.

As before, they reported to the Dockyard Commissioner's office and faced the same officious clerk. He sent them off once again to see Lieutenant Burns, who was not in his office. As the clerk had no idea when he would return the men resolved to leave and return the next day.

As they returned to their mounts another officer detached himself from a group of nearby workers and approached them.

"Gentlemen, I am Lieutenant Long, Second Officer here in the Dockyard. Who are you and what are you doing here?"

As they explained their purpose the man frowned. Obviously searching his memory, his face cleared as he remembered. "Ah, I recall now. Yes, Gerald mentioned you. If you're looking for Lieutenant Burns, sir, he is away and won't be back today. "

"Hmm," said Evan. "Do you know if there are any orders for us, sir?"

"Orders? No, no orders. Haven't heard a thing."

"Um, we were given to believe word of our presence would be passed to Captain Nelson? His ship was in port the other day, I thought."

"It was indeed in port, but I think he left for Nevis last night. I believe he's due back soon, but I can't really be sure. As for word of you I don't know if that was passed on. If Lieutenant Burns said it would be then I'm sure he likely did. Given the injuries you two have sustained perhaps there has been no rush to bring you back."

"Yes, perhaps," said Evan, trying not to let his dismay show. "Well, we shouldn't trouble you further. Please, if you do have opportunity to mention us to Captain Nelson we would be grateful."

As they went to mount their horses the same mongrel greeting them on their first visit came out and stopped beside them. As Evan and James smiled at the dog Lieutenant Long had a very different reaction, shocking both men by aiming a swift kick at the animal. The dog yelped and ran off to the safety of cover under a bush.

"Here, was that necessary, sir?" said Evan.

The Dockyard Lieutenant looked at Evan as if he was an imbecile. "It's a mongrel. The scruffy bastard's been hanging around here begging for weeks. No place for strays here as far as I'm concerned. Let one in and we'll have a menagerie around here in no time." Turning, he stalked off.

Seeing him leave James walked over to where the dog cautiously poked his head out of cover and let James scratch behind his ear, earning him some grateful tail wagging.

"At least the dog is glad to see us if no one else is, sir."

***

A week later they tried reporting to the Dockyard again, only to get the same vague response as to orders. Nelson, together with all the other warships in harbour had apparently not gone to Nevis. They instead had left for Barbados for the regular post hurricane season meeting of all Captains of the Leeward Islands Station and no one knew when they would return. When the two men got back to the hospital Betty saw their frustration. Wordlessly she sat the two men down and poured two mugs of ale for the thirsty, dejected men. Listening to their tale she grimaced and sighed.

"You two need a break from me and my cooking. I was talking to the doctor about you two and we both agree you need a change of scenery to improve your spirits. He suggested hiring a buggy and going to St. John's. Spend the day in town and sightsee. Maybe even stay overnight if you want. Stop at a tavern and have a drink. Find a place to cook you fresh fish right off the boat. I can even recommend one if you like. My youngest sister and her husband run a tavern right on Market Street called The Flying Fish Inn. I'm serious. You two listen up, I'm your nurse and I prescribe some vacation time away from this place."

The two men looked at each other and both shrugged at the same time.

"Sure," said Evan, a small smile coming to his face as he rubbed his chin in thought. "I could use a change of scenery. Let's do it."

After an early lunch the next day the two men borrowed a horse and buggy from the engineers and rode into town. The ride took a little over an hour through the low, rolling hills of Antigua, passing field after field of sugarcane waving in the breeze. Several of the plantations had large numbers of slaves working the fields and almost as one the two men came to a surprising realization; the vast majority of the slaves toiling in the hot sun were women.

"Mr. Ross, sir? I don't get this."

"Not sure I do either. We must be sure to ask Betty why that is."

The roads were much more congested once they got closer to the centre of town. The bustle of people was overwhelming after the relative isolation the two men had lived in for over two months. Navigating their buggy through the narrow streets and around the biggest potholes in the road while not hitting people on foot was a struggle. The closer they got to Market Street and the heart of the port the busier it got.

Most of the faces going by on foot were black. White men and sometimes women mostly occupied the few other buggies on the road similar to theirs. Both the businesses and people on the street were a riot of colour and variety. A blacksmith shop was next door to a general store, which was right next to a spice seller. A nearby bakery was dispensing fragrant, fresh loaves of bread. A huge number of stalls all jumbled together in a winding snake comprised the local fruit and vegetable market offering an amazing array of varieties, many of which the men couldn't put a name to. Near the waterfront was a sprawling, reeking fish market. A group of large black men were using massive cleavers to chop and clean an obviously fresh catch from one of the boats anchored offshore.

"My Lord, sir, look at the size of that shark!" gasped James.

Evan couldn't believe his eyes as he risked a quick glance in the direction James indicated. The shark was a hammerhead and well over twelve feet long. Both men shuddered inwardly; sharks filled the nightmares of every seaman.

"Mr. Wilton, that looks like an inn over there— ah, this is our destination. I see a sign that says it's the Flying Fish. Lets get out of this madness and see if they have a stable there that can take care of our horse and this buggy."

Betty's sister Emma wasn't available, but they introduced themselves to her husband Walton and he did indeed have a stable. A short while later they were away on foot. Being far too early for dinner, the two men decided to explore the town. The next few hours were spent simply walking about and taking in the sights.

The harbour quickly drew their attention. A wild array of anchored ships dotted the bay. Large British merchant ships sat moored at the docks right beside a host of shabby, stinking fishing boats, so decrepit neither man could understand how they stayed afloat. Baking in the early afternoon sun in the distance was Rat Island, with its defensive fortifications guarding the harbour entrance and barracks for the soldiers stationed there. Several taverns and small inns dotted the streets around the harbour to serve the obviously busy port.

Most interesting, though, was the presence of a large trading sloop clearly flying American colours tied up at the Customs dock. The two men looked at each other in wonder and shook their heads. "I know what you're thinking, Mr. Wilton, and the answer is I have no idea what they are doing here. Apparently enforcing the trading laws Captain Woods was talking about is easier said than done."

The rest of the town was a rambling mix of shanties and little businesses selling anything and everything. A stone church dominated the surroundings not far from the harbour. The town jail and local militia headquarters were combined into one ramshackle building with a row of gallows poles in the yard beside it. Hooded bodies swaying with the breeze occupied two of them.

Weary of trudging about and thirsty from the heat they headed back to the Inn. The shady, cool interior was welcome relief. Unlike most of the other rickety looking wood frame structures dotting the heart of St. John's, this building was in the minority with walls made of stone. Wide shutters on three sides were open to admit whatever breeze could be had. Several tables with chairs dotted the room, which was already almost full with an assortment of customers drinking ale or rum.

As their eyes adjusted to the shade of the interior they realized everyone inside had turned to look at the newcomers. A few even raised their eyebrows at the sight of unfamiliar faces before looking away.

"Good God, keep one hand on your money and the other on your sword, Mr. Wilton," muttered Evan from the corner of his mouth as they scanned the crowd and made their way to a table.

Wilton couldn't hold back a snort of laughter, but he agreed with Evan as he warily eyed the nearest tables full of ruffians. "Too right, sir."

At least half the crowd was clearly sailors from the ships in the harbour and from all appearances likely quite familiar with the inside of whatever jail existed in their last port of call. One of the tables held a group of soldiers obviously on leave from guard duty on Rat Island. Given the scars and tattoos covering the exposed parts of their bodies, they could easily have been mistaken for a group of pirates were it not for their uniforms. Several plainly dressed, thin black men occupied three or four tables off in one corner. Yet another table held an animated group of men playing a dice game.

Sprinkled among the groups of men were a number of women. Of interest some were black and some white, and several were rather attractive. Given they were in a tavern surrounded by sailors Evan knew what would be on offer if the price was right. What caught their attention next were the two barmen, who obviously doubled as enforcers for the tavern. By far the roughest looking of the lot, they were huge, vicious looking thugs openly wearing two-foot long clubs tethered to their belts. Each man also wore a sheathed knife at his side. As Evan claimed a table near one of the windows he smiled, knowing the barmen likely had more weapons out of sight. Both made a point of sitting with their backs to the wall so they could watch the crowd.

Betty's sister Emma, a much younger and rather slimmer version of her older sister, came bustling over to take their order and talk to them. "Gentlemen! My name is Emma. My husband tells me you're the fellows that stabled your horse and buggy. I'm sorry I missed you earlier. I was busy making sure preparations for tonight's dinner were underway. And how is my big sister? She never comes to visit me anymore! Did I get that right, you are her patients?"

Emma's eyes widened when they explained who they were and why they were indeed her sister's patients. "Lord, we don't often get an officer and his man gracing our establishment!"

Evan cursed himself for having let slip he was an officer. "Hmm, yes, well, let's not bandy that information about, shall we? If anyone asks we're just a couple of Navy boys on leave from the hospital, eh?"

"Of course, sir. It's safe with me. A couple of Navy boys it shall be. Since you are Navy, you would probably like rum? And maybe some juice or water to go with it? Ale perhaps? And how about dinner, are you staying for that? I have some lovely fresh fish tonight. Yes, you've been eating my sister's cooking, haven't you? Well, she's a far better nurse than she is a cook! I, on the other hand, know what I'm doing in the kitchen. I'll bet you've not had anything like my spiced chicken."

Raising a hand to forestall any further offerings, Evan smiled. "We are in no rush to go back to the hospital today, Emma. We shall place ourselves in your care. Please bring us some ale to start and when you think it best bring us a sampling of your dishes. Your sister did indeed tell us about your culinary skills and I think we have both worked up an appetite."

"I like you two boys already. You're in good hands so sit back and enjoy yourselves." Mugs brimming with ale soon appeared and the two men settled back to study the crowd.

They had barely managed a few sips before two black women came over and settled into the other two chairs at the table.

"Hello, gentlemen," said one girl with a smile. "This is my friend Alice and my name is Rachel. You two fellows look like you need some company."

The two men looked at each other, at a loss for words, until Evan finally coughed and stammered out a reply. "Uh, well, hello ladies. Ah, actually I don't think we were, um, in the market for company as it were."

Alice responded with a shrug and an innocent smile for both men. "Well, being company can mean lots of different things. Actually, we'd be happy if you just bought us a drink. We're thirsty and no one else around here has been willing to buy us one. Unless you two would prefer to drink alone?"

Her smile was so winning Evan couldn't help but laugh as he gave in and signaled for drinks for the two women.

"Forgive me, ladies. Where are my manners? We can certainly stand you a drink. I am Evan and this is James."

The decision to buy them drinks wasn't hard. On close inspection the two women were about the same age as the two men and both had pleasing good looks in their own ways. Both wore simple, sleeveless, loose dresses hinting at hidden, enticing potential underneath. As they chatted away the two men simply drank in their presence; the last time Evan had been with a woman was longer than he cared to remember and he knew this likely applied to James, too. As his nose twitched Evan realized the attraction was their alluring fragrance, a wonderful, fresh, feminine scent surrounding both women. He couldn't help thinking of the contrast between their scent and the ripe aroma of a hundred or more seamen on a warship with few opportunities for regular bathing.

The two women soon drew out the men's stories. Evan presented both of them as simple sailors on medical leave and Alice eyed him as he finished, a speculative look in her eyes.

"Hmm. You know, I could be wrong, but neither of you strike me as common seamen. I should know, I've seen plenty around here. It's all right whoever you are, your secret is safe with us."

Evan groaned and confessed the truth of who they were. "Lord, I hope we aren't that transparent to everyone else in here. I was hoping to be a little more discreet."

The women's eyes widened on hearing Evan was an officer and James was the son of one. Their eyes grew even wider at the story of how they had been wounded and what prompted it.

"Yes, we've heard about these rules, everyone in town has. A lot of people are concerned they will be bad for business."

Pausing, Alice indicated with her eyes and nod of her head a small group of sailors on the far side of the room. "The Americans certainly aren't happy."

"Yes, we noticed their ship. What are they doing here, do you know?"

The women looked at each other and both shrugged. "I think they said something about being low on supplies and being forced to put into port," said Rachel.

Evan grunted and raised a skeptical eyebrow, but said nothing. The first mugs of ale soon disappeared and another round was ordered. As the afternoon wore on small plates of food appeared at

76

intervals. Spiced, fresh grilled fish and chicken dishes dominated, but bread with a surprising array of different cheeses appeared too. Several customers came and went, with some even stopping to briefly join the little group and talk.

The conversation turned to life on the island and, remembering their ride into town, James asked why there weren't more men at work in the fields. The two women glanced at each other before Alice replied with her own question.

"Um, I guess you fellows don't know much about how things work around here, do you?" Seeing their blank looks she smiled.

"If you're black and you're a woman you get the dirty work. It's that simple. See, the owner man at the top has slaves to meet all his needs, right? But he has lots of different needs. The men are trained to do all the work that requires skills. Blacksmiths, carpenters, house servants, you name it. They don't think women are capable of anything that needs skill or training. So the women do the field work."

"Yes," said Rachel. "And then more often than not their work isn't done when the day is over, if you know what I mean."

The two men looked at each other and James raised an eyebrow.

"She wasn't kidding when she said the owner man has needs. That's right, if you're a black woman and the owner man fancies you, you won't be getting any rest at night."

"Not only him, though. The overseers have needs too," said Alice.

The two men looked at each other and shook their heads.

"Well, I find that— hmm, I don't know what. I accept what you're saying is true, but it doesn't seem right," said Evan. "At least there are people like Emma and her husband free of all that with their own business here."

This time the two women looked at each other quizzically, before Alice responded with a raised eyebrow. "What makes you think they're free?"

"Eh? What do you mean?"

"Emma and her husband are slaves. They don't own this place, but they do run it for the owner man. This is all owned by Mr. Roberts, the richest planter on the island."

The two men's mouths fell open as she continued. "You don't really think Emma would have the kind of money needed to build and maintain this place, do you? Emma and Walton actually lease everything from him, including all of the black people you see working here. They are both smart people and because of that they were trained for this. Both of them can read and do books for the business. And as long as Roberts gets his profits, they get to keep any tips they get as incentive for themselves, see?"

The two men sat back, stunned. A puzzled expression appeared on James's face as he sat forward again, with a quick glance at Evan as he spoke. "Uh, so if you don't mind my asking, how do you two fit into this?"

Alice smiled as she responded. "Gentlemen, we are slaves, too, and we are part of the overall operation. This establishment aims to meet all of your needs."

"Good God!" said Evan as both men's eyes bulged wide. "I'm at a loss here. I can't believe it's allowed to force you into something like this."

"Force? No, that's not true. Well, not exactly," she added, as Alice saw Evan's eyes widen again. "Everyone here had a choice, although it's not a hard decision to make. We could all be working out in the fields all day long instead of being here. And, like I said, we'd only end up on our backs with the owner man on top of us at night anyway. On the plantation we'd stand a good chance of being beaten every day, too. Being here we don't work in the fields and once the 'fee' for the establishment is paid, we too get to keep whatever extra tips nice gentlemen may give us."

She laughed as a choking look appeared on Evan's face. Coughing to hide his discomfort, he mastered himself and looked at the two women. "So, what about all the other businesses we saw in town? Are they all owned by the planters too?"

"Probably. I guess a few white men that aren't plantation owners own some of the businesses. Well, there's maybe a few black people that have managed to gain their freedom and they may be business people too," said Rachel with a shrug and a cryptic look. "Hmm, at least some have one way or another, but most everyone you see would be a slave."

Seeing the look on her face Evan realized she was hiding something. Curious, he hoped she would say more as he grappled with the possibilities in his mind, but nothing was forthcoming and James broke the awkward silence.

"Uh, can I ask what's maybe a dumb question?" said James. "There are white women in here that I'm fairly sure are in the same, ah, business as you two ladies. They can't be slaves, can they? How do they fit in?"

"You're right," said Alice, as she laughed. "They are indeed the competition, but we got to you first! They aren't slaves but they might as well be. They're all indentured servants. They have a binding contract with the owner man to be a servant. Their service arrangement is hardly different than ours, of course."

Evan paused to order another round of drinks and looked around with fresh insight as he gathered his thoughts. The inn had grown steadily busier and rowdier as afternoon gave way to evening and encroaching darkness outside. Every table was full and no spare seats could be seen. Slightly fuddled from all the drink, Evan began to think about the long ride back to the hospital.

Watching the two women, laughing and engaged in conversation with James, Evan was distracted by the hint of full breasts swaying beneath the simple dress Alice wore whenever she moved. Everything about her drew his attention; Evan realized Alice really was a striking, uniquely attractive woman. Softly curling dark hair falling to her shoulders framed her equally dark eyes, while a brilliant smile lit her face. Sensing his gaze she focused back on Evan, her smile widening as Rachel and James continued talking.

"Do you like what you see, Evan?" said Alice, leaning forward and grasping his hand. Her touch was electric.

Evan didn't trust his voice, knowing it would be thick with sudden desire. He nodded as Alice laughed and winked. "I'm glad. For me, I see a handsome man in front of me and I like what I'm seeing too."

Thoughts of returning to the hospital intruded a few times as the evening wore on. Several people stopped to talk and introduce themselves before moving on. On learning they were Royal Navy seamen several shook their heads, grumbled, and expressed concern over the Navigation laws. The din of noise grew steadily louder the more people drank.

The din was broken by a sudden disturbance on the far side of the room, which instantly drew everyone's attention. A belligerent, drunken seaman shouted incoherently and angrily slapped a woman at his table as she tried to spurn his attention. One of the bar men came over to speak to the man, who turned and pushed him away before reaching across the table and grabbing the woman's dress, tearing it down the front enough to partially expose her breasts. The bar man looked over his shoulder and nodded to his mate behind the bar, who in turn called into the kitchen. Two more men wearing aprons appeared and all three joined the first bar man at the table.

The offender found himself being hauled bodily out of his chair by the four men. Roaring in drunken anger the seaman struggled, but could do nothing as the four men each grabbed a limb. The customers in the tavern howled with laughter as the still swearing, angry seaman was carried out face down through the crowd, which parted quickly to make way for them. Several followed them out the door and more watched through the open shutters as the four men carried him over to a nearby rubbish heap and heaved him face first into it. A number of the watchers were the man's mates from his ship and they all bellowed with laughter at the sight of their groaning friend struggling to pick himself out of the reeking garbage as the four bar men stalked back to the tavern.

The two women grinned at their companions and Alice leaned forward, her breasts resting on the tabletop with the deep cleft between them exposed as she laughed.

"Now that's what I call incentive to be nice to us, wouldn't you agree?"

***

The light streaming through the shutters woke Evan. Sensing another presence in the room he rolled over to discover a pleasant, well formed breast with a tempting, dark brown nipple inches from his face. Reaching out he cupped the breast in his hand and brought the nipple to his lips.

Alice gave a sleepy murmur of pleasure and reached out to pull him closer, but kept her eyes closed. Evan pulled himself closer too and began to stroke her slowly as memory of the night came back. He couldn't recall exactly when it happened or what prompted it, but the feeling was like the sudden bursting of a dam. They paid their tabs and arranged for rooms for the two couples caring little for the cost; weeks of pent up abstinence had the two men in bull like desire to get to their respective rooms.

Evan recalled feeling some anxious moments about his missing limb and how he would manage, but desire overcame everything. He had also been concerned at how Alice would react, but she hadn't even seemed to notice. Evan was surprised she seemed more intent on actually enjoying being with him.

Evan had never slept with a black woman before. He continued stroking her gently, marveling at the softness of her light coffee coloured skin. His minimal experience with black people was limited to Betty and the few black sailors manning Navy ships like James and, now, this woman. On the ships doing your job was more important than what you looked like and to Evan, a child of the Navy, it seemed strange people with different coloured skin would be treated differently than anyone else for this reason alone.

This woman was indeed different, being a slave. Evan knew slavery existed; this was simply the way things worked. But his vague concept slaves were all mere field workers toiling out of sight away on plantations was obviously wrong. Blacks were walking about on all of the islands he had been to, but in past he assumed they were only servants. Evan resolved to learn more to fill in the obvious gaps in his knowledge.

One such gap was the brand. Shocked to find a two-inch square scar in the form of a capital R on her back near her left shoulder, he had traced it with his finger in between bouts of lovemaking. The burn had long since healed, but the pronounced scar was impossible to miss. She had shrugged when he asked about it.

"I've had that a long time, lover man. You could say I was a bit headstrong when I was a lot younger. I had this problem with being raped, you see. Mr. Roberts thought I was going to run away so he had that branded on my shoulder. Makes it a lot easier to identify his property, now doesn't it? The implication was I'd be feeling that branding iron again if I didn't toe the line, too."

As he stroked her shoulder one more time she stirred, giving him a smile as she finally opened her eyes, still groggy with sleep. "So do you still like what you see, Evan?"

"I did last night and still do today. I'm glad I stayed."

"Hmm, I'm glad you did too. One of the benefits of my job, lover man, is sometimes I actually like the man I'm with." Closing her eyes, she nestled even closer to him.

Evan looked at her speculatively for a moment before looking away. Finally he could resist asking no longer. "I appreciate you saying that, Alice. But I am really just another customer, am I not?"

This time her dark eyes stayed open, fully awake. Evan had difficulty reading her expression, but he thought he saw a faint hint of desperate vulnerability before she finally replied. "What do you think, am I just another whore?"

Evan took his time in reply. "Actually, no. Well, I should clarify. I don't often do things like this. But, in truth, I don't think you are, as you say, just another whore. You are too intelligent for that. I think you have some education and brains and have potential to be more than a woman making her living on her back. How is that possible, Alice?"

Alice's face was stone a few moments longer before it softened and she finally sighed. "My mom is a house slave for Mr. Roberts. She was taught how to read and write to help his wife. She does some of the bookkeeping too. I think his wife was lonely because he spends so little time with her. Well, my Mom and Mrs. Roberts learned a lot from each other and Mom passed it all on to me. She's still there."

"So where is your father? Do you have any brothers or sisters?"

Alice laughed. "Lover man, you really don't know, do you? Well, that's okay. Look, the reason I am this light coffee colour is because my Dad was white, you follow?"

Seeing his puzzled look she gave him a weary smile. "Evan, it is very likely my Dad is actually Mr. Roberts. In fact, Rachel is probably my half sister. Her mother works in the household kitchen with my mother. Did you not notice the resemblance?"

Evan pulled back to look at her and, thinking back, he saw what she was talking about. He nodded.

Alice smiled again. "So, lover man. Sure, you are just 'another customer'. But I had fun with you. For a one armed man, you do just fine! I think you are a good man and being a fine gentleman, I don't know why you would want much more to do with someone like me."

Pulling her even closer, Evan smiled in return and he reached for an enticing breast one more time. "Well, the night may be over, but perhaps I'm not done with you quite yet."

***

Two more trips to the Dockyard yielded no news for the men. Nelson and the ships under his command were still not back by early October. The Dockyard officers scowled at the interruption every time Evan and James appeared. Captain Moutray was nowhere to be found.

Bored, restless, and increasingly frustrated the two men hired their own buggy and horse to use whenever they wanted. They fast became regulars at the Flying Fish Inn after trying a few of the other local taverns, as the Inn had an atmosphere which kept them coming back. Sometimes the sailors would bring out their fiddles and play music. One man even had an accordion.

The women drew them back, too. Alice and Rachel began to watch for the two men to arrive. Some nights they already had other partners and all they could do is shrug at the discouraged faces of the men. Somehow, the desire to sample other women on offer simply was not there for Evan.

Mid October came with no change. Perched again at their usual table, the two men were accepted as regulars by the rest of the patrons and known simply as a pair of Navy men recovering from their injuries. The two had come to know a little of the regular crowd too and, as they originally suspected, a more villainous pack of thugs would be difficult to find. But this was a mixed crowd indeed. Some of the blacks were shifty eyed, constantly watching the entrance to the Inn and Evan suspected some of them were in fact escaped slaves.

Tonight the crowd seemed even more raucous than usual. The two women had already been snatched up by a rowdy group of American sailors arriving earlier in the day. This time not one, but two sloops were in port. Once again, the word in the tavern was the captains had claimed distress, but Evan observed cargo being offloaded from both ships as they passed by the docks.

The two men were thinking about leaving for the night when a number of American sailors began arguing with a group of British soldiers from the Rat Island barracks. What started the argument wasn't clear, but the dispute escalated fast. One of the barmen, sensing the tension, came over to try and mediate, but he was too late. A pitcher of ale sailed through the air, flung by one of the Americans, in advance of a wave of sailors all trying to get at one man in particular.

The soldier's mates weren't about to let him face the Americans on his own, but the crowd of Americans outnumbered them. A few British merchant ship sailors joined the soldier's side to make it a more even match. As they did the tavern's bar men waded into the fray and began wielding their wooden batons indiscriminately.

"Christ!" said James as an empty ale mug thrown by one of the Americans missed its target and smashed into the wall beside his head. "Time to get out of this mess, sir?"

"I fear that may be too late— watch it, you oaf!" shouted Evan as another of the Americans bulled his way past the bar men and crashed into their table, spilling ale everywhere. The American heard Evan's British accent and, struggling to his feet, took a swing and struck him a glancing blow to the side of his head. Evan tried returning the punch, but lost his balance and missed. Using the only weapon at hand James smashed his empty ale mug down hard on the sailor's head, staggering the man enough he fell to his knees.

Clusters of struggling men were everywhere. Evan and James fought their way through, throwing punches and shoving combatants out of their path every step of the way. Fortunately they were close enough to fight their way out the door as the melee spilled outside and onto the street. Outside, free of the bar men and their batons, several fights continued unabated. The American James had felled recovered and followed them into the street seeking revenge.

"Come on, then. No black bugger is going to get me down. Let's see how you do against a white man, you fucking animal."

"I think not," said Evan, pulling out his sword. "Go back and play with your friends. You're done with us tonight."

"You goddamn British cowards. Put that pretty stick away and take me on, both of you."

Stepping forward Evan placed the tip of his sword hard against the man's chest, enough for him to feel the sharp edge dig into his flesh. "I'm terribly sorry. Apparently I wasn't clear enough, but I shall be now. Bugger off or I'll carve you up. Is that clear?"

"I'll remember you two assholes," said the sailor, glaring at them in anger before turning to stalk back into the tavern. As he did the sounds of the local watch coming to quell the disturbance could be heard in the distance.

"Well, I'd say we're done here tonight, Mr. Wilton," said Evan. Turning to leave he realized a crowd of people drawn by the commotion were watching the whole affair unfold. "Let's get out of here fast."

As he spoke he caught sight of a carriage stopped on the far side of the crowd. Two officers in uniform and a well-dressed white woman were the occupants. With a start Evan realized one of the officers was Lieutenant Burns from the Dockyard and he was looking directly at him. The two men locked eyes for a few moments before the Dockyard officer turned, saying something to the woman beside him. She laughed before raising a hand to her mouth. The other officer in the carriage was Lieutenant Long.

Lieutenant Burns turned to look at Evan once more. A look of distaste came over his face, as if from smelling something bad. Evan watched in dismay as the officer growled an order to the driver and the carriage drove away fast.

James saw the whole thing. "Trouble, sir?"

"Shit, I hope not," groaned Evan. "Maybe. The last thing we need is a bad report on us. Let's get the hell out of here."

Chapter Five
October 1784
Antigua and Barbados

The first two months of Nelson's time on
Antigua were spent coming to know his Captains and
the officers under their command. Several dinners
together cemented a camaraderie Nelson knew would
serve them all well when needed. He also spent time
surveying the work done to date in the Dockyard and
giving thought to what else was needed. Many repairs
to the warships under his command were needed and
the enforced time in harbour due to hurricane season
was perfect for getting them done.

Despite best efforts to keep the men occupied
with work and occasional shore leave their
restlessness was a problem. Nelson organized regular
sessions of music and dancing for the men, along with
regular drills to work off excess energy. He even
commanded several plays to be performed. But a
restless sailor with access to too much rum was a bad
combination. Nelson didn't like ordering floggings,
but he knew he couldn't hesitate when necessary. The
trouble was he had been forced to order many more
floggings than there would have been were they out at
sea.

Before going to Barbados for the regular
October meeting of all ships on station at the end of
hurricane season, he endured several strained
conversations with Captain Moutray, his Lieutenants,
and the Dockyard Shipwright about the priorities of
construction work in the Dockyard and repair work to
the various ships on station. Captain Moutray was as
genial as ever, but the two Lieutenants could barely
conceal their disdain. The Shipwright could only

shrug and point out he was doing what he could with what he had. Similar conversations followed with Governour Shirley. All of them shrugged in the end and promised to do their best, but held out little hope things would progress with speed while the Order in Council was a thorn in everyone's side.

With the distaste of the floggings and the exasperating meetings still fresh on his mind, sailing off to Barbados seemed welcome relief. The purpose of periodic meetings of the ships on station was to share intelligence, discuss orders and priorities, and to sort out who was doing what for the coming months. But Nelson and several of the captains were astonished to find no discussion of interdicting smuggling as part of their tasks.

In response to a direct question on the subject Admiral Hughes downplayed it. "Smuggling? No, I don't think that's any of our concern, gentlemen. I'd say that nonsense is for those Customs fellows to tackle. We have plenty else to occupy us."

Seeing the surprise on everyone's faces, Nelson knew someone had to take the lead.

"Sir, I must protest. We have all been given orders to enforce the Navigation Order In Council most strictly." Several Captains nodded vigorously in support.

"Order In Council, you say? I'm not aware of that. It couldn't be that important even if there is one, I'm sure."

Nelson and his supporters were shocked by this bald-faced denial, but weren't backing down. Several produced their direct orders from the Admiralty and a few even had copies of the Order itself, already widely distributed through the fleet the year before. Faced with a determined assault and hard evidence the Admiral abruptly changed his story, claiming to finally recall seeing the Order. The captains carried away his ostensible backing, but they all knew lukewarm support when they saw it.

On his way back to Antigua Nelson stopped two different ships, certain they were American traders. His First Officer wasn't smiling as he reported back after boarding both, as it turned out both ships carried British registrations.

Nelson's eyes narrowed listening to his officer's report, especially the second time it happened. "Are you certain, sir? I'd stake my career that both of these ships we've stopped are American built."

"Sir, I agree. It's interesting that the paperwork of the entire crew states they are all from Upper Canada, except for the Captain. His paperwork says he is English. Their personal papers may all be forgeries, but they are too well done for me to challenge them. Of course, he kept a straight face as he told me the Order in Council didn't say anything about hiring Canadians to crew his ship. As for the ship itself, it has British registration papers and they don't look like forgeries to me. I see no way to detain them, sir."

Nelson could only grunt and reluctantly agree, resuming their journey back to Antigua. He brooded all the way over the frustrating difference between what the paperwork said and what his professional instincts told him was really happening.

But another worry came to the fore as his ship returned to the Harbour. Several sailors from the ships under his command came down with fever and it seemed unclear still how many would survive. Fever and sickness was a constant concern for officers in both the Army and Navy. At various times attrition rates from illness were close to fifty per cent.

Fortunately he had sailed from England with a full complement of men so he was hopeful he could weather this particular storm. Sailing a ship was complicated enough at full strength; sailing it undermanned brought a whole new level of stress.

With little he could do about the sickness he turned attention to the Dockyard and noticed right away how little construction work had been done while he was gone. Angered, he endured more conversations with the Dockyard officers. Proving even more strained than the previous ones, Nelson let his frustration show and made it clear he wasn't backing down. With time to brood on the lack of results on his way to St. John's to see the island Governour, Nelson sunk into a discouraged mood. The resulting conversation yielded similar results and ended with Nelson assuring the Governour he would be corresponding with the Admiralty on the lack of progress.

With his frustration simmering Nelson decided to stop at the Customs office to dig further into the situation, reasoning things couldn't possibly get worse.

Nelson realized he was wrong as he walked the few short blocks to the office and was snubbed three times by well-dressed white couples passing by. Recognizing his uniform and knowing he was Nelson, all three deliberately ignored his effort to nod acknowledgment and pleasantly smile. Two of the men scowled and grunted incoherently in passing, as if they had something stuck deep in their throats.

Coming close to the harbour Nelson saw an American flagged ship named the Amelia tied up at the Customs wharf. Sailors were offloading cargo in the sweltering sun. Angered, he entered the main Customs building. Fortunately, the Customs officer was free to see him.

"Captain Nelson, welcome, sir," said Lawson, a wary look on his face. "Dare I hope you have reconsidered my offer of assistance?'

His face fell as Nelson shook his head. "Mr. Lawson, what is that American ship I see tied up at your dock doing here?"

"Ah, they claim distress, sir. Wood and water, you know. They have the usual needs. They say they had bad weather they had to skirt around and have come much farther out of their intended path. Lost some spars, too. We can hardly say no to them, sir."

"Well, I think we can and we should, Mr. Lawson, especially since anyone can plainly see they are offloading cargo."

"Hmm, yes, well, I gave them dispensation to do so. Time is money, sir. They will make little or no profit if they have to back track to their original destination and our island has need of their goods, so where is the harm this once?"

"And are you charging them the King's duties, sir?"

"Ah, well. No, actually. They wouldn't make any profit, you see, and would refuse to sell their goods as a result. That outcome seemed a waste to me, especially as so many of the locals here have need of their wares. So, yes, I waived the duties this time, sir."

Nelson frowned at the Customs officer in response, his hard expression making the man blanch and sit back in his chair. "Mr. Lawson. What is the state of shipping traffic to and from Antigua?"

The Customs man was taken aback by the unexpected question. "Eh? Shipping traffic?"

Nelson replied with some heat to his voice. "Sir, I am asking you what the situation is. Aside from these irritating Americans, what has the shipping been like? Has it dropped or what?"

The answer was not what Nelson wanted to hear. After further browbeating the Customs man pulled out his records and revealed the grim truth. Legitimate shipping and the tonnage of wares being offloaded in Antigua was down substantially from the year before.

The Customs man as expected blamed the duties. Nelson sat back in his chair across from the man when he finally had the full picture and simply shook his head in disgust.

"So Mr. Lawson, if the shipping volume has dropped how exactly is it the locals here are continuing to have their needs met?"

The man shrugged. "Sir, I have no idea. Look, I can only deal with what I see, sir."

"Sir. You have a number of cutters at your disposal for interdicting smugglers. How many captures have you made in the past year?"

"Umm, none this year, actually. We've been terribly busy here in port, sir, and I simply don't have enough men or resources to be on constant patrol. I'm sure there are smugglers out there, as there always are, but they have proved rather clever."

"Mr. Lawson. How many times in the past year have American ships put into port claiming 'distress'?"

A trapped look appeared on the man's face as fumbled with some of his record books. "Ah, well, there have been a few. Is this really necessary to know, sir?"

"It is, sir."

After fumbling another three minutes of obviously hoping Nelson would give up the man finally pulled out some records with scribbled notes and confessed.

"Sir, keeping track of ships in distress is not my mandate, you understand. I have here some rough notes my assistants and I have kept, but I can't guarantee they are fully accurate." He spent another two minutes trying to count references and finally came up with a tally that was worse than Nelson had feared.

"Over two-dozen sir? My God!" Nelson was dumbfounded.

Taking a different tack the Customs man eyed Nelson speculatively. "Sir, I would like to repeat my offer of a few weeks ago to you. I am more than willing to help you get a dispensation from Customs. If that isn't agreeable, perhaps we could do this differently? I mean, really, this isn't the proper task for the Navy and I'm sure you have far more pressing matters on your plate to deal with. Why don't we work together, sir? If you write to the Admiralty expressing support for increasing resources to my meager operation I'm sure they would listen to a captain with your stature. Why, with intelligence from yourself, the ships under your command, and a proper Customs operation here I am positive we could make a real difference. What do you say, sir?"

Nelson stared at him, awestruck by the man's abysmal lack of competence and the blatant attempt to manipulate the situation. Reaching for his hat,

Nelson stood up and looked at the man with ice in his eyes.

"Sir, we all have our orders to fulfill. I suggest we both do so. I certainly intend to do my duty."

Nelson paused at the door and looked back at him one last time. "And Mr. Lawson? The next time I am in St. John's I do not want to see any American ships here, for any reason."

Nelson brooded the entire way back to English Harbour and by the time he got close, passing the small village of Falmouth Harbour, he was in a deep, black depression at the litany of problems he faced.

Reaching the Dockyard entrance and turning his horse and buggy over to the stable man his thoughts turned to the remaining thorn in his side. In his meeting with the Dockyard officers the two Lieutenants took overt glee, bordering on insolence, in reporting the presence of a Navy officer, supposedly recuperating from injuries. This officer was observed out of uniform in St. John's frequenting a local tavern with the worst sort of reputation. Worse, the officer was with a black man and both were seen involved in a wild street brawl involving common sailors.

The two Dockyard Lieutenants preened as they regaled their senior officers with the story, subtly insinuating Dockyard matters were better left without interference from 'active' Navy personnel. Nelson could only grit his teeth at the implied insult and vow to deal with it.

"Well," said Nelson, muttering aloud to himself. "I'll get to the bottom of that soon enough. Whoever he is he'd better hope I'm in a better mood than now when I see him."

**

The summons came two days later in the form of a Marine from the Boreas appearing with orders to report to Nelson forthwith. Evan knew it would come, having seen the ships return to English Harbour. He had presented himself at the Dockyard yet again and this time he approached the First Officer of the Boreas, who happened to be supervising work on shore at the time. Evan explained who he was and requested to see Nelson.

The First Officer searched his memory before his eyes widened slightly in response. "Ah, yes, I believe Captain Nelson mentioned something about an officer he would be looking for. He is extremely busy today, sir, but I will absolutely ensure he is made aware you seek audience."

Betty and James helped him dress in his best uniform with one sleeve pinned back. "My, don't you look handsome, Mr. Ross," said Betty. "Makes me wish I was forty years younger."

As he was rowed to the ship Evan studied it with longing and found time to wonder at how much he was missing being on board a ship. Climbing aboard with only one arm was challenging, but Evan took his time. The joy of being aboard a ship got stronger as he strode across the deck aft to Nelson's quarters. Bade to enter, Evan walked in and stopped in front of Nelson, saluting smartly. "Sir. Reporting as ordered, sir."

The Captain left him standing for a long few moments, obviously contemplating the man before him. Nelson frowned, but seemed to find no fault with what he saw as he gestured to the one chair before the desk. "You may as well have a seat, Mr.

Ross. I fear we will be in conversation for a while."
Nelson reached out a hand. "Your orders, sir."

"Sir, I can only offer my commission papers.
I was left with no orders."

Nelson raised an eyebrow and sat back in his
chair, his frown deepening to form a scowl. "No
orders? What is your story, please? I'm listening."

The edge to Nelson's voice alarmed Evan, not
understanding why his reception was so cold. Evan
spent the next few minutes explaining what had
happened to him and why. Nelson interrupted to ask
for more details and wanted to know if Evan could
find the bay where it had happened again. Evan was
puzzled at his interest, but assured him he could.

Finishing his story, Evan expressed his desire
to return to active service. The line he walked was
fine; in trying to show how eager he was to return to
duty he didn't want to be seen as pathetically
desperate. He knew he had to project absolute
confidence and certainty the loss of an arm would not
be a hindrance.

Nelson drummed his fingers on the desktop
and rubbed his chin for a few moments as Evan
finished. The frown seemed carved on his face. "So,
Mr. Ross. When exactly was it you were cleared for
duty, sir?"

Evan's eyes widened slightly, surprised at the
question. "Sir, the doctor advised I could do so
towards the end of September."

"Really. And why is it your presence here
only came to my attention a mere few days ago?"

"A few days ago?" said Evan, taken aback in
unfeigned surprise. "Sir, I don't understand. I've
reported to the Dockyard for orders several times, as
far back as mid September when I regained a portion

of my strength. I specifically requested my situation be brought to your attention each time."

"The Dockyard, you say. Whom exactly were you talking to, sir?"

Nelson's face hardened as Evan explained in detail what had happened on each occasion. Nelson drummed his fingers on the desk again as Evan finished, deep in thought, before he stared at Evan once more, his eyes like glittering ice.

"Mr. Ross. Imagine my surprise, sir, when I receive a report from these same Dockyard officers alleging they saw you, out of uniform, engaged in a wild brawl outside some scurrilous tavern in St. John's with some black sailor as your partner in crime. Help me understand, sir."

Evan knew he had to be forthright with Nelson, so he explained how the doctor had told he and James to take leave to lift their spirits as part of their recovery. Nelson's eyes widened at mention of the presence of the Americans and how the fight had started.

"You say there were not one, but two American ships in harbour?"

"Sir, yes sir. We watched both of them unloading cargo. I don't understand why that was happening, but that's what we saw. I was suspicious, but it was not my part to question what was going on."

"What were the names of the two ships, sir?"

"Why, one was the Mary Kay and the other was the Dolphin, sir."

Nelson couldn't stop the flash of anger appearing on his face. Seeing it Evan steeled himself, expecting to face the brunt of it. But Nelson leaned back in his chair and gazed away to master himself for a few moments.

"Mr. Ross. You mentioned a black sailor? Who is he? I could use some good hands right now. We've lost a number to the fever recently."

Evan almost sighed with relief. "Sir, he was injured with me." Evan explained how James's intervention had saved him and expanded on how James was more than a simple sailor. Nelson showed sudden interest when Evan explained whom James's father was.

"An officer, you say? What was his name and when did he serve?"

"Sir, Mr. Wilton showed me his father's commission papers. His name was Richard Wilton. I'm not sure what ships he served on, but I know he spent time here in this part of the world."

"Richard Wilton?" said Nelson with a start. "You are speaking of him in the past tense, sir?"

"Why, yes. Mr. Wilton told me his father died of the fever in Bombay."

A far off look came to Nelson's eyes. "Hmm, I wonder. Ask your Mr. Wilton what ships his father served on and let me know if one of them was a frigate named HMS Seahorse."

"Of course, sir," said Evan. "Sir, if I may speak freely?"

Nelson eyed him a moment, but he sat forward and finally nodded, so Evan continued. "Sir, I humbly apologize if any of my actions have brought disrepute to the honour of the service. The same applies if I have caused you grief in any way. I sense you might be displeased by my presence in St. John's out of uniform. As I was told to go into town as part of my recovery and take a vacation as it were, I felt it best not to wear it. I admit Mr. Wilton and I went into town several times. Our nurse encouraged us as she thought it would continue to help with our recovery and, as we had no orders, I agreed with her. I did my best not to advertise who I was. We told everyone we were a couple of sailors recovering from injuries."

"This is the truth, on your honour, sir?"

Evan sat straighter in his seat. "On my honour, sir. I swear it."

Nelson stared hard enough for a few long moments as if to bore a hole into Evan's soul, obviously deep in thought, before he sat back as he came to a decision.

"Very well, Mr. Ross. I believe you. And I welcome your talk of honour, sir."

A steely glitter came to his eyes as Nelson looked at Evan. "You will find honour is extremely important to me and, by God, I've seen far too little of it lately. You are a welcome and refreshing change."

"Thank you, sir. I only hope I can be of service to you or to one of the other captains. I realize there may be some who would question my ability to serve having only one arm, but I know I can still be of service, sir. It would be wonderful to be at sea again."

"Hmm, I fear that is not possible at this time, sir. The others and I have a full complement of officers right now and there is simply no room for you. As for your injury, you are right. There may indeed be some ready to throw you away. Like your former Captain, sir? No, no need to answer that question. That was unfair to ask and I already know the answer anyway."

Nelson paused a moment to regard the man in front of him before continuing carefully, emphasizing his words. "Mr. Ross, we are not at war right now and may not be for some time to come. But we will be. There are simply too many men without honour in the world. Worse, they all have simply too much greed in their souls. You've already given much for your country, sir. No one would think less of you for resigning your commission after an injury like this. Yet here you are in front of me, professing desire to continue to serve and give even more. Is this truly what you want?"

The iron in Evan's voice was clear. "I could not be more certain, sir. Give me an opportunity to prove myself. Command me, sir."

Nelson smiled and held out his hand for Evan to shake. "Well, I shall. I for one have no intention of throwing you away. Yes, we shall find some use for you, sir."

A far away look came to his eyes once more. "War is coming, Mr. Ross. Maybe not soon, but coming it is. I fear we may all be asked to give much of ourselves, even parts of our bodies like you. Our country will need everyone it can find willing to stand in the line of battle."

Recalling himself, Nelson rose to signal the interview was over and Evan followed suit. "Mr. Ross, I am off to St. Kitts tomorrow and I am not certain exactly how long I will be gone. Politics there is requiring my presence. I do not have time to draft you orders, but I shall upon my return. I have an idea, but need to think more about how I may best use you and your sailor Mr. Wilton. Yes, I think you may need his help. For now, I desire the two of you to find accommodation as near the Dockyard as possible. Time to move out of the hospital, sir. Hmm, I suggest take this accommodation for a period of six months. Present Mr. Wilton as your, ah, assistant or your clerk. Make it reasonable in cost, sir. The Crown shall reimburse you. I will send for you when I return and will draft orders for you once we have spoken again."

The two men shook hands once again. "Thank you, sir. I will not let you down in whatever task you set me."

"I have confidence of that. And Mr. Ross, you are free to continue visiting St. John's out of uniform."

Seeing the surprised look on Evan's face, Nelson laughed. "I am serious, sir. Yes, I think keep doing what you've been doing. Continue to represent yourselves as a couple of regular sailors. Maintain your contacts with the locals there. I shall explain my intent later. Well, maybe take a pass on the brawls, perhaps?"

***

The heavy clash of swords rang out, harsh and metallic. Drenched in sweat the two men danced back and forth, eyeing each other for an opening to take advantage of. Except this was not a smooth dance; after over thirty minutes of hammering at each other their steps were beginning to falter and their breathing was ragged. With a last burst of effort Evan tried to break James's guard and win past, but to no avail.

Signaling time for a break Evan stepped back, as did James. Even working out early in the morning and in the shade of their new home, the demanding drills sapped their energy exercising at the level they were. Thirty minutes of exercises and the standard naval cutlass drill followed by one on one against each other sapped their energy. They could hardly lift their sword arms with the heavy cutlasses any longer.

"All I can say is thank heaven you decided to stop when you did," wheezed James, still trying to catch his breath. "Another minute of that and you'd have had me."

"Except I couldn't have kept that up for another minute, James," said Evan, his chest still heaving as he slumped onto a bench and reached for a waiting pitcher of water. After downing several gulps he poured almost half the pitcher over his head before handing it to James.

Evan needed the workout and, more importantly, he needed the practice with the sword to adjust to having only one arm. He had long since begun adapting himself to daily tasks and grown accustomed to his loss, but using a cutlass effectively with only one arm was an entirely different matter.

"Lord, I don't know what I would have done were it my right arm that was lost. Even now I'm still having to adapt," said Evan.

The fight at the Flying Fish and his wild punch missing the American sailor forced the realization he would have to relearn how to maintain his balance in a fight. In hindsight, it appeared obvious what he did with his left arm served to counterbalance any action he took with his right. But at least he now understood he was going to have to work more at it.

James grunted agreement as the two men looked at each other.

"I think that doctor was right, Evan," said James. "My leg is a lot better, but something's still not right. I almost fell on my arse twice there. It doesn't want to bear as much weight as the other. This is going to take some getting used to."

But they were making progress. Both men felt much better from doing the strenuous daily workouts and their dramatically changed circumstances in the days since Evan's interview with Nelson lifted their spirits. Their relationship had evolved into a firm friendship and in private the usual barrier between officer and sailor disappeared. In public, James was Evan's assistant and clerk to anyone who asked.

Being close friends was unusual. Evan knew a casual observer, especially anyone from the Navy, would not have understood this. Even someone who understood the bond of their shared wounds and that James's father had been an officer would still have found the relationship strange.

But the friendship existed. Almost as one they realized they actually liked each other. So in private they were Evan and James; in public they were Mr. Ross and Mr. Wilton, and the expected distance was on display for all.

Betty wished them a fond goodbye from the hospital when she learned of their orders to leave. Evan explained their needs for accommodation and asked for her help finding something appropriate. Betty had given them a wide smile.

"I think I know a perfect place for you two."

The house was near the main road between the Dockyard and the village of Falmouth Harbour. The location about halfway between the two meant an easy walk between both. With a stone foundation and walls the house was sturdily built, and its two bedrooms, a kitchen, and a large main sitting area was all they needed. The home sat empty for several months after the old man living in it passed away and no one came forward to take it over. Betty negotiated a reasonable lease and the men moved in.

In the end Betty was not gone from their lives. She offered to serve as their housekeeper, but wouldn't have time to cook for them. She had laughed at the expressions on their faces.

"Don't look so relieved! Actually, I know who can help you out and, best of all, she's a better cook than I will ever be."

This was her niece, the daughter of Betty's sister Emma. She turned out to be a petite, dark eyed beauty named Anne with a broad smile, a younger version of her mother Emma. Evan almost laughed aloud as James and Anne locked eyes, ready to dive into each other's arms on the spot. Fortunately, her mother's looks weren't all she had inherited; her flair for cooking soon had both men looking forward to each mealtime.

Once they settled in the two men did as Nelson had bid them, strange as the order seemed. Hiring a horse and buggy for their ongoing use they began making the trip into St. John's periodically. On their way into town the first time the two men discussed their situation and the mysterious orders Nelson had given them.

"I don't know what exactly he has in mind, but he was really interested in the Americans," said Evan. "I think it likely whatever is afoot has something to do with them. But honestly, I don't care what he's got for us. I don't want to sound desperate, but maybe I am. I'd clean the heads on every ship in harbour with a toothpick if it got me a posting with him."

James laughed. "Find another toothpick for me and I'll help out."

The third time they made the trip into town they encountered a very different picture. By this time it was automatic to check to see who was in the harbour before they went to the Flying Fish. No American ships were in, but two large sloops flying

Dutch colours were tied up at the dock. A swarm of the usual boats filled with locals hawking anything and everything surrounded the two ships. Once again, the men observed cargo being offloaded, as if doing so was perfectly normal. The two men looked at each other and Evan nodded toward the Inn.

"I think we should see if any of that lot is hanging out at the Inn. We'll have to file this for future. I have a feeling whatever Captain Nelson is going to have us doing will involve paying attention to anyone and everyone that comes into port."

As the afternoon wore into evening the tavern began filling up once again and sailors from the Dutch sloops began filtering in.

Except, they weren't Dutch.

"God Almighty, James," hissed Evan under his breath, his eyes not leaving the crowd around them for a second. "Most of the sailors in here are bloody frogs!"

"Are you sure, sir?"

"Ah, I guess I haven't told you. I speak reasonably good French. My mother insisted I learn, thinking it would serve me well some day. Not bad with Spanish either, but my French is much better and I assure you, most of these men are speaking French. I think I'm hearing a sprinkling of Dutch in there. But that thug over there in the corner, he sounds like a Yankee. He's got that accent they all seem to have in the Boston area."

"Good Christ. So what's going on, sir?"

"I don't know, but I think Captain Nelson is going to want to hear about this. There's something odd about it all. So lets stay the night and watch." Evan couldn't resist spending another night with Alice, but Rachel could only shrug philosophically as

108

James decided to sample the wares of another woman.

After joining them at the table Alice raised an inquisitive eyebrow, seeing how distracted Evan was, continually watching the crowd. "You know, if I didn't know better I'd say you're more interested in them than me. Not making sense, lover man. Have I lost my charms?"

"Hmm? Ah, sorry, Alice. I'm checking out this unusual crowd in here tonight. Here, have you seen this lot in here before?"

"Sure. Not all that often maybe, but they've all been around in past. There are two ships and, more often than not, they are both here at the same time. Why, are they important for some reason?"

"Well," said Evan, not wanting to arouse her curiosity. "Professional interest. It is a bit odd they are here."

"If you really must know more about them why don't you go ask the Captain?"

"Captain? Where?"

"That fellow with his back to the wall over there in the corner. He's the Captain of one of the ships," she replied, gesturing with a nod at the man Evan suspected was from Boston.

Evan's eyes narrowed as he realized whom she was talking about. Scrutinizing the man, Evan knew he would want to recognize him instantly if he saw him again. Sensing Evan's eyes on him, the man turned his gaze to their table and the two men locked eyes for a few moments.

"Professional interest, huh?" said Alice, watching him with curiosity. "Well, I sure hope there'll be some of that left for me before the night is out."

Chapter Six
November 1784
Antigua

Nelson approached English Harbour with far less enthusiasm than the last few times he had sailed in. St. Kitts had tested his diplomatic skills, showing the flag for visiting Spanish diplomats. The diplomatic niceties seemed endless and Nelson hated it, but he knew diplomacy was all part of the job.

Returning to Antigua they did a sweep of the ocean around most of the island and its much smaller sister island Barbuda. His only success was in crossing the path of a distant American flagged ship he knew was probably heading for Antigua, but they thought better of it with a British warship off their quarter. They quickly altered course enough to allay suspicion and, as it was late in the day, Nelson decided not to give chase.

Dropping anchor once again in English Harbour Nelson scowled at the obvious lack of activity in the Dockyard. Despite it being early November the still air and stifling heat in the Harbour was overpowering.

"What a vile place," muttered Nelson.

"Sir? I'm sorry, I couldn't hear your order," said one of his officers.

Nelson shook his head. "Nothing, sir. I'm just enjoying the scenery and talking to myself. The deck is yours. I'm retiring to my cabin."

***

The summons to attend Nelson came early in the morning two days later. Dressed in his best uniform, Evan made his way to the Dockyard and found a party of sailors clearing the ground near the

110

entrance. Others were hauling stones from a large pile outside the Dockyard. The mongrel was watching the men in hope of being offered a treat and came out from the shade to wag his tail at Evan. He quickly lost interest in the new arrival as a few passing sailors stopped to scratch the dog's ear and feed him some small scraps of meat obviously brought for exactly this purpose.

Evan was grateful the interior of Nelson's cabin was cooler. Every window was open and, as a blessed relief, today a periodic breeze came in. Nelson himself had shed his uniform coat and was seated at his desk dressed in a loose fitting white shirt. The desk was almost fully covered with a mountain of paperwork. His ink stained hands were testament to an early start on dealing with his correspondence.

"Ah, Mr. Ross," said Nelson, looking up as Evan saluted. "Do sit down and please, make yourself comfortable. I'm glad you've come. Any break from this endless paperwork is welcome. Take your uniform coat off. I find it's impossible to wear that all the time in this beastly place. Too bloody hot here."

"Thank you, sir. I completely agree," said Evan, shedding his coat.

"There's a pitcher of cool water there with lemons in it, do help yourself. Right, down to business. How have you fared since we last spoke?"

Evan spent the next few minutes detailing how he'd secured accommodations as ordered and made continued visits to St. John's. Nelson's eyes widened in shock as Evan revealed what he had seen in his last visit to town.

"Goddamn, sir? Bloody frogs on these ships? I had not expected the French to be involved in this. Are you certain they spoke French?"

"Sir, I am. I speak French reasonably well. Spanish too, but not as good."

"You speak French? Excellent, that is good to know. And this American captain? What did you make of him, sir?"

"Sir, bear in mind I did not directly interact with him. However, the more I thought about it the more I realized this man was out of place."

"Meaning?"

"Sir, this man is allegedly the merchant captain of a trading ship. Now, I've met many merchant captains in my time, and he does not fit the mould. You would agree most tend to be much older, experienced men?"

"I would," said Nelson with a nod. "Continue."

"Sir, this man is young, perhaps in his late twenties or maybe he's thirty at most. But that's not all. He is extremely fit looking and he carries himself like a military man. I don't know if he was army or navy at some point in his life, but there is no hiding it. He has the bearing of a trained fighter and whatever he did, I am certain he excelled at it given the air of confidence he displays. Sir, I have nothing to base that on beyond what little I saw and my intuition, but I for one would be very careful about crossing this man. Captain, a man like this doesn't leave whatever service he was in and take ship doing routine merchant duty."

Nelson slowly nodded agreement as Evan continued. "But that's not all. Sir, I am convinced he was doing the same thing I was doing. He was watching the people in the room like a hawk. He was checking me out, much like I was doing to him."

Nelson sat back gazing unfocused out a nearby quarter galley window while drumming his fingers on the arm of his chair, obviously deep in furious thought. After a few long moments he turned back to Evan and sat forward once again.

"Well done, Mr. Ross, well done. This validates the course of action I have planned. I agree with your perceptive analysis of the situation. You've made a good start to your tasks and don't even realize it."

"Tasks, sir?" said Evan, noting Nelson referred to more than one.

"Indeed, Mr. Ross, I have three tasks for you and your, ah, assistant Mr. Wilton. This will be shore duty, as I'm sure you understand. Your first two tasks will serve as cover for the third."

Pausing to collect his thoughts, he sipped at a glass of water and continued.

"Mr. Ross, my orders state I am to do everything possible to accelerate the construction of the Dockyard facilities here. This is a strategically important station and must be made ready for the next conflict, which is as certain to happen as the goddamn mosquitoes will appear to disturb my sleep yet again tonight. The Dockyard Commissioner, Captain Moutray, is actually the man tasked with this duty. However, what is not publicly known is he has not been well and he really has not had the strength to see it through. It hasn't helped he is surrounded by those two buffoons who pretend to be officers. He has also suffered from a serious lack of support from the Governour and this pack of thieves that own the plantations."

"I see, Sir. How can I help you with this?"

"Why, you are my new liaison officer with the Dockyard, sir," said Nelson, a wide grin spitting his face. "I will provide you a set of orders specifying you are empowered to involve yourself in all aspects of Dockyard construction activity. They will advise you have authorization to command work to proceed under my authority. You will have full power to direct or redirect resources to achieve results."

Recognition dawned on Evan's face. "Ah, when I came into the Dockyard I saw some work parties from the ships. I assume that is your doing, sir?"

"It was. I will spare men whenever possible, but the real work will have to be done by slaves provided by the plantation owners. Yes, I know they've been reluctant, but I'll be dealing with them soon enough. I'm fed up with delay after delay. I shall provide you with a list of projects I want to see underway, but you should feel free to adjust this once you get into the details."

"Sir, are the Dockyard officers aware of this?"

"Not yet, but they will be when you make them aware. Captain Moutray and I have already been in conversation regarding this and I have his full support. As for those fools Mr. Burns and Mr. Long, the Commissioner and I have agreed they will be for you to deal with. The Commissioner seemed to enjoy the thought you would be the one to explain how the situation has changed, especially in light of their incredible failure to advise me about your presence here. Oh, they will argue and complain. Probably throw obstacles your way every chance they get. Your job is to get in their face, sir. Annoy them. Get them off their lazy backsides. Please."

Nelson laughed, before turning serious. "Mr. Ross, I firmly believe you can do little wrong in life if you simply grapple yourself to your foe and have at them."

Thinking back to how the two officers had treated him, Evan gave Nelson a grim smile. "Sir, I believe I shall enjoy this task."

"Ah, but that's only the first. So, I'm certain you have noticed I've been rather interested in your observations of foreign shipping in the St. John's harbour. The reason for that is the First Lord made it crystal clear my primary task here is to stamp out foreigners smuggling in this area. And make no mistake, sir, as far as I'm concerned the Yankees are foreigners. The problem is there are far too many connections between them and the local owners here. They're all bloody rebel sympathizers in reality."

Nelson shook his head in contempt. "Well, my task is now your task too."

Nelson explained what his First Officer had found on the two suspicious ships, certain they were American. "Something odd is going on with the ship registrations and I have a feeling that ninny in charge of Customs here has something to do with it all. Perhaps someone in the Governour's office is involved too. So, once again, I will provide you in due course with orders that specifically direct you to investigate the process of registering ships in this area. They will also state I want you to review records of who has docked where and offloaded what on this island. I want you to look for patterns of questionable activity. Of course, they will argue and complain and be obstructive. Once again, be annoying, sir."

Evan smiled. "I can do that, sir."

"Right, those are your overt tasks, for the consumption of anyone who wants to know what you are doing. Your third and most important task is covert. You've given me the sense you have built contacts with local people and we shall rely on this."

"Umm, well, to some degree, yes, but I would not call them extensive."

"Make them extensive, sir. Mr. Ross, I need information. There are people out there who know who is smuggling what and when. I want that information so I can stamp this out. I want information on smuggling on any of the islands in my patrol area and not only Antigua, although I expect that will be most of what you may find. What I want to know is exactly when and where a delivery is going to be made so I can stop by and invite these bastards to tea with me."

Nelson paused to smile. "So build a stable of informants. Find out what that goddamn Yankee Captain is up to. And while you're about it, look into why in God's name we suddenly have a crowd of Frenchmen in our midst. I don't believe for a second those are really Dutch ships."

Evan was taken a little aback as he digested it all. "So Mr. Wilton and I are to be spies, sir?"

"Mr. Ross, I know what you are thinking. Consorting with undesirables, skulking about, digging in the dirt as it were, hardly seems like something a gentleman would do."

"Well, yes, I guess that is my concern, sir."

"As it should be. We must guard our honour at all costs, for without it we have nothing. But here's the thing, Mr. Ross. To serve our country we must do what is needful and that means delving in the muck at times. I firmly believe one can do this and still serve honourably. In fact, we must do this. Information is gold, sir. I cannot seriously hope to fulfill my orders if I do not know my foe's mind and course of action."

Evan nodded. "I understand, sir. I confess my heart belongs at sea with a deck under my feet and this does seem, well, distasteful at best. But if this is what you require Mr. Wilton and I shall not fail you."

"I am confident of that, sir. I have one other avenue I shall explore to gain what I need, but it will only complement any tangible knowledge you bring me. Now, speaking of gold, you shall require resources for this." Reaching into his desk drawer he pulled out a small, but heavy bag tied together with a drawstring. The bag clinked with the sound of many coins as he dropped it on the desk between them.

"This should be sufficient for your immediate needs and, yes, I will need an accounting of your expenditures. Yes, Mr. Ross, I am talking about bribery, of course. Be judicious with the Crown's funds, please. Much as you have to explain your actions to me, I have to do the same to the Admiralty. Not everyone will need a bribe but, sadly, you will without doubt encounter people where gold is all that will serve."

Pushing the bag to Evan's side of the table Nelson continued. "So, your third and final set of orders I suggest should be for your eyes only, but use them as you see fit. All they will say is I expect you will provide regular reports to me regarding possible smuggling activity you become aware of. If you become aware of a smuggling transaction and there is time to intercept it you will convey this information to me immediately. My officers will be instructed to interrupt me regardless of what I am doing should a message from you arrive."

Nelson paused as a speculative look came over his face. "I suggest be careful about putting your sources names to paper. It is not out of question there may be foreign agents at work and if they realize what you are doing they may waylay you. This American Captain may indeed be an agent. If he is, you are to give him no quarter. We must put a stop to whatever mischief is planned. So perhaps use a cipher and prepare your real accounting only when you come on board this ship. I suggest you wear your uniform sparingly, if at all, and don't wear it into St. John's. For your first two tasks I suggest continue presenting yourself as you have been. You and Mr. Wilton are simply two Navy sailors still recovering from wounds. If anyone discovers you are an officer and wonders about the uniform tell them you are on temporary detached service doing civilian shore duties."

"I understand, sir."

"One final matter, sir. I will be corresponding with the Admiralty regarding all of this and am quite certain of their approval. I will further be informing them of your assignment to HM Antigua Naval Dockyard. Mr. Wilton is also assigned to the Dockyard and he reports to you."

"Sir?"

"Think of the Dockyard as your new ship, sir, a temporary assignment. As I explained in our prior meeting there is no room to assign you to any of the ships on station at this time. We already have a surplus of officers and, frankly, were we to do so it would upset our command structure badly. It would also result in such a flurry of angry protests from the civilians in the Admiralty that it would take me a decade to dig my way out from under the pile of letters that would arrive."

"But not to worry, sir," continued Nelson. "I shall make it clear your assignment is still an active service commission, not civilian. I know this is highly unusual, but I am absolutely confident of my actions. You will not be overlooked. Of course, being successful in achieving your orders will go a long way to override anyone that protests."

Nelson sat back, signaling the interview was over. "Is this all clear? Any questions, sir?"

Evan looked inward in thought before responding. "Only one, sir. What about all these American ships that keep showing up claiming distress? If that keeps happening it will defeat our purpose, will it not?"

Nelson chuckled and gave Evan a grim smile. "Yes, indeed, it would if I let it. That clown in the Customs office is probably getting rich on the bribes they are undoubtedly slipping him. However, dealing with that is my task and I shall do so at the first opportunity. The sign I have acted will be evident by the sheer volume of outraged screams you will hear. Your orders will be delivered forthwith, sir."

Evan laughed. Pulling on his uniform coat he saluted as he turned to leave. He paused at the door, remembering, and turned to look back at Nelson.

"Sir? I apologize, I almost forgot. You asked earlier about what ship Mr. Wilton's father served on, so I asked him. It was indeed the Seahorse as you suspected."

Nelson face fell and he sighed. "Hmm, I feared that would be so. Well, I must meet your Mr. Wilton some day."

'We are at your command. Good day, sir."
Turning, Evan left the cabin.

***

The sign Nelson prophesied came a little over a week later in the form of two shots from six pound cannons booming out across the bows of two American ships trying to enter St. John's harbour early one morning. The unexpected reports of the guns echoed across the water and about the town, startling everyone and stopping them where they stood.

HMS Latona had sailed into the entrance to the harbour and anchored near Rat Island two days earlier. Everyone eyed the warship with curiosity, but as it sat doing nothing they soon forgot and went about their business. The guns changed everything and had all eyes on the unfolding scene. A watching crowd quickly grew on the harbour front. What seemed incredible to the crowd was the realization only two cannon had fired, but more were ready. The gun ports on the entire side of the ship were open and all of the guns were out, fully manned for action.

The First Officer of the Latona was rowed over to the first of the ships and climbed aboard. The American Captain was outraged.

"What the hell was that for? Why in heaven's name are your guns run out? We are here in peace, sir."

"Sir," said the officer, after looking about. "You are ordered to turn your ship about and leave our waters immediately."

The man's surprise was so complete his mouth hung open speechless for a few long moments before he finally responded. "What? Why?"

"Sir, you and your sister ship are smuggling in contravention of the Navigation Order in Council. You will leave immediately."

"But— sir, this is outrageous! We are here in desperate straits. We need wood and water and food. How can you ignore our need?"

"We can do that because you are not in distress and you are in fact smugglers. We have orders to sink you if you fail to comply." The young officer looked around and scowled at the baffled faces of the crew and the captain, all of them still rooted to where they stood in shock.

"Well? You've been told, so get on with it!"

Turning, the officer left and was rowed over to deliver the same message to the other ship.

***

The meeting in the Governour's office in St. John's the next day was as testy as Nelson expected it would be. The Governour, Dockyard Commissioner Captain Moutray, the Customs officer Lawson, and three local plantation owners were all present. One of them was the vocal owner at Captain Moutray's dinner, John Roberts. Nelson went on the offensive as he walked into the room and saw who was present.

"Governour Shirley, good day. I understand you wish to discuss the events of yesterday."

As the Governour nodded and began to speak Nelson raised a hand to forestall him.

"Sir, what business do these men have at this meeting?" As Nelson waved a hand to indicate the three plantation owners their faces collectively dropped in open surprise.

"Good Christ," said Roberts, the shock showing on his face the most exaggerated of all. "The man asks what business we have here. Unbelievable."

The Governour raised his own hand to quell further interruptions. "Captain Nelson, I believe you have met some of these men. They are local plantation owners with significant business interests here on the island. They are directly affected by the events of yesterday, hence their presence."

"Governour, I am well aware of their thinking in this matter. However, they are not decision makers with power in this issue, so I fail to see why they would be here."

The Governour sat back in his chair and regarded Nelson for a long moment before nodding. "I agree with you Captain, you are right."

As he spoke all three men gave a start. The Governour raised a hand with a weary look to forestall them once again.

"Notwithstanding, sir, I value their thoughts and seek their counsel often. Can you forbear me in this one instance, sir?"

Nelson paused in thought for a moment before nodding as the Governour smiled in relief. "Thank you, Captain. Well, sir, you have certainly caught our attention with your recent actions. Have I got this straight, now? I have reports three American ships were denied entrance to St. John's in the last two days. Another was denied entrance to Falmouth Harbour yesterday."

"There was one other sent packing from one of the small harbours on the north side of the island also, sir. Governour Shirley, let's get to the point, shall we? We all know these ships are not in 'distress' and are in fact smugglers. You also know my orders. So why am I sitting here, please?"

The Governour cleared his throat and pulled out a sheaf of papers. "Well, sir, I took the liberty of expressing my concerns about your orders to your Admiral Hughes in Barbados some time back. He has conveniently now replied to me indicating he understands our situation and has advised he will be directing you to follow my orders to desist in your actions regarding the alleged smuggling activity. Has word of this reached you, sir?"

"Yes, I just received them, probably from the same packet ship that brought you your response."

The Governour smiled and looked at the men around him. "Well then, I'm glad we have that settled and there will be no repeat of the events of the last two days. I am pleased this has been settled quickly."

Nelson did his best to look apologetic. "Governour Shirley. I'm afraid this is not settled at all. Admiral Hughes is mistaken in his understanding of what my orders are and I will of course be writing to explain this to him. My orders are crystal clear and they are from the First Lord of the Admiralty direct. I shall of course write to the First Lord and explain this misunderstanding. And, for the record, even if I had not these crystal clear orders from the Admiralty I must confess some puzzlement. As Captain Moutray knows, I am an active commission sea officer. I do not take orders, ever, from civilian authorities. I really do not know what Admiral Hughes was thinking, but I shall explain myself to him."

The men around the table were speechless, looking around at each other in disbelief. Before the Governour could speak the plantation owner Roberts exploded in anger.

"God Almighty, sir! What in heaven's name are you thinking? You are disobeying the direct order of a superior officer! Are you insane?"

Nelson's reply came with a cold hiss of anger. "If I need advice on how to conduct my business from the likes of you I will ask for it. And watch your language, sir. Any more disrespect from you and you will face the consequences."

"Gentlemen, please. Captain Nelson," said the Governour. "Are you bent on this course of action, sir? Would it not be more prudent to await clarity?"

"Sir. I have my orders."

"Ah. That is clear, then. Well, thank you for coming today. We shall have to see how this works out."

"Actually, Governour, since I am conveniently here there is one other matter we should discuss."

"Oh?"

"As you know, the Dockyard requires expansion of its facilities. I have explained this is of strategic importance to the Crown and you know what my orders say regarding this. The expansion work needs to proceed faster."

"Yes, Captain, we are all aware of this. But, really, we all also know the work will have to done primarily by the slaves from the plantations. There are many demands on their time, but I am certain the owners here have done the best they could to free up the resources."

"I am afraid they will have to do better in future, sir. If I do not see improvement soon I will have to act."

The men around the table looked at each other, concern carved on their faces.

"Act, sir?" said the Governour.

"I shall not be unreasonable about this. I will be discussing needs with Captain Moutray in the near future and we will define exactly what we would like to see. We will of course be sensitive to difficult times, such as harvest periods where clearly no one is to be spared from the fields. But I must insist our needs be met. If not, my officers shall enforce my needs by attending the various plantations to impress the workers we require."

The three planters roared in shock. Pressing unwilling men to service in the Navy was a tactic the Navy had employed in past, but it had never been used in a situation like this.

Their leader Roberts gathered his wits first, his face red with anger, and he pounded the table with his fist hard enough to make the cups on it bounce.

"That's a bloody outrage! You can't take my property whenever you bloody feel like it!"

Nelson stood up and put on his hat to leave, looking around at the dumbfounded group of men. "No? Who is going to stop me? I have my orders, sir. Good day, gentlemen."

Feeling truly pleased for what seemed the first time in days Nelson left and headed for his next meeting, this time with the man in charge of the Royal Mail in Antigua.

***

Two nights later Nelson was alone at dinner with Captain Moutray and his wife Mary.

"Well, my friend, you've certainly stirred them up this time," said Moutray with a laugh. "My word, they were so blind with anger at you I'm surprised they were even able to see their way out the door."

"Captain," said Mary with a smile. "You have not changed. You hide a steel fist behind all that charm."

"Madam, your kind regard is like a refreshing swim in a cool lake." Turning, Nelson sighed and looked at his friend.

"Well, John, something had to be done. They won't like it, but they will comply. We will get this building program at the Dockyard moving and completed one way or another."

"I will do what I can, Horatio, you know I will. But I fear I may not be able to help you for long."

Seeing Nelson's wary, anxious look Moutray gave a small grimace. "Yes, I went to see the doctor yet again the other day. He is recommending a return to England. Whatever this is that is slowly sapping my strength is beyond his skill. He has suggested seeing a specialist in London. He also thinks this climate out here is unhealthy and may have something to do with it."

Nelson nodded in acknowledgement, concern still on his face and some heat in his response. "I certainly agree with that assessment of the climate. This awful heat, well. Our cool English weather doesn't breed the kind of abominable diseases one finds common out here. So what will you do?"

"I'm about to write for dispensation to end my tenure here early. I have no idea how long it will take for a decision, but I don't anticipate a problem. I expect we shall be gone by spring."

Nelson sighed. "I shall miss you both. I have so few real friends I can relax and be myself with. But I understand. You must do what is best for the two of you."

"We shall miss you too, Horatio," said Moutray. "I have to tell you we are concerned, though. These plantation owners are not true gentlemen. They will use every underhanded trick they can to get their way. Worse, you are proving a tangible and direct threat. If they can find some way to potentially ruin you they will certainly attempt it."

Nelson smiled. "Do not fear for me, my friends. You are right. These owners all do their best and pretend, but being rich and in business does not make them gentlemen. I am not afraid of them. I have boarded my foes with initiative and won through in past. Securing myself to my foes and having at them will serve me well in future."

.

Chapter Seven
November 1784
Antigua

Evan sat beside James at the table they had
added to the front verandah of their house as both
men cradled their mugs of ale and stared into the
distance. The table and chairs were a perfect addition;
the verandah of the house was a shady spot where
even a wisp of breeze made it pleasant to sit outside
and enjoy the view of Falmouth Harbour in the
distance.

Both were deep in thought. After Evan
explained the orders in detail James was silent for the
most part, digesting it all. Evan wasn't surprised; on
the journey back from the Dockyard his mind was
racing, going over the details of the conversation
again and again. James grunted acknowledgement in
the end and said he needed to think for a while. After
several minutes James finally turned, refilled their
mugs, and looked at Evan.

"Sir, can I ask your thoughts on all this?"

Evan gave him a curious look in response.
"'Sir', is it?"

"Ah, sorry, Evan. It's because we're dealing
with Navy business. Force of habit, I guess."

"Well, that's probably not a bad thing. We're
going to find ourselves in situations where the fact
we're friends will seem completely out of place. You
will have to be careful about that when we are in the
company of others. So, forgive me, I won't question
your use of 'sir' in future. In any case, you want
thoughts."

Evan paused for a moment, clearly struggling
with what to say. "This is something new to both of

us. I don't think I like it, not at all, even despite what Captain Nelson said about the necessity. Give me something straightforward, like life on a ship. Sailors are something I know and can deal with. Give me an enemy ship and I can deal with that too. But this business? Well, dealing with those clowns in the Dockyard and chasing after records about ship registrations are simple enough, of course. But skulking about, as he called it? Or making contacts with questionable sources or even bribing people? My God!"

"Well, I see we are thinking alike, Evan. But these are our orders. We're going to have to figure out how to do this. God Almighty, we simply have to succeed at this, Evan. I mean, what will happen if we don't?"

"God knows, so I agree, we are going to have to figure this out. Well, the overt tasks I think you can mostly leave to me, although I'd like you to be there with me when I explain my orders to those Dockyard fools. I want them to understand you are my agent in all matters and are to be treated as such. I think we'll be dealing with them for a long time, so it's best you be involved and understand what is happening on that front."

James nodded agreement, so Evan continued.

"As for the skulking about part, well, I welcome your thoughts. We've made a few contacts at the Flying Fish, but there are other taverns around. Perhaps you could spend some time checking them out?"

"Yes," replied James slowly, obviously thinking hard. "I think that makes sense, sir. You are an officer and there are too many people around here know that, even if you don't dress the part in town.

Me, I'm only an injured Navy boy hanging around to amuse myself while I get better, right? Best of all, I'm black. I can maybe connect a lot easier with the locals without you with me."

"Yes, that makes sense. Captain Nelson didn't say as much, but I suspect this is what he had in mind. So in addition, I think you should perhaps take a tour of the island. Same story, but add the idea you are bored and wanted to see some of the sights. You can make a few friends as you go and look for anything suspicious. Even better, you can look for likely spots smugglers could do their business without prying eyes."

James nodded agreement, looking thoughtful once again. "Evan, did you notice Alice and Rachel got kind of shifty that day we talked about runaway slaves? Or was that my imagination?"

Evan looked quickly back at James, realizing how perceptive the thought was. "Yes, I think you are right. Hmm, I wonder if there is something there? Maybe some sort of support networks for the runaways? If there is, we might be able to work with their network to have them get information for us. The question is, how do we access it if one exists?"

James coughed and looked at Evan as a grin stole over his face. "Ah, well, you know Alice pretty well by now. Perhaps she would be willing to help? You do have lots of gold to work with."

Evan laughed in response, knowing James well enough to be certain of what he was really thinking. "Yes, I could do that, couldn't I? And what about Rachel?"

"Ah, well, I've kind of moved on from that. Don't want her to get used to it. You know how it is."

"No? Well, how about Anne? She seems rather taken with you. Perhaps you could, um, get to know her somewhat better? She could be a source, too."

James struggled to keep the grin off his face as he straightened up, turned, and raised his arm in salute. "Sir? My orders are to seduce our cook, sir?"

"For King and country, Mr. Wilton. We must both do battle as we've been ordered," replied Evan, as the two men broke down and howled with laughter.

***

The sealed orders from Nelson arrived the next morning, delivered by one of the Marines from the Boreas. Evan broke the seals on the three separate packets and read them to James, but they contained nothing they did not already know.

Turning to James, Evan smiled. "Hmm, well, no point in wasting time. I think we should finish breakfast and stroll over to the Dockyard to acquaint our two friends there with our new role. I'm rather looking forward to this."

James smiled.

An hour later they were in the Dockyard offices sitting in front of the two Lieutenants. The senior, Burns, threw the orders at his colleague Lieutenant Long and stood up.

"What bloody nonsense. Excuse me, I intend to seek audience with Captain Moutray on this."

"Captain Moutray is already aware of this and is in agreement with these orders, sir," said Evan.

The Lieutenant's eyes bulged in disbelief before he turned and stormed out of the room. Lieutenant Long picked up the orders, shock and puzzlement struggling in equal measure on his face.

A minute later his jaw dropped open and, with his own eyes wide, it became his turn to stare at Evan.

"God Almighty! Is this a joke?"

Evan couldn't resist a pleasant smile in response. "I daresay Captain Nelson indeed has a sense of humour, but I don't think he uses it much when he issues orders, sir."

Lieutenant Long continued staring for a moment before throwing the orders across the desk to Evan. The three men sat in strained silence for a full five minutes as the sound of distant, raised voices came from elsewhere in the building. The short burst of angry voices didn't last long and a period of acute silence followed, until a much more subdued Lieutenant Burns came in and slumped into his chair. His face was flushed and shock, anger, dismay, frustration, and despair all seemed to play across his face in equal parts. With one look the Second Officer knew what had happened.

"Well, you can't say I didn't warn you, Lieutenant Burns," said Evan. "So, gentlemen, my assistant and I need a full debriefing from the two of you as to where you are at on all of the various projects. I would like to know how we stand with supplies and what you are doing about deficiencies. I want to know what your construction schedule is for the next three months. I also want to know what day-to-day Dockyard activity with ship repairs is planned over the next three months, especially if you expect it to affect the construction schedule. I want to know when you expect to get help from the local plantation owners and how much you expect. Oh, and so you know, you should consider my assistant Mr. Wilton as my voice in all matters should I not be present. If he makes a request consider it as coming from me."

The two men both groaned and held their heads in dismay.

***

Back at the house at the end of the day Evan and James slumped onto their chairs on the verandah. Anne was waiting and, seeing how tired they looked, she soon reappeared with a pitcher of ale. Both men drank deep.

"Thank you, Anne. You are an angel. My word, that tastes good," said Evan. "I've been looking forward to that for hours."

"Me, too," said James. "Good Lord, Evan. Those two are a right pair of annoying bastards, aren't they?"

"Yes, indeed." Seeing Anne waiting for orders he smiled at her. "You probably want to know if we're ready for dinner. The answer is yes, please. We've had a trying day."

James drank deep once again before turning to Evan once Anne was out of earshot. "You know what? I'm happy I get to do the skulking part of this job. I think you've got way more patience than I would have to deal with them. I wanted to throttle both of those idiots at least twice today."

Evan laughed. James wasn't exaggerating; the two officers had adapted quickly after their initial shock. Every possible reason to delay or deny Evan's requests were trotted out as the day wore on and Evan was forced to badger and threaten both of them continually throughout.

What hadn't helped was what they had learned. Evan was dismayed to find no real plan for the next three months, let alone the next three days. The two men acted on something only when a reaction to something else was necessary.

The state of Dockyard supplies was a perfect example. Repairs to a sloop had finally been completed and another was ready for repairs to its copper bottom. The problem was no one thought to check whether the supplies of copper on hand were sufficient to do the job and, of course, they weren't. Incredibly, the two men failed to adjust and assign the few regular Dockyard workers other duties while the supplies were coming in, meaning no one was actually doing anything while they all waited for additional supplies to arrive.

The Dockyard construction projects were in a similar state of disarray. Fortunately, Evan had learned enough to be able to report factually to Nelson and Captain Moutray. After dinner Evan sat at his desk in the house making notes, thinking about his recommendations and a possible schedule of work for the construction he knew was needed. James winked at him as he left with Anne to go for a drink at the Falmouth Harbour Inn.

Feeling refreshed the next morning Evan reworked his notes and finished a report, which he delivered to the Boreas. Stopping in to see the two Lieutenants he spent an hour pointedly going over more issues he hadn't covered the day before which had come to mind only after having time to think about what he had seen. The two men greeted him with sour faces and their resistance seemed no less than before.

His last task as he was leaving was to look over the site of the planned new pitch and tar building with the two Lieutenants. Evan was on the far side of the site with Lieutenant Burns when the same mongrel from before came up to Lieutenant Long, tail wagging and tongue hanging out, looking hopeful for a morsel of food. The Lieutenant, already in a bad mood, attempted to kick the animal. The dog barely got out of the way and snarled at the officer, standing his ground.

"You scruffy little shit," said Long. "Get lost!"

The dog seemed tired of the abuse. Dodging the kick he danced in with surprising agility to try and bite his foe. The two went back and forth at each other until the dog finally got hold of his pant leg and tore it.

"God Almighty!" shouted Long. "Right, that's it for you."

He stepped back, reaching to pull out his sword.

"Don't even think about it," said Evan, coming over to step between them. "You'll not be harming this dog, sir."

Lieutenant Long glared at Evan with bulging eyes, but stayed his hand. "What the bloody— that dog tore my pants. He's a goddamn stray!"

"Only after you tried to kick him first, sir."

The officer's face went red with anger, but he slowly mastered himself. "If you like this dog that bloody much I suggest you take him with you. The Dockyard is no place for strays. If he's still here tomorrow I will order he be removed."

"Let's not forget who is in charge around here, sir. But no matter, as it happens I like animals. I've often thought one of the hallmarks of a gentleman is how he treats creatures less fortunate and weaker than him. I shall adopt this animal."

Lieutenant Long scowled, but offered no response, too angry to speak. He turned and stalked back into the Dockyard, followed by Lieutenant Burns. Evan shook his head in disbelief as he made his way back into the Dockyard too, but this time he went to the worker's mess kitchen. Returning with a handful of small scrap bits of meat and a short length of rope he coaxed the dog out from under the shade of a bush. Offering the scraps periodically he enticed the dog into following him all the way back to the house. The dog submitted to the rope leash without protest, as if he was already used to it.

Pleased with the start he'd made on his tasks and having made a friend, Evan was in a good mood. As he came up to the house he frowned at the muffled sounds coming from the interior. His concern grew as he realized he was hearing the screams of a woman. Quickly tying the dog to a pillar in the shade on the verandah he stepped inside, only to realize the screaming of the woman was rhythmic and coming from James's room. Her screams were punctuated by similarly rhythmic, inarticulate grunts from a male voice.

Evan laughed as he realized what was happening, so he scribbled a quick note about the dog. He couldn't resist adding he was heading into town to make his own connections with the locals and telling James not to expect him back that night. The dog licked his hand as Evan left a large bowl of water for him.

By the time he made it to town the hour was well past the middle of the afternoon. He went straight to the Flying Fish and sought out Alice. Fortunately, she was still unattached for the evening and was pleased, displaying her white teeth as she flashed him a broad smile.

"Sure, lover man. I'm yours for the day and night anytime."

"Excellent. I have some business with the Customs fellow I'd like to get started on, but I will be here to share a dinner and, ah, the rest of the evening with you later."

Alice draped an arm around his shoulder, rubbing her breasts against his chest with a grin. "Customs? Good Lord, that and this Navigation Order is all anyone can think about around here now. Come back soon, lover. I've got way more interesting things for you to have on your mind."

The Customs officer Lawson was not as welcoming. Scowling as he read the orders Nelson prepared for Evan, Lawson finally shook his head and passed the papers back across the desk. Slumping back in his chair the man regarded Evan with dismay and frustration clearly evident on his face.

"My heavens, sir. Hasn't your Captain Nelson made my life complicated enough? I have angry ship owners and businessmen badgering me to do something constantly now. I am swamped, sir, completely swamped."

Evan was unsympathetic. "Sir. As with Captain Nelson, I have my orders. As you can see, the Captain is concerned there may be irregularities with ship registration. I am tasked with assessing the situation. Your cooperation will be duly noted and conveyed, sir."

Lawson scowled. "Well, I'll do anything I can to help our good Captain and, if I may be frank, sir, to get you out of my hair. What do you want to know?"

"I am not familiar with the process of ship registration. How does this work here?"

A devious look Evan did not like appeared on the man's face as he responded. "Hmm, well, when a ship is built or acquired, as the case may be, it must

137

be registered in whatever its home port may be. This process is the same in any British controlled port. In our case the responsibility to maintain and control a register rests with a section of the Governour's office. Of course, Customs is involved almost immediately every time a registration takes place. We have to know what is happening to ensure there is no untoward delay in the movement of shipping."

He stopped and paused a moment for emphasis. "That also means, of course, I will have the ability to properly enforce the Navigation Order in Council so dear to your Captain."

"Of course, sir," smiled Evan, not rising to the man's bait to argue the issue. "So while you have involvement the control rests elsewhere?"

"Exactly, sir, which is why you should be talking to Mr. Ellis in the Governour's office. Roger Ellis. He has overall responsibility."

"I see. Do any requests to register a ship ever come to you first?"

The devious look reappearing in the man's eyes told Evan the question hit home. "Umm, well, yes I confess there have been some come through my office first. These are people that don't understand the process, of course."

"Hmm, is there any fee for registration, sir?"

The man's face fell and a bead of sweat appeared on his forehead near his hairline. "Fee? What are you implying, sir?"

Evan gave him a cold look. "I imply nothing, sir. I merely asked if there is a fee. Why, did you think I was talking about you personally charging them something, sir? I'm sure that wouldn't be the case, would it?"

Lawson sat back in his chair, looking trapped once again as he tried to compose himself. "No, no, heavens no. Ah, well, yes, there actually is a fee charged by the Governour's office. Really, you must talk to Mr. Ellis about that."

"So Mr. Lawson, have there been a lot of registrations in the last year, sir?"

The man's face fell and with brows knit he began shuffling the papers on his desk about. "Hmm, well, there have been a few. Where did I put that information, now?"

"I can wait for it, sir."

The man sighed in resignation. Reaching into a side desk drawer he leafed through some files before pulling a folder out and placing it in front of him. Flipping through its contents, he pulled out a sheet and passed it over to Evan. No less than twenty-five ships had been registered in the port of St. John's in the past year. For the two years prior the combined registrations were barely a quarter of this total.

Evan pointed this out to Lawson who only shrugged and gave him a pleading look. "I have no explanation for that, sir. Perhaps Mr. Ellis will have a better understanding of why that would be?"

Realizing he wasn't going to get much more from the man and with it being close to the end of the day Evan thanked him for his help, rising to leave.

"I'd like to take this list with me, sir," said Evan. "I assume you have another copy for yourself?"

A look of consternation came over Lawson's face as he eyed the paper in Evan's hand. He clearly didn't want to part with it, but couldn't think of any reason to deny Evan's request.

Evan paused at the door and looked back at the Customs man wiping the sweat from his brow.

"I may be back if I have further questions, sir."

The man looked appalled. "Sir, forgive me when I say I very much hope not."

***

"So, lover man, are you going to spend the rest of the evening watching the other people in here or are you going to actually pay attention to me like you should?" said Alice, leaning across the table and showing her tempting cleavage once again.

Evan laughed. "No, Alice, tonight my interest is completely with you. Besides, it seems rather quiet in here tonight anyway."

"Well, not hard to know why that is. If the Navy is going to keep shutting the door on American ships that alone will slow business down a lot. From what I hear every business in town is suddenly suffering. Emma and her husband are complaining too."

"Hmm. What else are you hearing about this?"

Alice shrugged. "Well, everyone knows the smuggling is going on. They're all angry because the smugglers will merely use a different approach. The problem is the people running the businesses like Emma and Walton won't get anything because the sailors can't come in and drink. Or, for that matter, spend their money on me. So no, there aren't a lot of people happy about this at the moment."

"Huh. What about other shipping? Have those Dutch ships been back?"

"Not since you saw them. Like I said, not a lot happening around here suddenly. Say, why so interested, if you don't mind my asking? More of this 'professional interest' of yours?"

Looking carefully around first to ensure they couldn't be heard before responding, Evan turned back to Alice. "Actually, yes. And you may be able to help me."

Alice raised an eyebrow, but said nothing in response.

"I believe I can trust you, Alice, so what I'm about to tell you is in strict confidence, please. Yes, I have interest in learning more about the smuggling going on here. A lot more. In fact, I need details about when and where it will happen and who is involved. I don't know if you are in a position to help with that. If you aren't, perhaps you can point me to someone who can? I have resources that may help convince anyone who has information to part with. So, are you someone who can help here?"

Alice sat back in her chair, staring hard at him. For a moment Evan feared she was going to get up and leave, but their dinner began arriving. As the waiter left, Alice finally responded.

"I need to think about this. Can we eat our dinner for the moment?"

Evan nodded in reply. A spicy fish soup with fresh bread to start was soon followed by the main course. The plate held a fresh caught grouper breaded and fried, along with some strange local vegetables Evan had never seen before. All of it tasted delicious. For a change Evan ordered a bottle of wine to go with it and both of them savored drinking something other than ale.

Holding her glass high and staring appreciatively at it, Alice smiled. "I could get used to this, you know."

When the meal was finished she lingered, toying with her glass, relishing what was left of the bottle. She leaned close as he poured the remainder into their glasses.

"So lover man, the answer is maybe, yes, I can help you. However, I'd rather not talk here. There are too many ears in here that may be sharper than we think. Why don't we take our glasses upstairs?"

***

The need for information took a backseat to other needs as soon as they were alone in the room. A half hour later Alice sat propped up at the head of the bed, sipping her wine, with Evan's head resting on one of her breasts.

"Can I ask you a dumb question, lover man?"

"Sure."

"How come you keep coming back to me?"

Evan grunted and sat up, turning to look at her before pulling himself up further to sit propped up beside her. He replied as he reached for his glass of wine. "Good question. I seem to have become a regular customer, haven't I?"

"Yes. The only one I have, actually."

"Huh. Can I ask you a dumb question too?"

"Sure."

"Am I imagining things or do we both actually enjoy each other's company that much?"

"Hmm, I don't think it's your imagination."

"Well, that's what I thought, too. So there's your answer, I guess. I like you."

"I like you too, Evan. But you do realize it's not likely this will work much beyond where we're at right now, right?"

Evan grimaced and shrugged. "Maybe I want something to work out. Maybe you do, too."

"Evan, you and I are the wrong colour for each other. Plus, I'm a whore, for God's sake. Well, not by choice, but that means nothing. I'm a slave. You are an officer. Officers have expectations placed on them by the white man's world you live in."

Evan sighed. "That is true. So can I ask you one more dumb question?"

"Sure."

"Why did you ask me the question in the first place?"

Alice turned and looked away for a moment before responding. "Don't know. Well, maybe I do. I've never had anyone take an interest in me for, you know, longer than doing it takes. This is unusual. I guess I wanted to understand."

"Really? No special friend outside the 'business'?"

Alice gave him a weary grimace. "Lover man, who wants a whore as a special friend? I'm careful about it and make you all wear protection, but the risk of getting disease is always there. So no, like I said, you're the only 'regular' I've ever had, either as part of the trade or otherwise. Look, I don't want to be doing this any longer than I have to. It's better than being in the fields, like I said. I've been trying to save what little money I have in the hope some day I can do what Emma and her husband do. They're going to put in a word for me the next time the owner man wants to open another tavern somewhere. I've been learning from them how to cook and how to manage a place like this. Maybe some day I can have a better life. I don't want to end up working in the fields when I'm old and my looks have gone."

Evan sighed, thinking back to his hurried experiences with serving girls when he was much younger like everyone else. He had also joined the other midshipmen and officers in taking advantage of discreet brothels to be found in whatever port they were in when the need and the rare opportunity arose. Joining the Navy as young as he had and being constantly on the move left little opportunity to experience anything more substantial or permanent. Being with Alice consistently somehow felt more satisfying.

"Well, I guess we make the best of what we have," said Evan, a far off look in his eyes. "I have a feeling you'll make your goal some day. I don't know why, but I somehow feel it. In any case, I'd like to continue being a regular customer for you if you're okay with that."

Alice laughed and rolled over to straddle him, hands on his shoulders and breasts brushing his face. "Well, this is a business transaction so as long as you keep paying everyone will be happy. But I'll be that much happier and will do my absolute best to please."

As Evan responded and lost all thought of anything other than her body she laughed once again. "I think I'm going to like having a regular customer!"

***

"So you want details of the smugglers activity, huh. You do realize these are dangerous people to get mixed up with?"

Evan came over and poured her another glass of wine, having dressed and secured another bottle from the tavern after their last round in bed. Looking at her, he shrugged.

"So? I'm dangerous, too. Captain Nelson is dangerous. We're not afraid."

"Why is this so important?"

Evan wasn't sure why she wanted to know, but took a few minutes to explain what he knew.

"So to be clear," she said in a slow voice, obviously thinking hard as she spoke. "Making the owners pay the duties is making their life real difficult? It affects their ability to stay in business?"

"Well, so they say, yes. But that's not any of my concern."

"Evan, if they went out of business, what would happen?"

Evan frowned. "What do you mean?"

"I wonder if something better would finally result? If the owner men using slaves can't make their system work anymore maybe a better system would result?"

"Alice, you are way beyond me on this. Look, I'm really hoping you maybe have some contacts that could serve. Keep their ears to the ground. Pass on any tidbits of information about smuggling that is happening. When, where and especially who is involved is what I need. You've hinted there are maybe runaway slaves out there. There must be a network or something to help them. Maybe the network could help?"

Alice stayed silent a few long moments, obviously weighing a hard choice, before finally replying. "Let's say you are right, there is a network and I know who to talk to. It may be they're closer to hand than you realize."

Evan raised an eyebrow as she continued. "And it's perhaps not only a network to help runaways, of which there are plenty. The network is always on the lookout for ways to make the owner man's life difficult. Everything from 'accidentally' burning the master's meal to deliberate destruction of his property."

She paused a moment to offer him a broad grin. "Mr. Roberts has had to repair his sugar mill more times than he would like. And that is despite having a guard on it all the time."

"So, lover man, I need to talk to some people. Come and see me in two days. I may have someone for you to meet. I think you said you have 'resources' that would help?"

"I do," replied Evan, clearing his throat. "Umm, use of these 'resources' needs to be reasonable."

"I don't think you need fear that. I suspect what you are looking for would willingly be done for free, but every little bit helps."

"Two days, then."

***

Leaving the Inn the next morning Evan was pleased with the progress made. Heading for the Governour's headquarters he enquired how to find the man Lawson had advised was in charge of ship registration. Fortunately, he was in and able to see Evan after only a short wait.

Roger Ellis had the air of a born thief masked by expensive clothing and a perfect, manicured look. Evan disliked him from almost the instant he saw him. The man was silent as he read Evan's orders, looking up in the end to survey Evan from head to toe. The look on his face was as if he was seeing and smelling something faintly distasteful.

"Sir, why are you not in uniform?"

"I am on detached service looking into civilian matters at the behest of Captain Nelson and it was his orders I dress appropriately for the circumstances," replied Evan with a hint of steel in his voice. "Not that this is any of your concern, sir."

Ellis grunted in disdain, but said nothing. Explaining he had visited the Customs officer already, Evan asked the same questions of Ellis as he did of Lawson. The answers were much the same. Having confirmed what he knew Evan began to probe deeper.

"Sir, did the Governour not find it unusual that so many ships would suddenly be registered in the past year?"

The man shrugged. "The Governour? Sir, forgive me, but the Governour is a busy man. Far too busy to deal with petty details like ship registrations."

"I see. So do you find it unusual this is happening?"

The man shrugged once again. "It is not my job to question these things. I have a purely administrative function here, sir. Ensure the registration is in order and the fee is paid, of course."

"Of course. So, I'd like to know more about these ships that have been registered in the past year. Do you inspect any of them personally to ensure they are what they say they are?"

Ellis sat back in his chair, a look of shock on his face. "Good Lord, why would I do that?"

"It is part of your job to make sure, is it not?"

"Well technically, yes. But really, it's not necessary, not at all."

"Why?"

"Well, the ships registered this past year are all owned by distinguished, respected people here on the island. I have no reason to doubt their word, none at all. It would almost be an affront."

"Hmm. So of the ships registered how many were actually built here, sir?"

147

The man was taken aback and a trapped look appeared on his face. "Why is that relevant, sir?"

"Bear with me, please. How many?"

After fumbling with his papers for a few minutes Ellis finally reported only one of the ships was brand new. Owners on Antigua had acquired the rest from other sources.

"Right, these 'other sources', sir? Who are they? Where would they be located?"

The cornered look stayed on Ellis's face. "Umm, I don't have that information, sir."

Evan raised an eyebrow. "Why?"

"Well, it really doesn't matter to know all that, does it? As I said, I have no reason to question the actions of respected people here."

"So this information was not required?"

"Well," said Ellis, buying himself time by responding slowly and choosing his words carefully. "Technically, it is a requirement. I decided to waive the need for that as a lot of bureaucratic detail. Sir, the owners were all desperate to keep supplies for their operations flowing smoothly in the face of these draconian laws about smuggling. I felt it was in the best interests of all to facilitate that as it were."

"I see. Well, Mr. Ellis, I think I have what I need to know. Thank you for your time, sir."

"I hope I've been helpful and that you'll report as such, sir?" said Ellis, a questioning look on his face.

Evan couldn't resist raising an eyebrow once again, disgusted at the man's gall, but he kept his reply civil. "Indeed, sir, the information has been helpful. Good day."

Chapter Eight
November 1784
Antigua and Barbuda

Two nights later as promised Evan appeared at the Flying Fish, where Alice was waiting for him.

"You can relax, lover man," she said, seeing him look cautiously around the room. "I know you're wondering what's up. The deal is you're buying me dinner and we get down to business later." She grinned. "Well, you're buying me for the night, too, in case you were wondering. We'll talk upstairs."

Once in their usual room she forestalled him as he reached out to grasp a tempting breast in his hand.

"That's for later, you beast. First, business will be knocking soon, so sit down and relax." Raising a finger to her lips, she pointed at the door.

A short while later a tapping came at the door, so light they almost didn't hear it. Alice opened the door a crack and looked out, before opening it wide to admit a woman. Evan gave a start when he realized who was joining them, before smiling at the irony; he indeed was close to the network without realizing it. The woman was Emma. He started to speak, but Alice put a finger to her lips once again as Emma sat down on the bed. A short while later the tapping came again and this time Emma's husband Walton came through the door.

"Sorry for the mystery, Mr. Ross, but we have to be careful," said Emma. "So, Alice has told us a little, but there has not been much opportunity to get details. You seek information and help?"

"Indeed I do." Evan explained the situation and what he sought in depth. When he finished Emma and her husband looked at each other for a moment. Walton turned back to Evan.

"Mr. Ross. Forgive us for what I'm about to say, but we must know the answer to this. How do we know we can trust you, sir?"

Evan had anticipated the possibility and pulled his orders from Nelson from his pocket. Handing them back after both had a chance to read them, Walton continued.

"Okay, that helps. But how do we know the fact we may help you will stay secret? Alice tells us you asked about a network to help runaway slaves. Can you guarantee this will remain secret? What will Captain Nelson do with that information? You must understand, we are taking an enormous risk even having this conversation with you."

Evan remained silent for some moments, thinking about his response. Reaching a decision, he looked at the two nervous people sitting in front of him.

"I realize that and I appreciate it. You must understand I cannot guarantee your involvement will forever remain secret. Anything is possible and circumstances I may not foresee now may result in your exposure. What I can guarantee you is I will do my utmost to keep your identity and your roles secret. I am certain the Captain will appreciate the need to protect our sources, too. Frankly, I don't think a few runaway slaves would even gain or warrant his attention. You have seen Captain Nelson has tasked me with seeking information on smugglers. Your possible activities involving runaway slaves or any other activity you may be engaged in are not covered by his orders. I think as long as we stick to smuggling, I would have no need to report on, umm, other issues."

Emma studied Evan for a moment. "On your honour, Mr. Ross?"

"On my honour," replied Evan, sitting straighter as he spoke.

Emma and Walton looked at each other once again and both nodded. "Okay, Mr. Ross," said Emma. "We believe you are a man of honour. You have been good to Alice here."

"Thank you."

"So yes, we do have a network, such as it is. You may as well know most of us are people like Walton and me. People that run taverns and little food businesses for the owners all over the island are a big part of our contacts. We have access to food that can be slipped out of sight and provided to help runaways, see? Spoilage, you know. More importantly, we have contacts in the households of the owners. We can connect with eyes and ears everywhere. But we have one more question for you, sir. Why should we help you?"

Evan wasn't ready for the question. He sat taken aback for a moment, realizing he was a fool for not having anticipated it. Despite furious thought he could think of only one possible response.

"I have resources at my disposal. They are not bottomless, but I have authorization to employ them. We can talk."

The other three said nothing for a moment, until Emma broke the silence.

"Tell me, Mr. Ross, what is money to a slave? I could have all the money in the world and still be a slave to the owner man if he refuses to sell me."

Evan sighed. "I don't know what to tell you."

"Emma," said Walton, glaring in dismay at his wife.

Emma looked down at her hands before looking up once again. "I'm sorry. There isn't really anything you can say and you can't change the way things are. We only wish you could! We want to be free, Mr. Ross. So look, we will help you, but I want you to understand it's about more than the money. Oh, we'll take it from you, no mistake there. It will help. So you understand, if helping to put a stop to the owner man's smuggling makes his life difficult we're all for it. Even better if it helps bring an end to this insane system of keeping people as slaves!"

Evan nodded; they had a common foe, but for different reasons. Reaching into his pocket once again he pulled out a small, heavy bag clinking with the sound of coins. As he passed it to them he smiled.

"Consider this a start, a token of my sincerity. I should think this is sufficient to, umm, assist with gaining information wherever it may be found. Do you have thoughts on how to pass information to me when you have it?"

"Simple, Mr. Ross," said Emma. "You are already a regular here. You are known to favour Alice so no one will be surprised if you keep seeing her. If we have information for you we can meet in your room discreetly, like now. It will take us time to get the word out as to what is needed. Our contacts will need time and opportunity, so that may take a while. I suggest come by every couple days or so. If we have something for you Alice will let you know. If not, well, I'm sure the two of you will find something to keep yourselves occupied with."

Alice flashed him a huge grin.

"Actually, Mr. Ross," said Walton, seeing Evan nodding agreement to the idea. "I'm going to suggest you formalize a more ongoing relationship with Alice, as it were."

"Eh?" said Evan, as a trapped look came over his face. "Umm, meaning what, exactly?"

"Ah, nothing quite as constraining as you may be thinking, sir," said Walton with a knowing smirk on his face. "We suggest you contract with us to acquire her, ah, 'services' for an extended period. We can make it public that you have entered into this arrangement to anyone who asks, so we can explain why Alice is not available for duty, so to speak. I gather she told you she has been learning our business to someday run her own operation, right? That's perfect cover for her to move about doing business on our behalf when not busy keeping you happy. She can collect messages and make contacts with others in the network. She can even come and visit you at your residence on occasion, especially if we have urgent news for you."

Emma leaned forward and gave him a broad smile, which seemed more like a leer. "I'm sure we can negotiate a reasonable discount for a commitment to ongoing services."

Evan roared with laughter as the grin on Alice's face widened even further.

***

Evan kept busy while waiting for developments. He penned a report to Nelson about the ship registrations and another much more detailed one regarding the state of construction activity in the Dockyard, after spending several days walking into the Dockyard to check on progress and harangue the two officers. A small, mixed party of seamen from the ships under Nelson's command were detailed for shore duty to help get the work underway and Evan made certain they were used effectively. But Nelson had been on a short trip to Dominica on yet more political business, so the reports had only recently been delivered.

Despite this no immediate summons to attend Nelson came. Evan shrugged and thought no more of it, his mind elsewhere as he sat on the verandah watching the sun go down. His thoughts drifted to dark depression, not for the first time, as he absentmindedly rubbed the stump of his arm. Physically the wound had healed, but the depression still came without warning at times and, some days, it took iron will to even get out of bed. A desperate, trapped feeling washed over him, together with a yearning for a ship and the freedom of the sea, but Evan knew this was not going to happen without successfully fulfilling his orders.

Evan's mood brightened when James and the dog joined him on the verandah. James had been busy too, and had only just returned after being away several days. Despite having much to discuss, by unspoken agreement they instead sat enjoying the sunset as James fed scraps of meat to the dog. The beast greedily snapped up each piece as if he was starving, looking hopeful for yet more morsels of food. But he was definitely not starving; the dog had visibly put on weight in his short time at his new home.

"Hmm," said Evan, as he paused a moment with a speculative look on his face. "I think this dog wasn't getting fed regularly. Every meal it's like he'll eat till he's ready to burst. But he does seem used to being around people, though. I wonder if some previous owner abandoned him? Maybe when the dog lost his leg the owner figured he was done and turned him out."

"I think you're right, Evan. He took the leash and let you lead him away easily enough. It's about time we gave him a name, don't you think?"

"Sure. What do you suggest?"

"Well, he's a scrapper like Captain Nelson, Evan," said James. "So how about Nelson?"

Evan laughed and smiled. He realized the smile was his first of the day and he felt his black mood finally lifting. "Sure, why not? Nelson it is."

With this settled the two men briefed each other. Anne proved willing to help, but knew little direct information herself. However, she provided several contacts in various villages dotting the coast of the island and also made suggestions as to which taverns in St. John's might have potential for gleaning nuggets of information.

Acting on her information James traversed the island, spending three days trawling for information in St. John's alone. In the smaller villages James soon realized local fishermen were a prime source of what he wanted to know. For the price of a few drinks James learned much each time he connected with them. Several bays were identified as places smugglers either could use or, in some cases, certainly were using. The possibility of a reward for information leading to capture of a smuggler brought a gleam to the eyes of all of them.

The taverns in town were a different matter.

"Shit, Evan, you wouldn't believe it," said James. "The Flying Fish is a palace compared to some of those joints. And the locals using the Flying Fish regularly are like model schoolboys compared to the crowd of unsavory bastards in these other places. These sailors that work the local ships owned by the plantation bosses are a damn close-mouthed bunch. I had to be real careful not to push them. A couple looked real hard at me and I had to scramble to convince them my interest was innocent. And then there was the joint frequented by a bunch of the plantation overseers. All of the customers were white men. I had to back out of there in a hurry, let me tell you."

"But the good news is I think I've got a hint of something, Evan. Those two Dutch ships? They are indeed regulars here. Thing is, when I started asking questions about them most everyone got real shifty and here's the real interesting part. I was in there trying to spread money around to get information, right? Near as I can tell, they have been doing the same thing."

"Looking for information? Good Lord, what are they after?"

"Information about what the Navy has been up to and may be up to in future. Anything to do with our activity against smuggling seemed most of interest, but that wasn't the sole focus. They seem real interested in movements of our ships in general and they don't care who gives them the information. I think they're trying to make sure whatever they are up to happens in areas where the Navy is not present, so to speak."

"Hmm, I don't like this. The Captain will want to know."

"But that's not all, Evan. This gets better. I have names. That American Captain we saw in the Flying Fish? His name is Nathan Jones. He's definitely the Captain of one of the two ships. The even more interesting part is a Frenchman captains the other Dutch ship. His name is Marcel Deschamps."

"God Almighty. Well done, James."

"Evan? I was thinking. While I was digging up information I found out there are three brothels in town we didn't know about. I know where they are now."

"And you are thinking we should use some of our resources to have the ladies see what they can dig up from some of these frog sailors, yes?"

"Exactly!" said James, a beaming smile on his face. "I see we are thinking alike again."

"And that, of course, means you will have to spend time in each getting to know them first, doesn't it?"

James shrugged and the two men burst out laughing at the same time.

"If I have a choice between that or dealing with those useless shits in the Dockyard, I'll take the brothel duty any day."

Evan could only smile in response as he went inside to pen another report to Nelson.

As James left later to deliver the report one of the Flying Fish servants appeared with word Alice wanted to see Evan, so he took the buggy into town right away. She led him upstairs and within moments both Emma and Walton joined them.

"Evan," said Walton, keeping his voice low despite the door being firmly shut. "We got word one of the owners is having a cargo offloaded on Barbuda. I don't know if you know of it. It's a small nearby island that's part of the colony of Antigua. The drop off is at Two Foot Bay tomorrow night. The beach they are using is as far away as possible from prying eyes in Codrington, which is the only town on the island. The plan is to have a group of small fishing boats pick up the goods later and sail into St. John's to off load the parceled out cargo when no one is watching."

"My God, this is excellent. I must get word of this to the Captain. Thank you all!"

Evan returned right away to Falmouth Harbour and another report was soon on its way to Nelson. The response was swift. Two hours later the red serge of a Marine came into view up the path to the house. Evan stood and the man stopped in front of him in salute.

"Mr. Ross, sir?"

"I am Lieutenant Evan Ross, yes."

"Captain Nelson sends greetings, sir, and he desires to see you at nine o'clock tomorrow morning."

"Acknowledged. You may report I shall be there."

As the man turned to leave he saw the dog Nelson. "Ah, so this is where he got to! You gentlemen decided to give the beast a home, have you, sir?"

"Yes, he was in danger staying where he was so we have indeed given Nelson a home with us."

"You've named him Nelson, then?" said the Marine with a smile as he leaned down to scratch behind the dog's ear. "Ah, that's a good name for a fighter like him, sir. I shall tell the lads. We were all wondering what happened to him. We all tried to save a few scraps and feed him when we could. But you say he was in danger, sir?"

"Hmm, yes. The Dockyard officers seemed to feel there was no room for strays in their domain and were threatening his removal, so here he is."

The pleasant smile on the Marine's face melted away as Evan finished his explanation. With a bland look he paused for a moment before saluting Evan.

"Thank you, sir. The lads will be pleased to know he is in good hands. Good day, sir."

Evan nodded and the man returned the way he had come.

***

Nelson was sitting at his desk studying some paperwork when Evan was shown in the next morning. Once again, the desk was practically covered in paper.

"Ah, Mr. Ross. Thank you for coming, sir."

Evan held out a sealed envelope for Nelson to take. "Captain Nelson. I came on board early to prepare an accounting of my expenditures on, ah, sub rosa purposes."

"Excellent. Although, I must confess I hardly need more paper than I already have on this desk." Opening the envelope Nelson quickly scanned the document and grunted.

"Less than I thought it would be. You have one somewhat larger expenditure for a woman?"

Evan couldn't help blushing a little. "She is a key contact for us, sir. She is also a messenger."

Nelson laughed and winked at Evan. "You can relax, sir. We must work with whatever sources best serve. So you and your Mr. Wilton have indeed been busy. I am pleased with your progress on all fronts. Captain Moutray and I have come to agreement on what we want to see done in the Dockyard and the timing of the work. More importantly, we have identified our specific needs thanks to your detailed assessment. You may expect to see results on this in the near future. A list of the number of workers we want here together with a schedule of when we want them has been prepared and presented to the owners."

"I see, sir. Will they comply?"

Nelson laughed. "They say they will. They'd better. And your work on the ship registrations has given me something to work with on that front too. I suspect there were never any real sales of ships. I think we'll find these are still American owned ships and the only money that changed hands was to sell them a registration. I shall have to give the next step some thought."

"Sir? Permission to offer a suggestion?"

Nelson looked at Evan speculatively for a moment, before sitting back in his chair and nodding agreement.

"Sir, those ships could be almost anywhere serving other islands and it may be some time before they come back here. Rather than wait, perhaps it would be as simple as having Governour Shirley issue a revocation order for each of the ships with questionable paperwork? If you provide this order to each of your ships on station they could stop the ships wherever they are found. If they can't produce paperwork to support a proper registration their business can be stopped immediately."

Nelson continued staring at Evan for a long few moments, before sitting forward in his chair again. Nelson smiled.

"You prefer action, don't you, Mr. Ross?"

"I do."

"We are alike, sir. Yes, I think that's a good suggestion. I shall make it so."

Nelson paused a moment, rubbing his chin in thought. "And speaking of action, you have found something for us to move on. I should have given more thought to Barbuda as a possibility. Well done, sir, well done. Even better, you have more information on these mysterious 'Dutch' ships. Mr. Ross, those buggers are up to something. I can feel it in my bones. I desire you to make them a special priority. I don't know what bloody mischief they have afoot, but we've got to find out and stop it."

"We shall do our best, sir."

"You already have been doing your best and I have confidence you will continue to. You have justified my faith in you and I am of a mind to offer you a small token of my appreciation. I suspect you may enjoy it."

"Sir?"

"How would you and your man Wilton like to take a little trip with me, sir?"

***

"Good God, this feels good!" said Evan, as the night breeze off the ocean ruffled his shirt.

"Too right, sir," said James, standing beside him with a huge grin creasing his face.

They were standing on the leeward side of the quarterdeck of the Boreas, hanging onto the railings and doing their best to stay out of everyone else's way. Nelson had invited them along on the mission as reward, but specified neither of them were to wear uniforms. Nondescript civilian clothing was required. Before getting underway Nelson came over to speak briefly to them.

"Consider yourselves temporary civilians, please. I can't have any confusion on deck over another officer suddenly showing up nor do I want either of you to be chastised by the bosun for standing around. You will keep to a corner of the quarterdeck out of everyone's way," said Nelson.

Evan answered for both men as they responded with crisp salutes. "We are very much looking forward to this. Thank you from both of us, sir!"

Nelson smiled, seeing the excitement on their faces. Before turning away from the two men Nelson paused to look James up and down and in particular study his face. After a few moments he nodded.

"Well, Mr. Wilton. I expect Mr. Ross has told you I was asking about your father. Yes, I served with him when I was much younger. He was a good, good man. I can see him in your bearing and in your face. I was sorry to hear of his passing. I caught the fever too and was sent home from the East Indies. He must have caught it and died after I left. You should be proud he was your father."

James nodded and saluted as Nelson turned away.

Nelson had hoped for a cloudy night because the moon was full, but didn't get his wish. Clouds were about, but not enough to obscure the moon for long. Each time it peeked out a great, silvery, shimmering, and mesmerizing path of light from the moon reflecting off the surface of the water appeared. A small school of dolphins found the ship and decided to playfully race along beside it, leaping and diving with abandon through the moon's light.

"I could stand here all night watching this, sir," said James.

"Me too. Some officers used to complain about getting the night watches. But I never understood what there was to complain about if you were in the Caribbean, had good sailing, and had time to enjoy views like this. God, it feels wonderful to be back on a ship at sea. Well, we must enjoy this while we can, because I don't know when it will happen again."

The Boreas had left her moorings in English Harbour at dusk. After gaining freedom from the Harbour and getting underway on open seas, Nelson called his officers together for a conference to explain his intent. Evan and James crowded into Nelson's cabin with the others.

"Gentlemen, our two, ah, 'civilian' friends here have brought us word of possible smuggling activity. I have asked them to join us in case any of you have questions for them as we discuss tonight's operation."

"So, the landing of the contraband is allegedly set for two in the morning. The smugglers are using a nice, deserted beach on the east side of Barbuda. The problem they have is there is only one road to this beach and it leaves from the main town of Codrington. Our sources report much of the terrain on this part of the island consists of rather large, thick bush that conveniently has rather a lot of sharp thorns."

The men around the table all smiled and eager looks appeared as they began to see where Nelson was going with his plan. The Lieutenant in charge of the Marines, Francis Wolf, broke into a broad grin when he realized they were going to have a role to play.

"Yes, indeed, Lieutenant, you will be busy on that one and only road to the site," said Nelson with a smile. "Thus, we will first drop you and your Marines off in Codrington. Your orders are to make your way to Two Foot Bay at best speed. I anticipate a two-hour march based on distance of approximately five miles. This should give you some leeway. If you arrive at Two Foot Bay before we do or you are discovered you are not to engage unless forced to. Your purpose is to simply stop them from using the road as an avenue of escape. We, of course, will sail around the island at best speed and prevent escape by sea. The Sailing Master has assured me we can be on scene at approximately the same time given present wind conditions."

Nelson paused a moment to nod in the direction of Evan and James. "These gentlemen have advised there is evidently a break in the reef large enough to permit small boats to access the beach. We expect to find our smuggler landing cargo and hiding it out of sight in the brush. Their plot is to have fishing boats pick it up in smaller lots and bring it to the main island surreptitiously over the next couple of days."

"Gentlemen, I want all of these rats caught and put on display. I want this lot serving as a public message to all that smuggling is a bad idea. I desire no unnecessary violence, but if they put up a fight you are to respond accordingly, with maximum force if required. Any questions?"

The First Lieutenant raised a hand. "Sir? Do we need prearranged signals for any reason?"

"Hmm," said Nelson, rubbing his chin in thought and looking at the Marine Lieutenant. "Take some flares, Lieutenant Wolf. Use some blue and red ones. Blue to indicate your location if need be. Red will be for if you are in distress and require our help."

The Marine officer nodded agreement before turning to Evan. "Sir, do you have any sense of the size of force the smugglers will have?"

"Not precisely," replied Evan. "However, we understand this to be a large sloop they are using. Given this fact it is possible they could have as many as two-dozen crew or perhaps even more. I sorry we can't be more specific."

"Which is why you had best take your entire complement with you, Mr. Wolf," said Nelson.

The officer grunted and nodded. "Sir, I have no further questions. We will do our duty."

"Anyone else? No? Then let's be about it, gentlemen."

Landing the Marines on the edge of town was accomplished with brisk efficiency and minimal noise. No one could be seen about in the sleeping town or on watch in the harbour, so the first part of the operation was accomplished with the stealth Nelson desired.

Almost two hours later the Boreas rounded the coast and was driving towards the rendezvous with all eyes alert for any sign of activity. The Sailing Master signaled for the First Officer and after a brief conversation word was passed to call the Captain from his cabin. He soon appeared and came over to the Sailing Master.

"Captain, we are almost there. I think another five minutes. I recommend we reduce sail. This chart I have is a bit old and I am concerned about that reef."

Nelson nodded to his First Officer, who saluted and began issuing a series of orders. The moon once again disappeared behind the clouds and the minimal light from distant stars was insufficient to dispel the heavy darkness. While it hid their approach from the smugglers, it also hid them from the eyes of the warship. The officers on the quarterdeck used night glasses to try and penetrate the gloom when the action they were all expecting began with a hail from the masthead lookout.

"Deck there! Ship fine off the starboard bow! At anchor, I think!"

As all eyes focused in the direction he indicated a flurry of flashes came from shoreward, followed by the distant popping sounds of gunfire. Sporadic flashes and popping continued for the next minute as the Boreas grew closer and all could finally see the dim outline of a ship offshore. A sudden, brilliant flash lit the anchored ship forward of the waist, followed by the report of a larger weapon being discharged.

"Captain! That sounded like a swivel gun!" said the First Officer. Even as he said it the moon finally came out from behind the clouds, illuminating the scene before them clearly. A blue flare climbed high into the air from some distance down the beach followed quickly by a red one. Red flashes of guns discharging came from an area of the beach closest to the anchored ship.

The crew of the Boreas had long since been called to quarters and the guns made ready. Nelson looked at his First Officer, a grim look on his face.

"Fools. Mr. Wilkins, four guns with grapeshot. Two to deal that crowd on the beach opposing Lieutenant Wolf and the other two to put that swivel gun out of action, please. As we discussed, let's have one boarding party for the ship and another to support the Marines on the beach, please. Away with you, sir."

The crew of the Boreas drilled on the guns incessantly, so the shots came fast and with deadly accuracy. The flashes of the guns blinded everyone failing to look away in time. Seconds after they fired

166

the Boreas came about and two boats were launched. The swivel gun on the other ship didn't respond, but sporadic flashes of gunfire came from both the beach and the mystery ship. Lieutenant Wolf wasn't taking any chances with being cut down by friendly fire as another blue flare sailed high into the air, this time from much closer to where the Marine's foes were positioned. Another round of shots from the Boreas silenced all resistance on the smugglers ship and within minutes all gunfire finally ceased.

The rest of the night was spent dealing with the aftermath of the fight. The smuggling sloop turned out to be the Louisa out of Boston, with a mixed cargo of timber, clothing, and other dry goods. Three men were dead on the sloop, all cut down by the grapeshot from the Boreas. Four smugglers on the beach were dead.

As the First Officer went through their papers in detail he realized the three dead men on the ship all had highly questionable paperwork. When confronted with it the sloop Captain shrugged and glared at him.

"Doesn't matter much now, does it? Of course they were Navy deserters. I had no idea they were going to fire that swivel. They had it set up and took their shot before I realized what they were doing. Seeing your damn Marines must have set them off."

The rest of the sailors were mostly Americans, but one of the dead men on the beach also appeared to be a deserter.

"He's likely the bastard that started the shooting, Captain," said the First Officer, standing once again in Nelson's cabin with the other officers to debrief.

"I'm sorry, Captain," said Lieutenant Wolf when his turn came. "They had a picket hiding in the deep brush that fired at us before turning tail, so their whole force was ready for us when we reached the beach. I have two dead and three wounded, courtesy of that damn swivel gun. The wounded should all recover. I anticipated possible fire from the ship, but nothing of that magnitude. I take responsibility, sir."

"Nonsense, Lieutenant. No one could have anticipated that many desperate deserters would be present and that they'd have such a weapon on a trading ship. We will know better for future, sir."

By dawn the final boats were pushing off the beach and returning to the ships with the last of the cargo. Evan and James were tired, but satisfied. They were still staring out at the amazing, distinctive pink sand beach revealed by the daylight when Nelson came up to stand behind them. Sensing his presence, they both turned and saluted.

Nelson smiled. "Well done, gentlemen. You should warn your network immediately when we return. I think there will be some seriously unhappy people in Antigua when this action becomes known. Some of them may be suspicious it was no accident we were able to intercept this ship. I fear it will get much more difficult for your friends to glean information for us. This is going to be a war of attrition, I think."

He turned away, but as he walked away he called over his shoulder to the men. "And I do hope you enjoyed your little sojourn!"

Chapter Nine
December 1784
Antigua

Evan and James got dark looks in the streets of Antigua from people who knew they were Navy personnel as they made their way to the Flying Fish and found a table. Nelson was correct; no one in town was happy and many feared the impact to local businesses. Angry merchants and plantation owners glossed over the details that the smugglers fired first and that several were deserters.

As Evan read the local newspaper he realized the publisher was the most vocal of them all. The picture he painted emphasized Navy brutality enforcing the Navigation laws, urging his readers to be appalled over simple traders being killed. Evan shook his head in disgust; he was certain the man's print machine was working overtime to get his highly coloured version of the facts out along with his outraged editorial demanding the Governour do something. Evan knew the man was probably praying daily for more such incidents, even as he counted his mounting profits.

He snorted in disgust as he passed the paper to James and reached for his ale. "What a pile of horse turds."

Alice slid into the seat beside Evan and scanned the room carefully to ensure no one could hear them, but the hour was still early and the room wasn't full. Turning back she looked at the paper James was still reading.

"That may be horse turds, Evan, but even so there are a lot of people taking a good whiff of them.

Word is the publisher has had to print three times the usual number due to demand."

Evan grunted and shrugged as she continued. "I'm glad you gave us a warning. It gave our sources a little time to prepare a cover story. But the owners are definitely suspicious and they don't want to give up. As far as I know at least a dozen or more people have been beaten severely so far. It's likely a lot more people are still paying for it. But I have more news, lover man. We aren't sure what to make of it. First, there's a landing planned for Bush Bay on the north side of the island tomorrow morning. The ship is coming in from a stop at St. Kitts."

"What do you mean, you're not sure what to make of it?"

"Well, we also have word of one at Dutchman Bay, too. That's supposed to be tomorrow night right at dusk. The thing is these both came too easy or at least it seems that way. It doesn't feel right, coming so soon after this episode on Barbuda. Our sources weren't concerned; rather it's Emma and Walton that are nervous about this. With all the pressure we weren't expecting to get anything coming our way for some time."

"So you fear this could be planted information that will lead back to your sources?"

"Yes. But we don't know what to do about it," she replied, biting her lip as her face creased with worry.

Evan sighed. "I understand why you are torn about this. But there is only one way to find out if these are indeed traps. It's your call, Alice."

Alice looked down at her hands before looking up again. "The call has already been made. Emma and Walton have already agonized over it and told me to tell you. It's only I have a bad feeling about this. I know many of these people and I don't want to see them beaten to death or branded because of this."

Evan nodded and reached over to hold her hand, knowing nothing he could say would ease her concern. After a minute he looked over at James.

"I need to get this information to the Captain. Are you coming with me?"

James shook his head. "I think I'll trawl here in town for information. Upset people sometimes say things they otherwise wouldn't say."

Evan nodded and stood, throwing some coins on the table to pay for the drinks.

***

Four days later Evan was once again shown into Nelson's cabin. The Captain surprised him as for once he was not seated at his desk shuffling through the usual mountain of paperwork. This time the Captain was standing with his back to him and staring out the stern cabin windows.

"Captain? Reporting as ordered, sir," said Evan.

Nelson said nothing for several long moments, making Evan wonder if he was in for a dressing down. Based on events of the last few days Evan wouldn't be surprised.

"Have a seat Mr. Ross," said Nelson, a distracted, far away tone to his voice. With a sigh, he turned and came over to drop into his usual chair.

"Well, I guess your contacts were right to be concerned about the information fed to them. Have there been consequences as feared?"

"Sir, yes sir. Word has come that one individual in particular was subjected to most strenuous torture and has succumbed to it. We are not certain if he revealed his contacts, but we don't believe so. I think the plantation overseers that seized him are inexperienced torturers. Brutal thugs they may be, but their skill is limited to making people work, not talk. There have been several others severely beaten and injured. The network and its information will be slow to come back, sir."

"Yes, I feared this might come about at some point. These people are thugs, as you say, and I include the owners in that category. It is ironic that much of our wealth depends on this system and on people like this. But that is how it works and the country depends on it."

"I wonder if there is a better way than slavery, sir. It doesn't seem right, somehow."

Nelson shrugged. "I'm not a businessman, Mr. Ross, and I thank heaven I'm not. But this is the system and much of the wealth that flows into the Treasury to pay for us to be here comes from people that own slaves. It gives us the opportunity to defend the country's interests. I have every confidence that we will overcome our enemies and our country will lead the world in everything that matters. Maybe some day we'll lead on slavery, too."

Nelson grimaced, and sat forward. "Well, time to consider our business, Mr. Ross. I assume the town is still abuzz with outrage?"

"Quite, sir. I think the newspaper publisher should count himself fortunate we are creating so much business for him."

Nelson grunted. "Indeed. That ship Captain Sands seized was clearly a very good setup. They did an excellent job of pretending to be smugglers. They'd conveniently forgotten to bring their ship's papers with them, too. And as soon as Captain Sands gets them into St. John's harbour their Captain starts screaming about the outrageous behaviour of the Navy seizing legitimate ships. Of course, a plantation owner happened to be conveniently standing on the dock with the ships papers when they got in. Funny coincidence, eh? And the newspaper publisher somehow missed all these details in his reporting of the incident, despite showing up almost immediately to find out what was happening. Bastards."

"Ah, thank you for the explanation, Captain. I was concerned we had steered you wrong."

"Oh, not at all, Mr. Ross. You weren't to know. There is no lasting damage. Yes, the public thinks I am riding roughshod over their rights and there's a lot of pressure on Governour Shirley. He knows, though. I have made what happened clear to him. We carry on, sir."

"Sir? What happened with the ship that was allegedly offloading at Dutchman Bay? Did anything come about from it?"

Nelson frowned. "No, and that is why I was rather deep in thought when you came in. I am suspicious. There was no one at the rendezvous, but there was a ship in the area that eluded us when night fell."

"Suspicious, sir?"

"I am wondering if they were tipped off we were coming. Of your contacts that have been questioned were any of them the source of this particular tip to us?"

Evan frowned. "Now that you mention it, everything I was told about people being interrogated did seem tied to the fake smuggling ship. So it is likely the second tip was real?"

173

Nelson nodded. "I'd say so. But that leaves the question of how they knew we were coming."

The two men stared at each other for a few moments, both deep in thought, until Evan broke the silence.

"Sir, were all of your ships in English Harbour here that night?"

"Hmm, yes, I was thinking about that too," said Nelson, a far off look in his eyes. "The only two I have not working out of other islands were both here in English Harbour. I wonder? A fast horse relay of the information a ship had departed and was sailing toward Dutchman Bay? Carrier pigeons, perhaps?"

"So that means someone in the Harbour is watching and providing information about your movements, sir?"

"I fear so, Mr. Ross. The ship that escaped us behaved like they were guilty. I don't believe in coincidences, at least not when it comes to this business."

"Sir? Was your destination announced prior to departure?"

Nelson paused to think before shaking his head. "No, but it is possible someone talked when they shouldn't have. The only people that knew were my senior officers and I trust them implicitly. I— wait, damn it, I remember now. There was a conference with the Dockyard Shipwright and officers beforehand. My First Officer had some concerns about whether some repairs were fully completed. The Shipwright asked how far we were going and we told him the other side of the island." Nelson rubbed his chin in thought. "I wonder?"

"The Dockyard officers were there, sir?" said Evan, one eyebrow raised.

174

"Hmm," said Nelson, clearly thinking quickly for a few moments before looking hard at Evan. "Mr. Ross, if you and your man Wilton could ask a few discreet questions about what happened around here that night? Anything unusual, you know. And maybe check and see if anyone nearby raises pigeons."

Evan nodded. "We shall, sir."

"Well, we are making progress, Mr. Ross, slow as it may seem. I have another possible source of information I'm still working on that may be fruitful in the long run. We shall see."

"Sir?"

Nelson smiled. "Ah, well, what I'm about to tell you is strictly for your ears only and I mean only your ears, sir. But since you are effectively my intelligence officer you may as well know you should be most careful about what you say in letters you send through the mail."

Seeing Evan's puzzled look Nelson laughed. "My good friend the Royal Mail postmaster here is busy flagging correspondence between here and, um, foreign interests in the United States. I asked him to have a look at any plantation owners that correspond regularly with them and to find out what they are corresponding about. He is also looking at communications with other islands by these same people."

Evan sat back in surprise. "You mean, we can open and read people's mail?"

"National security, sir. We must do what is necessary. The government has been doing it for a long, long time. At any rate, I am hoping they will slip up and communicate orders and plans."

"Well, I'm glad it's not all down to whatever Mr. Wilton and I can glean, Captain."

175

Nelson smiled. "One must explore every avenue to achieving one's goals, sir."

"Sir, will that be all for today?"

"Actually, I have one other task for you. Do you recall I mentioned threatening the plantation owners with undertaking a press of workers for the Dockyard if they didn't comply with our requests?"

"I recall, sir."

"Well, that arrogant arse Roberts, the one who styles himself their leader, isn't cooperating, but the others are. Governour Shirley told me Roberts wants to make a political show of it. He wants me to send Marines to his plantation tomorrow morning so he can have witnesses there to attest to our heavy-handed treatment. Of course, it will all be written up as such in the newspapers. I am assured he will free up his allotment of workers after a token speech making it clear he is acting under duress."

"I see, sir. I am to help with this?"

"Why, yes," smiled Nelson. "You are my Dockyard liaison officer, aren't you? You are the one who detailed what needed doing and you gave recommendations on how many workers would be necessary. So I desire you to be my voice, sir. Marine Lieutenant Wolf and a file of Marines will be your backup. All you need do is show up with Mr. Wolf and request Mr. Roberts provide the half dozen workers he is scheduled to, as your job is to escort them safely to the Dockyard. Do not let them draw you into any nonsensical arguments. You are only following orders."

"Sir? If the Governour is wrong and they actually resist?"

"You and Mr. Wolf shall make them comply. Use force at your discretion, sir. In view of the political sensitivity of all this minimal force, if any, would quite preferable. But I will be obeyed. Any questions, sir?"

Evan rose to leave and saluted. "No, sir. Mr. Wolf and I will report as soon as we are able."

Nelson got up and returned to staring out his stern windows as Evan left the cabin.

***

Evan and Lieutenant Wolf approached the property with wary caution. Wolf had received the same orders and explanation from the Captain and neither man felt trusting about the situation. The Marines marching behind Lieutenant Wolf carried themselves with eyes forward; Evan, Wolf, and his Sergeant did not. Both officers agreed too much potential for someone to do something stupid existed. All three men's heads constantly swiveled back and forth as they marched up the wide drive to the house on top of the low hill, leaving their wagons and horses at the entrance to the estate. In the distance wide fields of sugarcane stretched as far as the eye could see.

Except, this was not a house they were approaching. Evan was amazed as he realized the opulence of what was in reality a small mansion. The wide expanse of well-manicured lawn and plants leading to the main entrance was overwhelming. The well-constructed stone building had the aura of an English country manor somehow miraculously transplanted to the tropics. Evan knew the building was nowhere near as large as many in England, but it performed a fair impression.

"Steady on, you men," said Wolf, loud enough for the Marines behind him to hear. From the corner of his mouth the Lieutenant spoke in a stage whisper only Evan could hear.

"Christ, how rich do you have to be to own a joint like this?"

"Right, here we go," said Evan as they finally entered into a wide, open courtyard with a circular drive surrounding a small garden filled with flowering plants. Working their way around the drive they came to a halt in front of the fifteen-foot high, wide doors fronting the entrance to the main hall. Wolf brought the Marines to a halt as Evan stopped and raised his hand. As no one came out to meet them, he grunted at Wolf to stand ready and walked up to the door. He didn't have to knock, as the door opened when he was within a few feet.

An impeccably dressed white servant met him at the door and enquired politely what Evan's business was. Evan smiled, but the tone of command in his voice carried a sharp edge.

"You know why I'm here, so let's get on with it, shall we?"

The servant's bland expression remained unchanged. "I shall tell the master you have arrived. Wait here," said the man with a disapproving look as he closed the door in their faces.

Evan smiled at the incongruity of the servant's command, given he was unlikely to be doing anything else. But over five minutes went by and nothing happened. Evan signaled Wolf to come forward and join him at the entrance. As Wolf gave him a questioning look Evan told him what had happened and the two men regarded the door. Evan took a deep breath and looked at the Marine officer.

"Well, I think we're going to have to get these buggers moving a little faster, don't you?"

Wolf grinned. The two men pulled out their swords and as one began hammering hard on the door with the butt of their swords. Almost a full minute went by before the door was quickly jerked open to reveal the same servant. This time he was scowling.

"Sir! I told you to wait!" said the indignant servant. Before Evan could respond the door was pulled open wider by the owner Roberts stepping forward and pushing his servant out of the way.

"Gentlemen. I am John Roberts. Can I help you?"

Evan was distracted for a moment by his first sight of the man. The distinguished, patrician features and greying hair couldn't hide his resemblance to Alice. Evan recovered his composure, realizing he should have expected this.

"Mr. Roberts," said Evan. "I am Lieutenant Evan Ross with the Royal Navy. This is Lieutenant Francis Wolf of the Royal Marines. I am given to understand you know why we are here, sir."

The owner looked both men up and down before responding, a wrinkled scowl creasing his face. "Yes, I had heard rumor you might come here to enforce your Captain's illegal seizure of my property."

Turning, he gestured to two men standing in the interior shadows to come forward. As the first stepped into the light Roberts waved a hand toward him in introduction. "This is Mr. Stanley Watson. He is the publisher of the local newspaper. He brought me word that this might happen and desires to report on the circumstances as they develop."

Evan and the Marine officer nodded in acknowledgement as Roberts gestured to the second man. "This other gentleman is Mr. Roger Ellis from the Governour's office. I invited him here as a witness for the purpose of keeping the Governour fully informed."

The two officers nodded and Ellis looked at Evan. "Ah, Mr. Ross. I wondered if it might be you attending here."

Roberts raised an eyebrow, looking at the two men as Evan gave Ellis a stony look in return.

"Mr. Ellis and I have already met. Mr. Roberts, I believe you are aware of our requirements. If you could have your workers brought to us we will be on our way and leave you in peace."

"My foreman is already bringing them around from the rear of the property. And I agree, the sooner you are gone from my land the happier we will all be. This illegal seizure is creating havoc for my business. It's but another form of taxation is what it is. Instead of only making my goods less competitive with your ridiculously high customs duties now you are hindering my ability to make money. My slaves are assets, sirs! By stealing the assets that make me money you are taxing me! Do you not see?"

"We are not here to discuss politics, Mr. Roberts," said Evan in an even tone, not rising to the man's baiting.

The men were all so focused on their conversation they did not realize they had company until the woman spoke.

"Father?"

The men turned as one to see a stunningly beautiful, young white woman astride a horse had ridden up and stopped. Evan had difficulty keeping the shock from his face as he saw the clear resemblance to Alice. He had no doubt; this had to be Alice's half sister.

Roberts walked over to offer his hand to help her to the ground and she looked expectantly at her father for introductions. He sighed in return.

"My love, you really shouldn't be here. This is business."

"Father. You can't keep me cooped up all the time. These are officers and gentlemen, are they not?"

Roberts acquiesced and introductions were made all around. Her name was Elizabeth. As Evan bowed and rose again to look into her eyes he felt an ache refusing to go away. This dazzling beauty with her long blonde hair was the woman inhabiting endless nights of dreams in every bunk and hammock on every warship in the fleet, come to life. And on closer inspection her resemblance to Alice was unmistakable. Evan felt lost.

As Roberts finished introductions a party of six frightened looking black workers surrounded by overseers on either side came to stand a respectful distance away.

"Lieutenant Evans," said Roberts. "Your workers are here. You shall return them two days from now as scheduled."

"Of course, sir. I bid you good day." Turning to leave, he was forestalled by Elizabeth.

"Ah, now I understand. This is all about your disagreement with Captain Nelson, isn't it, father?"

"Yes, my dear, but that's not your concern. We need—"

"Father, I have an idea! Why don't we invite these handsome officers to our Christmas ball this coming Saturday? I know you've had bad relations with the Navy, but perhaps a little gesture would help improve things? Please?"

Roberts looked trapped. The struggle was apparent on his face for a few moments until he mastered himself, but Evan knew he risked appearing ungracious were he to deny her.

"My dear, you are right," he replied, turning to stare with meaning at the newsman. "Perhaps a gesture on my part would serve well, wouldn't it? And I have never been able to deny you anything anyway, have I?"

Turning to the two officers, Roberts gave them a pleasant smile bearing no real warmth. "Well, gentlemen? You cannot deny my daughter either, I trust?"

Evan looked quickly at Lieutenant Wolf who gave a tiny shrug. Evan turned back and bowed once again.

"Sir. My lady. We are honoured by your generous offer. We will both have to ensure we have leave from our duties, but I don't think that will be a problem. We shall send word."

"Very good. The ball is commencing at seven o'clock."

Taking leave, Evan and Wolf turned away. As they marched back down the drive to their wagons they encountered a working party of slaves and more overseers crossing their path. Calling a halt to let them pass Evan and Wolf watched in horror as one of the overseers without warning raised his whip and struck at several of the slaves in the party, many of which were women. What prompted the outburst wasn't clear. The lead overseer saw their horrified looks and stopped to frown at the officers as the rest of his party left. As the road finally cleared he fell in behind the last of the slaves, but not before scowling one more time.

Evan shook his head. "Let's get out of here, Mr. Wolf."

***

The next night Evan was once again upstairs at the Flying Fish with Alice. Being in bed with her seemed surreal after having met Elizabeth. Aside from the obvious difference of their skin colour the two women seemed strangely both alike and, yet, not alike. The similarity of the almost regal bearing they shared was the eerie part.

Alice was a little despondent. The angry, questioning search for whoever was providing information was finally dying down, but many people had paid the price. Evan was thankful only the one slave had been killed, but Alice wasn't as grateful.

"Listen, Evan, the only reason more people weren't killed is because slaves are valuable property. Kill one and you are really taking a bag of your money and throwing it into the garbage."

Evan could only shake his head. "I'm sorry it came to that, Alice. The Captain thinks this is going to be a war of attrition."

"He's right," she shrugged. "We'll continue to get you information, but it may be a little slower coming than before."

As they sat in bed sharing a bottle of wine Evan told her what happened at the plantation. Alice sat bolt upright and turned to stare at Evan when he told her Elizabeth had invited the two officers to the ball.

"Seriously? The white bitch princess is trying to collect you too?"

"Collect me?"

"Oh, yes, she collects men. You'll see."

"Hmm. And I wasn't seeing things, was I? She has to be your half sister, yes?"

"No, you aren't seeing things. If owner man Roberts isn't the father of both of us then he must have a twin somewhere that did the deed."

"Huh. So I take it that despite the obvious blood ties you have no relationship with them?"

"Are you kidding me, lover man? Why do you think I was steered toward doing what I'm doing at the Flying Fish? Evan, we grew up together. She was a bitch then and she's a bitch now. As I got older the princess bitch and her mother didn't want me anywhere near them. Looking at me every day only reminded them of how much of a cheating bastard Roberts really is. Of course, somehow they don't see that he's a cheating bastard. If he went around screwing some other white woman, well, there would be a problem for sure. Running around screwing your 'property' is somehow different and therefore acceptable in their world. The thing is they don't want to see the results of that walking around them every day."

"I see."

"Yes, you will. Watch the blonde princess bitch in action. Try actually having a conversation with her. You'll see."

Chapter Ten
December 1784
Antigua

Nelson raised an eyebrow when the two Lieutenants reported on the outcome of their mission to collect the slaves from Roberts.

"Invited to his Christmas ball, are you? Well. I certainly hadn't expected that."

"I rather think it was his daughter's spur of the moment request, sir," said Evan.

"Hmm. The wounded hero and his dashing Marine officer companion caught her fancy, eh. I suppose I should be jealous, but I don't feel it. Gentlemen, I can see no reason to decline their invitation. In fact, Mr. Ross, you may be able to further our cause by making contacts. Get to know some of our foes better, so to speak. But I fear you gentlemen will be on your own representing the Navy. I'm not aware of any of my Captains or their officers receiving the same invitation. You may find yourselves beset on all sides. I can only ask you be extremely careful about what you say, with the politics being what they are at the moment. Otherwise, you are free to go win some feminine hearts, sirs."

With his warning still playing in Evan's mind the two men rode up to the entrance the night of the ball in a small buggy they had borrowed for the occasion, but they didn't even make it into the main drive past the gates. A large queue of expensive looking carriages was already being directed through the entrance, but they weren't allowed to join it. A well-dressed white servant took one look at them and the shabby little buggy they were in, and hastily directed them to a cleared field off to the side.

"Sorry gentlemen, access to the main drive is limited. Please park over there and walk in."

Evan and Lieutenant Wolf looked at each other in amusement.

"I guess we know where we stand in the order of things, now don't we?" said the Marine officer.

As they walked up the drive they realized in reality they would have been hard pressed to find a spot to leave their buggy. The road to the manor and the familiar circular drive was packed with even more expensive looking carriages. Several coachmen waited by each.

Both men wore their best dress uniforms and they stopped briefly at the entrance to look themselves over, making certain they were presentable. Satisfied, they walked in to find a large queue of well-dressed people waiting to be announced at the entrance to the main hall. Joining the line the two men looked around.

The entrance hall was overwhelming. A broad staircase led to the second floor. A huge chandelier with at least a hundred candles lit the room. Aside from the staircase only two other exits from the main entrance could be seen, one leading left and one to the right. The left entrance was where they were queued while the other was closed and guarded by an impeccably dressed white servant. Amazingly, there were two small marble statues on pedestals on either side of the staircase.

"Good Lord, Mr. Ross," said the Marine officer under his breath. "How much money do these people have?"

"A lot, I daresay, Mr. Wolf. Right, here we go," replied Evan as their turn to be announced finally came. Both men tensed, wondering what kind of reception they might get.

They needn't have been concerned. The crowd inside was already far too engrossed with themselves to pay any attention to two lowly officers. A few heads turned on hearing the words 'Royal Navy', but the only result was a few brief, puzzled frowns before people went back to their conversations. The two men were momentarily dazed by the opulence on display and simply stood rooted where they were.

The servant announcing them scowled and muttered in a low voice, intruding on their thoughts. "Move on, please, gentlemen".

The two men moved to stand with their backs to a wall, taking a glass of wine each from a waiter with a tray of drinks along the way. The long hall they were in was dotted with small groups of people wearing expensive, formal evening clothes talking and laughing. Several exits with open French doors led from the hall to other rooms. Music could be heard somewhere in the distance. The hall had expensive crown mouldings and more spectacular chandeliers to light the scene. Well-made chairs and small tables were along the sides of the room. The feel of overwhelming wealth permeated everything.

Deciding to explore further they wandered together through the rooms, nodding occasionally to people they passed. A few looked at them with open curiosity and frowns, recognizing the distinctive Navy and Marine officer uniforms. Some of the people carried plates of food and, realizing they were hungry, the two men went in search. They found one of the rooms held a series of tables practically groaning under the weight of the food. Both men stared momentarily open-mouthed at the range of meats, cheeses, and delicacies before them as they grabbed plates. Both men dug in after finding a small table Evan could place his plate on to eat.

"Oh, my word," said Evan. "Have you tried this cold lobster salad, Mr. Wolf? I could eat a mountain of it."

"That's next for me, sir," said Wolf in between mouthfuls. "Have a go at this soup. Apparently it's called conch chowder, whatever that is. The meat is a little chewy, but it really is quite tasty."

Finally sated almost to bursting the two men found another waiter with fresh glasses of wine and they began to stroll about once again.

"Good Christ, what have we got here?" came a voice from behind. The two officers turned to find a distinguished looking man and woman regarding them.

"You gentlemen are Navy, are you not? I thought so. Well, I am surprised. Roberts didn't tell me you would be here. Frankly, I'm shocked any of you are here at all."

Evan introduced Wolf and himself, explaining the circumstances of their presence. As they talked two more couples stopped as they came by to listen to the conversation.

"Ah," smiled the man, looking knowingly at the woman. "Gentlemen, I am Randall Johnson. This lovely creature is my wife, Mary. We own the plantation next door. Well, however you gentlemen got here I hope you enjoy yourselves. But, I'm curious. Do you share your Captain's views on this whole Navigation Order in Council business? Do you realize what an impact it's having on our businesses?"

"Randall, please," said his wife, with a mild frown of disapproval directed at her husband. "These men just follow orders and do their duty. They can hardly disagree with their Captain."

Johnson grunted before responding. "I suppose that may be true but, damn it, these men are officers. Officers are supposed to be able to think for themselves, are they not, gentlemen?"

Evan looked at Wolf, who wore an inscrutable look on his face as he responded.

"I am a simple sea soldier, sir. As your good wife has pointed out, my job is to do my duty."

Johnson' cynical smile told everyone this was all he had expected, but he turned to Evan regardless. Evan considered offering a similar response, but realized it would be unlikely to satisfy the man, so he took a deep breath before responding.

"Sir, you are correct. Officers are expected to think for themselves. We are also expected to provide opinions when asked, but we naturally will follow orders and, as my colleague says, do our duty."

"Ah. So you do have an opinion in this matter?"

"Sir, I do. The government cannot perform its critical functions if it has nothing to work with. Customs duties are a fact of life. We live in a sometimes dangerous world and the resources must be there to have, as only one example, a strong Navy to defend our collective interests."

"But Lieutenant, if the duties are so onerous we are forced out of business, what then? Look at what happened to our former American colonies."

"I agree something must be done to reach consensus as to what is fair, Mr. Johnson. I think no one wants to see open rebellion again. I have heard before there are public concerns that businesses are suffering and, if so, conversations to sort out a consensus on what meets everyone's best interests must be undertaken, in my humble opinion. But, sir, please forgive me on one point here. I can only form opinions based on facts, as I know and see them, right? Look around you, sir. Does this look like the home of a struggling businessman?"

Even more people had slowly joined in the growing crowd around them, listening to the conversation as it progressed. As Evan finished speaking several laughed openly.

"Oh, good shot, sir! Randall, he has your measure," called one man on the fringe of the crowd.

Johnson was good enough to smile ruefully in acknowledgement, but wasn't ready to give in yet. "I fear you do not fully understand the competitive nature of our business, sir. Reality is things change quickly and appearances can be deceiving."

Evan decided to press his advantage. "Indeed, sir. It is not my intent to put you on the spot. I for one am simply grateful Mr. Roberts's gracious daughter was good enough to invite us. Opportunity to build relationships can only help ensure we all understand each other and hopefully find a more positive resolution to this dispute."

Several more people chuckled, but this time Johnson's wife laughed the loudest. "Well, young man, I rather think it was my husband's intent to put you on the spot. You have managed to turn that about quite nicely."

Turning to her husband, she gave him a mild, but stern look. "Randall, I'll not have you baiting these young men any further."

"I surrender, my dear," said Johnson, as he rubbed his chin. He looked speculatively at his wife for a moment before turning to Evan. "Come to think of it, there may be some merit in what you say. Mary, we are having a ball in January. Why don't we invite these young gentlemen? In fact, perhaps an invite to Captain Nelson and his other officers would be helpful. I rather think he is unlikely to change his mind, from what I have seen of him, but it can't hurt, can it?"

"Randall, that is an excellent idea. Lieutenant Ross, please convey to your Captain that invitations will be forthcoming."

Evan had difficulty keeping his surprise at the turn of events from his face. The two officers stammered their thanks as the Johnsons left to freshen their drinks and the crowd dispersed.

"God Almighty, Mr. Ross. I don't believe that just happened," said Wolf under his breath, ensuring only Evan could hear him. "Well done, sir. I shall tell Captain Nelson how well you represented us."

Evan ran a finger along the edge of his neck collar, realizing he had been sweating as the conversation had worn on.

"Thank you, Mr. Wolf. I'm not sure I believe it, either. Well, I need to refill my drink. Let's go find some more."

Entering a room they hadn't been in yet in search of drink they found a mixed crowd of men surrounding the daughter of their host. Several Army officers of different ranks together with a crowd of young men who could only be the sons of local planters were clustered about all trying to garner her attention. A few other young, good-looking women were hanging about on the fringes of the group, but the star they all revolved around was Elizabeth. She was luminous in a long white ball gown. An expensive looking diamond pendant hung around her neck.

She saw them enter and called out. "Gentlemen, how wonderful! I'm so glad you came!"

With all eyes on them the two men joined the crowd and bowed to her. She introduced them to the men around her and Evan instantly realized none of them shared her joy at yet more rivals being on the scene. Evan was asked how he'd lost his arm and when he explained the reactions were mixed all around. The Army officers expressed dismay over his bad luck it had not happened in a 'proper' engagement while the planters as one frowned over the mention of smuggling.

"A bad business, sir. Things like this wouldn't happen if a more circumspect approach were taken while efforts to bring about more realistic policy are underway," said one.

"Enough!" cried Elizabeth. "I don't want to listen to silly politics all night. Mr. Ross, how long must I wait for you to ask me to dance?"

"Dance?" said Evan, taken aback. "Ah, I have to confess I haven't actually had opportunity to try that since my injury. I'm really not sure of doing well with that, Miss Roberts."

"Nonsense. We have three arms between the two of us. We'll manage."

Taking his arm she led him into the next room where a small band was playing.

Evan managed well once he got used to it. The problem was the same as he faced when using a sword, with the necessary counterbalance provided by a left arm not present. Fortunately, the band was

192

playing slow waltzes. Once he became comfortable he began to enjoy holding this stunning creature close with his arm. The eerie resemblance to her half sister was disconcerting, though. Worse, the gown she wore was low cut, exposing the tops of what promised to be a truly magnificent pair of breasts brushing maddeningly against his chest.

Elizabeth chattered away the whole time they danced about nothing of substance. Evan was made to compliment her on several topics lasting all of perhaps twenty seconds before she flitted to the next, including everything from the new horse she had acquired to her new ball gown. Racking his brain for something vacuous enough to talk about during their second dance Evan managed to get in a question about the size of her father's estate and how many slaves he had.

"Oh, I don't know," she replied, a tiny frown marring her face. "I don't pay attention to boring things like that. I think father said once he was now the biggest planter on the island. More than a thousand acres, he said. And slaves? Who cares? They're only beasts, you know. I don't know how they find time, but they breed so fast so I really wouldn't know how many he has."

"I see," said Evan, as he realized exactly how far apart this woman's perception of slaves and his own different experience with them were. Fortunately, the dance finally ended and a concerted rush of new suitors came for her. A handsome planter's son won the race and pulled her away to dance the already beginning next waltz.

Left on his own, Evan grabbed a glass of wine from a passing waiter and, thinking he might find Lieutenant Wolf near the food, he went in that direction. Wolf wasn't to be found, but he couldn't resist stopping to sample one of the many desserts set out. As he sat at a small side table taking a big bite of chocolate cake soaked with rum he saw one of the female black servants come by with a full tray of fresh desserts out of the corner of his eye. Until now he hadn't paid any attention to them, but something oddly familiar about the woman made him look closer as she put the tray down to make more room for it on the table. Evan walked over and stood beside her.

The woman turned and looked at him, surprised to have a guest paying her any attention. Evan knew in an instant why she seemed familiar; she was an older version of Alice. She wore a tired air and seemed care worn. She crinkled her eyes in puzzlement at his scrutiny until she realized he was missing an arm and her look changed to a hesitant recognition.

Still unsure, she gave him a tentative smile. "Sir?"

"You are Alice's mother, aren't you? I can see Alice in your smile."

The woman's eyes widened, but before she responded she looked around to see if anyone was listening. No one was paying them attention, so she let her smile widen, in exactly the same way Alice always did.

"You are her officer. She told me about you."

"Yes, madam. My name is Evan."

"I know. You have been kind to her. Men with kindness in their hearts are rare."

She looked around quickly to see if anyone was watching, but no one was. To Evan's surprise she leaned up and gave him a quick kiss on the cheek.

"It is so good to meet you, sir. Thank you. I must go or I will be missed." As she drew back Evan saw a tear forming in her eye.

Turning, she bustled away. Evan was still surprised at how similar mother and daughter were. Despite the years Alice's mother retained a regal kind of beauty and Evan wondered if she was still subject to the attentions of the plantation owner. Shaking his head, he went in search of Lieutenant Wolf. He found him standing in the next room talking to Angus Campbell, the Scottish Army Engineer Evan had met several weeks before on Shirley Heights.

"Well, Mr. Ross! We meet again, sir," said the man. "You look much improved."

"How was your grand moment in the light, Mr. Ross?" said Lieutenant Wolf with a smirk.

"Fortunately brief, sir. The woman is amazingly beautiful, but I fear she is perhaps less well endowed with intelligence. Well, maybe that's not fair. Let's say I think her interests are rather limited to fairly light matters and leave it at that. I'm not sure she'll even remember my name."

Both men laughed as Lieutenant Wolf offered his own experience. "I got in a few dances with one of the other women, too, Mr. Ross, and it was much the same. She collared me before I knew what was happening. I think she was trying to make the rest of them jealous. But were you seriously expecting better, sir? I hope not."

Evan shrugged, but before he could respond two more plantation owners stopped as they passed by, drawn by the Navy uniforms. The officers saw the two men weren't smiling, instantly making them all wary.

"Good Lord, what the hell are these two doing here, Jeffery?" said one.

"I have no idea, Samuel. Roberts never said anything about inviting Navy people. Heaven knows why he would."

"Gentlemen," said Evan, doing introductions and explaining how their invite came about.

The planter named Jeffery snorted in disdain. "That at least I can understand. The woman likes to surround herself with admirers. Although, were I you I wouldn't get my hopes up, gentlemen. We're more likely to have a blizzard and three feet of snow here before either of you will get a shot at her. Our friend Roberts will see to that."

"You must excuse us, sirs," said the one called Samuel. "I really can't abide talking to Navy people given what you are doing to us. The whole thing makes me angry and I'm going end up saying things that will get me in trouble. But mark my words, gentlemen. Trouble is what you will get if the Navy continues on its present course. Good evening, sirs."

As the two men stalked away the three officers all breathed easier.

"Well, that was pleasant. We seem to produce a real range of reactions from people," said Wolf.

"Indeed," said Evan. He turned and gave the Engineer officer an inquisitive look.

"Mr. Campbell? I seem to recall when we first met you mentioned you have been in this part of the world for some time. What is going on here? Do I have too simplistic a view of this? I don't understand why it seems impossible for the political people to sort this out. Is there some background to this?"

"Hmm. Well, yes, I have been out here a long time and have gained some understanding. I think you are right. History is influencing what is happening now."

"Indeed, sir," said Evan. "I would be grateful to gain further understanding and hear your thoughts. Let me find more wine for us first."

Returning a minute later with a waiter bearing a tray and three full glasses the two officers looked expectantly at the Engineer.

"To understand what is happening I think you need consider how these people perceive themselves. See, most of high society looks upon people in business as being, well, newcomers as it were. Not real people of quality with history behind them, you know? Granted, there have been many examples of people making enough money to fill a horse barn that have been given titles and acquired acceptance over time. But you agree that is the general perception?"

Evan and Lieutenant Wolf looked at each other and nodded agreement.

"The planters see themselves very, very differently—as entrepreneurs. People with initiative and bold in action. Decisive people willing to take big risks."

Angus paused to give them a wry grin. "Does that sound like anyone you gentlemen know? I'm surprised the Navy doesn't seem to get how alike you are in some ways." He laughed at the expressions on their faces.

"Anyway, in fairness, most of them have worked hard to get to where they are. So the key is they see themselves as independent people. And this type of fellow doesn't take kindly to other people making rules that make it harder for them to realize profit, let alone anyone trying to take their hard earned money through duties and taxes."

"So Captain Nelson is right to view these men in much the same light as the rebels in our former American colonies, sir? Wanting to run their own affairs and pay little if any taxes?" said Wolf.

"Yes. But there is more, see. If memory serves planters colonized this island around 1630 or so, but it was Sir Christopher Codrington that really got things going here about a hundred years ago. He got the sugar industry moving on both Antigua and Barbuda, which is why the town on the other island is named after him. He was a complete rogue, but he got things done. Actually, he is a perfect example of what I was talking about. He made a mountain of money and ended up with a knighthood. In the end he achieved at least some degree of respectability. That's the key, you see. They think there is no higher purpose in life than making money and once they've done that things like knighthoods and titles would only be rewards they think they deserve."

Pausing, he took a sip of his wine. "Anyway, he was joined by a large number of families that were turned out of their plantations on Surinam some decades earlier when we ceded it to the Dutch. Needless to say, this group was not happy. From their point of view they were betrayed by a government unwilling to do what was necessary to protect them and their interests. They basically had to start all over here and these families have long memories."

"And that sense of betrayal has stuck with them that long, sir?" said Evan.

"It has. It would be an understatement to say these people feel under appreciated by those who benefit from their efforts."

"Meaning, as one possible example, the Navy."

"Oh, yes. For many years these men had little or no protection. The nearest naval base was Jamaica, which as you know is over a thousand nautical miles from here. In fact, in the early years their only protection was what they organized for themselves and that was it. They used to get raided by a fairly warlike bunch of natives from Dominica on a regular basis, until they finally put a stop to it. The owners banded together and landed a force of several hundred men, ravaging a number of villages on Dominica. The natives got the message. One interesting piece of the story, if you can believe it, is that slaves formed a good portion of the attacking force."

The two Navy officers looked at each other in disbelief.

"Really?" said Wolf. "Why would slaves willingly go on a raid like that? I'd have thought their participation would be rather half hearted."

The Engineer shrugged. "Hmm. I think you need to understand how things work around here. The reality is it would have been in their interest to help out. Oh, make no mistake, there is no love lost between the owners and their slaves. But those men would have had their own interests. See, the slaves here have homes and families to care for, too. The raiders from Dominica wouldn't have been particular about who they were attacking, would they?"

"Huh. So they banded together to fight the greater threat. I guess I can understand that," said Evan. "But it still seems strange given how the slaves are treated."

"It's not the first time slaves have participated in attacks. I seem to recall mention of a few hundred involved in the invasions of Martinique and Guadeloupe back in, what, 1759 I think it was. It was frog privateers that motivated them that time. Look, lads, it's not in the plantation owner's interests to treat them like complete beasts all the time. Well, owners aren't all the same, right? Some are arguing for better treatment, you know. Give slaves access to doctors, churches, and hospitals. They already get Sundays off plus Christmas every year. The legislatures on several islands have passed something called a 'slave code'. They vary from one to the next, but the common features of the codes set out duties of slaves and the rights of owners. They also have provisions that specify slaves aren't to be abused, but I've never heard of anyone actually enforcing them. And yes, on the other end of the spectrum there are owners whose treatment of their slaves is rather questionable. Describing it as 'harsh' would be charitable."

"Mr. Campbell?" said Evan, a puzzled look on his face. "Everything you've said is helpful. But how is it this works at all? There must be thousands of black slaves on this island as compared to far fewer white owners. If as you say there is no love lost and the treatment is questionable, is an uprising by the slaves not a real danger?"

"Oh, aye, Mr. Ross," said the Engineer, an emphatic look of agreement appearing on his face. "That would be the nightmare that haunts every owner on this island every night, I'm sure. And you're right. There are probably fifteen times or maybe more blacks on this island than there are whites. The owners were actually a whisker away from all being murdered in their beds not that long ago in point of fact."

"Seriously?" said Evan, looking hard in a quick aside at Wolf who wore an equally frozen look.

"Oh, yes. Hmm," he replied, obviously searching his memory. "Yes, I remember, it was 1736! There was one fellow that was particularly active. What the owners didn't realize is he was a big tribal chief of some sort. He managed to sway enough of his followers into thinking they could pull it off. The somewhat amusing part of that is he did it using drums."

The two Navy officers looked at each other in puzzlement.

"Drums?" said Evan.

"Indeed! The slaves don't only make music with them. They can talk to each other using a musical cipher over great distances. Useful if you're trying to talk to someone far off with an impenetrable jungle in Africa between you, I should think."

"So, what is the amusing part of this, sir?"

"Ah," grinned the Engineer. "The owners thought it was all nonsensical, savage music. Part of slave culture, as it were. So whoever this chief was spent a lot of time ensuring his messages got out consistently around the island. He was about ready to proceed when some owner's wife got the bright idea to hold a cultural event so the slaves could put on display their music and dance for the owners."

"Can you imagine, sirs? Seating for a few hundred white owners and their families? A stage set up with a bunch of drummers and several grinning dancers? The owners weren't happy to find out later that the drummers were in reality 'talking' the whole time about what buffoons their masters were and that sweet revenge was right around the corner!"

"My word," said Wolf. "So what happened to stop it?"

The Engineer shrugged. "Someone talked at the last minute, of course. I don't know. I suspect someone feared the consequences of a revolt and what might happen to their family. Perhaps it was a slave for one of the more enlightened owners who heard rumour of what was happening? Some of the owners have actually freed slaves that served them well. I know for fact that over time some of these slaves have become like part of the family. Maybe one of them didn't want to see their 'family' hurt."

Pausing to down the rest of his wine, the Engineer put his glass down on the nearest table.

"Regardless of how it happened, the revolt was put down. Several public executions and a lot of harsh beatings put it to rest. The chief in particular was made to suffer for a very long time."

"Well, sir, we must thank you. This has been most enlightening. I confess I was puzzled at why the Navy has been held in such low regard," said Evan.

"Well, there is a certain irony here, don't you think?" said the Engineer. The two Navy officers looked puzzled as he grinned.

"The planters were complaining they didn't have enough protection, remember? Now, they have plenty of it with a major Naval base and an expanding, working Dockyard to boot. And they're still not happy! Perhaps a case of needing to be careful what one wishes for, don't you think?"

Heads turned as the three men roared with laughter.

An hour later the ball began winding down. The two Navy officers mingled a little more, drawing much the same mixed reactions. A few couples engaged them in conversations about what life was like in the Navy. Others talked about it being

Christmas and the importance of building more churches on the island. The problem was finding preachers willing to come to the island to meet their needs.

Both men made it to the dance floor with a few more of the young women present, but none proved of interest to either man. Conversations were about nothing of substance, much like Evan's conversation with Elizabeth. With a pleasant glow from having downed several glasses of wine they decided to leave, so they joined the growing queue of people at the door saying goodbye to the hosts. When their turn came Roberts gave the two of them a blank look.

"Well, gentlemen. I trust you enjoyed yourselves?" Not waiting for an answer he folded his arms. "I have to confess I wasn't sure what the reaction would be to having a Navy presence here. There are many people with deep feelings on our current troubles. And I hear my neighbour Johnson has invited even more Navy people to his ball in January, including Nelson himself? Well. I don't know what the man was thinking, but it's his ball. I suppose having our pleas fall on deaf ears once more is the worst that could result. Good evening, sirs."

Turning away, he greeted the next people in line without shaking hands with either Evan or Wolf.

"Pleasant people, what?" said Wolf as they walked down the drive to their buggy.

"Huh," said Evan. "All things considered it wasn't a wasted evening. I know a lot more people now and our friend Angus has given me a much better understanding of what is going on and why. And on top of it all, we got to drink some rather good wine and got fed a lot better than we'd get on board a ship."

"Isn't that the truth!" said Wolf, with a loud belch.

"And, best of all, we get to do it all again in January!"

Chapter Eleven
December 1784/January 1785
Barbados and Antigua

Captain Sands of HMS Latona strolled over to his First Officer on the other side of the quarterdeck and smiled.

"Mr. Hill. I think it time we reduced sail, sir. Our sailing master will be unhappy if I keep us at this speed coming into harbour. This goddamn Yankee has got into St. John's ahead of us, but we made good speed. We'll get to him before he has time to offload any of his cargo. We shall anchor right beside him. Take Sergeant Strand and a party of Marines ashore when you are ready and explain to the Captain he needs to leave."

Lieutenant Hill saluted and made ready to depart, but quickly realized Captain Sands was wrong. By the time he made it to shore with his party the Americans had already offloaded a dozen large crates, with more being swung up from the darkness of the hold. The American sailors had seen the warship sail in and anchor beside them, and were all to a man eyeing the approaching Marines with wary looks. Sensing something was about to happen a slowly growing crowd of onlookers gathered to watch.

"Who is the Captain of this vessel, please?" said Hill to the nearest sailor once he got close enough.

"I am, sir. Can I help you?" said an older man walking down the gangway to the dock.

"No, sir. I am Lieutenant Hill with HMS Latona. You are hereby ordered to depart at once, sir."

"What? Why? We are in need of water and other provisions."

"Really? You're so desperate to get provisions you decided to offload cargo first? And why exactly is it are you offloading cargo if you're merely here to get provisions?"

The Captain was taken aback at the question. "Umm, well, it is normal practice to try and sell our goods wherever we can in whatever port we put into, sir. Surely you understand that?"

"Huh. Actually, what I understand is you are trying to circumvent our laws, sir. You are ordered to reload your contraband goods and leave, now, sir."

"This is an outrage," shouted the Captain, looking around at the crowd and speaking more to them than to the Lieutenant. "My ship is in distress, sir! Besides, these people can without doubt use the goods we have on offer. Why do the good people of Antigua tolerate this nonsense?"

Several angry shouts of support came from the crowd, which was still growing with every second passing.

"Navy bastards! Leave them alone!" shouted a merchant seaman from a local ship as he stepped closer.

"I can use their goods in my business, sirs! Leave them be!" shouted another man. The crowd steadily pushed closer, the ones in the rear trying to see what was happening.

"Get back, the lot of you!" shouted the Lieutenant. "If we have to crack some heads we will. Captain, I gave you an order to reload that cargo and depart. If you don't comply we will dump your cargo in the bay and we will make you leave. Now get on with it!"

You assholes! I have friends here and I'm going to see what they have to say about this!" Turning, the man ran to disappear into the crowd. They swallowed him up within seconds.

Angered, Lieutenant Hill tried to snatch at his collar before he got away, but missed. Several men in the crowd shoved him back and he fell hard to the ground. The Marines waded into the fray and began using their muskets as clubs. Despite the advantage the weapons conveyed, the party was seriously outnumbered. Several desperate fights broke out as Lieutenant Hill regained his feet and pulled out his sword.

Lieutenant Hill knew Captain Sands would be watching from the quarterdeck to read the situation and he surmised the Captain would not like what he was seeing. The Lieutenant soon saw a much larger party of well-armed sailors with more Marines was on its way. Even so, the crowd fought hard, using whatever was at hand to fight with. Rocks sailed through the air as the fighting spread like wildfire all along the dock front. Several fights came close to nearby shops and many sustained damage.

Local militia marching up from behind the rioting crowd finally quelled the fighting. Caught between the two, the rioters realized they had no chance and fled in all directions. Looking over to the quarterdeck of the Latona, the Lieutenant could see Captain Sands shaking his head in dismay.

Lieutenant Hill groaned as he set about trying to bring order to the situation. "There's going to be hell to pay for this."

***

The meeting in Governour Shirley's office was unpleasant and brief. Most of the same people in

207

attendance at the last meeting with Nelson were present once again. Nelson reflected on the irony of sitting in front of them feeling as if he was on trial.

"Captain Nelson," said the Governour. "Surely you now understand why we are all concerned about how you are implementing your orders. The populace is clearly badly upset. This Order in Council is affecting everyone's livelihoods, sir, and there are hard feelings about this. The local business people are suffering, sir! Many have sustained damage from the riot. And who will pay, they ask? Look, I am the Governour here. I cannot tolerate riots in the streets! Please tell me you understand. Even better, please tell me you will change your approach."

"And I cannot tolerate this treatment, sir!" interjected the American Captain. "This is a violation of accepted international practices. I will be seeing my lawyer and complaining vigorously to your Consul about this matter when I return home."

Nelson scowled at the American to silence him before turning his attention to the Governour.

"Governour. I have read my Captain's report on this matter. The Captain and his crew behaved in all respects with propriety and in accordance with my orders. You want to know who will pay for the damages? I suggest send the bill to the fool sitting beside you. And as for—"

Several men groaned loudly as the American Captain bristled in anger. The Governour forestalled everyone by raising a hand before gesturing with a weary look at Nelson to continue.

"Thank you, Governour. This man agitated the crowd into clearly unacceptable behaviour and then ran off. He was already offloading cargo the second he got here, for God's sake! Look, Governour, how you deal with disturbances and riotous behaviour in your domain is your business. How I deal with smugglers and smuggling is my business. My orders are clear and I intend to see them through."

Standing to leave, Nelson turned a hard face to the American Captain.

"The Marine guard preventing you from offloading your cargo will be in place until first light tomorrow. Since you are still here and claim 'need', I have given orders to allow you to purchase supplies between now and then, but that is all. If you and your ship are not underway and departing Antigua by tomorrow morning, Captain Sands and HMS Latona will sink you. Good day, gentlemen."

Several men groaned and held their heads in despair as Nelson rose to leave the office. Glum looks were plastered on every face.

"Thank you for your time Captain," said Governour Shirley. "I trust you understand these gentlemen and I will remain here to discuss our options. Good day, sir."

Nelson nodded and left.

***

"What in the— oh, no, no!" said Admiral Sir Richard Hughes as he walked into the stern cabin of his flagship anchored in Carlisle Bay, Barbados. Sitting on his desk was a thick pile of at least two-dozen letters tied together in a bunch. A few other separate letters lay beside it. Two days ago when the Admiral was last on board his desk was empty. In the Christmas season the Admiral deemed it simpler to remain ashore to attend the endless round of balls he was expected to appear at as senior officer on station.

Hughes retraced his steps to the entrance of his cabin and ordered his Flag Lieutenant sent for.

Lieutenant Perkins was nearby and appeared quickly, before Hughes even had time to sit down.

"Admiral? You sent for me, sir?" said the Lieutenant as he saluted.

"Mr. Perkins. Where did this bloody big pile of paper suddenly come from? It's the Christmas season for heaven's sake. Haven't people got better things to do than send me letters at this time of year?"

"Hmm, the big pile tied together all came off that mail packet ship that came in early this morning. The three or four others are the usual reports and correspondence. One is from the Barbados Governour while the others I believe are the reports from your Captains on station with details on the state of their supplies as you requested, sir."

Hughes eyed the big pile suspiciously. "That came in on a packet ship? From where?"

"Antigua, sir."

Hughes groaned aloud. "Oh my Lord, what has that bloody man done now? Well, my day was going fine until now. All right Mr. Perkins, thank you. I'll be at my desk working through this nonsense. Hmm, have that packet ship readied for an immediate return trip. I have a feeling quick responses to this lot will be required. I'll send for you when I'm ready."

Perkins saluted and left as Hughes slumped into his chair and removed his uniform coat to get comfortable. The story became clear as he opened one envelope after another. Almost an hour later the Admiral threw the last of them on his desk and sat back to rub his tired eyes.

Local merchants, ship Captains, and plantation owners in Antigua had all written to complain about Nelson's actions. All of them wanted him to understand how their businesses were suffering and how outraged they were at the situation. The businessmen with property damage from the riot were also screaming for compensation. The message common to all was a fervent wish he would simply do something to resolve this, given he was the senior Admiral on station and therefore responsible.

One of the letters was from the American ship Captain who had incited the riot. His letter was full of righteous indignation over his treatment and he too was seeking compensation, except in his case he wanted it for loss of income. Threats of lawsuits that would potentially include the Admiral as a defendant and vigorous complaints to the American Congress filled out the rest of his letter.

The letter from Governour Shirley was the one giving him pause for serious thought. His letter didn't have the emotion and anger common to the others. Instead, this letter was almost apologetic. The Governour was doing the best he could to calm a difficult situation and support the Navy, but emotions were running high on the island. The Governour feared if matters worsened and martial law had to be declared the responsibility would rest squarely with the Navy, meaning the Governour would be pointing the finger of blame directly at Hughes for failure to act.

Hughes sat deep in thought for a few minutes. Rising from his desk he put his uniform coat back on as he called to the Marine standing at attention outside his cabin. When he appeared the Admiral ordered a party readied to row him ashore again.

***

"So you understand the situation, sir? Matters are progressing quickly. This small riot may or may not be an isolated incident. I am concerned this will get progressively worse. We cannot have the Crown at risk over this."

"Sir Richard, I understand," said Alan Hunter, senior Kings Counsel for the West Indies. The two men were sitting across from each other in the lawyer's office on Broad Street in Bridgetown. "And I am thinking you are here about the legal opinion on this whole Navigation Order in Council business you want from me, correct?"

"I am, sir."

"Hmm, well. I have not completed my research yet, sir. I did tell you this would take time."

"I know you did, but as I explained I am concerned that this is getting out of hand. I need something to work with. Is there no help you can offer me, sir?"

"Hmm," said the lawyer, pausing a few moments to reply, as he was obviously deep in thought. "Right, I cannot give you something definitive enough to be iron clad. I can certainly give you an opinion, though. That the Navy is involving itself in this business without reference to Customs is highly unusual and singular. I have not come across anything even remotely close to this situation in my reading to date and, I assure you, I have been diligent at that since our first conversation. Given how unique this seems to be the exercise of caution by all parties involved would certainly be wise. From a purely legal perspective, of course."

"Ah, of course," smiled Hughes. "And would you be prepared to put that opinion in writing? Especially your last statement about 'the exercise of caution', sir?"

The lawyer paused a few moments to mull the thought, rubbing his chin. "Hmm, I see no reason why not. I shall have to detail the facts as I know them and reference my research to date, but anyone with a proper understanding of the law will know straying into uncharted legal territory carries risks. So yes, I can provide you a letter to this effect. But if you don't mind my asking, what do you plan to do with this?"

"A letter from you would be excellent, sir, excellent. For my part I shall correspond with all of my Captains on station. I shall provide them with copies of your opinion and advise in light of this a modification in our approach is necessary until a definitive ruling is available. I will specifically direct that the Navy's role be limited to interdicting suspected smuggling activity only. Once a possible offender has been identified my Captains will be ordered to have them sent into the nearest port. The local Governour or his representative can then review the case and make decisions as they see fit, in consultation with local Customs people. I will correspond with the various Governours to explain the new approach. Do you have any concerns with that, sir?"

"No," said the lawyer. "Between us, I think that's an excellent compromise approach, Sir Richard. Making the link to Customs and giving the local Governour back control of what is happening in his domain I think brings this back onto much firmer legal grounds."

The lawyer gave the Admiral a smile. "Of course, my letter won't be saying any of that, you understand."

"Of course," smiled the Admiral in return. "Can I have your letter before Christmas, sir?"

The smile disappeared and the lawyer spread his hands wide in dismay. "Admiral, it's almost

Christmas. I do need a little time to give thought to my exact wording. You were fortunate to catch me in the office today."

"Right after Christmas, then? Please, sir. Our friend Governour Shirley has fear of further outbursts of violence."

The lawyer paused a moment in thought before nodding. "You are right. Yes, right after Christmas it shall be, sir."

***

Nelson was once again standing before his stern windows, his back to the door when Evan entered. Announcing himself and saluting, Evan waited for Nelson to acknowledge his presence. The Captain lingered a few moments longer before turning and gesturing to Evan to be seated. Nelson still seemed distracted and deep in thought as he joined Evan at the desk. Finally recalling himself, Nelson nodded to Evan to begin his report.

The last time they had met was before the ball at Roberts's plantation and Evan had much to report. Work in the Dockyard was moving forward, although still not as fast as Evan preferred. The two officers and the plantation owners were proving adept at throwing small roadblocks in the way, but Evan felt he had their measure.

"They are getting inventive with excuses as to why they can't provide as many workers as they are scheduled to and, of course, when I'm not around my colleagues in the Dockyard are only to happy to assure them how understanding we are and that it's all okay. I've had a general message sent to all of them that any future shortfalls will result in an increase to their allotments amounting to what they shorted us plus an extra ten per cent to help get us back on schedule. I specified a party of Marines and myself will arrive on site to ensure the increased requirement is met and, so far, they seem to have gotten the message. I didn't think suggesting the Marines could be used for this purpose would exceed my brief. Have you any concerns, sir?"

Nelson smiled and shook his head so Evan continued.

"Sir, we have done what we can to investigate whether there was collusion to forewarn the smuggler at Dutchman's Bay last month. Unfortunately, we have nothing definitive. There is indeed a fellow that raises pigeons not far from where Mr. Wilton and I reside. We questioned him, but he became suspicious and we chose not to push it. There is also a rather shabby old inn at Falmouth Harbour that seems to have more horses in its stable than one would think necessary. It could therefore be one or both have involvement. We think setting a trap may help, sir. The next time there is word of a smuggler landing we could leak word out and set a watch on both to see what happens. The downside, of course, is the smuggler may get away. Alternatively, we watch both when we know you are sailing and see what happens."

"Hmm. Let me think about these options, Mr. Ross. But please continue."

Evan began to report on the ball they had attended, but the Captain raised a hand to forestall him.

"Lieutenant Wolf has already provided me a full report, sir. Part of me is amused you have secured an invitation for us all while another part is loathe to have any more dealings with this pack of troublemakers than I must. Well, it will do the officers of our little squadron good to get off their ships and enjoy the company of society. Who knows, it may even do me some good, too. And, yes, I do agree with Lieutenant Wolf that given the circumstances impressing this man and gaining invitations is a noteworthy achievement."

"Thank you, Captain. One other item to report on is that of the two Dutch ships. They have not been back in port, but the word is they are expected in the next week. I wish I could report success on learning more about their activity, but I cannot. We will have all eyes on their behaviour when they do show up, sir."

"Please do. Anything else?"

"Yes, one last thing. This is a bit disturbing. One of our sources is a, umm, resident of one of the local brothels, sir. She's a black woman. She reports a vague conversation with one of the French sailors. She thinks he may have been one of the senior officers on one of the ships. He asked her a question that was odd, so I went to question her directly when I heard the report from Mr. Wilton."

Nelson raised an eyebrow. "Indeed. Odd in what way?"

"Sir, he asked her what she thought might happen if the blacks on the island were armed. When she looked shocked at the question he apparently said he thought it disgraceful the way blacks are treated and changed the subject."

"Good Christ!" Hardening, Nelson's face appeared chiseled from stone.

"Sir, I have our other sources keeping a watch for any hint of problems. There are vague hints of a loose group of young men talking about changing the established order. We think many are slaves that have run. Of course, a group of angry young men talking is perhaps not unusual, but taken with what this frog said perhaps something is afoot."

"Hmm. What would the motive be? I wonder if this is an attempt to destabilize the situation further. Well, in any case, this is well done. Carry on, sir. We simply must find out more and stop them."

"Captain, if I may ask a question?" Nelson nodded so Evan continued. "Sir, I have heard reports we have been ordered to hand intercepted smugglers over to local authorities for a decision on what to do with them?"

Nelson laughed in grim amusement and pointed to an opened letter on the corner of his desk. "Your sources are correct, sir. Our good Admiral Hughes has produced a legal opinion that tells us we are in uncharted waters and to be cautious. He is using that as basis to order us to be cautious, as he somehow thinks what this bloody paper pushing lawyer says should supersede my direct orders from the First Lord. I tell you, Mr. Ross, this pains me more than you know. I believe in respecting the chain of command. We have all been taught to obey orders above all, haven't we?"

Evan nodded as hard steel came to Nelson's voice. "Well, we shall not be obeying this particular order. I have already crafted a response that makes this perfectly clear and it will be on its way to Barbados at first light tomorrow. Mr. Ross, I have orders from higher authority than my Admiral and they are crystal clear. Yes, an officer is expected to interpret and apply orders as the situation demands, and I respect that Admiral Hughes believes he is doing that to the best of his ability, but he is wrong.

Officers are also expected to display good judgment and to that end he is failing badly."

Nelson paused to shake his head in dismay.

"He knows and understands what our orders say and is deliberately attempting to circumvent them. Worse, he knows the residents of these islands are American by connection and would join the rebels if they had the power. The postmaster has given me an initial report of his observations. There is indeed a steady flow of correspondence back and forth between the American states and here. Much of it is in rudimentary ciphers, but we have cracked some of them. The plantation owners are placing orders in cipher in their letters and the responses, in cipher, confirm ability to deliver. It's the dates and the ship names we are struggling with as they have a second more complex cipher in use. They are also providing intelligence to the Americans about the dispositions of my ships and how we have been approaching the situation."

Nelson paused a moment, the fire in his eyes emphasizing his words. "Well, it pains me even to speak of all this, especially as it involves a much senior officer, but given your role I believe you must understand the nuances of what is happening here. I speak with full expectation of candor on your part. Governour Shirley is aware of all this, of course."

"Captain, you may rely on my discretion and I do appreciate your confidence. This must be extraordinarily difficult, sir."

"It is bad enough we have enemies that seek to undermine us on every side. But when people on our own side that should be offering us support are in fact doing the exact opposite it is disheartening."

Nelson stood up and walked over to stare out of the stern windows once again. He paused a few long moments before continuing.

"Honour, sir. Honour and strength in knowing that above all one is doing what is right in the service of our country will sustain us. That, and disdain for caution, sir. I think I told you before, did I not? You can do no wrong by laying yourself alongside your foe and having at them. Mr. Ross, we shall have at them at the ball next week, eh? You are dismissed."

"Thank you, Captain."

Evan rose and saluted, but Nelson was still standing with his back to Evan, staring out the stern windows and bearing the endless, heavy burden of command.

Chapter Twelve
January 1785
Antigua

The manor house owned by plantation owner
Randall Johnson was only marginally less opulent in
size and scale than the one at the Roberts plantation.
Both were similar as the entrance to the grounds was
limited and only so many carriages could be
accommodated closer to the manor to drop people off.

Evan and Lieutenant Wolf were invited by
Nelson to join him traveling in his carriage to the
plantation along with the other officers from Nelson's
ship. Both men were amused when a steward tried to
deny them entrance and send them off to a side field
to park as had happened at the Roberts ball. Nelson
stuck his head out the window and scowled at the
steward before turning to his driver.

"Ignore this fool. If he doesn't get out of the
way, run him over," barked Nelson. Once their driver
maneuvered his way into a spot near the main doors
to the manor, garnering several annoyed looks from
other drivers and the inhabitants of their carriages, the
men disembarked and headed for the entrance.

As they entered Nelson muttered under his
breath to Evan. "Stay with me for the first half hour
or so. Let me know if you see trouble."

This time the crowd paid far more attention as
they were announced. The faces wore a mixture of
disdain, bored curiosity, and intent interest. What was
common to all is everyone seemed stiff and few were
smiling. Nelson ignored it all with his own haughty
disdain as more of the Navy officers followed in his
footsteps.

Nelson worked the crowd like a maestro. Evan knew his Captain exuded an almost mesmerizing charm, but he had never seen him employ it as a tool so effectively and with so many people. Despite what they may all have felt about how he was impacting their businesses and lives, many found themselves drawn to him. But no shortage of people with strong wills and charm of their own were in the room. One of the more senior plantation owners tried taking Nelson down a little.

"Captain Nelson," said the man, as a large crowd formed to listen. "I must say I was somewhat surprised when I heard you were to attend, but now that you are here I am glad that it is so. Opportunity to mend relations is never to be passed up."

Nelson smiled. "I agree, sir. We must all work together in common cause to further the interests of our country, wouldn't you agree?"

"Mm, yes, but it is all a question of what is in the best interests of the country, is it not?"

Without waiting for reply the man continued. "Really, sir, the Crown will be well served if our businesses can flourish. We are happy to do our fair share, but barriers to doing business are a big issue for us. Captain Nelson, you are a young man and your business is to defend us. We are all impressed with the zeal you have shown prosecuting your orders, but honestly, sir, is this good judgment? You have many much older, and if I may dare say, many people wise from years of hard experience at hand. Their advice should not be discounted I would think. Does it not occur to you that perhaps you should take their advice and stay your hand, at least until we can make London finally understand our issues?"

Nelson's smile was cold. "Sir, I appreciate your thinking, but I can assure you I feel no lack of confidence in myself or my decisions. I have been a Post Captain of various warships since I was twenty-one years old and I am now twenty-six. I dare say my own 'hard experience' has served me well and will continue to do so in future. Besides, sir, my orders are clear and they come direct from the First Lord of the Admiralty. As you may know, he is getting on in years and if I'm not mistaken, I should think he is rather older than you, sir."

This earned him a few chuckles of muted laughter. The man gave a wry look to concede the point and was going to continue, but Mary Moutray came over to take charge.

"Gentlemen, must we always talk business? We so rarely have the Captain and his senior officers in our presence. Perhaps we should get to know each other better? And I for one must insist on a dance with the good Captain later."

Her effort to divert conversation to less sensitive topics didn't last long. Nelson continued working his way through the crowd, followed by Evan and a few of the other Navy officers. Inevitably they came across the planter Roberts standing in conversation with two other men. Evan stiffened in recognition as he realized one of them was the American Captain he had seen several weeks before at the Flying Fish. The other man was not familiar, but it seemed possible he could be the captain of the other Dutch ship.

As Nelson finished talking to one of the plantation owners wives and made to move toward Roberts, Evan was able to whisper a few brief words of warning in his Captain's ear. Nelson gave no outward sign other than to plaster a cold smile on his face as he walked over and began shaking hands all around. Evan's guess was correct; the second man was indeed the French captain of the other Dutch ship. Once they were all introduced Nelson focused his attention straightaway on the two men.

"Gentlemen. I have heard rumour of your presence on occasion in Antigua."

The two men looked quickly at each other before turning back to Nelson as one. The French Captain Marcel Deschamps took the lead, spreading his hands wide in a gesture of mock puzzlement.

"You have heard of us, Captain? Why would a couple of simple traders like us be of interest to a busy man like you?"

The cold smile on Nelson's face remained in place. "Interdicting smuggling activity attempting to circumvent our laws is my primary task. Obviously, it is therefore my business to be aware of who comes and goes in my domain, sir. Even if they really are 'simple traders'."

"How could there be doubt, sir?" said the American with his own cold smile on his face.

Nelson laughed. "Gentlemen, you are interesting whether you realize it or not. Come, come, how often does one see two Dutch flagged ships that appear to be operating in concert? Even more interesting, one ship has a Frenchman for Captain and the other has an American captain. And I hear most if not all of the sailors crewing your ships are French, too. There is a story here, is there not?"

This time Captain Deschamps responded. "Well, there is not much to tell, Captain Nelson. I have a Dutch cousin with more money than he knows what to do with. When the peace came he decided to embark on a trading venture out here and he needed people with experience to captain his ships. I have gained a little over the years as a trader so he lured me away from my former employer. My friend Nathan and I have known each other for many years through our trading connections. So I in turn lured him away. Many of my men had no allegiance to my former employer so they followed me to our new venture."

"It wasn't hard for my friend Marcel to lure me away, Captain," said the American Captain Jones. "Times are hard in America and one has to find work wherever one can. I was grateful when Marcel contacted me."

"So you see, Captain," said Captain Deschamps with a smile, spreading his arms wide in innocence once again. "We really are simple traders."

"But it is a struggle for them, Captain," interjected Roberts. "These men are legitimate traders, but how much longer they can continue is open to question because of the customs duties. If I can't afford to buy their wares, they will have to go elsewhere."

"We all have decisions to make, regardless of who we are, sir," said Nelson, before turning back to the two ship Captains.

"Well, gentlemen, I still find your story most interesting. I know men with the depth of real experience when I see them and I think your cousin has done well to find such two men to captain his ships, hard times notwithstanding. Tell me, Captain Deschamps, is the Marquis de Castries still Secretary of State for the French Navy?"

The unexpected question caught the Frenchman off guard, his expression showing a sudden wariness. Still, he recovered himself quickly.

"Umm, why yes, I believe that is his title and yes, I think he still is, Captain," said the Frenchman.

"I see," said Nelson, as he turned quickly to the American. "And you, Captain Jones. Tell me, are the Committees of Correspondence still alive and active in America?"

The American stiffened visibly and his eyes narrowed before he responded. "I believe I have heard of them somewhere before, sir. I'm really not sure of what exactly they do or whether they are still active in whatever that may be."

"Indeed," said Nelson, looking from one man to the other. "Well, gentlemen, be assured I am familiar with the activities of both of these organizations. The French Navy is alive and most active and, yes, Captain Jones, I rather think the Committees of Correspondence are still around in one form or another and still doing business."

Nelson stepped marginally closer to both men before continuing. "Forgive me, gentlemen, but I would like you both to understand my interest. Our respective nations are at peace now and this is good. But it would be a grave concern to me, very grave indeed, were I to discover these organizations were actively pursuing objectives openly or otherwise, in my domain, contrary to my King's interests and the peace we all want to maintain."

Nelson stepped back and spread his arms wide in innocence, just as the French Captain had done earlier. An innocent smile played on his face, but the steel was still in his voice.

"But then, gentlemen, you are both mere 'simple traders'. That being so, I am certain there won't be any misunderstandings between us, will there? I bid you both good trading, sirs."

As Nelson and his party moved away Evan looked quickly over his shoulder. The planter and the two captains all wore frozen expressions on their faces. The American Captain in particular stared hard directly at Evan before turning away. As they approached another group of people Evan pulled closer to Nelson once again.

"Captain, I think this next lot is mostly a crowd of American ship captains."

"Thank you, Mr. Ross. That was a timely warning."

"Captain, if you don't mind my asking, what are 'Committees of Correspondence'?"

"Ah, remind me of that later and I will explain when we have a moment alone."

Evan was right; the four men were indeed American ship captains. The welcome was as cold as the looks on their faces and talk soon shifted to their grievances, which Nelson predictably brushed aside.

"Captain Nelson," said one of the Americans. "You do realize our options are growing fewer and fewer. We all loathe dealing with lawyers and paying their fees, but if that is what we must do then be assured we will not hesitate."

"Sir. My defense is I am doing my duty as ordered. If you do go that route it will end up being a quite simple case."

The two groups soon parted company. Nearby was much friendlier ground; a small group of local Army officers welcomed Nelson with open arms. While in public they did their best to remain neutral in the dispute, Evan knew privately they couldn't have been more pleased to see the Americans being put in their place. The group was soon rapt in attention around the young Captain as his charm worked its magic once again.

"Yes, gentlemen, I am not engaged only on dealing with smugglers. The French are out there, sirs, and they are active."

"The frogs, you say?" said an Army Major. "God damn, what are they up to now, sir?"

"Watching what I'm doing as much as I'm watching them, at the least. I came across a French sloop a couple of months back that I'm quite sure was shadowing me. I got tired of that in a right hurry, as you can imagine, so I turned about and went after him to find out what he was up to. We both had our flags properly displayed, but at sea one is required to render a salute. He was supposed to fire a blank round first to render honours to me as the larger warship. Well, this fool didn't do that."

"Really? What did you do?"

"I fired a live round into his rigging! Heaven only knows what he was thinking. I dare say he had to change his trousers before being rowed over to see me."

The Army officers were still laughing as Nelson continued. "And then there was the frog frigate that I caught surveying for anchorages in our waters on the other side of the island a couple of weeks ago. I sailed up and anchored right beside the bugger. Opened my gun ports and ran all my guns out as we dropped anchor. Had them with their pants down that time, I did. Told him the next time I catch him doing that I won't be stopping at merely opening my gun ports!"

As the conversation continued Nelson looked around and caught Evan's eye. "Mr. Ross, I think we are through the worst of the gauntlet now. You are free to mingle and chase the ladies as you see fit."

Evan decided the wiser course was to find some food. Once again the banquet table was loaded with a virtual mountain of exquisitely prepared delicacies. An ample bowl of steaming lobsters cut into chunks for dipping in a melted butter sauce caught his immediate attention. Delighted, Evan found a small side table he could eat a small plate of it at and still hungry, he filled a second plate with bread and cheese, almonds, and cake. Finally sated, he found a glass of wonderfully smooth, dry red wine. Evan suspected it of being a contraband French vintage, but this didn't stop him from appreciating it. As he wandered into another room he almost bumped into the two captains of the Dutch ships. Evan nodded and was about pass them by when the French captain forestalled him.

"Mr., ah, Ross, was it? Please, join us for a bit."

Evan turned back to join them, wary but outwardly showing a blank face.

"Your Captain Nelson is an interesting fellow, but I fear he is far too suspicious of everyone."

Seeing Evan's stone faced reaction the French captain rushed to reassure him. "I mean no offence to him, of course. We understand. It is his job to be suspicious, yes?"

The American Captain standing beside him smiled in mute agreement as the Frenchman continued.

"It really is unfortunate relations between our respective countries are so bad. The world is a hard enough place as it is without suspicion and mistrust. Would it not be better if we worked together?"

Evan raised a skeptical eyebrow. "Worked together? Really? And what would you propose?"

"All of our countries are struggling to recover from the effects of war, yes? Would it not be better to encourage a freedom of trade with each other? An economic zone with the common goal to improve the movement of goods between us with minimal taxes would be welcomed by many men of business in these parts, and not only on British islands."

Warming to his subject and seemingly encouraged by the neutral look on Evan's face, the Frenchman continued. "Think of it as an experiment, sir. We could try it in the Caribbean islands on a small scale. My friend Nathan and I trade with many of the islands—Guadeloupe, Martinique, Puerto Rico, you name it and we've been there. Trade should know no boundaries. I know the merchants and businessmen on those islands would welcome the opportunities to find new markets for goods and from talking to the plantation owners here they clearly feel the same way. Everyone, even the slaves, could benefit from expanded trade. We want to do business and not make war is what we say. So is this making any sense, sir?"

Evan permitted himself a little smile in response. "Perhaps. You make it sound much easier to do than I suspect reality would dictate. Everyone has interests, including nations, right? Finding those common interests and in particular finding trust will not be easy. But gentlemen, while I agree in general that war is not good for anyone, it is not clear to me how my country would benefit from this."

"One must start somewhere, sir," said the American Captain. "With more trade you could lower the duties. We think your government could make as much if not more because of volume. Would you not agree?"

"Maybe. But change really must come from the work of politicians and diplomats. Gentlemen, I am a simple sailor. You really should press your arguments home with the diplomats."

"Ah, but you are much more than a simple sailor. You are an officer, sir!" said the Frenchman. "Officers have influence. Look at your Captain Nelson, for example. His opinion carries much weight and he is certainly having an impact on local affairs. You obviously have a relationship with him. Come to think of it, what exactly is your role, sir?"

Evan was instantly wary, seeing the intense interest of the two men in their eyes. "You are correct, gentlemen. I do currently report to the Captain, but I am not assigned to the Boreas. I am attached to the Naval Dockyard as the Captain's liaison officer. The Captain is senior officer on station and I am his voice in all matters involving the Dockyard."

"Really?" said the American, a slightly skeptical look on his face. "I thought I'd heard the Dockyard already had a full complement of officers."

Evan eyed him carefully, noting his foreknowledge of Dockyard affairs with suspicion. "They do, but the Captain has many responsibilities and the Dockyard is a much busier place now he is here. I assist him with other administrative matters when needed."

"Other administrative matters? I see," said the American, not bothering to hide the openly skeptical look on his face. "Well, that all sounds like a fairly limited role for an experienced sea officer. Would your talents not be better served at something more challenging?"

"Ah, we are at peace, sir, and opportunities are not as frequently available as they are in times of war. I was fortunate the Captain chose to attach me to his service after my injury."

"Ah, but the point is you do have influence with the good Captain, yes?" said the Frenchman. "Please think about what we were saying, sir. Every little bit of help we can get towards improving relations and bettering trade is welcome."

"Well, I fear you gentlemen are seriously overestimating my influence. The Captain does pay attention when I speak, but he is like most others in my experience. It is most unlikely he would welcome attempts by a junior officer to sway his mind on an issue. But, really, gentlemen, I think you both know this, don't you? Both of you have had military experience, correct? I can sense it in your bearing."

The two men looked at each other before turning back to Evan. The American Captain was the first to respond this time.

"Well, I confess I was serving on a small gunboat during the war, sir. The action I saw was limited, of course. We couldn't hope to match you at sea, obviously."

"I had a little training, sir," added the Frenchman smoothly. "My father wanted me to join the Army and I tried, but we lived by the sea and that was where my heart was. My heart was also not into being a warrior, either. He finally understood and sent me to sea on my cousin's ships."

"Indeed," said Evan, wearing his own mildly skeptical look.

"Mr. Ross, you underestimate yourself. You have influence and ability to make an impact, perhaps not much on Captain Nelson I grant you, but on affairs overall. In fact, I suspect your influence is relatively much greater than what you get paid. You know, there are many on this island and on others like St. Kitts that I suspect would be very generous to someone in a position of influence prepared to facilitate rather than hinder their cause."

"Facilitate, you say? In what way?"

"Oh, I'm sure there are many ways you could help. You have knowledge of operations, sir. You also have charge of activities that could be of interest. Sometimes your Captain Nelson wants things done in a hurry, when really being a little more circumspect would be best. But those are all small details that can be sorted out later. The important thing would be to ensure the right people understand where you stand."

"I see. And are you two gentlemen part of this generous group of the right people?"

"Us?" said the American, spreading his arms wide and displaying an innocent smile. "We're simple traders, sir. My friend just speaks of what we know from conversations with many of the businessmen hereabouts."

Evan was about to reply when he was forestalled by the touch of woman's hand on his shoulder. The hand stayed on his shoulder as all three men turned to find Elizabeth Roberts had joined them.

"Captain Deschamps, Captain Jones, how good to see you both again!"

"Mademoiselle!" said the Frenchman. "You are still the most beautiful woman in all of the islands!"

"Your flattery will get you a dance at some point tonight, monsieur," said Elizabeth, smiling at the Frenchman before turning a pouting look on Evan. "But first I must insist you stop monopolizing the handsome Lieutenant Ross so he can dance with me. He danced with me only once at my father's ball and then most cruelly ignored me the rest of the night."

"Miss Roberts," said Evan, smiling broadly. "The crowd of suitors around you was rather thick. And many of them were officers far more senior than a humble Lieutenant."

Elizabeth laughed, as did the two merchant captains.

"That is usually true, especially when it comes to Mademoiselle Roberts here, Lieutenant," said the Frenchman. "But it is the plight of the moth to forever circle the light, is it not?"

"Perhaps, my good Captain Deschamps," said Elizabeth, as she looked at Evan. "But I have choice in which moth I shine my light on. A high rank is not necessarily something I pay attention to."

"Ah, the handsome and dashing wounded hero!" said Deschamps, with a grin. "I completely understand."

The French captain turned to Evan once again. "Well, Lieutenant, we are keeping you from winning the young lady's heart and risk her displeasure if we remain. I think my friend Nathan and I will go find a drink and leave you two alone. But please remember our conversation and give what we said some thought. We will let our friends know. If you have interest you need merely express it to any of the local planters like Mr. Roberts or Mr. Johnson or even ourselves if we happen to be in port. Good evening, sir."

Evan watched the two men leave, his face a hard mask as he considered what he had learned. Elizabeth brought his attention back to her by exerting pressure with the hand still resting on his shoulder. She also moved tantalizingly closer to whisper right in his ear, brushing a breast against his side as she did. She was close enough her feminine scent almost overwhelmed his senses as it stirred his desire. Even better, the enticing breast remained firmly planted against his side.

"My dear Lieutenant, if I didn't know better I'd say you were more interested in them than in me. Now why in heaven would that be, I wonder?"

Evan coughed and turned to look her in the eyes. "Ah, I am sorry. These gentlemen made an interesting business proposition to me, which caught me a bit by surprise. I shall make amends."

"Well, you seem to be interesting enough to everyone. My father was even talking about you, too." The pouting look returned. "Business! That's all I ever hear about. Mr. Ross, take me dancing and talk to me about something other than business for a change before I lose all patience, please!"

Evan was surprised by the reference to her father's interest, but acquiesced and led her onto the dance floor. This time they danced several dances in a row, much to the chagrin of a crowd of suitors waiting to take Evan's place, but she kept brushing them off. She kept their conversation light; she wanted to know more of his life at sea, a topic he needed little prompting to talk about. His simple love of the sea was soon apparent and to his surprise she listened with few interruptions. Before finally being pulled away by a planter's son she gave him a winning smile.

"Lieutenant Ross, thank you for the dances. You clearly love what you do. We must have tea or go riding some day."

Evan watched her go with mixed feelings. Her growing interest in him was puzzling. She was a truly desirable woman and would be a prize catch for any would be suitor. He had no doubt her father would settle a generous dowry on her, a tempting enough thought.

But Evan knew the reality. Her affections were not what mattered. This woman would find herself married to another plantation owner's son or perhaps being sent back to England to make her way in society under her mother's constant supervision. A wounded, lowly Lieutenant with few prospects for advancement had no chance.

He knew part of him desired her. But another part of him wasn't sure he wanted the chance. Every time he thought about Elizabeth the face of Alice somehow came to mind.

Shaking his head to clear his thoughts he went in search of Captain Nelson, seeing the ball was winding down and people were beginning to leave. Nelson's eyes lit as Evan appeared.

"Time to leave, Lieutenant. We don't want to overstay our welcome, do we?" said the Captain, a small grin of amusement playing on his face. "I have my First Officer rounding up the others."

Evan saw they were alone for the moment so he briefed the Captain quickly on what he had learned. Nelson's eyes narrowed when Evan revealed the attempt to subvert his loyalty.

"Indeed. I must think about this, Mr. Ross. We shall talk further about that."

Looking around Evan saw they still had a few moments alone. "Captain? About the Committees?"

"Ah, yes. The Committees of Correspondence are something that evolved on the rebel side during the war. Each of the various states had a need to coordinate their internal affairs on several fronts, everything from the state of their supplies to their thinking on any given issue. Of course, the states needed to coordinate amongst themselves too. Over time we believe they more or less coalesced into one larger entity. I don't know if they still call themselves by that rather innocent sounding name, but I'm fairly certain they still operate in one form or another."

Nelson's First Officer stepped forward to join them with news their entourage was ready to leave. They made their way out the door saying their goodbyes to their hosts as they did.

Once outside they had a few moments wait before the carriage was brought up. Evan saw he still had Nelson to himself while everyone was otherwise occupied, so he broached one more question.

"Sir? So why did Captain Jones react as he did to your questions?"

Nelson smiled. "Because, Mr. Ross, while the Committee for Correspondence has many tasks, the primary job became spying. As for the Frenchman, we are aware the French Navy on occasion directly employs people engaged in sub rosa activity. I asked those questions to test them both and, given their reactions, I rather suspect both of them are spies of some sort for their respective masters, sir. Yes, we must talk later."

Chapter Thirteen
March 1785
Antigua

The little group of three people standing on the dock in English Harbour stared up at the trading sloop moored beside them being readied for sea. No one was smiling and Nelson knew it was for good reasons.

One of them was Captain John Moutray, clearly looking unhappy his command of the Dockyard was ending early. His illness had not abated, so his reluctant request to be sent home had been approved.

His wife Mary also looked sad, but for a much different reason.

"Goodbye and God bless you, Horatio," said Mary Moutray as she gave him a hug. "I shall miss both you and the warmth and sunshine here. I know you both think it is bad for your health here, but I simply cannot look forward with pleasure to the rain and grey skies next winter in England."

As the third member of the little group Nelson felt more wistful than sad, but did not show it.

"Well, Horatio, I see they are signaling it's time for us to board," said Captain Moutray. "You still have a hard road ahead of you here. I wish I could be here to help, but it is not to be."

"I know, my friends. There really is no one to replace you here. I have no one I can truly open up to. But with command comes loneliness and we all know it. You must look after yourselves and not concern yourself with me."

As Mary stepped into the bosun's chair slung over the side to haul her aboard she called out. "I shall write!"

Nelson waved as she was lifted aboard. "I shall miss her, John. You did well to find such a woman. I can only hope some day to be as fortunate myself. Someone to share my hopes and my life would fill a void that seems as great as the night in my soul."

"Have you no prospects, Horatio?"

"Well, there is one lady over on Nevis that caught my eye on my last trip there. I really didn't have opportunity to pursue the matter, but if chance arises I perhaps will. She evinced little or no interest in me, but then we really had no time together. We shall see."

Captain Moutray turned to Nelson one last time as the empty bosun's chair was swung over to the shore once more.

"Well, Horatio, you know we wish you all the best. I promise I will brief the First Lord in detail on what is going on out here as soon as I can. You need more support and you certainly aren't getting it from the local politicians or populace. If nothing else a chat with the First Lord may have some direct effect on that fool in Barbados you report to. Even if he did relent over that legal nonsense about being cautious back in January he will continue to be a source of aggravation to you, I fear. Well, I have a few other contacts within the government and be assured they will hear of this too."

Moutray paused to stare mournfully into the distance. "I don't know if I'll ever have another command, Horatio. I've given thirty years of service, but I fear I may soon be on the beach for good."

"I sincerely hope not, John, you deserve better. And I truly value your support. Thank you."

"Sooner or later, Horatio, you will find yourself back in England. You must visit us!"

Nelson nodded and the two men shook hands. Moutray stepped into the bosun's chair and waved as he was hoisted aboard. The sailors began casting off the lines holding it in the shore's embrace as others let fall the sails.

Nelson stood alone as the ship made its laborious passage out of the Harbour. Before it finally turned out of sight two tiny figures on the deck waved one last time to the lone figure still standing on shore. Nelson waved back, truly alone again.

***

Alice's mother knew what she was doing was dangerous. She looked up to see the owner Roberts and his leading overseer as they entered his office for a meeting. She was bent over dusting furniture in the far corner of the anteroom and they had not seen her. The opportunity to listen in came because they left the door to the office open, thinking no one was about.

Quietly she worked her way around the room to get as close to the office door as she could. She began to sweat with fear as she realized they were discussing arrangements for a smuggling operation on St. Kitts. As soon as she had the details she worked her way toward the other doorway to get away to safety, but she met another female black servant at the entrance. She tried signaling the other servant to remain silent, but the woman began talking.

The sound of her voice drew immediate attention. Both women found themselves gripped on the shoulder and roughly turned hard about to face the overseer. The man's strong fingers dug harshly into both women.

"What are you two doing here?" said the man, suspicion darkening his face and menace heavy in his voice.

"We're only doing our cleaning, sir," said Alice's mother in fearful reply.

"Were either of you in this room? Did either of you hear anything?" said the overseer, watching their faces closely for any hint of guilt. Both women were too fearful to answer so they meekly shook their heads.

The overseer glared hard at both before finally releasing his grip. "If I catch either of you snooping around you will pay in ways you don't want to think about."

With one final harsh look he turned about and stalked back to the adjoining room where Roberts waited, slamming the door shut hard as he entered. The two women rubbed their aching shoulders and turned back to their duties.

***

The meeting the next morning in Nelson's aft cabin on the Boreas was strained as Evan and the two Dockyard officers Burns and Long could all see the icy displeasure on Nelson's face. Nelson wasted no time getting to the purpose of the meeting.

"Sirs, I have received orders from the Admiralty and I can tell you now there will be no new officer arriving to replace Captain Moutray. I have been ordered to assume direct command of the Dockyard and all of its personnel, in addition to my duties as Captain of the Boreas."

The utter dismay on the faces of the two Lieutenants was obvious. With a flash of insight Evan realized both had pinned hopes on either getting a new Commissioner more favourable to them or, even better, they were hoping one of them would be appointed to the position.

But Nelson was not giving them time to recover. "So, gentlemen, I want you both to understand my expectations. Progress has been made since Lieutenant Ross became involved, but I have read the reports of everyone and can see with my own eyes what has been done. I judge the only reason things have moved forward is due to the efforts of Mr. Ross. I am doubtful that you two would have accomplished anything of consequence were he not involved. Thus, you both need to understand I simply will not have any further obstructive behaviour from either of you. You had plenty of warnings about what was expected of you from Captain Moutray. Gentlemen, I tell you your careers are at stake, here. Fail me any further and you will face the consequences."

Nelson paused to glare at the two men. "Do either of you have any questions?"

Both men shook their heads.

"Fine. There is one last thing, then. Lieutenant Ross has been serving as my liaison officer until now. I am changing his role. Henceforth he will serve as my First Officer in the Dockyard and you two will report directly to him."

The two Dockyard officer's faces fell in open shock. Lieutenant Burns was the first to recover, his face flushed crimson. "But—but I'm the First Officer! I'm sure my commission dates before his!"

"Say 'sir', damn you!" barked Nelson.

"Ah, sir, I apologize. But, really, is this not unusual, sir?"

"You question my orders at your peril, sir! I am in charge here and you will follow orders. I want an active service commission officer running day-to-day affairs in the Dockyard and Lieutenant Ross fits the requirement. You two are civilian appointments and you certainly won't get active commissions from me. The date of your commission is irrelevant in these circumstances. If either of you has a problem with this feel free to write London for reassignment elsewhere. Is that clear?"

The two chastened officers nodded wordlessly so Nelson sat back and folded his arms. "You are dismissed, gentlemen. Not you, Mr. Ross. Please stay behind."

Once the door closed Nelson slowly began to calm down. Visibly relaxing and rising, he removed his uniform coat. "You may wish to take advantage of removing your coat to make yourself comfortable, sir. The weather is getting warmer again and it really seems beastly still in this vile place today."

"Thank you, sir," said Evan with a grateful smile. "You are right, it is warm in here. I think my two colleagues were finding it particularly hot."

Nelson laughed. "Keep the heat on them, sir! I simply cannot abide people that have no sense of duty. Right, what have you for me today, sir? We have not had much action for some time now."

"Yes, Captain. I think the owners and the men they have involved with smuggling activity have adapted and become close mouthed about their actions. I can't be sure, but I think the reason we haven't seen much action is the locals needed to reassure the ship owners they had their house in order, so to speak. They wanted assurances everything was being done to plug leaks."

"Hmm, yes, that would make sense. Come to think of it, that would tally with some cryptic written references my friend in the Post Office has advised me of. But it can't go on forever. They want supplies and they don't want to pay duties."

"Exactly, Captain, which is why I have news for you. Despite their best efforts, I have word of a large drop of goods on St. Kitts. The handover is set for tomorrow night on the north side of the island. It's a deserted beach called Sandy Cove. My source believes there is to be a hand off to a legitimate British trader who will falsify his records to reflect duties are already paid. This is coming from a source at the Roberts plantation."

"Excellent, Lieutenant, excellent. Roberts, eh? Why am I not surprised? It's too bad we can't go after Roberts himself, but we must protect our sources. Well, I shall be joining them for the occasion."

"Sir, if this tip proves to be true this will be the first time we've had concrete evidence of a link to another island."

"Indeed. My Captains patrolling the other islands have been encountering similar smuggling activities, but not on the scale we have here and on St. Kitts. To date we have not seen a direct link like this. I suppose we shouldn't be surprised they are trying something different. We must carry on and be vigilant, sir. Stamping this out before it becomes rampant throughout all of the islands is critical. And how about our two 'Dutch' friends, Mr. Ross? Any word of them?"

"Not as yet, sir. I confess I am a little puzzled. The locals report these ships are fairly regular in their visits every couple of months. We have many eyes watching for them, sir."

"Excellent. Well, I shall depart for St. Kitts first thing in the morning tomorrow. I think you should post a watch as you suggested on the fellow with the pigeons and the inn with all those horses. Lets see if any messages are sent about where I am heading. If you can don't let them know they have been observed. Even if a message is sent it is unlikely they will be able to stop the train of events."

"As you wish, Captain. Sir, have you given any more thought to using me as a double agent?"

"Yes. As tempting as it is to have you pretend to agree to facilitate matters for the plantation owners, I think we should hold that possibility in reserve and employ it only if we must. My concern is this could be a trap."

Evan nodded. "Yes, that thought crossed my mind, too. I suspect the newspaper headline would be something like 'Nelson's Dockyard Officer Seeks Bribes from Honest Businessmen'. The smear would implicate you as the real target, sir."

"Yes, they will try to smear me every chance they get. I see no point in helping them. It's too bad we can't turn that into a headline like 'Dishonest Businessmen Try Bribing Nelson's Dockyard Officer'."

"I doubt that would sell enough newspapers, sir."

Nelson offered a grim smile. "Indeed. You are dismissed, sir."

***

The unexpected, sudden sound of distant drums coming from different parts of the island late in the night woke people everywhere and the sound brought fear. Several plantation owners and overseers hurriedly dressed and parties were sent in search, but the drums weren't active long. The drummers melted away into the darkness.

On the Robert's plantation, frustrated by lack of success, the lead overseer Whyte turned to the group of armed men with him on the search, his face dark with anger.

"Follow me. We're going to get some answers."

Heading straight for the area slaves were quartered Whyte kicked the flimsy door in on the first hut he came to and the occupants screamed in fear and surprise as he burst in. His followers needed no orders to do the same to other nearby huts. Whyte roughly dragged a woman from her bed and out the door into the open. The woman screamed piteously as he began beating her with the heavy, three-foot cane he carried.

A male slave stumbled out of the darkness of the hut and fell to his knees in front of Whyte, hands raised in desperate prayer.

"Please, sir! She has done nothing, I beg—"

Whyte's punch caught him full on the nose, breaking it with an audible, sickly crunch. Spraying blood, the slave fell to the side in a crumpled heap. Around him the night was filled with screams of pain and terror.

Turning back to the woman he dragged her into a central clearing and whistled sharply several times to catch the attention of the other overseers and issue orders. Within minutes a crowd of terrified, moaning slaves were huddled together on the ground in front of Whyte. Light from flickering torches the overseers lit showed the fear on their faces as Whyte stepped forward to address them.

"You know what we want. Somebody needs to talk, now."

The frightened, desperate slaves had no idea who the drummers were, but they could tell him what the vague, ominous message delivered by the drums said.

Be ready, for the time is coming when the white man will pay.

***

The drums woke both James and Evan too. As this was the morning Nelson was departing for St. Kitts they had no time to discuss it until they could get into place at the shabby old Falmouth Inn to spy from an open window. While sharing breakfast they could see anyone coming from the Dockyard to either the Inn or the nearby home of the pigeon keeper. As they waited the two men discussed the puzzle of the drums.

"I suggest let me trawl about in the town bars tonight, sir," said James. "We've had no warning of this, but I have a feeling this has to do with that Frenchman's talk of arming the blacks. I wonder if those Dutch ships are back?"

"Yes, see what you can find out. I'll check with Alice to see what she knows. I— ah, look what we have here. Lets stay in the shadows and see what happens."

James turned and looked out the window in the direction Evan indicated, careful to stay as hidden as he could. "Well, if it isn't that pompous little pile of shit clerk. And look, he's gone over to talk to the stable hand. Do you think he's our man?"

As they watched, the clerk exchanged a few coins with the stable man and mounted a horse.

247

Within moments the clerk was disappearing down the road at a steady trot.

"Hmm. I wonder?" said Evan. "That fool doesn't strike me as anything more than a message boy. I wonder if there is more than one traitor in our midst here. Well, we'll see what the Captain makes of this."

***

Entering the Flying Fish much later in the day Evan saw how subdued the atmosphere was. The drums had rattled everyone more than Evan realized. The usual crowd was present, but even the rowdiest of the lot were toning it down. The question on everyone's mind was whether the drums would be heard again tonight and, if so, what they would say.

But this wasn't what interested Evan the most. The two Dutch ships were indeed back in port and Evan was certain it couldn't be a coincidence the drums had begun at the same time. The American Captain Jones appeared at the Flying Fish once again, coming in as Evan and Alice were sitting at dinner. He offered them an amiable nod when he saw them as he made his way to a table across the room with his First Officer. A while later, seeing they had finished dinner he came over with his mug of rum and asked to join them. Evan nodded.

"Welcome back, Captain Jones," said Evan, although the tone of his voice was anything but warm.

"Thank you, it has been a while. The life of a trader, yes?"

Evan introduced Alice, but the American waved his hand in dismissal. "I already know who she is, Lieutenant Ross. How could I not? The most beautiful woman on the island and I find you've already grappled her firmly to you. You are fortunate you noticed her before I did."

Alice smiled beatifically. "Flattery is always welcome, Captain."

"Where is your friend Captain Deschamps, sir?" said Evan. "Does he not enjoy a night in port after so long at sea like you?"

The American smiled. "Oh, most certainly, sir. However, his tastes are, umm, much more refined than mine."

"In other words, he prefers the most expensive brothel in town?"

This time the American laughed out loud and shrugged. "Oh, I'm fairly certain he knows where they all are, expensive or otherwise. But I think he also knows more than a few ladies in any given port we visit. But Lieutenant, as much as I enjoy talking about women I actually came over here to see if you've given any thought to our last conversation."

"Ah, yes, I have. I'm sorry, but I really can't see how that could work, sir," said Evan, a wry look on his face. "I appreciate the thought, but I belong at sea and in the Navy."

"Hmm. Do you really think you will be able to find a berth with someone, given your injury, sir?"

Evan shrugged. "I can but try, sir. My heart is at sea."

"Well, Lieutenant, I think you are a capable fellow. If things do not work out for you perhaps joining Marcel and me at sea would work. If you prove yourself we could even consider fitting out a third trading ship with you as Captain. The Navy isn't the only choice if the sea is where you are truly at home."

Evan was speechless, pausing a moment to consider his response. "That is very generous of you, sir. I think my heart is at sea as a Lieutenant in the service, but I shall have to give this some thought."

"That is all we can ask." He stood and picked up his mug to leave. "Well, I shall let you and the lovely lady enjoy the rest of the evening together."

***

With a bright half moon to light the way the Boreas hunted its prey and fell on them with vengeance. A shot across the bow brought an end to any thought of running on one ship, but the other was making desperate attempts to get underway. They were too late.

"Well, isn't this interesting. This lot is trying to run from us. We may have a pack of deserters here. Bring us alongside and ready boarders, Mr. Wilkins," said Nelson, alive with the sudden prospect of action.

The Boreas rounded to and grapnels flew across. Within moments a host of boarders were jumping down onto the deck of the smaller ship as sporadic gunfire and the clash of steel rang out. Nelson himself led a party fighting their way straight toward a knot of smugglers clustered on the quarterdeck.

"Surrender, you fools," shouted Nelson, as he sprinted up the steps with his sword at the ready, followed closely by his coxswain and several sailors.

The response was a savage lunge from one of the men in the crowd, which Nelson barely managed to parry with his own sword. Nelson and his opponent slashed back and forth at each other as the quarterdeck became a muddled scene of struggling combatants, but it couldn't last. Nelson caught the man with a vicious backhand cut, felling him with a crash to the deck. Three other smugglers were already down and the remaining outnumbered smugglers fell back, dropping their weapons in surrender.

Flushed from the unexpected action, Nelson shook his head. "Right, lets sort these bastards out and find out what we've got here."

***

Late in the night Evan and Alice were awakened from deep sleep by the sound of tapping on their door. The tapping was soft, but insistent.

Evan opened the door to find the scared face of Emma waiting for him.

"Sir," she hissed. "You must come. Your man James wants you."

Worried, Evan quickly donned his clothes and followed her to another room. James was inside having his arm bandaged by Emma's husband Walton. The two men looked up as Evan and Emma came into the room.

"God Almighty, James!" said Evan. "Are you all right?"

"I'm okay, Evan," said James. "This is but a scratch."

"Well, it's a bit more than a scratch, Mr. Ross," said Walton with a grim smile. "But it is a flesh wound that will take some time to heal. He's got a five-inch grazing slash in the flesh right below his shoulder. Fortunately it's his left arm and he's right handed so this won't slow him down too much."

"What happened, James?"

"I got too close to a couple of people talking and they didn't like it. Real nasty bastards, they were. I think they may have been escaped slaves. The reason I got this is my damn leg gave out on me when I needed it most. But I gave as good as I got."

James offered Evan a grim smile before pausing a moment as he turned serious. "Sir, it was worth it though. There's a drop of weapons tonight. This is only a small shipment. Apparently it's a token of support. Whoever is behind it is pushing this bunch of fools to do something to show they are serious. If they do, more supplies will be forthcoming."

"My God, this is going to get ugly. James, was there any hint of this happening on other islands?"

"No, sir. Like I said, I got the sense this is a trial to see what happens. If they succeed, well, who knows where this will go? But the better news is I think I have someone identified that will serve as a source for us. I'm going to need to work on him. His help will come at a price, of course."

As he finished speaking everyone's heads turned to listen to the sound in the distance. The drums were talking once again.

***

Evan was in his office at the Dockyard the next afternoon when the messenger shoved past the clerk outside and burst in the door.

"Lieutenant Ross? Is it true Captain Nelson and his squadron are away?"

"Who the hell are you and what are you doing in here?" barked Evan. As he finished speaking an angry Marine guard burst in and grabbed the man roughly by the collar.

"Sorry, Lieutenant. This fool rushed past us to see you when we told him Captain Nelson was away. I'll show him out of the Dockyard."

"Unhand me, you idiot. I am a messenger from the Governour."

Evan scowled, but signaled to the Marine to stand easy. "If you're from the Governour he needs to find better help, because you are the only idiot in this room. I could have you stripped and flogged for unauthorized entry to a military facility."

The man blanched white seeing the ice in Evan's eyes, but Evan waved at him to sit. "Right, you're here now and yes, the Captain and his squadron are away. I am currently senior so you'll have to give me your message."

"Sir, the Governour desires Captain Nelson to attend him at once to discuss what happened last night. I assume you will suffice as senior officer present."

"Good heavens, man. Speak clearly. What happened last night?"

The messenger's eyes widened. "You've not heard? Lord, everyone else on the island knows. There were attacks on two plantations last night. Two overseers and their families were cut to pieces in their beds on one plantation. Worse, on the other an owner and his entire family were shot to death. The women were raped before they were killed."

Evan was silent a moment as the implications sunk in. "You may advise the Governour I will attend him as soon as possible. This Marine will escort you out."

As Evan rode his buggy into St. John's he passed several armed, angry parties of whites roaming the island. Very few blacks were about, but twice he came across mobs beating black men they had obviously caught in the open.

Entering the Governour's office Evan saw several planters including Roberts in attendance. He took a deep breath to steel himself, knowing the meeting wasn't going to be pleasant.

"God Almighty!" said Roberts, before the Governour could even get started. "We have murders in the night with weapons that have undoubtedly been smuggled in and where is the dauntless Captain Nelson? Probably off chasing after legitimate traders when he should be spending his efforts protecting us!"

Evan stared at Roberts, but was saved from having to respond by the Governour.

"Lieutenant, thank you for coming. You have heard what has happened?"

"Sir, I have. Do we know what the drums were saying the night before?"

"We do. The message was that retribution is at hand. That was all. I have ordered armed parties of Army and militia to patrol to maintain order and give the people a sense of protection. But I must confess I agree with Mr. Roberts and the others in the room here. It would be far better if the Navy were to put a stop to smuggling of weapons, especially guns, onto the island."

"I can't believe the Navy is slipping so badly as to let arms, even a small amount, be smuggled onto the island!" growled one of the other owners, shaking his head. "And Captain Nelson is nowhere to be found with the island in such need. Probably off putting on a fine show where he is least needed."

"Governour. Gentlemen. I share your concerns and I will ensure the Captain is made aware of this the second he returns—"

All heads turned as another plantation owner burst into the room and strode up to the Governour's desk. "Sir, I apologize for this interruption, but we have news I think you want to hear. One of my ships has just come in from St. Kitts. Captain Nelson intercepted two ships there last night, but this time it is different. He has confiscated both the cargo *and* the ships and brought them into Basseterre Harbour early this morning. The rumour is he is sending it all to the prize court there!"

The news turned the angry plantation owners into starving sharks with a bleeding fish barely out of their reach. Oddly, Roberts was the exception, remaining cold and silent throughout.

After ten minutes of more ranting from the owners, Evan rose to leave. "Gentlemen, as I said, I shall ensure the Captain is made aware of your concerns. The rest of the Captains on station shall be made aware of what has happened and I am certain they will make every effort to put a stop to this. Good day."

Returning to their quarters in Falmouth Harbour Evan prepared a written report on the events since Nelson's departure, to be given to him the moment he returned. He entrusted it to James who was trying to rest his arm. The dog Nelson was at his feet and a bottle of rum on the table beside him to keep the still painful cut under control. James assured him he would have the report in Nelson's hands as soon as he returned.

Concerned more repercussions could follow in their network Evan decided to make his way back to St. John's. Back at the Flying Fish he stabled his horse and buggy, finding it was late enough dinners were already being served inside. The crowd was noisier than usual, abuzz over events. No one paid him any attention as he looked around the room for Alice. His arm was gripped hard as Emma surprised him, breathlessly pulling him close.

"Thank God you're here, sir!" she said in a low, quick whisper. "I couldn't stop him!"

"What? Stop who?" said Evan, concerned at the fear he saw in her face.

"That animal Whyte, the lead overseer for Mr. Roberts!" she hissed. "He just barged in and demanded to know where Alice was. He had a knife and was going to cut me if I didn't tell him!"

Evan went cold. "Christ! Are they upstairs?"

She nodded and Evan sprinted for the stairs, taking them two at a time. At the top of the stairs he saw the door to their usual room was open. As he got to the top he heard a hard slap and a woman's voice cry out in pain. Certain the voice was Alice's he pushed himself even harder. Rushing to the door he called to her and as he came in he heard the crunching sound of a fist hitting flesh, followed by another inarticulate cry of pain.

Alice was crumpled on the floor, holding the side of her face and sobbing. Standing over her was the overseer Evan had met on his first trip to the Roberts plantation. The man took his attention away from Alice and focused on Evan when he heard him enter.

"What the hell do you want?"

"Get your hands off her. Now!"

"I think not, one arm. This is my master's property and I'll do whatever I please with it. So piss off."

"I said, get your damn hands off her!" said Evan as he crossed the room.

The overseer shoved Alice out of the way and pulled a knife from his belt.

"I warned you, you stupid bastard!" said the overseer as he lunged with the knife straight for Evan's heart.

But Evan had seen the move coming. Dancing to the side out of harm's way Evan gave him a hard shove as his opponent's momentum carried him off balance. The overseer fell into the wall hard, but he didn't stay down for long. He bounced back up as Evan pulled his own dirk from his belt. The two men circled each other, taking wild slashes in the confined space and trying to get the other off balance.

Evan was at a disadvantage. In a more open space with his sword he could hold his own, but in a knife fight with little room to maneuver it would only be a matter of time before they would begin to tire. An opponent with a free hand would be able to use it to his advantage and shove the other off balance. A quick, following knife thrust would finish the job. Knowing this, Evan grew more and more desperate to find some opening to gain an advantage.

The overseer knew it too.

"Yeah, Navy boy. You're screwed. I'll have you soon enough," he grunted out in between lunges.

But even as he spoke he gave a small start and the feral grin on his face melted into a look of puzzlement. He pulled away, arching his back for a moment before crumpling to the floor in a heap. A knife was buried to the hilt in his back.

Alice had come up behind him unseen, finding strength in her anger to drive a knife she always kept close at hand into him. Stepping away, one hand to her face, she appeared a mess. Her nose was bleeding and the damaged side of her face was quickly swelling, turning an angry red colour. Her eye was already almost completely swollen shut. Her dress was ripped open and her breasts were hanging free. Painful looking dark bruises were already appearing on one. She looked at Evan and held out her arms as Evan put down his weapon and rushed to help her over to the bed.

"God in heaven! Are you okay?" said Evan, as she nodded in response. "Please sit here while I go find something to clean you up."

"Thank you for saving me," she said. "Please tell me he is dead."

Evan went over to feel for a pulse, but knew he wouldn't find one. The knife was well placed, finding his heart. Evan looked over and shook his head.

Alice rose shakily to her feet and stepped close enough to spit on the body before collapsing back to the bed. "Bastard!"

Evan returned a few minutes later with water and towels. Emma had gone in search of Walton when Evan had bounded up the stairs and both of them appeared at the same time as Evan. The two innkeepers were appalled at what had happened.

"Lord, what are we going to do?" said Emma, her voice edged with fear. Walton was speechless, standing at her side.

Evan took a deep breath, knowing he had to take charge. Bending over the body he began searching the dead man's pockets. "Don't worry. We'll figure something out. Did anyone see him come in or go upstairs?"

Walton responded first as the two innkeepers gave each other questioning looks. "I was in the stables. I had no idea this was going on till Emma found me."

"He came in the back through the kitchen, just before you got here," said Emma. "I think he was trying for surprise. So our people in the kitchen probably saw him, but I doubt they paid much attention. As for the people in the main room he wasn't there for long so I don't think anyone there would have noticed him. He found me in the back office and then he went straight upstairs."

Emma turned to Alice, a sick look on her face. "Alice, I'm so sorry. I should have lied and told him you weren't here. I was scared. He threatened to cut me."

Alice waved a hand in dismissal. "Don't worry, Emma. There was nothing you could have done or said to stop him. He still would have searched the place."

"Are the people in the kitchen going to be a problem?" said Evan, still working his way through the man's pockets.

"No. They are both dear friends. They will admit to nothing."

Evan finally stood up and turned to the group, holding out both hands for them to see what he had found. "Well, this is interesting. I think this is a bag of money and this appears to be a notebook of some sort. It has lots of entries. He doesn't seem to have anything else of consequence in his pockets."

As Evan pulled the drawstring open on the bag their eyes all bulged on seeing the contents. They expected to find coins; what they had not expected is they would be gold.

"Oh my Lord!" said Walton. "That's got to be a small fortune! Why would he have that on him?"

"I don't know, but this maybe provides us the perfect way out of this. With him carrying a bag full of money around robbery would be a logical motive for his murder. But Walton, can we just get him out of here with no one seeing us? We need to get him as far away from this place as possible right away before anyone comes in search."

Walton grunted as he quickly thought it through. "Yes. We can haul him out the back stairs and down to the stables. I've got a cart we can use. We toss him in the back and cover him up."

"Have you anywhere we can dump him where he won't be found?"

"Sure. The road out to Fort Bay is pretty deserted, especially this late at night. No one has any plantations or homes around there and there are lots of patches of thorn bushes. I can work my way into the middle of one and dig a hole for this scum. As long as no one sees me and I cover my tracks well, he'll never be found. But I will need you to help me get him down to the stables."

After removing the knife and binding the wound to staunch any further bleeding Evan and Walton picked up the dead man and carried him out of the room, leaving a small pool of blood on the floor. Evan found it awkward with only one arm, but Walton had the dead man under his arms and Evan was able to hug the man's feet to his chest and they got underway. Progress was slow because they wanted to make as little noise as possible. Both men were sweating from the exertion, but they managed to get him into the cart unseen by anyone. After throwing a shovel into the cart Walton carefully looked outside the stables, but no one was about. He nodded to Evan and jumped into the seat. In moments he had slipped into the darkness.

Evan waited a few moments to ensure no one had been hiding and watching before heading back to the room. Emma was working hard to clean up Alice. The bleeding had stopped and her dress was temporarily repaired, but it would be a long time before she would look herself again. The two women gave Evan a questioning look as he came in and he nodded wordlessly in response.

Emma looked at the bag of gold and the notebook sitting on the bed. "Evan? What are you going to do with those?"

"Hmm. I don't know, but I'd better keep them. If any of you are found with them they'll have you hanging on the pole outside the jail before you know it."

"Evan?" said Alice. A sick, worried look was on her face. "I didn't have time to tell you, but I'm afraid for my Mom."

"What? Why?"

"She was the source for the last tip about St. Kitts. That scum must have somehow found out she was involved. He told me he'd already questioned her and he figured I was involved too. Then you showed up so that's all I know. Evan, I have to go to her."

"God, no!" said Emma. "If you show up there looking like this they'll be suspicious right off. Leave that with me, girl. I'll have someone look in on her and find out what happened."

"Hmm. I fear Emma is right, Alice. In fact, I am concerned whether anyone else knows what he did or whether anyone knew where he was going. Emma, I need to get Alice out of here, quickly. Someone else may follow and start asking questions."

Emma obviously saw the need as she nodded vigorously. "You are right. So what is my story?"

"Alice, what were you doing before this all happened?"

"I've been up here in the room for several hours."

"Excellent, so it's unlikely any of the crowd in the tavern would know you were here."

Evan turned to Emma. "Right, I came in looking for Alice, but she wasn't here so I left the back way. If anyone asks about the dead man he came in looking for someone, you have no idea who, and couldn't find them so he left the way he came in. You have no idea what he wanted or where he went. Does that work?"

Emma took a moment to think, but nodded slowly. "Okay. But what are you going to do with Alice? And what will I say if anyone comes looking for her?"

"Well, that's easy enough. I've already paid to acquire her services for an extended period. The story is I decided to pay you a little extra to have her as a live in service doing housekeeping and so forth. So she comes home with me. She can lay low with me until this blows over and she heals. That means all that's left is to get her out of here unseen. We don't want anyone seeing what has happened to her face. Can we maybe dress her like a man? Find a big floppy hat or something to help cover her?"

Minutes later they were all in the stables. Alice was sitting in Evan's buggy, disguised with spare men's clothes Emma had found.

The two women looked at each other and Emma reached up to grasp Alice's hand.

"I'll send word as soon as I can. Now get going you two. I've still got some blood to clean up."

Chapter Fourteen
April 1785
Antigua

Alice's mother fared worse than Alice. Much worse. The overseer had beaten her badly and brutally raped her before coming for Alice. Her body would be much longer in healing, but despite the injuries her spirit remained.

Evan felt fortunate the dead man had apparently not told anyone what he was doing or where he was going. Piecing it together, Evan surmised the man had learned of the seizure on St. Kitts and acted on impulse on his intuition Alice's mother had in fact overheard what was said. Roberts was suspicious of the coincidence that Alice's mother was found beaten and raped at the same time his overseer disappeared. She was questioned hard, but they had nothing to go on. Her torn clothes and serious bruises from the harsh beating supported her story that the reason for it was her attempt to spurn his attentions. Search parties scoured the grounds and the town, but nothing was found.

Alice was slow to heal. Her anger on learning what happened to her mother combined with her own injuries was obvious and slow to dissipate. Evan did his best to give her time to heal, but the bruising on her face lingered for a long time. Almost two weeks later she finally came to him and held him close.

"I'll be myself again some day, Evan. The bruises are fading. I hope you'll still find me pretty."

Evan reached up and gently touched the still marred side of her face. "You are even now still the best looking woman on this island."

The tears fell as she led him to the bedroom.

Afterwards they sat on the porch. The dog Nelson had fast become Alice's dog, following her everywhere she went. They all laughed at the dog's sudden allegiance to her, but his unconditional, simple love did much to heal the invisible wounds. The dog was helping in the same way for Evan, whose own nightmares and unexplained feelings of anger had finally diminished to a point where the episodes were far less frequent.

They took to going on long walks with the dog. James sometimes joined them, but he was almost fully healed and keen to get back to trawling for information. In particular he wanted to track down his potential informant and secure his aid. Whoever he was, the man had an irregular schedule and James had not been able to find him again.

Sometimes in the early mornings or late in the day when the heat was more bearable Evan and Alice took to riding up to Shirley Heights to sit and look out over the harbour, watching the ships come and go. They were watching the sunset on the Heights one evening when Evan stiffened as he used his telescope to look at an approaching ship. He didn't need long to see what he needed.

Alice put a hand on his shoulder. "Is it finally him?"

"It is. He will want to see me first thing in the morning."

***

Leaving the house early in anticipation of his orders the next morning Evan met the Marine sent to fetch him at the Dockyard gate. The Marine retraced his steps with Evan in tow, passing several small work parties busy with construction in the Dockyard.

Nelson had been in St. Kitts for almost three weeks. Evan was puzzled at this with so much happening on Antigua, but he knew Nelson would have his reasons. Nelson had sent word by a mail packet ship he would be gone an extended period and ordered reports to be sent to him in St. Kitts until further notice. Evan had done so, but no explanation was forthcoming for the extended absence in return.

Nelson was busy with yet another pile of correspondence when Evan was shown into the cabin. "Ah, Mr. Ross, that was quick. Waiting nearby for me were you?"

"Anticipating my orders, sir."

Nelson chuckled as he finished what he was doing. Pushing the pile to the side, he sat back and smiled.

"Well, you've had a busy time of it while I was gone. I'm sorry you had to listen to all the complaining in my stead over the incident with those murders. I take it there have been no further incidents or clues as to who did it?"

"None, sir. I am told the people, and in particular the overseers that were murdered, were particularly brutal, so it is perhaps no surprise they were the victims. It was likely slaves on their plantations that did the deed, but no one has admitted to it despite another round of harsh beatings."

"Hmm. So it is likely Mr. Wilton had good intelligence then. This was maybe a small, one-time shipment and the murders were proof the recipients were serious. And no more drums?"

"No more drums. Coincidentally, or not, our Dutch ships came and went while that happened. Unfortunately, we still do not have any idea of their future schedule. They are guarded about their plans.

We heard rumour they were off to Dominica, but can't be certain."

"Well. We shall have to be vigilant. Ah, I had a question about your latest report, sir. You were quite vague and indicated a verbal report would be better?"

"That was deliberate, sir. I took your warning about being careful in my correspondence and other people reading it."

Nelson raised an eyebrow and sat forward with interest as Evan detailed what had transpired. Nelson winced when the details of what had happened to Alice's mother were provided.

As he finished, Evan gave Nelson a troubled look. "Sir, I am concerned about this. If word gets out as to what happened I fear for what could happen to my sources. For better or worse, it's true this man was killed. But it would be a travesty to punish Alice for it."

Nelson shook his head. "Mr. Ross, your concern does you credit, but you should not lose sleep over this. As far as I'm concerned we are at war with these smugglers and he is a casualty of it. From what you say it sounds like our enemies have not succeeded in identifying our involvement or that of your source, so all is well. I assure you, though, I will vigorously support both of you should this become open knowledge and charges result."

"Thank you, Captain. It's true I am not concerned for myself, but your support is like gold to me. Speaking of which, what do you want me to do with it, sir? It's not a huge fortune, but it is still a tidy little sum."

"Hmm, good question. I am puzzled as to the source of this. It seems odd this man would have had that much money, and gold in particular, on him. Well, regardless, I want no part of it. Normally this would by right become property of the Crown, but this feels like tainted money. Do as you see fit with it. Find some way to use it for our purposes and to good ends. Maybe help some of our informants that suffer in the course of helping us."

"Sir, I shall do so. Ah, if you would permit a question, sir?"

Nelson nodded so Evan continued. "I understand your mission to St. Kitts was a success?"

"Oh, of course, I apologize Mr. Ross. I have much on my mind, but I must remember to keep you abreast of developments. I did not have time to correspond with you while I was away. Yes, indeed, we caught the smuggler and the legitimate ship he was transferring cargo to with their pants down. There were several deserters among the crew of the American ship, including the now deceased Captain, which is why they were stupid enough to fight us. And condemning both ships as prizes in the St. Kitts prize court certainly caught everyone by surprise!"

Nelson laughed. "Yes, I know what you are thinking. Most people thought prize courts apply only in time of war, but that's not true. The practice is not to use them much, if at all, during time of peace. Well, I'm changing that. It took me a while, but I convinced the prize court judges I was right. They had to research it! That's what kept me on St. Kitts for so long."

To Evan's surprise Nelson paused to grin and wink at him. "Well, that, and a certain lady I've had my eye on. She lives on Nevis. You may find I'm spending more time over there, Mr. Ross. Anyway, there is an appeal outstanding, but I think we'll have that dealt with by the end of the month. So, you also mentioned in your report a vague reference to a book?"

"Yes, sir," said Evan, pulling the dead man's notebook from his pocket and handing it to Nelson. "I have not been able to decipher it, sir. It appears to be some kind of rudimentary cipher."

Nelson flipped through the pages intently, studying it closely. "Have you noticed some of these references appear to recur throughout, sir?"

"Yes, sir, but I don't know what to make of that."

"Hmm. Give some thought to the possibility this could relate to a shipping schedule. I am thinking perhaps these nonsensical names that recur refer to ships."

Evan was crestfallen not to have thought of it. Nelson saw the look on his face and gave him back the book. "I shall leave you to it."

***

Evan was still working on the notebook three days later when a knock came at the door to their house. He waved Alice into the bedroom and once she was hidden he opened the door. A well-dressed servant was waiting.

"Sir? I'm told Lieutenant Evan Ross is quartered here?"

"Yes, and I am he. Can I help you?"

The man handed him an envelope. "I am to carry your reply back with me."

Evan had to stop his jaw from dropping when he read the note. "I see. Ah, yes, please tell the lady I shall attend tomorrow at the specified time and offer my thanks for the invitation."

The servant nodded and left. Evan was still standing and rereading the note when Alice came out of hiding, a questioning look on her face. Wordlessly Evan handed her the note. Her face turned to stone as she read it.

"That bitch!" Alice looked up, ice in her eyes. "What are you going to do?"

Evan shrugged. "I replied I would be there. Look, I know how you feel about Elizabeth, but I have to go. There's something strange about this. A young society woman with a rich father wants to have tea with a lowly Lieutenant and one that's in the Navy to boot? Alice, the enemy has invited me into their camp and I'm a spy. I have to go."

Alice grimaced, but she nodded in agreement.

The next day Evan was back at the Roberts manor knocking on the door. The same servant that delivered the message answered.

Evan was apologetic. "I'm a little early, I'm afraid. I didn't want to be late and I made good speed getting here."

"I'll take you to the sitting room, sir."

As they walked down the hallway they heard male voices coming from a room they were about to pass. As they reached it Roberts and the French Captain Deschamps came through the doorway. Seeing Evan, they stopped in surprise. Evan instantly noticed the looks of consternation on their faces, although they swiftly disappeared as they mastered themselves. He also noticed the bag.

His couldn't stop his eye from being drawn to it. Roberts was holding a bag of the same shape and material as the one Evan had found on the dead overseer. And Roberts couldn't stop the jingle of many coins together as he tried his best to hide it out of sight behind his back. They all knew Evan had seen the bag.

The Frenchman was the first to recover. "Mr. Ross! This is an unexpected pleasure. What brings you here today?"

Evan smiled. "Sir, Mr. Robert's daughter sent me a kind invitation to have tea with her. How could I refuse?"

"Refuse an invitation from the prettiest woman on the island? That would be impossible! She makes me wish I was twenty years younger, sir."

"Hmm," said Roberts, a wary look on his face. "Yes, I was aware Mr. Ross was coming, but I think you are a bit early, sir."

"Yes, Mr. Roberts. I made better time than I thought I would. I apologize if there is any inconvenience. Mr. Deschamps, I have to confess I wasn't expecting to see you here either. I thought you and your colleague had left for Dominica."

The Frenchman's eyes narrowed slightly at Evan's knowledge of his destination, suspicion briefly forming on his face. "Ah, we did, sir, we did. My colleague is still there attending to business. I came back briefly to conduct, ah, some further business with Mr. Roberts here. We are keen to build support for what I was talking to you about some time back. But this was only a short call in port and I must take my leave."

Nodding to the two men, Evan made to leave. "Indeed. Well, I wish you good sailing, sir."

Evan followed the servant further down the hall and as he turned into the waiting room he glanced quickly back. The two men were still standing and watching him go. Neither was smiling.

A few minutes later Elizabeth and an old, white female servant soon joined him in the sitting room.

"Mr. Ross! How good of you to come. This is my chaperone Mary. She was my nurse when I was young. I thought we could go for a little walk about the grounds before tea?"

"An excellent idea, Miss Roberts."

"Please call me Elizabeth. And I shall call you Evan, sir."

Evan nodded and offered his arm as they began to stroll down the path. The gardens surrounding the manor were a well-maintained riot of colour. Flowers were everywhere. Red, white, and pink flowering bougainvillea plants abounded. Orchids with yellow flowers on top waved in the light breeze. Tall tamarind trees with brilliant red flowers provided much needed shade.

The talk was as before, light and of no consequence. Evan quizzed her on life on the plantation and he soon learned her days were comprised of an endless series of balls, riding, walks about the grounds, and occasionally attending church.

Evan soon realized she felt stifled and overly sheltered on the island, and was desperate for news of life in society in London. He was little help on the topic, having had no real experience of this kind of life so he turned to what he knew best. She was soon enthralled with his stories of life at sea. She found tales of the constant pranks the young midshipmen played on each other hilarious.

When they returned to the manor sitting room a large tray bearing tea and an array of tiny cakes and delicious chocolate cookies awaited. After politely sampling a few and sipping his tea Evan decided to try probing for her motives.

"Elizabeth, I must confess I was surprised to receive your invitation. Pleasantly, I assure you, but surprised nonetheless. Yes, I know what you said when we last met, but really, I am shocked your father is even permitting us to take tea. Am I missing something?"

An odd look stole over her face and Evan could see she was torn inside somehow. He had to wait a few long moments until a look of resolve came to her face.

"Yes, Mr. Ross, ah, I mean Evan. You are right that this perhaps is unusual. It comes from a conversation I had with my father because of what happened to Mr. Whyte."

Wary and alert, Evan couldn't keep from raising an eyebrow at mention of the dead overseer.

"He was such a dear, dear man and he was so good to me. He never had any children so he always treated me as if I was his own. My parents asked him to take the task of being my godfather. You really had to have known him as I did to get past that gruff exterior."

Evan was stunned by the contrast of what this woman's experience of the man was compared to what he had seen. "I see you have obviously felt his absence greatly. But what does this have to do with me, Elizabeth?"

"It made me think, Evan. I don't know why he has disappeared, but it has been yet one more thing to make everyone angry and suspicious. I don't like everyone around me being angry all the time. I don't like it when a man that was like a father to me simply disappears. So when I talked to my father about how unhappy I am he surprised me by bringing you up. I think he noticed I spent a lot of time with you at the ball, and to make me feel better he suggested I should invite you to tea. You, well, you seem— different, somehow. You make me laugh. You are not like all the other suitors and, yet, you are a man of influence. Captain Nelson obviously trusts you. "

"I find it interesting your father suggested this, Elizabeth."

She looked away as she sipped her tea and toyed with her napkin for a moment before looking back at him. "I know it was his suggestion, but I am happy he made it. You are an interesting man, Evan. I do like you, you know."

Evan was saved from replying by the opening of the door. Her father walked in and took a seat. "Well, I hope you two had a good stroll about the grounds and a pleasant chat. I thought I would join you for a few moments."

"Of course, sir. We are honoured."

"Actually, I would prefer to speak alone with Mr. Ross for a bit, my dear. I will come for you when we are done."

As Elizabeth closed the door behind her Roberts wasted no time in getting to the point. "Mr. Ross, I understand from a conversation with Captain Deschamps you have declined our offer. Why?"

"Ah, well, I guess it comes down to the Navy being my career and life choice, sir."

"Hmm, I wish you would reconsider. I think your potential is wasted in an organization as hide bound and stuck on antiquated rules as the Navy. Their thinking has not caught up with the times. A young man could make a fortune with the right friends in the right places. It would be far more than what a life in the Navy could bring you. And really, Mr. Ross, I am impressed, as are we all, with how you have adapted to the loss of your limb. But be truthful, please. Do you really think you will find a berth? What Captain will want a one armed officer?"

"I'm not afraid of challenges, Mr. Roberts."

"Exactly, which is why you should consider what I am saying. Really, life aboard a warship can't be pleasant. Long periods of deprivation from the finer things in life. And then there is the lack of women. Sir, following the path I am outlining for you would not be easy, either. It will be hard work. But the rewards will be there! Why, there is even my daughter to consider. She seems to like you, which is good, because she is dear to me. But we all know you are a mere Lieutenant right now. If you seek to win her you must do better, sir!"

Evan was almost speechless, but somehow he found his voice. "I shall give further thought to what you say, Mr. Roberts."

"I'm glad, sir. The future could be bright for you. Notice I said 'could be'. You may have heard talk of setting up an economic zone in this area to experiment with trade, sir. It's a brilliant idea and we shall be pushing hard to make this a reality. You'll be hearing more about this."

"I see. Well, this has been interesting, but I should go. Duty calls."

"Of course," said Roberts with a smile as he rose and made to leave. "I will send Elizabeth back in."

Roberts shook hands with Evan and left the room. Moments later Elizabeth reappeared

"My father tells me you must leave? So soon?"

"I have my duties to attend to."

"Well, I will see you to the door. You know, my father is excited about this notion of an economic free zone. Yes, I know about it! It's practically all he talks about. I hope he can find a way to make it work. Maybe he can with your help, Evan. Yes, I know he is seeking your help, too."

At the door she grasped his hand and wouldn't let go. Unexpectedly, she leaned up and kissed him on the cheek, still holding his hand. As before her breasts brushed his chest and she let them stay there for a long moment before pulling away.

"Thank you for coming, Evan. Please give thought to what my father said."

She gave his hand one last firm squeeze. Evan nodded and turned to leave.

***

Alice shook her head in contempt over the effort to manipulate Evan. "What did I tell you about these people, lover man? Damn, I can't decide who I hate more, my father or my half sister."

Evan gave her a hug and, grinning, let his hand slide all the way down her back to her bottom, grasping it firmly as he steered her toward the bedroom. "They had nothing to offer that interests me. You, on the other hand, well."

Three days later Evan was at his desk at home when he finally cracked the cipher in the notebook. Nelson was right; the nonsensical, repeating names in the book could be matched with ships. By scouring past records of dates ships came into port along with known locations of specific ships caught smuggling, he was able to decipher most of what the book contained. Two of the ships listed in the book belonged to Captains Deschamps and Jones, but only limited references to them were present and they were all old. Although he needed to test what he had learned, Evan was confident he had what he needed.

He was shocked at how many smugglers they had missed. Evan knew the Captain would be pleased with what he found, but true to his word Nelson was indeed over on St Kitts once again. Even better, though, the notebook listed ships and dates almost three months into the future. If Evan had indeed cracked the cipher, Nelson would be ecstatic to find he could be waiting to capture his foes this far in advance.

James walked in and sat down, throwing a newspaper on the table as he reached for a glass of water from the jug in front of Evan.

"Damn, it's getting warm out there. Well, there it is, as you thought it would be. There's a big article in the newspaper all about this economic zone and free trade. There's a long editorial on the same topic, too. Calling on the Governour to jump into bed with other Governours on islands like St. Kitts and basically tell London to get on board with the idea. So you think this frog and his gold is somehow behind all this?"

Evan shrugged and told James what he had found in the notebook.

James's eyes gleamed. "Maybe we can get the Captain to take us on another trip, Evan? I need to feel a deck under my feet again."

"That would be good, wouldn't it?" replied Evan with a conspiratorial grin. "Well, we shall see."

Chapter Fifteen
April 1785
Antigua

Nelson was indeed pleased at the news the notebook held promise. The news was timely as the Post Master reported the cipher the planters were using had changed for unknown reasons. Until they cracked it the mail would no longer be a source of intelligence.

The news of Evan's visit to the Robert's plantation was of even more interest. Nelson frowned in disgust on learning the planter was potentially accepting money from the Frenchman.

"Goddamn meddling frogs. If I had some way to ban the whole lot of them from this island I would be a much happier man."

He was also interested to learn Roberts had made another bid for Evan's loyalty. Nelson eyed Evan speculatively before leaning forward across the desk to speak.

"Well, Mr. Ross. Roberts is right about some things. Life in the Navy is lonely, isn't it? And it isn't likely to make you rich any time soon, if ever. It hasn't made *me* rich yet, that's for certain. Are you considering his offer seriously?"

"Sir. I am a Navy officer, sir. I still prefer the feel of a deck under my feet."

Nelson nodded and laughed. "Well, if that isn't a subtle hint it's time to offer you another little trip to enjoy catching a few smugglers again I don't know what would be."

***

Once again Evan and James were standing on the quarterdeck of the Boreas soaking in the joy of being on a warship at sea. Both men were silent, simply enjoying the moment.

But this was more than a little trip. Nelson decided to engage in a little deception of his own to ensure no one would warn off his target. Word was put about the Boreas was off to St. Kitts and on leaving harbour they sailed in the right general direction. They also left much earlier in the day. As soon as they were out of sight of land Nelson changed course to follow a leisurely route to the late evening drop location specified in the book on the far northern tip of Antigua.

This meant it would be a day of sailing for the sheer joy of it. The wind was cooperating, allowing the ship to sail at a brisk eight knots. Nelson came over from his side of the quarterdeck to join the two men.

"Lovely day for sailing, what?"

"Sir, it is," said Evan.

"Mr. Wilton, we have some time, sir. Tell me more about yourself, please."

James was a little surprised, but nodded. "Certainly, Captain. What would you like to know?"

The two men spent almost the next half hour talking. Evan soon realized he wasn't a part of the conversation so his mind drifted in and out of touch with their talk, simply enjoying where he was. But he felt the shift as he realized the conversation was ending and his mind snapped back to attention, as Nelson was about to leave.

Stepping back a little, Nelson stood with folded arms giving James an appraising look. "Well, Mr. Wilton, you are indeed a man of some experience. You are doing your father credit, sir."

"Thank you, Captain. That is my goal."

"Well, gentlemen, as much as I would dearly love to spend the day out here enjoying the sailing, my desk awaits. If I let it go too long it will be buried in a mountain of paperwork."

Nelson turned to his First Officer. "You have the deck, sir. I will come up an hour before we are due at our destination."

Once Nelson was gone Evan raised an eyebrow at James, who was watching the Captain depart and looking a little bemused. "What was that all about, James? I have to confess I didn't pay a lot of attention."

James shook his head. "I don't know. He kept asking me all these questions. At first it was about my career in the Navy, but then he started asking me questions about things like ship handling. Stuff like why holding the weather gage is important in a fight and what I would do if I found myself on a lee shore in the middle of a battle and the rest of the officers were killed or too injured to deal with it. It's a good thing I spent all that time as a master's mate or I wouldn't have been able to answer most of the stuff he asked about. It was almost like a test."

"Huh," grunted Evan. "Well, the fact he's interested in you can't be bad."

Four hours later the smuggler was exactly where they expected him to be at the appointed time, caught in the act with almost half the illegitimate cargo already on the beach. Nelson led the boarding party despite protests from his First Officer.

"Yes, I know this is your job, Lieutenant, but you can't have all the fun. Besides, I've done my penance in my cabin dealing with enough paperwork already today."

Nelson was the first up the side of the American ship, only to be closely surrounded by angry sailors on the deck all shouting at him to leave. Nelson saw a few held clubs and small axes, but no firearms.

"Get back, you oafs! Where is your Captain?"

One of the Americans stepped closer, nose-to-nose with Nelson. He was so angered he sprayed spittle as he responded. "Get off my damn ship! You have no right—"

Nelson grabbed the man by the collar with his left hand and, pulling him closer, kneed him hard in the groin. As the American crumpled moaning to the deck Nelson freed his left arm to elbow the first sailor coming to his Captain's aid in the face. The man fell to the deck spraying blood from a broken nose as Nelson pulled out his sword with his right hand and slashed at two other sailors coming for him. The razor sharp sword tip caught one of them on the arm as both men fell back in desperation. A fast growing stain of blood appeared between the sailor's fingers as he howled in pain.

"Right, who wants it next?" said Nelson, his sword at the ready.

Behind Nelson the harsh report of a gun turned everyone's heads. Nelson's Marine officer had gained the deck and, raising a second loaded gun, he pointed it at the crew as he lowered the other one he had already fired to catch their attention. "Stand down, you fools."

As the prize court appeal in St. Kitts had still not been settled Nelson decided to only confiscate the cargo and send the American ship away. Back on the Boreas Nelson was flushed from the action. Once they were underway again Nelson came over to see Evan and James.

"Well done once again, gentlemen," he said with a pleased grin. "Hopefully it will take them a while to realize we have knowledge of their schedule. And I will be eternally grateful if you can find more opportunities for me to see a little action instead of endless bloody paperwork!"

***

The next night the drums sounded yet again, setting the entire island on edge.

Evan and James headed for town early to delve into what was happening. Their first stop was the Governour's office where they were in time to learn yet more vicious beatings had yielded a translation of the message. Once again the meaning was revealed to be simple, telling only of more action to come soon.

Splitting up, James went in search of his potential informant while Evan questioned everyone he could as to the whereabouts of the Dutch ships. But both men came up empty.

Meeting later at the Flying Fish both men were frustrated and puzzled. They were almost the last ones in the tavern due to the lateness of the hour and both were tired.

"I don't get it, damn it all," said Evan. "I was sure we'd find those buggers from the Dutch ships here again."

"There was no reference to them being here in the notebook, Evan."

"I know, damn it. And you had no luck with finding your man, eh?"

James shook his head. "I scoured every joint and source I've got out there, Evan. He's gone to ground for some reason. I'll keep looking. No one seems to have any information on who is using these drums."

With most of their clients gone Emma and Walton were finally able to join them.

"So you two had no luck?" said Emma. Seeing both men shake their heads she continued. "Well, as before we've picked up a hint something is happening, but that's it. If I was a plantation owner I wouldn't be sleeping easy tonight."

"Well, we have little choice but to keep at it," said Evan with a sigh.

"Are we staying here tonight, Evan?"

Evan sighed. "No, I think we should get back to our quarters. I have a feeling the Captain may want to see me tomorrow morning. Well, you can stay if you want."

James opted to take a room for the night so he could be up and prowling for more information early. Paying the bill Evan said his goodbyes to the others as they lingered over the last of their drinks.

"Don't get up, I'll see myself out the back."

The moonlight Evan needed to find his way to the stables out back saved him. A faint rustle from a nearby bush was enough to make him slow his pace and, as he did, a male voice came out of the darkness.

"Lieutenant?"

Evan turned to face whoever had called out as a glint of light striking the steel of a blade in motion caught his eye. In desperation Evan threw himself to one side and stumbled to the ground. The blade whistled past him hard in a downward stroke, barely missing his left shoulder. If he still had a left arm to lose it would be gone.

Rolling desperately to his feet Evan shouted inarticulately at his attacker. "Bastard!"

Evan had to dodge quickly again, this time to avoid a straight on, forward thrust coming at his chest. He had no time to wonder at why he was being attacked; all he knew was the need to survive. But his opponent momentarily lost his balance with the forward thrust, displaying his lack of training in swordplay. The opportunity was all Evan needed.

Evan fell away and to the side, trying to be a moving target, as he finally got his own sword out. Evan knew endless practice in the navy cutlass drill would serve him well. The two men's blades met and clashed several times, the dim light of the moon making their efforts ever more difficult and desperate.

Distant, alarmed voices were coming closer and Evan could sense his opponent wavering, realizing he had failed in his task. Evan seized the advantage, pressing the man hard. His assailant finally broke and tried to run, but he chose his time poorly. Evan had intended only to wound the man, hoping to take him prisoner and find out why he was attacking him. Instead, his assailant went in an unexpected direction and grunted in sudden shock as he ran right onto Evan's thrust, crashing instantly to the ground.

Two lanterns appearing at the back entrance to the Inn lit the scene as the man fell. James was in the lead, waving his drawn blade about in search of a foe. Walton was right behind him with a vicious looking machete in one hand and a lantern in the other, ready for anything. Emma held the other lantern. When they realized the only assailant was already down, they turned as one to Evan. He was breathing hard from the exertion, adrenalin coursing through his system.

"Christ, Evan!" said Walton. "Are you all right? What the hell happened?"

After several deep breaths to slow his breathing Evan finally pointed with his blade at the body on the ground. "I'm okay, only winded. This bugger tried to kill me. I got lucky and saw him coming before he succeeded."

James bent down to check the man, but he knew what he would find. "Well, you got him before he got you. He's stone dead, Evan."

"Search him, James. Christ, I think I'm still in shock."

As if she had read his mind Emma appeared at his side, a mug of heavy rum in her hand. As the fiery liquor coursed down his throat Evan gagged a moment before taking a second deep draught.

"Ah, that's better. You're an angel, Emma. So who is this fool, anyway? Has he any papers on him?"

"No," said James. "He hasn't much actually. A few coins in his wallet and that's it."

"I recognize him, Evan," said Emma. "He's French."

"French! Are you joking?" said Evan, going cold at the implications.

"At a time like this? No!" said Emma. "I'm telling you, I've seen him several times before. This bastard has been a customer here. He's one of the men off those Dutch ships that come in here. Or at least, he's in here all the time with sailors from those ships. And, he has a French accent."

"Damn it, this is getting stranger and stranger. I tell you, I scoured the port for word of those ships being docked anywhere on the island. If they are around they are in hiding."

"Sir?" said James. "I know you were thinking about going back tonight, but I think a change in plans would be a good idea. I suggest we both stay here."

Evan could only nod agreement.

"Mr. Ross? What do you want to do with him? Shall I find a deserted spot for him too?"

"No," replied Evan, after pausing a moment to consider what to do. "Call the watch. Sorry, I know this is going to make it a long night, but we need this to be public. The next time those goddamn Dutch ships show up here we're going to have some questions for them and they'd better have answers."

As he finished speaking the far distant sound of the ominous drums throbbed once again in the night.

***

Evan didn't have long to wait to ask his questions. At first light the Dutch ship captained by the American Nathan Jones tied up, but the second ship captained by the Frenchman Deschamps was nowhere to be found. Evan was all for heading straight for him, but the town was in an uproar once again and a Marine from Nelson's ship came to find Evan.

"Orders, sir. Captain Nelson thought you might be here and desires you join him immediately at the Governour's office. There is a meeting about to start."

By the time Evan arrived a large group of planters were crowded in with the Governour and Nelson was already facing the brunt of the planter's collective anger, demanding the Navy focus on more important tasks like weapon smuggling. Another attack had taken place the night before and this time the target was the Robert's plantation. Roberts and his men were alert and prepared. Still, one of his men was killed by a shot from a musket and two men were wounded with grazes from pistols. Three attackers were killed in a trap Roberts had prepared, but they thought more had been injured before escaping. The three dead men turned out to be young, runaway slaves.

Evan added more fuel to the maelstrom of anger by revealing what had happened to him. As he finished explaining what happened the Governour held up a hand to forestall more angry outbursts from the planters and looked at Evan.

"Sir, are you aware of any reason why this man would try to kill you?"

"No, sir. It's possible I may have seen this individual around town or at the Flying Fish on occasion, but I'm quite certain we have not been introduced."

"Spend a lot of time at the Flying Fish, do you, Mr. Ross?" said Roberts.

Nelson stepped into the conversation. "Mr. Ross is about town frequently on business related to the Dockyard and on tasks I provide to him, sir. I don't know why this has happened any more than the rest of you, but if it involves a Frenchman I want to know what he was up to."

"Maybe he was a deserter and was trying to rob Mr. Ross?" said another of the planters.

"Perhaps," said Nelson. "But the attacker seemed to know Mr. Ross. I am concerned the attacker wanted to confirm who he was before trying to kill him. That would make this a planned attack on one of my officers. I want to know why."

"Well, whatever this is all about I don't see a link of any sort to the attack on Mr. Roberts and his people," said the Governour.

"Gentlemen, this is all speculation at this point," said Nelson to the group.

Nelson turned to Evan. "Mr. Ross, I don't think your presence will be necessary for the rest of this meeting. Lieutenant Wolf here and the two Marines you saw outside came with me as protection. I suggest you take Lieutenant Wolf as a witness and go question this American captain. If nothing else he needs to decide what he wants done with the body, if the attacker was indeed one of his men. I expect I shall be here a while, so report back here."

Evan looked over at Lieutenant Wolf and both men rose. Saluting, they turned and left as one.

Minutes later they were at the port requesting permission to see Captain Jones. He came down the gangway to the dock and looked quizzically at the two officers.

"Gentlemen? You asked to see me? Mr. Ross, I really am only here for water this time. I do hope you don't think I'm smuggling or something. We're not doing any trading and I expect to be away shortly."

The man's face grew grim and turned to stone as Evan explained what had happened.

"So I am hoping for a few answers, Captain Jones. If you could join us at the local militia station morgue to confirm his identity that would be a start."

The Captain nodded. "Sir, lead on. I fear I know who this is."

"Do you now? Well, you can tell us more as we walk to the morgue."

The three men turned and left the port to walk the few short blocks to where the dead man waited.

"Mr. Ross, I believe this may be Francois Vachon. He was a sailor on my ship. The last time we were in port we couldn't find him when it was time to depart. He was not happy with me, I'm afraid. He was not trustworthy. Some of the others on the crew had accused him of stealing from them and you know how serious an offence that is to sailors. We don't often have to resort to flogging on a trading ship, but I had no choice. They would have killed him had I not made him pay the price."

"I see, Captain. So why do you think he would pick me as a victim?"

The American shrugged as they reached the morgue. "I have no idea, sir. Perhaps you were in the wrong place at the wrong time."

"Indeed. And why do you think he would have tried to confirm who I was before striking at me?"

"Sir, I have no idea."

As the three men waited to be escorted to see the body, Evan turned and looked the American in the eye.

"Well, Captain, I'm sure you can forgive me for saying this, but my initial thinking was quite the opposite. I think he was waiting for me in particular and he wanted to make sure it was me, and only me, he was going to kill."

The American looked away briefly before responding. "Sir, I am at a loss to explain that. It may be he recognized you. Perhaps he thought that you being an officer you might have more coins on your person than others."

Evan gave a noncommittal grunt, but was prevented from further comment as they were led down the stairs into the morgue proper. The room was windowless and cool, being below ground. Even so, the body of the dead man was already decomposing and the smell was strong.

"If we could get an identification quickly, please, gentlemen. This man needs burial rather soon," said the morgue attendant as he lifted the sheet covering the dead man's face.

The American Captain stepped forward for a close look before stepping back with a sigh. He turned to Evan and nodded. "Yes, that is Francois. I wish it were otherwise."

Turning to the morgue attendant the American pulled out a coin purse and withdrew a small handful of coins. "I would like to leave some funds to ensure he receives a decent burial. Will this do?"

From the sudden light of greed in the eyes of the attendant Evan knew the sum would serve. "Quite, sir. That will guarantee everything you could want for this man."

"Thank you. Well, I should return to my ship as we must be on our way soon."

The morgue attendant began pulling the sheet back up over the dead man, but Evan held out a hand to stop him.

"Sorry, there is one more thing. Please pull the sheet down. I want to look at this man's back."

The attendant looked puzzled, but did as he was told. Together Evan and the attendant shifted the dead man onto his side. The man did indeed have the tell tale scars of the lash on his back, but they were old and long since healed. Evan nodded and they shifted him onto his back again. As the attendant finally covered the dead man with the sheet Evan turned to the American captain, who was simmering with obvious anger.

"Was that necessary, sir?" rasped the American.

"It was. This man tried to murder me and I want to be certain of the facts. You claim to have flogged him, but those scars are quite old."

The American shrugged in anger. "So it was a long time ago. So what?"

"Sir, are you telling me a man that angry with you would wait that long to make his move, and somehow in the meantime he wouldn't give further cause for discipline? Forgive me, but I know what sailors are like as well as you. I find this difficult to believe, sir."

"Well, you can believe what you like. Look, he was one of the quiet ones that hold a grudge. I couldn't read the damn man's mind. See here, I've had enough of this place so I'm going back to my ship. We will be away before the day is out. We won't be coming back to this island for some time. Good day, sirs."

Turning, the American Captain stalked out of the room. Evan was still frowning at the door where the American had departed as Lieutenant Wolf finally spoke up.

"Mr. Ross? This place stinks. Let's get out of here."

Chapter Sixteen
May/June 1785
Antigua, St. Kitts, and Barbados

Nelson won the appeal in the prize court on
St. Kitts in early May. With this in his pocket he
immediately seized an American ship docked in the
Basseterre harbour, the Eclipse out of Philadelphia,
and sent it to the prize court. The ship was legally
registered on St. Kitts by one of the planters, but
Nelson found proof the crew was all American.

Sailing for Antigua the next day he put word
out his policy would henceforth be different. A
summary of the case result was prepared and added to
a direct message smuggler ships would be seized
without exception or recourse henceforth. Distributed
through Antigua by the newspaper and by posters in
St. John's, word spread like a brush fire with a devil
in charge of the wind to fan it. Worried looks on the
faces of ship owners, businessmen, and plantation
owners told of their sudden fear of what this would
mean. Many knew of the prize court case on St. Kitts,
but dismissed it as of no concern on the assumption
they would win the appeal.

The depth of fear and anger over the change
made sitting at the Flying Fish four days later a less
than pleasant experience. Several dark looks from
those who knew who he was were sent in Evan's
direction. Fewer people knew who James was, but by
sitting at the same table as Evan he felt the anger too.

"Maybe we should lay low for a while, Evan,"
said James, glancing about the room. "There doesn't
seem to be a lot of happy people in here."

"Hmm, you may be right, but we cannot lay
low for long. Now that the Captain has his court

ruling I'm pretty sure he will want to press his advantage. On the other hand, I don't know how much we will be seeing of him. He sailed back to St. Kitts again yesterday."

James's eyebrows rose. "Again? He's only been back for three or four days. What, does he have better pickings over there or something?"

Evan grinned. "For the moment I think the answer is yes on a couple of fronts. You know that Yankee ship he seized right before he came back? He told me they found paperwork on it indicating there are more shipments coming right after it. This is all rather convenient for the Captain because romance seems to be in blossom over there. Remember I told you he'd taken a fancy to some woman living on Nevis? Her name is Fanny Nisbet. The Captain gets rather starry eyed when he talks about her."

This time James was amused. "Starry eyed? The Captain? Are we talking about the same person?"

"We are," said Evan, still smiling.

"Huh, well, I don't know about getting attached to one woman. That wouldn't work real well with life in the Navy, now would it? I prefer keeping my attachments brief. But then, what about you, if you don't mind my asking? It's been two months since Alice moved in. Looks to me like she's practically building a nest. Not that it's any of my business, of course."

Evan shrugged and toyed with his mug of ale. "Yes, I've noticed that. I don't know."

"You think we'll ever get a ship, Evan? If we do, that'll be an end to it, won't it?"

"Well, sure. We're getting the job done for the Captain. I have a feeling he's going to be a good patron for both of us if we can just keep it up. We only have to keep getting it done and he'll find something for us. Sooner or later his posting here will end and maybe he'll take us back with him."

Evan paused a moment and looked thoughtfully at James. "And yes, I'll have to sort out what I'm going to do about Alice sooner or later. I'm not sure she's entirely safe yet. That bastard Roberts made a point of commenting on how much time I spend in this place. That means he may have someone watching us here now. If I bring her back here and spend more time hanging around her, word of that may work its way back to him and he may make the connection. On the other hand, we didn't really advertise the fact she moved out of the Flying Fish and in with me, but if Roberts somehow finds out we may have a problem."

James grunted. "So what will you do?"

"I don't know. Well, I have time. She's been good to me and I'll sort this out one way or another."

***

Word of Nelson's actions on St. Kitts over the next two weeks sent owners on Antigua into a frenzy of anger. The American ship owners in particular were incensed. Facing them in his office Governour Shirley groaned inwardly, as he knew they weren't going to be happy.

Using the intelligence gained from the captured ship in concert with Captain Sands on HMS Latona and Captain Collins on HMS Rattler they seized four American ships trying to smuggle their goods onto St. Kitts. All four ships were brought to the prize court for disposal.

"This is our livelihood, sir!" screeched one of American owners, as a large, angry group of other ship and plantation owners crowded behind him in the meeting. "What are you going to do about this?"

"I completely understand, sir. As you know I have been making ongoing representations to both London and to Admiral Hughes in Barbados. I shall continue to do so and, believe me, I shall ensure everyone is aware of your dire situation."

"Not good enough, sir! Damn it, this has gone on long enough. You'll be hearing from us."

Turning, he stalked out the doors with the others scowling and following close behind. The Governour sighed as he watched them go, while reaching for paper and a quill pen to write yet another letter.

***

Two weeks later Nelson returned, but Evan waited two more days before Nelson sent word to attend him.

He was with the Captain going over a status report on construction in the Dockyard when the Americans made their move. The Boreas was tied up at the main dock with a gangplank down to the shore so access to the ship was easier. Being so close they were able to hear the sound of several angry voices coming closer and closer. Nelson looked up and frowned at the sound, but made no move to check on what was happening.

"My First Officer will let us know if we are needed, Mr. Ross."

They were indeed needed. A muffled and obviously heated conversation on the dock ensued and a few minutes later a knock finally came on the cabin door. The First Officer Wilkins was admitted, holding an envelope in his hand and wearing a flushed, angry look on his face.

"Captain. I don't know what's in this envelope, but I don't think you're going to like it, sir."

Nelson raised an eyebrow, as his First Officer was not normally a man to show emotions. Waving Lieutenant Wilkins into a chair Nelson took the proffered envelope from his hand and began reading.

The explosion of anger wasn't long in coming. "God Almighty! The gall of these audacious bastards!"

As fast as the fury had come, it disappeared by the time he finished reading the envelope's contents. Nelson stood and paced over to the stern windows to stare into the distance for a long few moments while the two officers looked at each other in wonder. Finally he returned to his desk and slumped back into his chair, still wearing a distracted look and staring hard at the letter in front of him. Evan could stand it no longer.

"Captain? Is there anything we can help you with, sir?"

Nelson looked up, almost startled, before he took a deep breath and sat back in his chair. For the briefest instant Evan thought he saw the look of a trapped animal cross Nelson's face. "Help? I appreciate it, but I fear this will require more help than either of you gentlemen can offer. Mr. Ross, these greedy Americans are suing me, sir! It's outrageous, bloody outrageous!"

The two officers were shocked, but a look of sudden realization crossed the face of Nelson's First Officer.

"Oh my word, that explains it! Captain, there's a crowd of bailiffs outside in the Dockyard. Their leader said he was here to arrest you, but he didn't say why. I tried everything to get him to explain, but all he said was for you to read the message in the envelope."

"A crowd of bailiffs? In the Dockyard, sir?" snarled Evan. "Who in God's name let them in?"

"Ah, your Lieutenant Long was with them, Mr. Ross. I presume he was there to show them where to find the Captain. He didn't explain himself."

His face blazing with wrath, Evan made to stand up, but Nelson waved him back to his seat.

"Well, gentlemen. The envelope contains a message that is actually a warrant for my arrest. The Americans have banded together and are suing me for forty thousand pounds. Because of the great sum they are pressing me for they convinced some fool of a judge I would be a risk for flight, hence they want me to rot in jail until the court hears the suit."

The two officers faces dropped in open alarm when Nelson mentioned the sum involved. Forty thousand pounds was a staggering sum of money. Even a tenth of the amount would be enough for a man to live comfortably on for a long time.

"Sir?" said Evan, his shock evident in the hushed tone of his voice. "What will you do?"

"Fight back, of course. For starters, you are going to send these fools packing from the Dockyard. Ask Lieutenant Wolf for a file of Marines to back you up. Then I'm afraid it will be back to work at my desk for me. I have yet more letters to write. They will have to support me. It's that simple. I suppose I should have expected these arrogant fools to try something like this. No matter, gentlemen. We shall prevail. You are dismissed."

Evan was still steaming as he walked down the gangplank to the dock with the Marine Lieutenant Wolf and another half dozen Marines in tow. A crowd of no less than seven bailiffs were milling about, held back only by the two Marines standing guard at the foot. Lieutenant Burns was with Lieutenant Long and both men were standing off to one side watching for developments.

As soon as Evan stepped past the guard on the dock the crowd surged forward and their leader came to stand nose-to-nose with him.

"Where is Captain Nelson, sir? We haven't got all day. We have a legal warrant for his arrest. I demand—"

Evan grabbed him hard by the throat, choking off the rest of the sentence. The man reached up trying to claw Evan's hand off his throat unsuccessfully.

"If you don't back off the only thing you'll be demanding is help for your broken face, you arsehole," hissed Evan as he roughly shoved the man backwards, letting go of his throat as he did.

The bailiff stumbled back, grabbed as he hit the ground by his supporters. Rubbing his throat and coughing, he got to his feet and glared at Evan.

"Look, we're merely doing our job. We have a warrant to arrest the Captain—"

"I don't care if you have a magic wand that makes you a fairy princess, you fucking idiot! You are not authorized to be on Navy property. Get the hell out of the Dockyard, all of you. Now, sir."

"We have a legal right to bring this man to justice, I tell you. Your Dockyard Lieutenant let us in here! I—"

"Lieutenant Wolf, I think we've heard enough of this shit, don't you?"

"Absolutely," said Wolf, his best parade ground voice bringing fear to the bailiff's faces.

"Marines, to the front. Show these damn fools the way out."

The bailiffs fell back in a stumbling shambles as the file of Marines stepped forward, weapons at the ready as they began shoving their foes backwards even further.

"All right, all right, we're going!" said the leader. "But your Captain Nelson had better be on the lookout. If we catch him we will do our duty. Let's go, men."

"Lieutenant Ross, my men and I shall escort them out. I think we will have to beef up the guard on the Dockyard henceforth. I wouldn't put it past this lot to try anything."

Evan watched them leave for a few moments to assure himself no further problems were coming, before stalking over to the two Dockyard Lieutenants. He was too overwhelmed with anger to do anything other than let the ice of his wrath show through his eyes for a few moments before he finally spoke.

"What in heaven's name were you thinking, you fools?"

The two men looked at each other, before Lieutenant Long responded with a puzzled look on his face. "Sir? Uh, they had a legal warrant, sir. It seemed best to let them in so the Captain could deal with it."

"Yes, Mr. Ross, Mr. Long here asked me about it and we both agreed it would be best."

Evan stared at the two men in disgust, shaking his head. "Lord, I am beginning to understand why Captain Moutray was at his wits end with you two idiots. This is Navy property! They have a civilian warrant. It has no weight, no weight at all, on Navy property. Do you hear me? I don't give a damn if someone shows up with a circus marching band at the entrance to the Dockyard in future, gentlemen. If they don't have approved Navy business to be here you bloody don't let them in! Is that clear?"

The two officers both nodded, although from the look on their faces Evan wasn't sure they agreed with a word of what he had said.

"Christ! Get out of my sight, both of you," said Evan in disgust.

***

Evan soon realized Lieutenant Wolf was right; the extra guard on the Dockyard was indeed necessary. The Americans weren't at all happy the attempt to arrest Nelson was rebuffed and demanded continuous efforts to fulfill the warrant. The bailiffs took to showing up at odd times hoping to catch the Captain in an unguarded moment. When this didn't work they settled into a haphazard pattern of simply waiting, in hiding or otherwise, outside the Dockyard for random periods. Nelson became a prisoner on his own ship.

A storm of correspondence between Nelson, the Admiralty in England, Governour Shirley, Antiguan businessmen, plantation owners, and Admiral Hughes in Barbados was soon flying back and forth.

***

Admiral Hughes was in a good mood until he walked into his stern cabin and saw the huge pile of letters sitting on his desk.

"Oh, not again!" Wheeling about, he sent for his Flag Lieutenant, who soon appeared in the Admiral's door and saluted.

"Perkins! Please tell me this isn't what I think it is."

Lieutenant Perkins looked apologetic and shook his head. "I'm sorry, Admiral. All of that is from the mail packet that came in from Antigua."

The Admiral groaned, staring at the pile as he walked around his desk and slumped into his chair. "Now what has he done? Damn it all. The man has no diplomatic skills. All right, Perkins, have some tea brought to me. I'll be having at this for a while."

"At once, Admiral. Ah, sir? I don't want to ruin your day any further, but another mail packet has come into harbour in the last hour. I think this one is from England."

"So I'll have even more to deal with, will I? You're full of good news today. Next it will be a plague of poisonous toads infesting the ships or something."

"Sir?"

"Just get on with it, Mr. Perkins."

Almost an hour later Hughes had worked his way through most of the letters and the situation was clear. As before, everyone was outraged and demanding Hughes do something. The Americans were particularly incensed. Making it clear the lawsuit was against Nelson for the moment, the threat was they would widen the scope to include Hughes if he didn't support them. The Admiral was rubbing his chin in deep thought and considering whether to take another shot at the legal approach when Perkins knocked on his door.

Mercifully, the pile of correspondence in his hands was considerably smaller than the pile Hughes had already worked his way through. The Admiral sighed nonetheless.

"Better have some more tea brought, Mr. Perkins."

Sorting through it quickly Hughes soon identified what could wait and what needed his immediate attention. As always, correspondence from the Admiralty topped the pile to read first. Most of it turned out to be the usual instructions associated with running a complex, far flung operation like the Royal Navy. But one thin, personal note from the First Lord of the Admiralty to Hughes was what turned the Admirals' day from being merely bad to a disaster.

The Admiral's face fell in dismay and he groaned loudly as he digested the contents. "No! Damn it all, no!"

As the Admiral spoke his servant was bringing the fresh tea in and the man stopped, frozen with concern he had done something wrong.

"Sir?"

"Oh, for Christ's sake, put it down and get out!"

The Admiral sat back in his chair in frustration, staring at the letter from the First Lord. Any choice in how to deal with the matter was gone.

The First Lord's letter directly ordered Hughes to support Nelson in his efforts to stamp out smuggling at all costs and made it clear any failure on the Admiral's part to fulfill his orders would result in serious consequences for the Admiral and his career.

Sitting forward and reaching for paper and quill pen the Admiral reluctantly got down to business.

***

Early June had arrived by the time word of it all reached Nelson. Nelson was gratified the Admiralty had stepped in to reaffirm support for him. A separate letter from the First Lord to Nelson made it clear what he was expecting of Hughes.

"That's good news, sir," said Evan after Nelson stopped by Evan's office in the Dockyard on his way to St. John's and told him what had happened. "Perhaps this will turn the tide once and for all."

"I hope so, Lieutenant. I think this is the result of Captain Moutray advocating on my behalf with the Admiralty and the Government. I must remember to write and thank him for his efforts. I'm not sure it will make these damn Americans and their lawsuit go away, but perhaps if Admiral Hughes and the Governour are forceful enough the Americans will reconsider. I think all we have want of is the spine to stand up to this nonsense. So, you sent a note you have more intelligence for me, sir?"

Evan handed him an envelope. "I do, Captain. This is in addition to the three coming this month that we know of courtesy of the notebook. Perhaps these were shipments added because of our seizures? In any case, we have word of a possible single shipment to be dropped off on Barbuda. It would make sense, I suppose; there are only so many places where a ship can moor and cargo can be offloaded with ease. There is also another coming into St. Kitts. My report contains all of the details, sir."

Nelson studied the contents for a few moments before looking up. "Captain Sands can deal with the drop on Barbuda while I make St. Kitts my next destination. Hmm, I'll be back from St. John's in time to leave at nightfall. Sail into Basseterre Harbour first thing in the morning and see what I find."

Evan smiled. "I'm sure there'll be something, sir."

***

Nelson was a caged lion.

Sailing into Basseterre Harbour at first light brought success as he caught three ships all madly trying to offload their cargo and depart. His First Officer dealt with it all and returned to report, pleased with his success, but his smile melted away when he gained the quarterdeck. Nelson was standing looking shoreward, scowling and breathing hard, opening and closing his hands in mute frustration and rage.

"Captain? Is something amiss?"

"Nothing you have done, sir. It's them," Nelson replied, pointing to the shore. A crowd of armed bailiffs stood in the shade of a building patiently watching the Boreas.

"I sent the Third Officer over to question them while you were busy, Mr. Wilkins. Apparently these goddamn Yankees, curse them, have made their warrant effective on all of our islands and that means I can no longer visit Mrs. Nisbet on Nevis. I shall not subject the people I want to visit to a scene involving that lot chasing me about. Damn them!"

***

In the days following a firestorm of correspondence continued to fly about between everyone involved, fanned by over a half dozen more successful seizures by Nelson. At the heart of the storm was the letter from Admiral Hughes acknowledging his orders, which proved to be a masterly display of obfuscation. While it started with promise and his support was alluded to, on reading further the picture became murky. The Admiral's support was hedged with a host of qualifications and nuances, and by the time everyone reading the letter reached the end they had the beginnings of a headache from trying to understand exactly where the man stood. Everyone involved received the same confusing, waffling response so in the end nothing changed. The Governour chose to remain neutral and any public support from him was tepid at best. As a result, everyone around him saw Nelson was increasingly unhappy and angry.

But in yet another meeting with Nelson toward the end of June Evan sensed a change in the Captain as they met once again.

"Captain, it's not my place to comment perhaps, but you seem in a much improved frame of mind today. Have we good news, sir?"

"Good news? Well, we shall see. I had not realized my frustration was that obvious. Yes, I suppose I have been out of sorts. This damn lawsuit and being cooped up like a prisoner on my own ship has been more than a little wearing of my patience. And with hurricane season fast approaching the thought of being confined in English Harbour until October is appalling. Mr. Ross, it is truly galling to finally find someone to perhaps share my life with and I am reduced to communicating with her only on paper!"

Nelson paused for effect and smiled, a twinkle of mischief lighting his eyes. "But I am resolved on my course, sir. I had to think long and hard about the possible consequences, but there is no other way. Fortune favours the bold, sir, and I am nothing if not that! Seize the initiative and press your enemies hard, Mr. Ross. That is the key."

"Well, you know I like that approach, sir. So what will you do, if I may ask?"

Nelson grinned. "The die is already cast, Mr. Ross. I need the full legal support of the Crown to beat this frivolous lawsuit down. I don't have the resources to pay an army of paper pushing lawyers and even if I did, I don't see why I should be the one paying them. I am acting on the King's business. So if I can't get help from my Admiral I will find it elsewhere."

He paused a moment to smile. "I have written directly to the King, sir."

Chapter Seventeen
August 1785
Antigua

The number of seizures was dropping fast. The deliveries detailed in the notebook ceased to have any relevance. Nelson organized his resources to have one or more of his ships at each of the locations listed, but after the third time no one appeared Evan knew something had changed.

At first Evan was concerned at the sharp decline, but a visit to the Customs office told the story. The numbers of legitimate British trading ships with British crews working in the port had increased dramatically. The plantation owners and local businessmen still weren't happy, but it seemed clear Nelson's strategy was working. They all still needed the supplies to keep their operations afloat. The ship seizures were what made the difference; people could afford the loss of confiscated cargo, but risking loss of a valuable ship was too much.

Oddly, the drums too were silent.

"What do you think, Evan?" said James as they puzzled over it one night.

"I don't know. We're at the start of hurricane season now so I doubt we'll see action. Who would be crazy enough to smuggle arms this time of year? But I confess I don't know why we've had such a large gap since the last time. Maybe they've decided to lay low?"

"Maybe they've gone for a larger load to drop? Those weapons the owners seized after the last attack weren't French made, Evan. The militia officer told me they were American made and we are dealing a Yankee Captain, after all."

"Well, you're just full of cheerful thoughts. I hadn't considered that possibility. Yes, it would take them time to sail to all the way to Boston or wherever and back, wouldn't it? Let's hope you are wrong."

***

Word of another possible smuggling drop came from local intelligence and once again Evan was concerned when Nelson's ship sailed word of this would be passed onward to the smugglers. The opportunity to catch the spy red-handed had not been there before, but Evan was determined to put a stop to it once and for all. As the interception was to be shortly after nightfall the late evening dusk was upon them by the time Nelson departed, a perfect time for Evan and James to hide and watch outside the Dockyard.

Soon enough the clerk from the Dockyard made his appearance and this time he went to the pigeon handler's home. Evan and James followed him to the door and, peering in the window unobserved, they saw the man give the pigeon handler a note. With pigeon in hand the man began tying the note to its leg, but before he could complete the task the two men burst in with swords drawn.

"What do you mean barging in here? You can't do that!" said the angry pigeon owner.

Evan kept his sword pointed at the man as James walked over and grabbed the bird from his hands. Pulling the message off the bird and opening it, James took a few moments to read it before smiling and showing it to Evan. When he finished reading it Evan looked hard at the man.

"This sword says I can indeed barge in here, fool. And this little message says you are both complicit in spying on the Navy contrary to the King's interests. You are both under arrest."

The next morning Evan was sitting in his office at the Dockyard with Lieutenants Long and Burns in front of him.

"So you two are telling me you had nothing to do with any of this, eh? The clerk was quite adamant he was delivering the note on your orders."

The two men looked at each other before Lieutenant Burns looked back at Evan and responded. "Sir, I think this man is desperate. He is making things up to save himself."

"I see. Well, gentlemen, you are on notice. I do not have direct proof of your involvement. The note made no mention of either of you. I have no reason to believe this man, but I have no reason to disbelieve him either. It will be up to you to ensure I don't start to believe him, because if I do the consequences will be grave. Very grave. You are dismissed."

Evan was dismayed at being unable to pin either of them down. He had pressed them hard, but both were either well practiced liars or they really were innocent. Evan vowed they would not escape him whenever the next opportunity came.

***

Nelson was standing and staring outside his stern windows once again. The oppressive heat of English Harbour in early August made him feel sluggish. With no response to his plea for help from the King the wait was becoming an ever heavier, constant burden on his mind. Should the King turn down his request for legal help he would be ruined, as he simply didn't have the resources to pay the lawyers. Worse, if the King felt his approach unseemly the damage to his career would be lasting. He would never receive another ship and may as well resign his commission.

But he could see a bundle of letters from the mail packet ship recently arrived was already on its way to him. Soon enough, a knock sounded on his door. His First Officer entered and saluted as he left the bundle on the Captain's desk. Nelson dismissed him and stared at the bundle for a moment, before settling into his chair. He sorted and organized the pile quickly. In the midst of the usual quantity of personal correspondence and letters from the Admiralty was a thin envelope bearing the Royal seal.

Nelson shoved the rest to the side and took a deep breath as he opened it. The envelope held only one page and it took only moments to read.

"Yes!" shouted Nelson, hammering his fist hard on his desk. Reaching for the various letters from the Admiralty he quickly opened and scanned their contents. Filled with new energy he couldn't contain he stood and called for his First Officer. Nelson was pacing back and forth in deep thought when Lieutenant Wilkins came in.

"Sir?"

Nelson couldn't keep the feral grin off his face. "Ah, Mr. Wilkins. Have Lieutenant Wolf and a party of Marines readied to escort me into St. John's. It's time to have at our foes once again, sir!"

***

A week later the heat in the courtroom in St. John's was stifling.

Nelson's first action was to ensure everyone was aware of the contents of the letter, but Admiral Hughes and the Governour had received copies direct from the King. Although they could see it for themselves, Nelson made certain they understood he would use it with maximum effect and his message was clear. He wanted to see full support for his efforts or they would face the consequences.

The letter from the King emphasized he wanted the full resources of the Crown brought to bear to crush the lawsuit. The lead Crown Counsel in Antigua had taken the message to heart. He brought his entire legal team to the fight and the lone lawyer with his one assistant for the penny-pinching Americans was no match. The legal arguments the Crown lawyers trotted out were as stifling as the air in the room, while Nelson's testimony was the coup de grace.

The legal community in St. John's was small and everyone knew everyone else. The judge knew the King had written in support of Nelson. Nelson's presence in the courtroom was commanding, as he gripped them all with his testimony. The mountain of factual evidence he presented in support of his case sealed the fate of the Americans. The judge quibbled over a few points of legal minutiae, but he ruled quickly in favour of Nelson.

The Americans were disgruntled and publicly vowed to appeal. They also threatened further diplomatic complaints, but they had lost and they knew the likelihood of overturning the decision was nonexistent.

The judge also rescinded the order for Nelson's arrest. Nelson walked out of the courtroom and smiled. Freedom was indeed sweet.

***

That night the drums beat several times yet again, haphazardly and for various lengths of time. Everyone on the island was on edge.

Evan worked at his desk in the Dockyard all day, waiting for word of developments. A messenger from the Governour came to report none of the plantations were attacked in the night, which made Evan furrow his brows in puzzlement. But the same message of retribution was all the drums spoke of and given the sheer volume of activity it seemed certain something big was afoot. James was already in town, having gone the day before to trawl for information, so Evan waited on edge hoping he would learn more.

The wait ended abruptly toward the end of the day when James himself rushed into his office, shutting the door behind him. Evan raised an eyebrow and made to speak, but James thrust a piece of paper in front of him.

"Evan! I got here as fast as I could. We've got them! My God, you won't believe this! But we've got to act fast."

Evans eyes widened, but he turned his attention to the piece of paper in front of him. As he read the contents he hastily stood, a look of outraged shock appearing on his face. The paper was meant to be a flyer for distribution, complaining of harsh oppression by the Navy and the government. Where the line was crossed was a call to arms to form a resistance to tyranny. Worst of all it ended with a call for all of the British islands to establish a new political entity, with freedom of trade and limits to taxation as the rallying points.

"Oh, my God! Where did you get this?"

"From Emma. This was copied from a draft someone found. Evan, the word is there is a group of plantation overseers meeting at the Flying Fish tonight. They think this has something to do with it.

And guess what? That bloody Dutch ship captained by the frog is back."

"Shit. What about the other one?"

"No sign of him. But that's not all. I finally pinned down my source, Evan. He's one of the runaways and he doesn't really want to be a runaway. He's running scared and it cost me a bigger pile of gold than the penny pinchers will be happy with, but he's come through. There is a drop of weapons tonight and word is it will be a big one."

"Hmm, I wonder how coincidental it is that our American friend isn't in port while his counterpart is and we have this happening."

"Evan, we've got to move on this. The word is both of these could be happening even as we speak."

"Time to see the Captain. Let's go."

Nelson acted fast, calling a hurried conference of his officers and Captain Sands from the Latona. They were too many to sit so it ended up a standing meeting.

"So, gentlemen, you have heard the situation. Lieutenant Ross, Lieutenant Wolf will provide you a party of Marines to lead to the Flying Fish immediately. If our sources are correct and a seditious meeting is underway you will break it up and deal with the traitors as you see fit. I don't care whose heads you break. I want this stamped out now. Any questions?"

"No, sir," said Evan.

"Captain Sands, you will proceed immediately to the location Mr. Wilton has provided us, which fortunately is not far from here, and deal with any ship you find on the scene. You will shoot first and ask questions later. I would go, but the Boreas is not ready for sea right now, curse it. Mr. Ross has the

Dockyard working efficiently and as you saw when you came on board a number of our yards are down and being repaired."

Turning, Nelson looked at his Marine Lieutenant. "Mr. Wolf, I am concerned Captain Sands will not get to the drop in time. He needs time to recall his sailors from leave and I fear there may be several already well into their cups in local taverns. You will therefore take the rest of your Marines supplemented by whatever number Captain Sands feels he can free up from the Marine complement on the Latona. Mr. Wilton will lead you to the location. You also will shoot first and ask questions later. We simply cannot have a large supply of weapons fall into the wrong hands. Are there any questions, gentlemen?"

The grim crowd of officers all shook their heads.

"Dismissed and God speed, sirs."

***

The light of an almost full moon helped James and Lieutenant Wolf, although it kept disappearing behind clouds periodically. Marching down the road to the deserted beach two hours later they could hear the sound of the waves lapping at the shore. They also heard excited voices in the distance. Stopping to load weapons, Lieutenant Wolf ensured everyone was ready and gave orders to remain as quiet as possible for as long as they could.

As they warily marched into the open, heads swiveling back and forth in search of foes, Wolf muttered to James under his breath. "I don't think this lot knows what they are about. They don't have a picket posted to warn them."

The scene before them was as James's source claimed it would be. A big pile of boxes and bags were on the beach, surrounded by a large, excited group of close to two-dozen men milling about. In the distance, hard to make out, the faint outline of a darkened ship could be seen. James thought it looked much like one of the Dutch ships, but he couldn't be certain. As a sliver of the moon shifted out from behind a cloud James saw a small boat rowing in the direction of the waiting ship.

Marching closer and closer, still without being detected, Lieutenant Wolf muttered in James's ear once again. "I'd say the drop has already been made. Would you agree, Mr. Wilton?"

"I agree, sir. I wonder how long it's going to take these fools to realize we are here?"

Lieutenant Wolf grunted in amusement and as he did, someone in the happy group finally saw the red serge of the Marine's coats and wailed in terror.

"In the King's name!" shouted Wolf. "You are all under arrest! Surrender or face the consequences!"

The scene exploded in confusion as three of the dark shapes around the pile of weapons discharged weapons in the direction of the oncoming Marines. A man beside James cried in agony as a shot struck home and he fell out of line.

At the same moment Lieutenant Wolf screamed in his best parade ground voice.

"Fire!"

The volley from the Marines tore through a group of men foolishly charging the line. Everyone still standing was blinded from the flashes of the weapons. Others were running in all directions to escape. A desperate fight ensued as the moon finally reappeared from behind the clouds. James faced off against a man with a sword, but his opponent soon realized he was no match for James. The man threw his weapon down and ran for it, but a Marine coming from behind hammered him hard with the butt of his gun to stop him cold.

As the Marines got the situation under control Lieutenant Wolf fired a flare high into the air. As James joined the Lieutenant handed him the flare gun and ordered him to reload it as fast as possible.

"That damn ship is going to get away. Where the hell is the Latona?"

James saw the Lieutenant was right. The mystery ship was already underway, still showing no lights.

"Damn! Are you ready, Mr. Wilton? Aim high in the direction that bugger is going. Maybe the Latona is out there and will see it."

A minute after James fired a much brighter series of flashes appeared in the distance, followed instantly by the booming reports of the cannons.

"Damn, sir," said Lieutenant Wolf. "Will he catch him?"

James could only shake his head. "I doubt it, sir. I think that broadside was almost at the maximum range of the Latona's guns. I would say Captain Sands probably realized the smuggler was going to get away and he rounded up to take at least one crack at him with a full broadside. They might have got lucky and had some shots tell."

"He couldn't chase him down?"

"Sir, that ship has too much of a head start. During the day it would be another matter, but at night with the damn moon going behind the clouds like it did again just now? Not a chance. The ship had no lights. All they have to do is change course a few times and Captain Sands would have an impossible task to hunt him down."

"Well, we've put a stop to this nonsense. The Captain will be pleased with that at least. Right, let's sort this mess out."

***

Evan realized the Flying Fish was crowded as he burst in and scanned the room, his party of Marines coming in fast behind him. Walton was standing at the back of the room behind the bar and, with all eyes on Evan, no one saw Walton point surreptitiously to a table in the far corner of the room.

The table had six men at it, all drinking mugs of ale or rum. Evan realized quickly he recognized some. Most of them were men he knew were overseers on plantations, but one of them was a Frenchman from one of the Dutch ships. Like everyone else in the room, they all wore surprised looks at the sudden appearance of Evan and his heavily armed party of Marines.

Marching fast straight to their table he snatched at the pieces of paper he saw sitting on the table. The shock of Evan's appearance and their indecision were the conspirator's undoing. Belatedly, they tried to claw the papers back, but they were far too late. Evan stepped away and quickly scanned the two he had snatched up. They were both the same as the copy the network had provided.

Evan looked up at all of them, steel in his eyes. "Traitorous bastards! You are all under arrest!"

This time the overseers were quick to respond. All six of them boiled out of their chairs as the closest of them took a wild swing at Evan. The blow only glanced off the side of his head, but it made him stagger to the side and forced him to struggle hard to retain his balance.

The Marines pushed past Evan to get at the six men struggling to get away. Several of the overseers pulled knives or clubs from their belts. Full mugs of ale were smashed into men's faces as others were clubbed brutally with the butts of the muskets. Someone's gun discharged and one of the bystanders striving desperately to get away from the battle fell with a gasp, clutching his stomach as the blood ran through his fingers. As another of the overseers crashed to the floor a bag he was carrying burst open and a shower of gold coins spilled everywhere.

The man who had taken the wild swing at Evan was the Frenchman. Shoving two combatants out of his way he came for Evan to try and wrest the evidence from Evans hand, pulling out a long, wicked looking knife as he came closer.

But Evan shoved the papers into his pocket, pulling out his sword and parrying a vicious slash barely in time. Evan knew the Frenchman was at a disadvantage having only a knife, but he kept Evan off balance by pressing forward hard, hoping Evan would slip. Evan stumbled against a table and seeing his chance, the Frenchman lunged forward in a stabbing thrust. The knife speared through Evan's uniform to cut his side. Roaring in anger Evan kicked at the man and chopped as hard as he could at the point between the man's neck and shoulder. The Frenchman dropped like a stone as blood fountained from his neck and he stayed down.

Recovering himself, Evan discovered the fight was over. One of the overseers had also been killed. Of the remaining four, two were stretched on the floor unconscious from blows to the head. Marines on either side guarded the other two. Both men gingerly rubbed nasty bruises growing on their faces before their hands were pulled behind them to be tied.

"Search these buggers," growled Evan.

"Sir, you're bleeding," said one of the Marines.

"It's only a scratch. Deal with this lot first."

"Good Lord, sir, look at this!" called one of the Marines. Holding up a small bag taken off the dead man on the floor, the Marine reached in and pulled out a fistful of large gold coins. The bag was eerily familiar, clearly of the same make as the one Evan had taken from the dead overseer who attacked Alice. Only this bag was bigger.

"Sir? These buggers all have bags of money too!" said another of the Marines, busy searching the two already tied up overseers.

Evan stalked over to the two subdued prisoners. "If you cooperate it'll go easier on you."

The two prisoners glared back at him, smouldering with anger. One of them spat on Evan's boots, which earned him a crushing punch in the face from the Marine guarding him. Staggering from the blow, he fell to his knees.

Evan looked at the other prisoner. "How about you? You fancy a broken nose like him?"

"I'm not that stupid."

"Excellent. Perhaps you'll be smart enough to talk."

"Like I said, I'm not that stupid."

"Pity. Perhaps after you think about dancing at the end of a noose for a while you'll change your mind."

"A noose? What the hell are you talking about?"

"That's usually how people caught committing treason end up."

The man began to sweat as a look of fear crossed his face. "Look, this isn't what you think. My owner only wants to promote a better way to do things."

"Really. And that happens to involve taking up arms like this notice I caught you with says, eh?"

"A figure of speech, sir."

Evan laughed. "Good Lord. Caught in the act with an incriminating flyer and bags of French gold as payoffs and you're telling me that? Be sure and remember to try that line on the judge, you arsehole."

The man gave a start of shock, but Evan had already turned away to issue orders.

"Well done, lads. Let's get this place cleaned up and haul this lot off to the jail. After tonight's work I'm sure Lieutenant Wolf will agree with me you've earned an extra tot when we get back to the ship."

The men grinned and a couple responded in unison. "Thank you, sir!"

With the prospect of an extra tot of rum as motivation the Flying Fish was soon put to rights, except for the bloodstains on the floor. Those would take rather longer to clean away.

Back at home much later that evening Alice fussed over his wound, cleaning it and changing the bandages hastily applied at the Flying Fish with care.

"Alice, it's just a flesh wound, really. I'll live."

"If its that minor why are you grimacing every time you shift position? You're the only regular customer I have, lover man. Remember? So shut up and sit still while I finish this."

Evan reached up to stroke her face. "Thank you."

***

Two days later Evan returned to the Flying
Fish, alone this time. The room was much quieter in
mid-afternoon, but even so almost half of the tables
were occupied.

Everyone turned to look and conversations
stopped when Evan walked in. Faces were frozen,
waiting to see what he would do. He looked around
the room and quickly found what he was looking for.
Walking over to the table occupied by the French
Captain Deschamps and the American Captain Jones
he pulled out a chair and joined them. Wary glances
and numerous raised eyebrows appeared, but with no
prospect of anything happening other than a
conversation everyone's attention shifted slowly
away.

Evan winced as he made himself comfortable
and ordered a mug of ale. The flesh wound suffered
in the fight was still bandaged, but healing well even
though he still got twinges of pain if he wasn't careful
in how he moved. After Emma dropped his drink off
he looked at the two men.

"Gentlemen. Thank you for accepting my
invitation today."

The Frenchman offered a rueful glance in
response while the American rolled his eyes and
looked away.

"Lieutenant Ross, you are clearly a gentleman
with a sense of humour," said the Frenchman. "I
usually would approve, but I'm afraid in these
circumstances I find it difficult to laugh. We could
hardly refuse, now could we?"

Evan shrugged apologetically. "Ah, you refer
to HMS Rattler anchored nearby and blocking your
departure, sir? Yes, there is that. Captain Nelson felt

it prudent to ensure you gentlemen remained in port for a bit longer while we sorted out a few things on our end."

"I hope this won't be much longer, sir," said the American. "We have orders to fulfill on other islands and bills to pay. The longer we sit here the more the cost with no income."

"Ah, not to worry, sir. We only need to have a friendly chat here and get a few things straight with each other."

"A friendly chat?"

"Of course, sir. We can do our best to be civilized about this, don't you think?"

Both Captains nodded, faces frozen into expressions as neutral as they could make them.

"So, I'm quite sure you know we've had some interesting things happening on the island lately. A large cache of weapons dropped surreptitiously on a deserted beach to a waiting group of runaway slaves bent on murdering people in their beds is certainly interesting. The mystery ship dropping these weapons somehow managed to get away. Did you gentlemen know HMS Latona got a broadside off before the ship disappeared? Admittedly it was from maximum range."

"Yes, we did hear something to that effect," said the Frenchman.

"Indeed," said Evan, turning to look the American in the eyes. "Captain Jones, I find it interesting your colleague was in port the night this happened, but you were not. Even more interesting, you appear in port the next morning with what looks like a number of shot holes in your sails. How did you come by those, sir?"

"I had an encounter with a Spaniard off Puerto Rico, sir. It was a misunderstanding, of course. I don't know what the fool was thinking when he fired. They can be touchy and unpredictable. Perhaps he thought I was a privateer."

"I see. Well, I hope you've had time to make repairs while you've been waiting."

"Ah, yes, we have, thank you."

"Excellent," said Evan, as he turned back to the Frenchman.

"Captain Deschamps, you of course know of what happened in the Flying Fish here two nights ago. Please accept my condolences on the loss of your man. Have you any idea why this man was present here?"

"I do not, sir. My men are free to do as they please when they are not on duty."

"I see. Well, I found this most strange. A man from your ship is caught with several senior plantation overseers with seditious flyers and mysterious bags of gold. The flyers speak of taking up arms to actively bring about political change. In fact, they were talking about exactly the kind of political ideas of free economic trade and better relationships with your respective countries you gentlemen were promoting. The only difference is you two did not speak of actively forcing change, while this flyer did. When I arrested them they resisted with weapons. So do you really find none of this even a little curious?"

"Lieutenant Ross. It's true we like the idea of freedom of trade and better relations. But you must understand I can control the behaviour of my men while on duty, but I cannot control it when they are off duty and away from the ship. And I certainly cannot tell them what to think. I am as shocked as you that he was involved in whatever this is all about. He must have had strong political views, I expect. My crew and I will miss him nonetheless."

Evan remained looking hard at the Frenchman for a few moments before nodding slowly.

"I see. Tell me, gentlemen, what do you think these men were doing with all that gold? It is beyond belief six men would normally have that much gold on them while sitting in a tavern."

The two Captains looked at each other and turned back to look at Evan.

"Sir, we have no idea," said the Frenchman.

"Hmm. It was interesting we found a large satchel beside the chair your man was sitting in, Captain Deschamps. It contained yet another bag of gold. I wonder if perhaps it belonged to your man, sir?"

The Frenchman looked wary and took a moment to respond.

"Well, I can't say for sure, sir. But if you believe it was his I would be happy to take charge of it in trust and ensure his widow gets the funds."

Evan laughed. "Forgive me, Captain. Your concern and willingness to support the man's widow does you credit. But I'm afraid we will be keeping the gold. After all, we don't know for certain it belonged to your man, now do we?"

The American was growing perceptibly impatient and could contain himself no longer.

"Lieutenant Ross. We have answered all of your questions. Can we not end this so we can be on our way?"

Evan smiled. "Yes, Captain, I agree the time for questions is past. But I think you should stay a bit longer and hear a little story that may piece all of this together. Wouldn't that be of interest, sirs?"

The two men nodded, faces still frozen and neutral.

"As with many things, gentlemen, this story is all a question of who has what interests. The plantation owners on these islands have plenty of connections to their American friends, built up over the years when relations were less complicated. Frustrated they can no longer deal with their contacts and paying what they consider onerous customs duties, perhaps a group of people hereabouts appealed to the Americans for help. Not having the best of relations these days with their former homeland, it is possible these American friends turned to their French friends for thoughts on how to address this situation. And the end result is two Captains, one from each country, are given the task of finding ways to help the locals hereabouts. Are you with me so far, gentlemen?"

"Interesting, sir. Do continue," said the American.

"As I'm sure you both know the interests of nations sometimes differ from those of individuals. In this story it is possible events were set in motion in a couple of ways. A little gold from the treasury buys a lot of allegiance from people already disposed to turn their coat, wouldn't you agree? Especially when those people are already feeling stretched financially. So the idea is to have them agitate publicly for a better deal like freedom of trade and when they get a deaf ear in return a local revolution is set in motion. By the time a currently somewhat weakened England hears of revolts on the islands they are presented with a new arrangement. Not independence, no one would agree to that. It would be rather more of an experiment. The tempting argument that would be held out is to give everyone a little more autonomy and then England can sit back and watch more taxes flow in from the increased volume of business. Meanwhile, American and French businesses are growing tentacles on the islands and local authorities are finding creative ways to hold back funds for local initiatives or whatever reason they dream up. Interesting, eh?"

"Yes, that's quite a story, sir."

"Ah, but it's not over. This is a complicated story. See, these friends of the locals I mentioned weren't content merely to bribe people to get what they want. No, they had to help matters along. Create motivation to follow through with commitments. So local runaway slaves with vengeance on their minds are given covert support. It would be minimal at first, of course. They need to demonstrate they are serious, so a couple of small drops of arms are made. And meanwhile Captain Nelson is pushing hard to shut down smuggling activity, so it's the perfect time to shove the plantation owners into action. An attempt to murder one of the Captain Nelson's officers is made to show they are serious. I imagine the political masters of these friends were looking for results faster too, so a big drop is arranged despite it being hurricane season. Arm a crowd of angry slaves and the locals would all have to take up arms regardless. Once the locals are in the mood, they carry on and take out their frustration on the local Government and the Navy and simply take over."

"Lieutenant Ross, this is all interesting, but it seems beyond belief these friends would support enemies of the same people they are bribing," said the Frenchman.

"Ah, but remember what I said about the interests of nations not necessarily coinciding with those of individuals. It wouldn't be the first time a few people were sacrificed for a larger objective, now would it?"

"I see," said the Frenchman. "And is this the story we shall be reading in your newspapers sometime soon?"

"Ah, well, not quite. Word of success in putting a stop to rampaging runaway slaves murdering innocents in their beds is a given, of course. Reassurance to all that this has been stopped in its tracks will be provided. A major brawl at the Flying Fish will be brushed off as a drunken incident involving intoxicated foreign sailors in a dispute with local plantation workers. No, it has been deemed necessary to keep some elements of this story sub rosa as it were. In this story, though, notice has been taken at the highest levels of government of French and American collusion in an attempt to achieve the real goal of this, which was to destabilize the British Caribbean islands in any way possible and disrupt the flow of taxes to His Majesty. Yes, this shall be a matter for the diplomats to chat about, sirs."

"I see, Lieutenant Ross," said the Frenchman. "And what is to become of these fictional Captains and their ships in this story of yours?"

"Ah. Well, if it were up to me the consequences would be far, far worse than they are. As I said, there is no interest in making everything widely known. So an immediate departure from Antigua and a ban of one year trading on or with any British islands is the outcome. The ships will be escorted out of our waters by HMS Rattler."

"And how is this justified, Lieutenant Ross? You have no proof," said the American.

Evan laughed, but his eyes narrowed and no warmth was in his smile. "We were shocked to find the Customs paperwork going back over six months was not in order for both of these fictional ships. Highly questionable entries that may or may not have been falsified were present. We simply can't have any of that, now can we?"

Evan sat back and pulled out some coins to leave on the table to pay for his ale. "One last thing. I suppose it would be prudent to make sure you fully understand the thinking, gentlemen. Should the Royal Navy find these two ships in British waters during the period of the ban the loss of trading privileges will seem trivial. Our warships are being given standing orders to shoot you first and ask questions later. I wouldn't be surprised if the ships were sunk before anyone on board had a chance to answer questions."

"Well, thank you for this telling us this fascinating story, Lieutenant Ross," said the Frenchman. "You are an interesting man. But we should be going. Perhaps we shall meet again some day."

Evan stood in response, looking hard at both men. "Yes, I agree you should be going. And if we do meet again some day I'm sure it will be just as amusing as this has been. The Rattler is waiting. Good day, sirs."

Chapter Eighteen
October 1785
Antigua

"I still can't believe it, Sir James. It's so appallingly unfair as to be beyond belief. I am of a mind to— ah, here we are. Come in gentlemen and take a seat."

Evan was apologetic when he saw a much older, well-dressed civilian was sitting across the desk from Nelson. "Captain, I'm sorry to interrupt. We didn't know you were already engaged with someone else."

"Not to worry, this gentleman will be joining us in our meeting today. Mr. Ross, Mr. Wilton, this is Captain Sir James Standish. He is retired, which is why he is in civilian clothes. I was just telling Sir James how frustrated I am."

"Horatio, forgive me, but you've been stewing on this ever since we left Barbados. You're going to have to let this go and move on sooner or later."

"I know, I know, damn it. But it's not only me, is it? Public credit should go where it is deserved, and these men sitting with us are far more deserving than him!"

Nelson turned to Evan and James. "I'm sorry, you have no idea what I'm talking about of course. As you know, we have returned from our regular October meeting in Barbados with all of the ships on our station. The Admiralty is pleased that the smuggling has dropped to almost nothing locally through our efforts. Even better, word has come the Americans have formally dropped their nonsensical lawsuit. We put down a potential slave revolt and put a stop to a nasty French and American plot. So you think with all this success we would receive the credit, right? No! It's Admiral Hughes that is being congratulated by everyone from the Admiralty to the King himself for his leadership putting a stop to all of this!"

Nelson sat back, a look of frustration on his face as he turned to Sir James once again. "Unbelievable. Sir James, you have no idea what an obstructive buffoon the man has been."

Sir James gave Nelson a wry smile. "Well, actually, I have had some experience with the man and nothing you are saying comes as a surprise. But Horatio, you know this is all about the politics. They have to do that so everyone can save face. It's the customary thing to do. The important thing is the right people know of the real story and who is worthy of their approval. I think you have a bright future to offer Mrs. Nisbet."

Nelson's face lit with a broad smile. "I hope so. She is such an inspiration and I am so fortunate she accepted my proposal. I am very hopeful we can gain approval to wed soon."

"I am certain you shall win through, Horatio. But politics aside, you know the reason I am here is to offer some recognition and reward to those who deserve it."

Nelson took a deep breath before responding. "You are right, Sir James. It's not enough to be a seaman. I guess I must master being a politician, too. Well, enough of my complaints."

Nelson turned back to Evan and James. "Gentlemen, you at least are being recognized for your efforts and we must reward you accordingly. Now, I know what you are both thinking. You want a posting to a ship. Any old ship would do, correct?"

As they nodded agreement Nelson gave them a rueful smile. "Of course you would want a ship. Unfortunately, that simply isn't possible. The situation is unchanged. We are at peace and all of the ships based here are all still fully manned. You may have noticed I seem to have more than the usual four or five midshipmen, have you not? In fact, I have no less than thirty midshipmen stuffed into the Boreas. Before I left England I had a ridiculous number of requests to place people's sons and favourites. It's the product of peace, sirs. So even if I had a vacancy in my officer ranks I would have no room for you. The screams I would hear from everyone that thinks their favourite should get the promotion would be loud enough to be heard all the way from England. I talked to the rest of the Captains in Barbados and we are all in the same situation."

The two men couldn't keep the disappointment from their faces.

"I see, sir. You did warn us of this," said Evan.

"Ah, but we do have something to offer you. Lieutenant Ross, you and Mr. Wilton form an effective team. You both did extremely well handling covert activities and your cover assignment as officer in charge of the Dockyard worked well. We would like to keep this arrangement in place. Sir James, would you care to elaborate from this point?"

"Certainly. Before I go further I should first explain my current role. Captain Nelson mentioned I am a retired Captain, which is true in that I no longer serve at sea. I am, however, employed by the Foreign Office these days. Our diplomats have found on occasion that having someone with knowledge of the sea and nautical matters is helpful to have around, especially here in the Caribbean. Advice on matters outside their expertise, right? I have on occasion also been employed in active intelligence gathering situations much as you two gentlemen have been involved with lately. As a rule Navy Captains are pretty much their own intelligence officers, but when the novel approach Captain Nelson has taken here was brought to our attention it set a few people to thinking."

Sir James sat forward and looked speculatively at the two men before him. "So what does this mean for you, Mr. Ross? It means we would like you to accept an extension of your commission as officer in charge of the Dockyard. Your colleague Mr. Wilton will stay with you. You would both continue doing exactly what you are doing. You maintain a cover of being in charge of the Dockyard while continuing to serve in an intelligence capacity. You will find yourself spending more time with diplomats providing them advice and support. I can't be everywhere at once, now can I? If covert action is required for whatever reason you will act as needed. It is likely this may mean travel periodically to other islands. Think of yourselves as specialists in intelligence activity involving naval matters. So is all that making sense so far?"

The two men nodded.

"Excellent. You will essentially have two masters. You will report to me for all intelligence or Foreign Office related matters. For the Dockyard you will continue to report to whoever is senior in command of the ships on station here. Should that officer require your assistance on intelligence matters you will of course provide it."

Sir James turned to Nelson. "Have I covered it all?"

"I think so, except for duration. Gentlemen, the assignment is proposed to cover the next three years, which will undoubtedly exceed my tenure here. Hmm, I think it important you understand the situation fully. You do not have to accept this, but as I said there is no ship for you. If you don't accept it the most likely outcome would be to send you both back to England. Yes, people in high places have noticed you and that may serve to get you both a posting at some point down the road, but there are no guarantees and it may be a long time."

Evan and James looked at each other as Nelson paused. James nodded and Evan turned back to Nelson. "Sir, we accept. We had already discussed the possibility you would not have a ship for us. You are right we would both much prefer a ship, but opportunity to serve in any capacity is welcome."

"Very good. Ah, Mr. Ross, you will be needing this in your new role."

Nelson took a sealed envelope sitting on the desk beside him and handed it to Evan with a smile.

"Sometimes, at least, the people in high places do get it right when it comes to rewards. Congratulations, *Commander* Ross. Yes, that envelope contains your commission papers and written orders concerning your new role."

Evan was astounded. "Good Lord, Captain. I don't know how to thank you."

"Ah, don't thank me, sir. What you have there is straight from the First Lord. Apparently he felt that if you were to continue in this role it should be clear to everyone who was going to be senior in charge of the Dockyard. Yes, it's all a bit unusual, but sometimes doing things differently is good."

Nelson turned and looked directly at James. "And then there is you, Mr. Wilton. There are many people on this island that don't know they have you and Mr. Ross to thank for saving their lives. The First Lord was interested in rewarding you, too."

Reaching for a second envelope sitting on his desk Nelson smiled as he passed it to James.

"So how does it feel to be *Lieutenant* James Wilton, sir?"

James's jaw dropped and his hand shook as he took the envelope from the Captain. He looked at it for a long few moments before looking up at Nelson.

"Sir, I don't know what to say. This feels like a dream."

"Well, I know what to say. Congratulations! You have done well and your father would be proud of you. Yes, I know this is a bit unusual too, given you have never served as a midshipman, but you are far too old to start you at that step in the process. Normally you would have to sit before a board of post captains and pass for Lieutenant like everyone else, but I assured the First Lord you know as much or more than any midshipman I currently have, so there you have it. And yes, this is an active commission so you will be Commander Ross's First Officer. You will be senior to those two fools already in the Dockyard."

Nelson paused a moment in thought before looking to James once again, obviously recalling a point he hadn't mentioned. "Ah, I must clarify that last point. So you understand, sir, we won't be making your commission as an officer public any time soon, you understand? Commander Ross is already known to be an officer, but you are not. You can thus

333

continue to serve as you have unencumbered by the higher profile your partner has."

"So, gentlemen, Sir James and I have a few other matters to discuss and you two will want to go celebrate. Take a couple of day's leave with my blessing. Sir James will want to spend more time with you briefing you in detail on the people you may be dealing with in future and the general intelligence situation, but that can wait."

Evan and James took this as their cue to leave and both stood.

"Thank you, Captain," said Evan. "From both of us. I know you said to thank the First Lord, but we know this wouldn't be happening without your support."

Nelson nodded, but his face grew a frown. "Ah, I almost forgot. There is one other small matter I must bring up with you two. There's a rumor in the Marine ranks on the Boreas that you two now have a pet. I hear it's some mongrel you acquired and what I found of interest is his name. Gentlemen, is it really true you have a *dog* named Nelson?"

Nelson was still frowning as he waited for a response. Evan and James looked at each other in dismay, but Evan knew he had to tell the truth. Licking his lips nervously and groaning inwardly, he turned back to the Captain.

"Sir, it is true. He was a stray that needed a home. We realized he was a tough survivor and a real fighter, sir. Somehow we thought of you when we were grasping for a name for him and it seemed to fit. We apologize if we have given any offense, sir."

"A real fighter, you say?" said Nelson, still frowning. Unable to contain himself any longer he burst out laughing.

"Sounds like my kind of dog, sirs! You are dismissed."

***

As the door closed on the two much relieved officers Nelson turned to Sir James, who was still chuckling at the obvious relief of Evan and James.

"Horatio, you are incorrigible. You should be ashamed of teasing them like that."

Nelson grinned. "Can you imagine it, Sir James? Everyone thinks I have no sense of humor."

***

The ride to the top of Shirley Heights to watch the sunset had become an early evening ritual for Evan and Alice. Arriving at the crest they knew they had an hour or so before the sun finally disappeared. With a few puffy clouds sprinkled on the horizon the sunset promised to be glorious once again. Alice herself looked glorious; Evan had bought her a new white dress made with high quality material. The dress contrasted against her light brown skin perfectly.

But Alice's mind was not on the scenery or her dress. She was still bubbling at the news James had brought before they left.

"Evan, I still can't believe it. That is so wonderful for Emma and Walton. They must have saved every coin that came their way to buy their freedom. And they saved enough on top of that to open their own little inn and tavern, too? What clever people."

Evan finished securing the buggy and they walked to the lookout to sit in their favourite spot.

"Yes, clever is one word for it," said Evan with a laugh. "I'm sure they were saving everything they could, but a little sudden windfall always helps too."

"A windfall?"

"Ah, well, you didn't hear what I'm about to tell you, you understand? You recall the incident at the Flying Fish when I arrested the traitors? Well, the bag of gold one of them had burst open and coins went flying everywhere. The Marines and I were rather busy dealing with those bastards and had no time to pay attention to what happened to the gold. By the time we got things under control I rather think more than a few of those were already scooped up by Emma and Walton. They were the only ones sticking around once the fighting started. All the other customers lit out of there in an eye blink. Well, there was also that pack the frog spy had, too. I have a memory of Emma coming up and handing it to me as they were cleaning up. She's the one who told me there was another bag of gold inside."

Evan laughed as he thought back to the look on Emma 's face when she handed him the bag and told him of the contents. Evan remembered Nelson's suggestion to look after the people risking their lives to give him information and, knowing exactly what was happening, he responded with a wink. Emma had smiled.

"So no one missed any of the gold?" said Alice, a look of wonder on her face.

"Ah, well, we had no idea how much was supposed to be in the bags and I wasn't about to go and ask that bloody frog captain or any of the plantation owners around here about it. Captain Nelson was more than pleased with the amount we surrendered to the prize court. His share ended up being a tidy little sum. And besides, Emma and

Walton deserve a little something for their efforts, don't you think?"

"Well, sure. I hope it works out for them. We all dream of freedom and they've got it now."

"And then there is you, my dear. You deserve some reward, too. With Emma and Walton gone I think you going back to work at the Flying Fish would be a bad idea."

Alice turned to look directly at Evan. "I confess that would be something I'd like to avoid. So where are you going with this, Evan?"

Evan reached into his pocket, pulling out an envelope and handing to Alice. She sat forward to take it, sitting on the edge of her seat and looking at the envelope with a questioning look on her face. Raising one eyebrow, she looked quizzically at Evan.

He grinned. "So, does the air taste a little sweeter knowing you are free now?"

Alice looked at him in disbelief as Evan nodded firmly in response. She slumped off her seat and fell to her knees in shock, one hand held to her heart as the tears formed in her eyes.

"Oh, my God! Is it really true?"

Without waiting for an answer she rose to her feet and reached for him. Evan began to rise to meet her, but she crushed him into her breasts in a bear hug and holding him tight for what seemed an endless time.

The sound of muffled laughter broke the spell. "Ease up, woman, I need to breathe!"

Alice finally relented, switching to a series of hard kisses as the tears continued to flow.

"Evan, I don't know how to thank you!"

"Ah, well, I can think of a way," he said with a leer on his face.

"Yes, I like that idea," she said, finally disentangling herself as they sat down once again, still brushing away the tears. "Evan, how is this possible?"

"Well, I do have resources. I'm not a rich man, but I'm not poor either. I confess I've been thinking about doing this for a while. But the necessity to dip into my own funds wasn't there, really."

"Oh? So where did you find the money?"

Evan laughed. "Everyone forgot about the bag of money we found on that bastard overseer Whyte that hurt you, remember? I don't think the Captain quite realized how much it was, but he ordered me to use it to help the people helping us. I couldn't think of a better way to do that than this in the end."

"Evan, how did you manage to convince my goddamn father to sell me to you? After all that's happened I would have thought he'd decline the offer out of spite."

"You're probably right, which is why he doesn't know any of this. All he knows is you have been sold to an unidentified buyer. Emma and Walton and I joined forces, you see. It was a combined offer for the three of you actually. We went through an intermediary to make the deal. The three of you were expensive at fifty pounds each. Relatively young, healthy slaves that were making him money command a high price. But sadly there are more where you came from and he undoubtedly made a tidy profit."

"Bastard. But I'm glad to be rid of him. Thank you!"

A strange look of sudden understanding stole over her face as the implications of it all sunk in, so abruptly it stopped Evan from responding. He offered her his own quizzical look, curious to know what she was thinking.

"My word, I'm going to need to find work," said Alice. "I wonder if Emma and Walton will need help?"

Evan laughed. "Ah, yes, I haven't got to that part yet. The new inn they are opening is actually a partnership. There was enough left from Whyte's bag of money to make you one of the three owners, Alice. We had to, actually, as Emma and Walton didn't have quite enough money left to do it alone. But they were real happy when I suggested that as a solution. The three of you will have to sort out who does what, but I rather think that won't be a problem. Like I said, they were most happy to have you as a partner."

"Lord, you've not only given me my freedom, but you've given me a future," said Alice, clutching his hand as more tears began to form.

"Ah, I have one last thought you may like, too. There is still a small bit left from the bag of gold. I am pretty sure it's not enough to free your mother, but as she is older she wouldn't necessarily command the same price. And your new business partnership may require some extra funds to keep you going until you see some profits. But if all goes well I am thinking that might be a good use for the rest of the money. Whatever, it is yours to do with as you see fit. And if need be, well, I do have resources of my own and I am willing to add them to help free her."

"You've thought of everything, haven't you? I suppose I shouldn't be surprised."

"Well, not quite everything," said Evan with a grin. "You know that rather dumpy place in Falmouth Harbour they have the nerve to call an inn? Emma and Walton negotiated taking it over. The plan is to fix it up. They were tired of the craziness of St. John's and Falmouth Harbour needs a decent inn. I think you'll do rather well there. So all you need is a name for it. I like The One Armed Sailor myself, but James suggested The Dockyard Dog Inn. After I thought about it I decided that would be more appropriate, don't you think? Well, it won't be up to me to decide that anyway."

"Sounds good to me. So I'll be able to move in there soon, will I?"

Evan cleared his throat and paused a moment before responding.

"Ah, well, I wasn't thinking there would be a need to do that, unless you want to, of course."

A hint of tears forming in Alice's eyes came once again. "I think I'd prefer to stay with you."

Evan nodded. "Well, I'm glad you want to. I've kind of gotten used to having someone about. And I'm quite glad that someone is you. But we have a problem, you know, and I don't know what to do about it."

"You're a sailor. And sailors need ships. And sometimes they sail away and never come back."

Evan turned away to look seaward as he spoke, holding his open hand out to as if to draw it closer. "My heart is at sea, Alice. It's all I've ever known. I know you've not experienced it. My Lord, the feel of the deck of a warship as it meets the waves. I love watching the flying fish the ship scares up. It's like an addiction, I think. Being in sole command of a huge warship in the middle of the night when everyone else is asleep. I could watch the shimmer of the full moon on the water endlessly. Ah, I'm wandering here."

"Yes, I know your heart is there. When you talk about it like that it makes me want to try it, too. See different places. All I've ever known is this island."

"Well, here's the thing, Alice. I'm a Commander now. That means if I get another commission after this one—and please God this time it's a ship—I will be in charge. It likely won't be a big ship, maybe a sloop or something, but it will be mine! I've been working toward that for a long time. But women on board warships are frowned on. I'll be honest with you, as a Commander I could in fact have a woman living with me. There would be no one to stop me. But it would be wrong to flaunt what I have and they do not in front of my men every day. Some Captains out there have done it, but to my knowledge it's always been a recipe for disaster."

Evan shrugged and paused to rub his chin in thought. He shook his head.

"Look, I'm stationed here now for the next three years, but what then? I don't know how this is going to work and that maybe isn't fair to you. Heaven knows I've never had anyone I cared about like this or for this long. It's not normal for a sailor. So I don't want you tied down."

"You know, there are lots of men out there that wouldn't even concern themselves with this. Use people until you've gotten everything you want and then dump them."

Evan shrugged. "I guess I'm just not built that way."

"I know. And then there is the fact you are the wrong colour, you know."

"Ah, yes, there is that too. Alice, as a more senior officer stationed here for three years now it is likely I will find myself invited to more social functions and balls, things like that, yes?"

"And coming in with a black woman on your arm would be a problem, wouldn't it?"

"Yes. A big problem. As much as that annoys me, I don't know what to do about it."

"I do. Don't concern yourself about me. I don't want any part of the owner's world and I'm not going to pretend to be something I am not. Just keep that white bitch's hands off you and we'll get along fine."

Evan laughed. "I think you need have no fear on that front. Even if she really is interested in me I rather think her father would put a stop to it. And for the record, I will admit she is a beautiful woman, as are you. But I think there is more to this than what one finds on the outside and I haven't come across anything of interest on the inside."

Evan reached out to grasp her hand. "But I'm still not sure where this all leaves us."

"Evan, I know the answer. It's simple. We take this a little at a time, that's all. Look, you amazing man, you've already changed my life for the better. I don't have to make my living lying on my back anymore! Lord, I own part of a business. So I am happy to enjoy this while it lasts. I have nothing to complain about with you and never will."

Evan nodded and both of them stood. He pulled her close to watch the last sliver of the sun drop below the horizon.

"Well. Yes, I think you're right, my love. So let's see what the future has in store for us."

The End

Author's Notes

This novel is based on real events and on a few real people involved in them. The timeline of the events was as described in the book and I made every effort to stay true to the historical facts.

Smuggling as a result of the Navigation laws was indeed rampant and it took a long, concerted effort to get it under control. The plantation owners on the islands did have many ties with the new American nation. The British government did in fact need the wealth the sugar industry brought.

Slavery was a harsh reality. I found it interesting to learn slaves did not all toil on the plantations. Some really did run little businesses or serve in a wide range of capacities, all in the name of making money. That forms of slavery still exist in some parts of the world today appalls me as much as what was happening over two centuries ago, but that is another story.

The French and American Captains, with their plot to destabilize the islands, are products of my imagination. But nefarious plots and active spies were undoubtedly present. Spying is the second oldest profession, after all. Admiral Hughes, Governour William Shirley, and Captain John Moutray with his wife Mary, however, were all real people who behaved more or less as described herein.

Then there is Horatio Nelson. For readers of this work who may not know already, I assure you Nelson was very real.

I confess when I started work on this project I had not envisioned Captain Horatio Nelson, hero of the British people and eventually a Lord and Admiral, having as many appearances in this novel as he does. In hindsight this was rather silly of me.

Nelson was an amazing individual. This man was dominant in the world of the British Navy in the period up to his death and, to my mind, he was leadership personified. Unfaltering dedication to purpose and principle, a degree of professional competence putting him at the pinnacle of his profession, and the way he led his men are his hallmarks.

He truly cared for the men under his command and they knew it. On more than one occasion in his career, even after he became a Captain, he was at the front of his men leading them into the thickest of the fighting in boarding actions. At the Battle of Trafalgar in 1805, where he crushed the combined navies of France and Spain once and for all, he made himself a target by wearing full dress uniform on his quarterdeck so his men would know he was standing in the line of fire with them. The British people did not celebrate the Trafalgar victory; they mourned the loss of Nelson in the battle.

Given this, I should not have been surprised his part in this novel ended up being significant. Knowing how many people still revere Nelson I confess I felt a little daunted as this evolved, but I decided to follow his advice to just have at it. I hope my portrayal does him the honour he richly deserves.

The same applies to the men of the British Royal Navy. As a small point of interest I sometimes wonder how many of my fellow Canadians understand the impact Nelson and the men of the Royal Navy following him had on our collective destiny. I refer in particular here to those serving in the War of 1812 defending us against the American invasion.

This conflict was considered a relative sideshow to the greater fight going on against Napoleon Bonaparte in Europe. While a number of other participants were involved in it, the Navy had a large role. I think it reasonable to suggest if the Royal Navy had not been as dominant courtesy of people like Nelson and the Trafalgar victory, the outcome of the 1812 war may have been very different and I might instead be writing this book as a citizen of a much larger United States of America. For my part, I *like* being a Canadian and I do have an appreciation for what these long dead warriors of the sea accomplished.

If you want to know more about Nelson and the fascinating times he lived in I can recommend a couple of nonfiction books. I drew on many sources for this novel, but The Pursuit of Victory by Roger Knight and Most Secret and Confidential by Steven Maffeo were particularly helpful.

I must also acknowledge the influence several other authors have had on me, all of whom have works involving the Royal Navy in this particular era. I've been devouring the works of C. S. Forester, Dudley Pope, Douglas Reeman, and Richard Woodman for many years. My two favourites are Julian Stockwin's particularly good Thomas Kydd series and Dewey Lambdin's equally good Alan Lewrie series. I do hope they keep them going for many more years, given I am completely addicted to the works of these authors.

As a final note I offer my thanks to several people, too many to list, who read the draft of Dockyard Dog and gave me great thoughts and feedback. Karen Autio gave me invaluable editorial insight with her evaluation of my draft.

So what is next for Commander Evan Ross and his newly minted Lieutenant James Wilton? I don't know if it has come through the pages of this work clearly, but I love the Caribbean. What a wonderful, diverse, and beautiful part of the world. Plenty of fascinating characters and history to work with, which are all good reasons to keep Commander Ross and Lieutenant Wilton assigned to the Caribbean for some time to come. You can follow them as they face new challenges in The Sugar Revolution, sequel to Dockyard Dog.

I hope you enjoyed Dockyard Dog.